PROCESSION OF THE DEAD

D B Shan is another pseudonym for Darren Shan the author of two hugely popular series for children: 'The Saga of Darren Shan', and 'The Demonata' which have been read by millions of people around the world in over twenty different languages. *Procession of the Dead* is his first work for adults and was previously published in 1999. The author has extensively revised the text for this 'director's cut' edition.

D. B. SHAN

Procession of the Dead

The City: Book One

HARPER
Voyager

This novel is entirely a work of fiction.
The names, characters and incidents portrayed in it are
the work of the author's imagination. Any resemblance to
actual persons, living or dead, events or localities is
entirely coincidental.

HarperVoyager
An imprint of HarperCollins*Publishers*
77–85 Fulham Palace Road,
Hammersmith, London W6 8JB

www.voyager-books.co.uk

This paperback edition 2008

1

First published in Great Britain in 1999 as *Ayuamarca: Procession of the Dead*
by Millennium, an imprint of Orion Books

This revised edition copyright © D B Shan 1999, 2008

The author asserts the moral right to
be identified as the author of this work

A catalogue record for this book is
available from the British Library

ISBN: 978-0-00-726130-7

Set in Meridien by Palimpsest Book Production Limited,
Grangemouth, Stirlingshire

Printed and bound in Great Britain by
Clays Ltd, St Ives plc

Mixed Sources
Product group from well-managed
forests and other controlled sources
www.fsc.org Cert no. SW-COC-1806
© 1996 Forest Stewardship Council

FSC

FSC is a non-profit international organisation established to promote the
responsible management of the world's forests. Products carrying the FSC
label are independently certified to assure consumers that they come
from forests that are managed to meet the social, economic and
ecological needs of present and future generations.

Find out more about HarperCollins and the environment at
www.harpercollins.co.uk/green

The chapter titles in this book are of Incan origin.

They are the names the Incas used for the twelve months of the year.

I have taken the liberty of switching the months of March and April around.

cap huchuy pocoy

If The Cardinal pinched the cheeks of his arse, the walls of the city bruised. They were that close, Siamese twins, joined by a wretched, twisted soul.

He dominated my thoughts as the train chewed through the suburbs, wormed past the warehouses and factories, then slowly braved the shadows of a graveyard of skyscrapers. Enthralled, I pressed my nose to the filthy window and caught a glimpse of Party Central. A brief flash of monstrous majesty, then the gloom claimed all and it was gone. That was where he worked, lived, slept and decided the fate of his cringing millions. Party Central — the heart of the city.

Stories about The Cardinal were as legion as the corpses buried in the city's concrete foundations. Some were outlandish, some cruel, some spectacular. Like the day he played a pope at chess and won a couple of countries. The president who spent forty days and nights prostrate on the doorsteps of Party Central in supplication for having angered The Cardinal. The actor who was guaranteed an Academy Award if he kissed The Cardinal's ass. The suicide bomber who froze at the last moment when The Cardinal shot him an icy look — they say he cried as he was led away, finger pressed hard on the detonator, unable to release it until he was alone.

The one that came to mind as the train slowed and switched tracks was a minor tale, but entertaining, insightful and, unlike a lot of the myths, probably true.

One day a messenger arrived with an important missive from a prince of some oil-rich kingdom. He was escorted to the fifteenth floor for a personal meeting with The Cardinal. This was no mere courier — he was a member of the royal's loyal cabinet, a carefully chosen envoy.

He went in and started speaking, eyes to the floor, as was the custom in his country. After a while he glanced up at his host and stopped in shock. The Cardinal was listening but he was also being blown by a hooker.

The Cardinal frowned when the messenger stopped and told him to continue. He did but falteringly, stuttering, unable to take his eyes off the naked whore going down on the big boss.

The Cardinal quickly lost patience and told the mumbler to leave. The messenger took offence and launched into a scolding tirade. The Cardinal lost his rhythm and shot out of his chair, bellowing like a bull. He crossed the room, grabbed the messenger by the lapels and tossed him head-first out of the window. He sent a note to the prince, telling him not to send any more fools his way, and an invoice to cover the expense of cleaning the mess on the pavement.

It was the type of cheap story you heard at every news-stand in the city. But I loved it anyway. I loved all of the stories. They were why I'd come here — to emulate The Cardinal and maybe one day build my own sprawling empire of sweet, sinister sin.

The sky was grey when I alighted from the train and was enfolded by the arms of the city and its guardian Cardinal. I stood my ground a few minutes, letting my fellow passengers stream past, a solitary rock in the river of disembarkation. I tried isolating specific sights, smells and sounds but my eyes, nose and ears kept flicking every which way, taking in everything, focusing on nothing. Only the taste stood out, of dry diesel, hot plastic and wood sap. Bitter but oddly pleasant at the same time.

As the last few stragglers passed from sight I decided it was time to make a move. There were things to do, people to see and a life to begin. I hoisted my bag and ordered my willing legs into action.

There was no guard at the gate. I stopped, looked around, ticket held out, a country bumpkin with an ironically unhealthy respect for the law. When nobody came to collect it, I pocketed the stub and kept it for posterity's sake, a memento of my arrival.

I left the station and entered the grim, grey streets beyond. It would have been depressing any other time. Dull buildings fit only to be demolished, cloud-laden skies, cars and taxis suffocating in their exhaust fumes, pedestrians wheezing and grimacing as they staggered by. But to me, that day, it was vivid and fresh, a canvas·to paint my dreams on.

I looked for a cab but found a miracle instead.

The crowd drew me. Against that grey, lifeless backdrop they stood out, huddled together, babbling and pointing. I could see the source of their agitation from where I stood by the station's doors, but moved closer to get a better view and be part of the gathering.

It was an exact, concentrated shower of rain. It fell in a literal sheet, about five feet wide and a couple deep. The drops fell in straight silver lines. I looked up and traced the thin streams to the clouds as if they were strings hanging from massive balloons.

A woman to my left crossed herself. 'It's a waterfall from Heaven,' she murmured, wonder in her voice.

'More like God taking a leak,' a man replied, but the glares of his colleagues silenced the joker and we watched in uninterrupted awe for the next few minutes.

Just before the shower stopped, a man stepped into it. He was small, dressed in loose white robes, with long hair that trailed down his back and flattened against his clothes under the force of the water. I thought he was just one of the city's many cranks, but then he extended his arms and raised his face to the sky, and I saw he was blind. Pale white orbs glittered where his eyes should have been. He was pale-skinned, and when he smiled his face became one unblemished blob of white, like an actor's painted face in those old silent movies.

He turned his head left, then right, as if scanning the crowd. I moved closer for a better look and his eyes immediately settled on me. His hands fell by his sides and . . .

I'm not sure what happened. It must have been a shadow, or dust in the drops of rain, because all of a sudden his eyes seemed to come to life. One second they were pure white, the next there was a brown spot at the centre of each, spots which flared and spread until the eyes were full.

He stared at me with the new eyes. He blinked and the brown was still there. His hands lifted towards me and his mouth moved. But before I could cock my ears he stepped out of the rain and back into obscurity. People moved between us and when they parted he was gone.

Then the rain stopped. A last few drops made the long descent and that was it. The crowd dispersed and people went on their way like nothing had happened. I remained longer than the rest, first checking for the blind man, then in the hope of a repeat performance, but finally I gave up and hailed a taxi.

The driver asked where I was going. He spoke strangely, accenting lots of words, grimacing whenever he stressed a syllable. I gave him the address but asked him to drive me about a bit first — I wanted to see some of the city. 'Your money,' he said. 'What's it to me what you tourists do? I'll drive you till night if you like. Least, till eight. That's when I knock off.' He was a sour sort and didn't make any effort to start a conversation, so I concentrated on the city.

It soon started raining – ordinary rain this time – and everything was obscured and warped. Street names, houses, traffic lights, scurrying pedestrians — they all looked the same. They blended into an alien landscape and I felt my eyes start to sting. Leaving the sightseeing for another day, I asked the driver to take me home. *Home* meaning Uncle Theo's place. Theo was the man I'd come to the city to live with. He was going to teach me to be a gangster.

Theo Boratto had been a gangster of great promise. Making his mark early on, by the time he was twenty-five he commanded a force of fifty men and was the scourge of the respectable southwest of the city. He was ruthless when he had to be, but fair — you needn't fear him as long as you didn't cross him. Most importantly he had the blessing of The Cardinal. Theo Boratto was a man on the way up, one for the future.

He was a good home man too. He loved his wife, Melissa, with a passion. He fell in love with her ears first. 'She had small ears, Capac,' he told me. 'Tiny, thin, delicate. They broke my heart, just looking at them.'

He wooed her vigorously and, though she wanted nothing to do with his world of violence, he won her. Their wedding made the society pages of all the papers. He spent a fortune to give her the kind of reception she hadn't asked for but which he believed she deserved. The Cardinal himself provided the cake as a present, hiring the city's best baker to design the iced marvel. The band played flawlessly and there wasn't a single clumsy dancer to be found. The women were beautiful in their designer dresses, the men handsome in their tailored suits. It was a day that made you realize what living was all about.

Their love lasted four wonderful years. Theo still went about his dirty business, burning down houses, breaking limbs, selling drugs, killing when he had to. But he was one of the happiest gangsters the city had ever seen. If you had to be bullied and beaten, there was no finer man than Theo Boratto for the job.

The only thing missing was a child. And that was when it all went to hell.

They didn't worry about it in the early days. They were certain a child would come in time. Melissa had faith in God and Theo had faith in the fertile Boratto testicles. But as the months became years, their faith wavered and questions were asked.

Doctors said they were fine and advised them to keep trying, not to worry, a baby would come along eventually. But years turned, the world changed, and the nursery stayed empty. They tried faith-healers, ancient charms and different sexual positions, read every kind of book on the market and watched the videos, prayed and made promises to God. Finally, when they'd almost given up hope, a sturdy seed broke through and made itself a home.

They threw a wild party when the test came back positive. They moved into a bigger house and bought everything the stores of the city had to offer. Happiness had returned.

It was a brief visit.

There were complications with the delivery. A trembling doctor presented Theo with his options — they could save the woman or the child. No maybes, no mights, no false hopes. One would live and one would die. It was up to Theo to choose.

He nodded slowly, eyes red, heart dead. He had one question — was it a boy or a girl? The doctor told him it was male. 'Save the baby,' Theo said, the last words he would utter for many months.

His wife was buried before his child was christened, and Theo's soul went with her. He was a broken man afterwards, prone to fits of depression. The child might have been his saviour, the light to bring him through the darkness, but fate robbed him even of that. The baby was a weak, scrawny thing. It came into this world on the shoulders of death, and death hovered ominously over the child. The doctors kept the dark gatherer at bay for a fragile seven months, but then he was returned to his beautiful, cute-eared mother, having spent more of his short life within her womb than without.

Theo let things slide. Money seeped out of his hands and into those of greedy, enterprising others. His house was repossessed, his cars, jewellery, clothes. The last deliberate act he committed in those days of descent was to give the child's toys away to charity before someone ran off with them. There was that much left in him which gave a damn. That much and no more.

Starvation and harsh winters forced him back into work. He did enough to eat and pay for a mouldy single room in the cheapest motel he could find. Nothing which required thought. He gutted fish in factories by the docks until the stench got him evicted from his most humble abode. He sold fruit and veg in a cheap street market, sometimes flowers. After five or six years, he returned to a life of crime, going along as an extra on thefts and break-ins. It was a long way from dining with The Cardinal and walking the hallowed halls of Party Central. But Theo didn't care. It kept him fed and warm. That was enough.

Then, inevitably, a theft went wrong. He was apprehended, tried, sent down for eighteen months. Prison re-made him. He took to thinking during his long days of incarceration. He saw where his life was stuck, what he had become, and made up his mind to change. He knew he'd never overcome his grief entirely. He doubted if he could ever be truly happy, or rise as high as he'd been before. But there was middle ground. He didn't have to be this low. If he wasn't going to do the simple thing and kill himself, he might as well do the decent thing and carve out a life worth the effort of living.

He made contacts, talked his way into deals and scams, made sure he had something to go to when he left, jobs which would lead to others and start the ball rolling again. It took years to pull himself back up. The big guns didn't trust him – he'd cracked once, they figured, and might again. He was a risk. But he kept at it, moved from one job to another, proved his worth, clawed his way up the ladder until he was in a position to put forward ideas and initiate his own deals. He employed a few thugs, bought a couple of suits, invested in guns and was back in business.

He built it up over the next few years, expanding his terri-tory, crushing weaker opponents, advancing slowly but surely. When he felt secure, he decided to bring in an heir, someone to carry on when he was gone. In the absence of a son he chose one of his many nephews. He spent a few months sizing them up, then settled for one with a touch of the wicked in his features, with what might prove to be steel in his blood, with a will to succeed at any cost. The nephew he chose was Capac Raimi. *Me*.

Theo wanted to be angry with me for arriving late, and he was scowling as the cab pulled away, stranding me at the foot of the house. But he was too excited to remain hostile, and by the time I was halfway up the steps he was grinning like a kid at a birthday party.

He threw his arms around my body and clutched me tightly. For a small, skinny guy he had a lot of strength. When he released me I was astonished to see him weeping.

That was one thing I hadn't expected from a hardened, twice-come gangster like Theo Boratto. He wiped the tears away with a trembling hand and sobbed, 'My boy, my boy.' Then, sniffing and smiling weakly, he led me into the house, shutting the door gently behind us.

In the sitting room, with the lights up full and a real log fire spitting tongues of flame up the chimney, I got my first good look at him. It had been years since our last encounter. I could hardly remember what he looked like. It was as if we were meeting for the first time.

There wasn't much to him. He was no more than five foot six, slim, very haggard. There was a parting in his hair that Moses would have been proud of, a long stretch of skull with a few brownish spots. The hair at the sides was grey and smartly cut. He blinked a lot, eyes of an owl, and it was nearly impossible at times to see the globes behind the shutters. He was clean shaven, with the shining skin of a man who shaved at least twice a day. His suit was conservative. Light leather shoes, a red handkerchief ornamentally placed in the upper left pocket. The perfect picture of a stereotype gangster. All he was missing was the slit-skirt moll with a sneer and a drooping cigarette.

'What do you think of the city?' he asked when we were comfortable.

'Couldn't see much of it,' I admitted. 'It was raining.'

'It's huge,' he said. 'Growing all the time, like a cancer.' He paused, maybe thinking of death and Melissa. 'I'm glad to see you, Capac. I've been alone so long. I always hoped I'd have a son to take over, but things didn't . . . You know the story.

'Things have been bleak ever since,' he continued. 'I don't mean the business — that's grown nicely. I'm talking about family. Family's what really matters. I've been alone since Melissa. My brothers never followed me into the business.

They went to college, got proper jobs, real lives. We were never close. My sisters . . . they write me now and again.' He shook his head sadly. 'I'm a lonely old man. Nobody to live with, nobody to live for.' He leaned forward, patted my knee and smiled. 'Until now.

'What do you drink?' he asked, getting up. 'Tea, coffee, wine?'

'A beer if it's going.'

'Always!' He laughed and fetched a couple of bottles from the fridge. I gulped most of mine with one thirsty swig and sighed happily. It seemed an eternity since my last one. Theo went slower on his, making it last.

'How old are you, Capac?' he asked shortly after I'd started my second bottle. 'Twenty-seven, twenty-eight?'

'Thereabouts.'

'A good age. Not too old to teach, nor young enough to be a nuisance. One of the reasons I chose you. Not the only one – I wasn't about to pick my successor solely on account of his age! – but a factor.

'It's a hard business,' he said seriously. 'I don't know what your expectations are, but it's not glamorous. The higher you rise, the glossier it gets. But we're at the lower end. Most of our money comes from protection. We threaten people – small shop owners and businessmen – and collect cash in return for not busting up their premises. If they don't pay, we have to make an example of them. It's about violence. Whatever else we profess to be, at the core we're violent people.

'But although we're an illegal business, we *are* a business. We account to the taxman like everybody else, so we have to keep books they can find no fault with. Neglect the paperwork and they'll be on us like jackals.

'There are employees to take care of. We've got expenses, overheads and legal fronts to maintain. It's a hell of a lot harder than running a legitimate business. The bigger teams can afford sharp lawyers to handle that for them, but not us – we have to do it ourselves, be everything, hood, lawyer, businessman, clerk. The profits can be high but only if you run things right, if you don't screw up and leave yourself open to attacks from the law or your opponents. Or The Cardinal.'

He stopped, cocked a finger at me and said, 'Never fuck with The Cardinal, Capac. *Never*. Don't muscle in on his territory, don't challenge even his lowest lackey. If one of his men asks to be cut in on a deal you spent months setting up and perfecting, you agree like a shot, even if it means taking a loss. The Cardinal runs everything and owns everybody. A lot of young men get a bit of power, some money and start thinking, "That Cardinal ain't so tough – we can take him."

'Those young men die. I'll say it again, so there's no confusion – don't fuck with The Cardinal. Steer clear of his crew as much as you can. If your paths cross, show them all due respect. Because if The Cardinal ever gets on your back, he'll ride you into an early grave. No surer thing.'

'Have you had any dealings with him lately?' I asked.

He hesitated and glanced away. 'No,' he said. 'We had a word a few months back through a third – hell, a fourth or a fifth – party. But no direct contact. I'm not big enough to be of interest to him.'

He was lying. I didn't know why, but I made a note to pry a bit deeper later. I had a lot of respect for my Uncle Theo, and knew I was going to learn a lot from him, but I had my sights set on higher targets. I most certainly did intend to fuck with The Cardinal's boys if I ever got the chance, regardless of Theo's warning. The Cardinal was the only route to real power here. If you didn't chance your arm and get involved with him, you'd be running penny-ante protection rackets forever.

Theo swirled the beer in his bottle, staring into its golden depths, and promptly changed the subject.

'*Capac Raimi*,' he said, drawing it out. 'An odd name. I haven't come across anything quite like it before. A Raimi or two, but they normally have recognizable first names, Joseph or Joel. How'd you get a name like that?'

'My father.' I frowned. 'He was a Raimi and, well, I don't know where the Capac came from, but I guess it's some old name or they got it from a book. Didn't my mother tell you?'

He coughed uncomfortably and a shifty look flashed across his eyes again. 'I didn't see much of your mother after she married,' he said. 'We fell out of touch. Families go that way sometimes. What was your father like?'

'He . . .' I tried to draw a mental picture of him. 'A nice guy. He died when I was young, so I don't remember that much about him, but he was a good man.'

'And your mother?' Theo asked, leaning forward, his eyes sharp and unblinking for once.

'She was . . . a *mother*.' I laughed uneasily. 'What's any mother like? She . . .' I stumbled to a halt. I felt uncomfortable, as if I had something rotten in my past that I wanted to keep quiet. 'She was *your* sister,' I said. 'You know as much about her as I do.'

'Of course,' he said too quickly. 'I just wanted to know if she'd changed since I last . . . since she . . .'

He grunted, downed the remainder of his beer, got another couple of bottles and asked no more questions about my family or my past.

I took to crime as if born for it. I was a natural, learning quickly, acting instinctively. I paid attention when Theo spoke and remembered everything he said. He taught me how to deal with employees, customers (we never spoke of victims, they were always clients or customers) and rival gangs. How to balance the books, use legitimate fronts to funnel our profits, and avoid trouble with the long and many arms of the law.

The city was a sprawling, multi-layered monster, anarchic to the untrained eye, but orderly if you eased up close and studied it in detail. The money was centralized in the north where most of the wealthy lived, whether their funds had been generated legally or otherwise. No class prejudices there — if you were rich enough, you were welcome. The streets were spotless, the lamps always worked, cars obeyed the speed limits. No pushers, no pimps, no street hookers. Nobody ever bothered the good folk of the north at home. Even break-ins were rare — the consequences outweighed the rewards to be reaped.

The blacks ruled the east and south-east. They weren't wholly segregated but were as near as could be. The city had an ugly history of racism. Huge riots back in the early 80s resulted in dozens of deaths and destruction of property on a scale usually reserved for earthquakes. Things had calmed down since and colour was no longer the lethal issue it had once been – better schools, improved career opportunities and housing developments had taken the sting out of the race bee – but years of oppression and hate couldn't be washed away as easily as people wished. Some things were slow to change.

The centre of the city was the business sector, the land of banks, office towers and over-priced restaurants. Huge buildings, most built during the last fifty years, functional and frosty.

The north-east, south, south-west and west were the suburbs. The wealthier commuters gravitated towards the south-west, the poorer to the eastern regions. The north-west had its share of migrant workers but was largely undeveloped territory, lots of open fields and parks. Several universities nestled out there, an amusement park, a couple of large sports stadia.

Along the river stood the factories and warehouses, many old and rundown. The city had been built back in the days when boats and power were synonymous. The older factories were being reclaimed and gentrified, but it was a slow process and it faltered with every dip in the economy.

The other divisions – the gang lines – were harder to define. The eastern areas were the domain of the black gangs, too many to count, most small and short-lived. A number of leaders had made efforts over the years to organize and unify the smaller gangs, but The Cardinal was quick to eliminate such threats. He preferred to keep the blacks fractured and in conflict with one another.

Elsewhere it was your usual mix. Strong and weak families, a few large clinical organizations, dozens of street gangs who'd self-destruct before they could amount to anything. Hundreds of drug barons and thousands of pushers. Gangsters built on a foundation of prostitution. Some who'd made their fortunes selling arms. The big thieves who dealt in diamonds and gold, and far more who thrived on protection and petty theft.

The Italians, Irish, Cubans and Eastern Europeans were well represented, but none ruled. There was only one kingpin in this city, beyond the touch of all others, and that was The Cardinal. He controlled the centre directly, the rest as he wished. He was the ultimate individual, proof that one man *could* do it alone, regardless of the help or hindrance of others.

Theo worked the south-west. It was where he'd grown up, along the streets his first boyhood gang – *The Pacinos!* – had patrolled. It was one of the quieter areas, not as much money to make as elsewhere. But there were bank managers and bored housewives with vices, lots of youngsters coming through with expensive habits. The police could be bought cheaply enough and the local councillors were eager to please. There were worse places to get an education.

Theo and I were together most of the time. He was preparing me for the day I'd be able to operate by myself. He figured another six months and I could start running the show for him, guided but with an increasing degree of autonomy. Until then I was his charge. He kept me under close watch, in his company most of any waking day, his literal right-hand man.

We were uncomfortable around each other at first. We'd gone, in the space of a day, from being strangers to partners. Like an arranged marriage. It was difficult spending so much time with a person you didn't know, thrust into a relationship where loyalty, honesty and trust were automatically required. But as the weeks rolled by, we got to know and genuinely like each other. After a month we didn't have to pretend to be friends – we were.

Theo was a strict mentor. He forbade involvement with women. Sex was fine, prostitutes and one-night stands were acceptable, but nothing more. He said it was too soon for romantic commitment. There was a time for love and a time for learning. This was the latter. A woman would distract me at this stage, take my mind off work and confuse my sense of purpose. I didn't agree but he was the boss and I'd made the decision to take his word as law, so I bit my tongue and followed his orders.

Anyway, I was so busy, I doubt I would have had time to chase the ladies. Love requires time and energy, neither of which I had much of following my laborious daily chores and lessons.

Our patch expanded while I was working for Theo. We took over a couple of old, rundown areas and implemented plans to build them up and attract new businesses. We bought out retiring or weak bosses, recruited their forces,

assumed responsibility for their debts, collected their dues.
We moved into drugs, feeding the addictions of the city's
dream-chasers. We got involved in a bit of gun-running and
smuggled a few caches of arms into the city. Like Theo had
said, it was a dirty business, and the better things got, the
dirtier it became.

Though my role was primarily that of an observer, I couldn't
help but get involved. You couldn't move in these circles
without bruising your fists every now and again. Fights would
break out unexpectedly and I'd have to stand my ground
and deal with the situation. Addicts were the worst.
Everything could be going fine, you had the merchandise
and they had the money. You'd be talking, smiling, closing
the deal, and they'd suddenly whip out a knife or a chain,
and off it went.

I was able to handle myself. In my time with Theo, I never
took a bad beating. I kept fit, ate sensibly, worked out at
home every night. I had quick reflexes and a quicker eye. I
took a few hard blows, but mostly to the stomach where
they didn't mark me. My face was as pristine as the day I
arrived, nose straight, ears unchewed. I'd get caught eventually – everybody did – but so far I'd got away lightly.

I hadn't killed anyone. I'd smashed many bones, clubbed
a few heads, tossed a couple of souls from speeding cars. But
Theo held me back from killing. He said he didn't want to
throw too much at me too soon. It was one thing teaching
a crazy crackhead a lesson he'd remember, another to pull
a gun and end his learning forever. Killing was sometimes
necessary, but should always be delegated where possible.
He'd only killed two men personally in all his years. He said
it was two too many.

'Deaths come back to haunt you,' he often muttered. As
worthy an epitaph as any.

*

The big fish was The Cardinal and everything we did (despite Theo's warning that first day) was designed to bait him. There was only so much we could do as an independent organization, only so far we could go on our own. If we were to grow and move in stellar circles, The Cardinal had to acknowledge us. Until that happened, until the call came to visit Party Central or attend dinner at Shankar's, we were trapped in the shoal marked small-fry.

The call to greater things came on a Tuesday. It was nearly six months since I'd arrived. We'd toiled like slaves, building, plotting, planning for the future. We worked well together and brought out the best in each other. I'd rekindled Theo's desire to be successful, and he'd taught me what was possible and what wasn't, separating my wiser ideas from my foolish fancies. His experience and my hunger made us a potent combination.

We knew we were on the right track when Neil Wain contacted us. Wain wasn't one of The Cardinal's men, but he was a ganglord of some note. You had to be wary if you got on the wrong side of him. He had The Cardinal's seal of approval and in the city that was everything. Dealing with him brought us one step closer to Party Central. Wain was a test — we were being sounded out. If we proved ourselves competent, there'd be more to come. Wain was the door to a new world of upper echelon corruption, politics and total control. The world of Cardinal crime.

He wanted us to handle a drugs shipment. He'd arranged for it to be brought into the city but there was too much for him to distribute by himself. We were to take a third, pay the bulk up front and cut him in for a percentage of our profits. He was asking a lot but money wasn't the issue. We wouldn't make much out of the deal in the short run, but long term it could be our most profitable move ever.

We met him at an abandoned wharf warehouse, late

Tuesday night. It had been a struggle getting the money together in so short a time – part of the test – but we cracked a few heads, called in favours and did it.

Theo was excited beyond words. His eyelids were blinking up and down so fast, you almost couldn't see them. His hands were twitching and I could hear his heart beating from ten feet away. 'This is it, Capac,' he told me, squeezing my arm. 'I never thought it would come so soon. It's because of you. Don't deny it! We were going good until you came along, but you've made us go great.'

'You're flattering me,' I protested. 'All I do is follow orders. I'm nothing special.'

'Don't you believe it,' he said. 'Whatever we get tonight, wherever we go from here, it's down to you. This is your night. Enjoy it. Hell, *relish* it.' He bit his lip to stop his eyes watering. He hadn't been this emotional since our first encounter. 'Come on. Let's go meet our destiny.'

We left our limo – hired for the day because you simply *had* to have a limo if you wanted to be a *real* gangster – and walked into the abandoned warehouse with three of our men. Wain was waiting for us, standing patiently beside his own car, briefcase in hand, smile on face. Theo broke into a near-trot and strode ahead of us, arms outstretched, too thrilled to maintain a solemn, businesslike air. 'Neil!' he boomed. 'Neil, by Christ, it's great to see you! How long's it been since –'

Bullets tore his chest apart as if it were a paper bag. His arms flailed and his legs buckled. Blood sprayed in all directions. The gunfire continued, even though he was obviously dead. He was spun around like a whirling dervish. I saw his face and the bewildered expression he was to carry into the next world. Then a couple of bullets wiped it away, expression, face, everything.

Two of the three men with me acted calmly and professionally, diving to the sides, reaching for their holstered guns as they moved. The other soiled his pants, fell to his knees and sobbed for mercy. They all died, caught in a lethal hail of metal pellets from the heavens.

Five seconds later I was standing in a pool of blood with four corpses beginning to steam in the cool night air. The echoes of gunfire were dying away, the walls swallowing the sounds hungrily.

I was stunned. Five seconds earlier I was on my way to fame and fortune. Now I was a standing corpse-to-be. I looked at my uncle, limp and lifeless, and wondered where we'd gone wrong. We'd had no quarrel with Wain. Our paths had never crossed. What was his beef?

I realized, after a few hazy moments, that I wasn't dead. I looked around the warehouse, blinking stupidly. The snipers were strolling down the stairs from the second landing, smoking, laughing, claiming kills. Neil Wain was standing the same as before, unruffled by the bloodshed. He gazed at me without any apparent interest, then turned at the sound of approaching footsteps.

A burly man came out of the shadows, a face like granite. He nodded curtly at Wain, walked past and stopped before me. He looked me up and down. 'You Capac Raimi?' he asked.

I stared at him, mouth open, about half a light year behind the action. I had to be dreaming. I'd wake up in a minute and –

He slapped my face hard. 'Are you Capac Raimi?' he asked again, louder this time, not used to repeating himself. I saw murder in his eyes, death if I kept silent. But I couldn't speak.

Another man crossed the room. He wasn't much older than me and had the look of a society gangster. He laughed as he considered me, spat at my feet and cocked his hat back at an angle. 'This ain't him, Tasso,' he said. 'This's just a bum. Let's kill him and split. I've got a date.' He raised his gun so the muzzle was pointing a centimetre beneath my chin. 'Can I do the honours?'

'Hold, Vincent,' the older guy said.

'Why? It ain't him. This is just some kid with a speech problem. We're wasting time. Let's –'

'I . . . I'm Capac Raimi,' I wheezed.

They looked at each other, unconvinced. 'You got any proof?' the older one asked.

My hands scurried to my pockets, searching for cards and tags I knew I didn't have – I'd never been one for credit cards or clubs that required membership. No driver's licence. I probably had a passport lying back in the house, but I couldn't have sworn to that.

The assassins saw my hands shaking and began to snicker. 'Shit, Tasso,' the younger one said. 'This guy's just some chump who wandered in.' He cocked his weapon and nudged my left ear with it.

The elder statesman shook his head and smiled bleakly. 'You haven't got anything on you to prove who you are? Everybody carries credit cards. You must have at least one piece of plastic.' He raised an arm and cocked a finger at me. 'Your life depends on it, boy. Cough it up or . . .'

'I don't have anything,' I said, voice steady, preparing myself to die with dignity. I looked my murderer in the face and grinned. 'So you might as well go ahead and shoot, you bastard.' I could have given myself a standing ovation. I was about to die, but I was going in style, head held high, and many a man would have paid a fortune to do the same.

The granite-faced killer scratched his chin. 'He said you'd say that,' he muttered. 'That's what the guy in his dream did. Him and his damn dreams. OK!' He clapped his hands and signalled the milling gangsters back to their cars. 'Vincent, you're with me.' Vincent nodded obediently and spun off towards one of the limos parked against the warehouse walls, hidden in the shadows of the slaughter house. 'Wain, take care of the money.' He kicked Theo's case across the floor. 'Make sure The Cardinal gets his cut.'

'What?' Wain's face puckered. 'But I was doing him a favour! We helped him out, damn it. I thought the least he'd do –'

'You thought wrong,' my captor snapped. 'Business is business, Neil, with its right ways and wrong ways. Cutting The Cardinal in – that's the right way. Short-changing him is as wrong as you can get, short of pissing on the devil on your way down the steps to Hell.'

'OK,' Wain grumbled, picking up the case. 'I'll see The Cardinal right. I'm no fool.'

'Glad to hear it. I guess we'd better be off then, Mr Raimi. Would you care to go first?' He beckoned towards the limo which was pulling up beside us. I looked at the man, then the limo, then Neil Wain. I didn't know where this night was heading or what lay in store for me, but seeing as how things were so far out of my hands, I decided I might as well go along obligingly and enjoy the ride. Pulling my coat tight around my shoulders, shivering from the cold and shock, I stepped into the car.

We'd been driving through the silent streets of the city for about ten minutes, nobody saying a word. I was starting to feel uncomfortable. The initial spate of shock which had numbed me to Theo's death was receding, and it was easier to talk than dwell upon the memory of his confused expression and ruby-red blood. Recalling the name Vincent had used back in the warehouse, I cleared my throat to break the silence and asked hesitantly, 'Are you Ford Tasso?'

He looked over in my direction, face expressionless. 'Yes.'

'The famous Ford Tasso,' Vincent snickered. He was driving. 'His name a curse in a hundred languages. Come one! Come all! Bow down and –'

'Shut up,' Tasso said softly, with immediate effect. He'd put up with a lot of Vincent's nonsense, but only to a point, and Vincent was cunning enough never to push his luck.

Ford Tasso. The Cardinal's number two. The strong arm of the city's unofficial king, feared almost as much as the only man he would ever call master. If The Cardinal was a myth, Ford Tasso was a legend.

I examined him in the sliding glare of amber street lights. He was getting on in years, at least in his late fifties. A big man, six-two, bulky like a bear. Thick hair, black as soot. He was sporting a pair of sideburns, relics of the disco age, and a thin moustache. His face was cold and hard. He breathed lightly. Black suit, white shirt, gold cufflinks, rings and chains. Dead eyes.

This was the man who'd run the city with The Cardinal for the last thirty years, who'd killed or bulldozed all in their way. He looked the part. Two words came to mind as I sat back and summed him up. They were cold and blooded. But I kept them to myself. He'd had a nickname once, when he was young – the Lizard Man. He didn't like it. The last man to mock him was found dead a couple of days later, his stomach emptied of organs and filled with snakes and iguanas. He'd been plain Ford Tasso ever since.

They drove me to Party Central. Heart of the city. Home and work place of The Cardinal. The safest place in the world for the invited. Death for any foolish enough to trespass. Vincent pulled up by the front to let us out. Ford dismissed him when we were on the pavement. 'Will you want me later?' he asked.

'Nah,' Ford replied. 'But be at Shankar's early tomorrow. We've got a busy day.'

'Ain't we always?' Vincent grumbled, slamming shut the door. He squealed away in a cloud of burning rubber.

I looked up at the massive building. I'd seen it many times but never this close. It was old, full of architectural curves and angles, a bitch to design, a nightmare to build. Imposing glass windows, red brick lower down, rough brown stone higher up. It looked like a renovated church, but I knew every window was reinforced and wired. Every floor was protected by the most expensive alarm systems available. Men with guns stood ready to shoot down intruders, any time of the day or night. It was an impenetrable fortress. Rumour had it there was even a nuclear fallout shelter buried beneath its floors, equipped to last a hundred years.

Two doormen controlled the massive front portal. They were dressed in red, capped and gloved. Harmless and friendly. The five armed guards to either side of them weren't so welcoming. These were members of The Cardinal's own personal army, the Troops. It had taken The Cardinal a long time to receive government backing for the recruitment and arming of his own personal force. He'd had to buy half the city's politicians and kill the rest. There'd been civil marches and protests from the police. It resembled a war for a while.

The Cardinal wanted his own official army. Everybody else – understandably – was less enthusiastic. Eventually The Cardinal won, like he always did, and the Troops came into being. Five hundred strong and increasing all the time. Ford Tasso had been their commander-in-chief in the early days, before moving onto bigger things.

There were more Troops in the foyer, posted at regular intervals, alert and poised to open fire at the first sign of trouble. I wasn't about to give them any.

The ground floor of Party Central was all tiles and marble, and your feet clacked whenever you moved. From there on up, however, it was carpet. The building was famed for its carpets, imported from Persia and India. They covered every inch of the floors above, even the stairs and in the toilets.

Shoes were outlawed above the first floor. All employees

and visitors had to check in their footwear at one of six reception desks before they could go up. There were no exceptions. Socks or bare feet, nothing more, not even a pair of slippers. And Christ help you if your feet smelled — everybody in the city knew at least one amputation story. The Cardinal had an allegedly sensitive nose and didn't appreciate foul odours in his innermost sanctum.

Ford Tasso and I handed over our shoes and took receipts. The receptionist placed them on a constantly moving conveyor belt and they were swept through to the back for storage. Ford got his bearings, I stared around in wonder, then we were heading for one of the building's many lifts.

It was late but the foyer was busier than most places were during the day. Businessmen with laptops were gathered in small groups, discussing the state of the markets. Off-duty Troops relaxed in the lounge near the back. A dozen or more receptionists manned the various desks around the floor, checking everyone in, arranging appointments, taking phone calls, keeping in contact with the hundreds of agents at work in the field.

The lift was from a different time. Large, carpeted, with cushioned walls and soothing music. There was an operator present at all times, using a cranking lever to guide his ship up and down the twenty-three storey shaft. He was amiable but I could see the bulge of a gun beneath his jacket.

Theo had loved that lift. He'd told me about it several times. He once said, if he could choose where to die, it would be in one of Party Central's marvellous old lifts. The memory brought a lump to my throat and I had to struggle to focus. It would have been nice to grieve for Theo, but these could be my last few minutes alive and I wasn't about to waste them mourning the dead. If I survived, there'd be plenty of time for Theo. My uncle would have expected nothing less of me.

'Good evening, Mr Tasso,' the operator smiled. 'Which floor?'

'Fifteen,' Tasso grunted.

'Certainly, sir.' He shut the door and spoke into a micro-phone. 'Floor fifteen. Mr Tasso.'

'Identification,' a dry, computer-controlled voice answered.

Ford spoke his name. A small panel beneath the micro-phone clicked open and he pressed down his fingers. There was a brief pause, then the lift began to rise, much smoother and faster than I expected. Like the building's exterior, this might look like a throwback to simpler days, but it was modern and efficient beneath the surface, an oiled monster in an antique mask.

Fifteen. That was The Cardinal's floor, hence the security measures. Hellfire. No underlings on the fifteenth. I was being taken to the top man himself.

The lift arrived. We got out. It slid back down.

Two Troops stood to either side of the doors, guns cocked. Three more were opposite. Apart from them, the place was deserted.

The air conditioners were set a couple of degrees lower than normal – I felt goosebumps creep across the back of my neck from the chill. The carpets were scented but lightly, the smell of fresh washing. I wriggled my toes in the plush material. Pinched myself to make sure I wasn't dreaming.

Ford Tasso started ahead of me but I wasn't ready to move yet and stood my ground. He stopped. Looked back. Raised a speculative eyebrow. 'Well?'

'What's happening?' I asked. 'An hour ago I was on my way to a run-of-the mill meeting. Now my uncle's dead, my future's in tatters and I'm on the fifteenth floor of Party Central, presumably about to meet with The Cardinal himself. What the fuck's going on?' I felt it was a reasonable question.

Tasso shrugged indifferently. 'Don't know, kid. The Cardinal said to bring you in and that's what I'm doing. Why he wants you, I neither know nor care. I don't question the ways of The Cardinal.'

'But he must have said something. There must be some –'

He shook his head. 'If you live long enough, you'll realize The Cardinal don't need a reason for anything. And he certainly doesn't have to explain himself. Now come on and quit with the questions. You'll find out the answers soon enough.'

He led me down long corridors, past war chambers, function halls and several computer rooms. The fifteenth floor was an office building of its own, independent and self-supporting, geared to meet all The Cardinal's needs. People moved in the various rooms that we passed, but silently and unobtrusively, like shadows. There was a sense of the sacred to the place.

Tasso led me to a room marked *'BASE'*. A secretary sat outside, busy at her PC. There was always a secretary on hand. The Cardinal often worked right around the clock, in touch with contacts in all the different time zones the world could offer.

She knew who we were without looking up. 'Hello, Ford,' she said, fingers never slowing.

'Hi, Mags. He ready for us?'

'Yes. But it's just the guest. You're to stay here with me.' She looked up and winked. 'Maybe he's trying to push us together. We'd make a good match, huh?'

He chuckled gruffly. 'OK, kid,' he said. 'You heard the lady. In you go.'

I walked over to the door, raised my hand to knock, paused, looked to Tasso for a guiding word. *'In!'* he barked. I took a breath, opened the door and entered the dragon's den.

hatun pocoy

As the door closed I looked around with wide eyes. I hadn't known what to expect, so I should have been ready for anything, but I was still taken by surprise.

The room was black with puppets. They were everywhere, dangling from the walls, slumped over on the floor, lying drunkenly on the huge desk in the middle of the room. Apart from the puppets it was sparse. No pictures hung alongside the marionettes. No computers, plants, water coolers or statues. There was the desk – at least twenty feet long – and several plastic chairs lined against the wall to my right. Two more chairs by the window, one plastic, the other plush, ornate leather. Little else of any note.

Apart from The Cardinal.

He was stretched out in the leather chair, feet crossed, sipping mineral water. He waved a gangling arm, inviting me over. 'Sit,' he said pleasantly, indicating the plastic chair. 'Do you like my display?' he asked, nodding at the puppets.

'Nice,' I gasped without looking around. My mouth was dry, but I managed to force out a few more words. 'Very . . . decorative.'

He smiled. 'Your eyes betray your lack of interest. You

should learn to control them. Now,' he said, lowering the glass, 'take a long look at me. You must be full of curiosity. Give me the once-over, Mr Raimi, and tell me what you think.'

He raised his arms and posed. He was tall, six-five or more. Thin to the point of emaciation. A large nose, hooked like a boxer's. His hair was cropped, shaved to the bone at the sides. He had a protuberant Adam's apple. His head was small for a big man, narrow and pointed, with too wide a mouth. His cheeks were little more than taut, paper-thick flesh. His skin was a dull grey colour. He was dressed in a baggy blue tracksuit and scuffed running shoes. He sported a cheap digital watch on his right wrist. No jewellery. He had long fingers, bony and curved. His fingernails were chewed to the quick. The smallest finger of his left hand bent away from the others at the second knuckle, sticking out at a sixty degree angle. He was in his late sixties or early seventies but I wouldn't have pegged him for a day over fifty.

After I'd scanned him, he lowered his hands. 'My turn,' he said and examined me closely. He had hooded eyes, like Uncle Theo's, but when he focused they opened wide and it was like staring into twin pools of liquid death.

'Well,' he said, 'you're not what I'd expected. How about you? What do you think of me?'

'You're thin,' I said, matching his own nonchalant tone. I didn't know what the game was, but if he wanted to play it cool, that was fine by me. 'I thought you'd be fatter.'

He smiled. 'I used to be plump, but with running the city and everything, I don't have time to worry about small matters like food anymore.'

He lapsed into silence and waited for me to speak. Trouble was, I couldn't think of anything to say. I held his gaze and tried not to fidget. In the end he put me out of my discomfort.

'So you're Capac Raimi. An Inca name, isn't it? From the days of Atahualpa and the Ayars?'

'Not that I'm aware of.'

'Oh, it is,' he assured me. 'I read all about the Incas a few decades back. Their founding father was Manco Capac. Some group's building a statue of him here later in the year. This city's full of Incan links. You'll fit in well with a name like yours.

'You know what the Incas' motto was?' I shook my head, dazed by the surreal conversation. *Manan sua, manan Iluclla, manan quella*. It means don't steal, don't kill, don't be lazy. Totally impractical apart from the last part. But that was the Incas for you.

'Enough.' He smacked his hands together. 'You want to know why I brought you here, why I had your uncle and all his men killed but not you. Right?'

'The question crossed my mind,' I admitted.

'Any guesses or theories?'

I shook my head negatively.

'Good. I hate guesswork. Never pretend to know more than you do. I've no time for fools like that. There's nothing wrong with good old-fashioned ignorance. You can't learn anything if you think you know it all.'

He fell into silence again. As before, I said nothing, but as the minutes passed I remembered something from the warehouse. I thought about it for a moment, then cleared my throat and chanced my arm.

'Ford Tasso said something.'

'Oh?' He looked up. 'Mr Tasso is well-versed in the ways of silence. He doesn't waste words. If he spoke, it must have been important.'

'I didn't take much notice at the time, but now that I look back . . . He said something about dreams. About you dreaming about *me*.'

The Cardinal's face darkened. 'I spoke too soon. Mr Tasso obviously hasn't learned as much about silence as I thought. Still,' he mused, scratching his chin, 'maybe it's for the best. I was wondering how to get around to the dream without seeming like a lunatic.

'I'll tell you about it,' he decided. 'You might find it hard to believe, but this is a world of wonders, Mr Raimi. Those who deny the impossible do the majestic magic of the universe a grave disservice.

'Last week I had a dream. I'd already made plans to kill your uncle. It was a minor matter, one I hadn't given much thought to. Then, as I slept, I dreamt of his murder. I saw it as if watching a film, the warehouse, the unsuspecting Theo, the assassins in the aisles. He entered with his men. I heard the guns blare. I saw Theo and his team drop, mown down like lambs.

'Just as I was turning on my side and preparing to move onto a brighter dream, I noticed one of Theo's men still standing. Bullets were exploding all around but he stood there, smiling, a cocky son of a bitch.

'He strode towards me. I was looking him straight in the face, my dream camera zooming into an extreme close-up. Closer still, until his face filled the world of the dream, smiling and confident.

'Then I awoke. The first thing I thought was, I could do with a man like that. A man that hard to kill, that cocksure and invulnerable . . . he had something to offer. So I checked on Theo's men, his confidants, the ones most likely to come with him to the meeting. Mr Tasso provided me with a list of names which I scanned quickly, following the logic of the dream. One stood out. *Capac Raimi*. An Incan name. A name of power and portent.'

He pointed at me. 'That's why you're here, Mr Raimi. That's why you're not rotting in the warehouse, surrounded by chalk-wielding detectives. My dream and your unusual name.

'Would you like a job?' he asked politely.

'You're joking,' I spluttered once I'd recovered from the shock. 'You're spinning me a wild tale, waiting to see if the dumb hick buys it.'

'Why should I lie to you?' he asked.

'For fun. To confuse me. To see how I'll react.'

He chuckled quietly. 'Is it so hard to believe, Mr Raimi? We've all had *déjà vu* and lived out scenes from our dreams. Why shouldn't I dream of you?'

'Because you're The Cardinal,' I snapped. 'You don't dream about people like me. We're not just beneath you, we're buried a hundred miles underfoot. Even if you happened to dream of Theo and the massacre, even if you *did* see a figure walk unscathed through a rain of bullets, you wouldn't bring him here and offer him a job. It isn't logical. In fact it's dumb.'

I waited for his wrath to fall. The Cardinal was a man with a huge temper, who blew up at the least provocation. I'd just called him a dumb, illogical liar. I was history.

But instead of attacking, he pondered my words, fingers crooked, lips pursed. When he finally spoke, he asked a question. 'Do you know the secrets of the universe?'

'What?' I blinked.

'Are you privy to the secrets of the universe? Can you account for the workings of nature, the movements of the heavens, the advent of life? Do you have an insight into the inexplicable which the rest of us lack? If so, I would pay much for such information.'

'I don't see what –'

'You don't see *anything*,' he snapped. 'You're as blind to the wonders of the world as the rest of us. We know nothing,

Mr Raimi. We have theories, guesses and opinions. We hold beliefs, each as valid and ridiculous as the others. We trust scientists to delve into the pits of time and space, tinkering with great questions like children playing with sand.

'In all my years I've met just one man who seemed to really *know*. He was crazy, a drunk working on the docks. He had trouble tying laces and buttoning his coat. He spoke in fits and riddles, but every word struck me to the core. I listened a very short time, then had him executed. I was afraid of him. If I had listened much longer, I'd have gone mad too. Truth is too much for minds as small as ours.'

His eyes were burning into mine. His long fingers were wrapped around the arms of the chair, biting into the soft fabric.

'I gave up on truth after that,' he said. 'From that day I resigned myself to a life of ignorance and blind acceptance. If I couldn't understand the universe, I decided I'd roll along with it and make the most of its own unfathomable rules. I'd no longer seek answers. I opted to wear my ignorance like an armband.

'Do you know what the secret of my success is?' he asked, changing tack again. I shook my head numbly. 'Knowing how to ride the waves of luck. Everything in this world ties together at some level. I'm sure you've heard the old chestnut about a bird's wingbeat in Australia determining the weather on the other side of the globe. An exaggeration, but as good an example as any.

'It all interconnects. Everything links, sometimes neatly, more often obscurely. A Jew makes fun of a child called Adolf and millions die in the death camps. An apple falls and gravity is understood. A filth-encrusted boy has a dream and The Cardinal is born.'

He stopped, rose, walked to the window and stared down at his city. I didn't know what he was rambling on about.

He was like a mad street prophet. What the hell had I walked into?

He stood at the window for close on twenty minutes. I remained perfectly still. I sensed danger in any untoward action. I was dealing with a fanatic, but he was the most powerful man in the city. *Cautious* didn't come close to what I had to be. Finally, after a silent eternity, he returned to his chair. Crouching forward, he said, 'I'm going to tell you how I run my empire.' He looked around, leaned closer, tapped my knee and whispered, 'Very carefully.'

He laughed and sat back. 'Everything's connected,' he repeated. 'That is what my time on this planet has taught me. It all hooks up somewhere along the line. From the smallest man to the greatest, there are bonds. No man's an island, if I may borrow an obvious phrase. We're all tied to each other, the world we inhabit, maybe even the planets and stars — I'm no believer in astrology but I don't discount it either.

'I try to manipulate the rules of chance and coincidence. I make my choices based on whims. I choose my friends and foes according to instinct. I run this city as the roll of the dice dictates. I've made myself a slave of fortune, Mr Raimi, and have reaped the rewards.

'Example. Some years ago I bought a derelict tenement building near the docks. I planned to renovate it and make a vast profit. A few months later, before construction was set to go, I met with an old gang lord. He drank a few too many vodkas and began talking about this building. He'd had plans and was on the point of buying out the old owner when I stepped in. He offered to buy me out for three million. "I'll give you three big notes," were his exact words. I declined. The building was worth much more than that.

'He went his way and I went mine. I gave it no further thought. A week or so later, I was out walking – as I did once upon a time – when a bum approached and asked for a hand-out. "You got a three-note, mister?" he asked.' The Cardinal crossed his eyes and squeaked as he imitated the hobo. He'd never make a career out of impressions. 'Have you ever heard of a *three-note*, Mr Raimi?'

'No.'

'Neither had I. But they were almost the same words as those I'd heard a week before. Coincidence?' His face split into a smile. 'I rang the old gang lord and asked if his offer still stood. He thought I was joking — like you did tonight. I assured him I was genuine. He agreed hastily, happily. He was getting a bargain. There was no catch, no hidden agenda. I was blowing millions.

'A few weeks later the building burnt down. An electrical fault. The new owner wasn't worried. He'd planned to knock the old whore down anyway. It meant he'd have to pay a bit more to clean the place up but in light of the profits to come, that didn't matter.

'But when they were digging down to clear out the foundations, they discovered it had been built on – I shit you not – an ancient burial pit. There were thousands of corpses beneath that old wreck. As if that wasn't bad enough, it turned out to have been a burial ground for *plague victims!*'

He burst out laughing at that point and pounded his fists against the sides of the chair. 'The fucking *plague!*' he gasped when he got his breath back. 'Once word got out, the project was dead. The council declared it both an historical site and hygienically suspect. The press dug up rumours and wild tales, the sort any old building has attached to it — mysterious deaths, murderers and rapists who lived there, etc. To cap it all, my old friend had to fork out for excavation costs.

'It set him back millions. Would have done the same to anyone. Even *my* pull couldn't have made a success of it. So, thanks to a street bum's mumblings, I was three million to the good instead of many more to the bad. I ignored logic, put my fate in the arms of chance, and emerged the stronger.

'Do you start to see, Mr Raimi?'

'You couldn't have known that was going to happen,' I protested. 'A crazy thing like that. You couldn't have predicted –'

'Of course not!' he interrupted. 'Have you listened to anything I've said? I just got through boasting of my ignorance. I know next to nothing about the workings of the world and the forces which bind us together. I'm not a fortune teller. I can't see into the future. That's not what my tale was meant to imply.

'I act on observed phenomena. I don't draw conclusions, think, hypothesize or question. When something happens –' he snapped his fingers '– I jump. When I become aware of a coincidence, I look immediately to incorporate it into my plans. Everything ties together, Mr Raimi. That is the first and only law. If you accept that – if you believe it – you can start to *use* it.'

He rubbed his forehead with his bony fingers. I could see the frustration behind his eyes. He was trying to impress upon me his secrets. He wanted to convert me. *Why*, I couldn't tell.

'The world has laws of its own,' he resumed. 'We don't have to understand them. We just need to obey them. Like with the three-note. There was nothing to say the two men were linked by the coincidence. But I took it as a sign that they were. At some unknown level they were connected by various strings of the universe. Sensing that connection, I acted. By acting, I profited.'

He stopped again and took a drink. 'That's how I do business,' he said softly. 'People see the killings I make on the markets and real estate. They look at the powerful friends I cultivate then abandon shortly before their unexpected falls. They wonder how I know so much, how I'm so often one step ahead, anticipating success and failure prior to everybody else. They assume I'm a cunning speculator, with a team of wise advisers. They're wrong. All I do is follow my instinct and play along with my hunches.

'Would you care for a drink?' he smiled.

While The Cardinal fetched a beer from the fridge in the office outside I went over his words and tried to make sense of them. He might be playing with me, selling me a wild tale designed to test my gullibility factor. But he seemed genuine.

When he returned I said, 'It wouldn't work. It couldn't. By the law of averages you'd have to lose more than you made. You'd have no control. It just wouldn't work.'

'But it does.' He gestured at the office. 'You must remember, these are not the ravings of a gambler with his latest sure-fire can't-lose scheme. I'm living off the fat of decades of proven success. This isn't a possibility – it's fact.

'It's not as simple as the three-note example suggests. I used that because it was colourful and illustrative. In most cases the links are much more slender, far more subtle. Recognizing and interpreting them is a near-impossible task. It's easy to make a mistake, choose wrongly, miss an opportunity.

'You have to ignore the risks, put your brain on hold and follow your instincts, even when your head insists you do otherwise. Sometimes you get burnt. I've been singed many times. Roasted once or twice. You have to live with the fire. Because if you start thinking too much or playing safe, you're lost to its wondrous charms forever. You become part of the real world again, the mundane, the ordinary, from where there's no escape.

'You're here tonight because I had a dream of a strange man, then found a man with a strange name. Will you serve

me faithfully? Be an addition to the firm? Help make me
another few million?' He shrugged. 'Time will tell. Time tells
all in the end. I feel you're right, that you're the man from
my dreams, but –'

'That's plural.'

'Excuse me?'

'You said *dreams*. I thought you'd only had one.'

The Cardinal stared at me like I was some hideous viral
strain. 'Slips of the tongue are the nuggets men like myself
kill for,' he said coldly. 'They should be sought zealously,
always cherished, never idly revealed. I made a mistake and
said something I didn't mean to. You noticed — congratula-
tions. But you revealed your knowledge and that was foolish.

'Keep your secrets under wraps,' he told me, pulling mind-
lessly at his loose trousers. 'No slip of the tongue is ever truly
irrelevant. That might save your life one day or at least prevent
you throwing it away, as you very nearly just did.'

'You'd kill a man for commenting on one of your slips?'
I asked sceptically.

The Cardinal smiled like a shark and said, 'I've killed men
for far less than that, Mr Raimi. You take your life in your
hands when you come to work for me. But that's a risk
you're more than willing to run, isn't it?'

I said nothing and in my silence he found all the confirmation he required.

Later The Cardinal summoned a third member to our small
meeting. He introduced the woman as Sonja Arne. We shook
hands before she took her place in the chair she'd drawn up
when entering the room. She was good-looking, in her forties,
lightly made up, hair greying. Her face was sharp and atten-
tive but kind around the lips and eyes. She was dressed in
a smart skirt and neutral blouse. A sombre, serious businesswoman.

'Miss Arne,' The Cardinal said, 'this is Capac Raimi. He's going to be working for you. I want you to teach him the business. Introduce him to the right people. Make sure he learns the moves and secrets of the trade. I want him to be your star pupil. If he picks up the tricks of the trade quickly, fine. If he doesn't, beat them into him.'

'No problem,' she said, looking me over. 'He's presentable and that's a start. A less aggressive suit, a touch of colour, a haircut . . . Let me hear you speak.'

'Sure. You want me to ramble on a bit or would you like some recitals? I know some good Dr Seuss.'

She nodded approvingly. 'A good voice. I don't think we'll have any problems. A few weeks under my watchful eye and he'll be one of the best salesmen this city has to offer.'

'*Salesman?*' I frowned and looked at The Cardinal.

'Miss Arne heads my insurance division,' he explained. 'She's going to teach you how to sell insurance.'

'*Insurance?* What the . . . Oh.' I grinned. 'You mean protection.'

His face darkened and I knew immediately I'd made a *faux pas*. I backtracked rapidly. 'Not that . . . I mean to say . . . if you want to call it insurance, that's fine. I won't –'

'*Mr* Raimi,' he growled, 'if I meant to say *protection*, I would have. I've never been afraid to call a spade a spade. Protection accounts for a sizeable percentage of my income, yes. But I don't want you to engage in such affairs at this time. Later, perhaps, but for the moment you'll concentrate on insurance. Miss Arne will teach you how to sell. She'll introduce you to our different and varied policies, show you how to push them, then set you loose – in an entirely legal capacity – on the good citizens of this city. Do you follow?'

I stared at him, confused at first, then angry. 'That's why you brought me here?' I snapped, forgetting my place. 'To become a fucking insurance agent?' I heard Sonja gasp but

I didn't care. Let the bastard kill me. I wasn't about to become a salesman, not for The Cardinal, God or the Devil. 'Listen,' I began, but The Cardinal raised a commanding hand and stopped me.

'Mr Raimi,' he tutted, 'there's no need to get so excited. I understand your concerns. I realize this isn't what you were expecting. But you must learn to trust me. I am older than you and vastly more experienced. I know what I'm doing.

'Miss Arne, will you tell Mr Raimi how you started in this company?'

'I was a prostitute,' she said. That shut me up. I gawped at her. This neat, precise, cultured businesswoman — a whore?

'It's true,' she replied in response to my unvoiced query. 'I came here looking for secretarial work. The Cardinal took me aside and offered me a position in prostitution instead. He outlined the terms of my contract, how much money I could expect to make, working hours, promotion prospects and the like. Although I'd never considered it before, I took him up on the offer.'

'You had many customers?' he asked.

'Plenty. I was good. I was popular.'

'And how did you end up here, in your current position?'

'I saved,' she said. 'When I had enough money to retire, I told you I was through and asked for another job. I'd taken a few courses in my spare time, picked up a lot from my clients, and felt I had something to offer other than my body.'

'And she had,' The Cardinal said, addressing me again. 'Miss Arne has an incredible head for figures and the ability to see through bullshit in seconds. I placed her in one of my insurance firms. Five years later she was running it. The moral? It's not where you start out – it's where you end up.'

He picked one of the puppets up off the desk and toyed with it. He manipulated the strings expertly, fluidly moving its hands, feet and head. He made it do a dance, grinning fondly. When he was through, he tossed it to the floor and carried on as if there'd been no interruption.

'Insurance is a fascinating field, Mr Raimi. It can teach you all you'll ever need to know about people. Successful insurance agents study their customers and find out what makes them tick, what frightens them, what entices them. They learn *why* people act the way they do. It gives them insight, ideas, understanding. Men in the protection business simply go around with guns and collect money. There is no finesse, no style, no learning. They scare people and take their cash. You could spend a lifetime in protection, make a fortune and build your own empire, and you still wouldn't be as useful to me as a man with a year of insurance under his belt.

'I want you to *learn*, Mr Raimi. I want you to experience the world of legality and honest men. Then, when you're ready, I'll let you dive beneath that surface to the world beneath, of desires, dreams and death. It's a dark, dangerous world and you'll drown if you jump in too quickly. Insurance first. Protection and other fields later. That's how I want it to be. That's how it *will* be. Agreed?'

I wasn't happy. But, given the time, place and the man before me, who was I to argue?

'Agreed,' I said shortly.

'Good.' He rubbed his hands together and raised an eyebrow at Sonja. She took the hint, stood and awaited permission to withdraw. He turned to me for the final time that night, a king dismissing one of his servants.

'You may go now,' he said. 'You begin work tomorrow, whenever Miss Arne summons you. A morning meeting at Shankar's, I imagine.' He looked to her for confirmation and she nodded. 'Mr Tasso will escort you to your new lodgings. He will also contact you in the near future, depending on how you fare in your day job, and teach you a few things other than insurance. That is all, Mr Raimi. Learn quickly. Work hard. Believe.'

And that was it. He'd lost interest in me. I rose, heart beating fast, knees shaking, and followed Sonja out to where Ford Tasso was waiting for us.

'Still alive, kid?' he smirked.

'Christ,' Sonja said, dabbing at her forehead with a crisp handkerchief. 'You never get used to that. It's been four years since I was in there last. I didn't know until he started talking if he'd called me in to promote or kill me.' She smiled weakly and squinted at me. She almost looked jealous. 'There was no question of him killing you though. He's got the hots for you. Even called you Mr Raimi.'

Ford's head came up. '*Mr* Raimi?' he echoed.

'What's so unusual about that?' I asked.

'The Cardinal calls those he likes by their first name. He uses surnames for people he's doing business with. Only those closest to him get called Mr, Mrs or Miss. I was with him eight years before he started calling me Mr Tasso. It's a mark of approval, a sign you've arrived and are here to stay. I've never heard him use it with some kid he's had dragged in off the street.'

He pinched my chin, tilted my head left and right, then grunted. 'Looks like you're going places, kid. I figure it's just as well I didn't let Vincent waste you. Come on.' He punched me on the arm. 'Let's get you settled in for the night. How does the notion of a room at the Skylight grab you?'

'Sounds good,' I mumbled, then let him lead the way down to the ground floor, where we collected our shoes and hailed another limo.

Party Central, Shankar's, the Skylight. They were the three architectural pillars on which The Cardinal's empire rested.

I couldn't have dreamt of entering any of them just six hours earlier.

The Skylight hotel was a huge box of metal and glass, encircled by a sea of gleaming cars. The city was full of hotels but the Skylight was where the cream came. Large, widescreen TVs in every room for starters, with a digital video library you could access whenever you liked. Four bars. Three swimming pools. Two gyms. A world-class restaurant. A wireless system and telephone lines which were the safest in the city, regularly scanned for bugs by the best experts money could buy. Free drugs compliments of the management (police never raided the Skylight). A spa frequented by movie stars. Computerized locks on every door. No theft or unauthorized soliciting — the Skylight was guarded by the Troops.

Ford said nothing while we checked in. The girl behind the desk smiled, took my signature and fingerprints, then asked if I had a passport-sized photograph. I didn't, so she took my photo with a digital camera. A bulb flashed, capturing my startled expression, then she printed it on her PC.

We were there eight minutes max. During that time I saw two TV stars, a big-name actress who'd have been mobbed anywhere else, several gangsters (all at least five times as powerful as Theo had been), more millionaires than I'd seen in my previous six months in the city.

When the receptionist handed me my pass card, a bemused Capac Raimi gazed up at me, his name, prints and room number lying neatly down the left.

'This is your credit bar,' she told me, tapping a thin metallic line. 'Present this at any of the leisure facilities and you'll be taken care of.'

'How much credit do I have?' I asked.

'Unlimited,' she replied.

'Can I afford this?' I asked Tasso.

'The Cardinal's picking up the tab.'

'Are all his subjects treated this well?'

'Just his pets. Come on. I've a bed to get back to.'

The lift was ordinary compared with the one in Party Central. Large, modern, clean, but unattended and without dramatic operational procedures.

We got out on the eighth floor. It was a short walk to my room. I ran the card through the scanner at the side. There was a sharp buzz, the door slid open and we entered. It was small, nothing special, a let-down after the glamour of the lobby. A few prints, ordinary carpets, plastic flowers in a vase.

'What do you think?' Ford asked, dimming the lights.

'It'll do,' I said, trying not to sound disappointed.

'You can order up stuff if you want,' he said. 'More pictures. Statues. A four-poster bed. You can even change the carpets. They've got a catalogue of extras – you'll find it in one of the drawers – designed to please.'

That sounded more like it! 'At any rate, it's better than Uncle Theo's new resting place,' I joked.

'You don't seem too upset by his death,' Tasso remarked.

I shrugged. 'I'd only known him a few months. We were in a dirty business, we knew the risks. It's the way things go.'

Ford nodded. 'You've got the right attitude.'

'The Cardinal certainly thinks so,' I said smugly, 'and he's never wrong.'

'No,' Ford contradicted me, 'he's often wrong. But who's gonna tell him?'

'What do you think he's got in mind for me?' I asked.

'I don't know, kid. The Cardinal doesn't confide in anyone. You learn to live with that and take no offence, or you get out quick. Speaking of which . . .'

He left and I was alone for the first time that long and unbelievable night.

I moved about the room in a daze, replaying my conversations with Ford Tasso and The Cardinal. At times I was sure I'd dreamt it all, that I'd died by the docks and this was my final dream. I'd wake up any minute and . . .

I realized I hadn't been to the toilet in almost – I checked my watch – nine hours! I rectified that, then washed my hands, brushed my teeth and prepared for bed. I was about to climb under the covers when it struck me that, in all my months in the city, I'd yet to watch a sunrise. I dragged a chair over to the window, pulled back the curtains and sat down for nature's finest show. My head was still spinning and my fingers were shaking from delayed shock. I let my head loll back a moment to relieve the tension in my neck and before I could stop myself I was asleep and the sun was left to rise without an audience.

airiway

A maid woke me at seven to say Sonja Arne was expecting me for breakfast at Shankar's in forty-five minutes. If I was late, I'd have to go hungry until lunch.

I splashed water over my face, scraped the crust from my eyes, brushed back my hair, didn't shave – I'd call it designer stubble – sprayed under my armpits, slipped into my gear from the night before and was set to go.

The concierge spotted me in the lobby – I don't know how she knew me, since she wasn't on duty when I arrived – and asked if I required a limo. I said I'd take a cab instead – they were more my style – and one of the bell-boys hailed one for me. As I relaxed and stared off into space, I thought I recognized the back of the driver's head. He looked like the guy who'd picked me up half a year ago when I first came to this jungle of metal, glass and brick.

'Do you get many fares around the Skylight?' I asked, sounding him out.

'Nah,' he replied gruffly. 'Most of that lot are too high and mighty for a car like this.' He had a curious way of accenting random words. I was sure it was him now.

'How about train stations? Do you –' I began as he stopped for a red light, but he cut me short.

'Look,' he snapped, 'just can it. I want nothing to do with your kind, OK? I'm giving you a ride, let's leave it at that.'

'No need to get aggressive,' I grumbled. 'I was just trying to be friendly. I didn't mean –'

'I don't care what you meant,' he interrupted. 'I'm not interested.' He honked at a pedestrian and was getting ready to wind down his window when the lights changed and he had to move on or risk being bulldozed by the river of cars to our rear.

'You work for The Cardinal, right?' he sneered. 'Big man. Throws his money around like confetti. And everybody grabs, smiles and puckers up to kiss his hairy old ass. Sickening.'

'You sound like you've had a run-in with him,' I said.

'Me? Nah. I'm just a cabbie. I've never even seen him.'

'Then what's your problem?'

'What he's done to this city. This was a good place to live. It had its problems, sure, but the scum knew their place and stuck to it. These days they run riot. Dirt everywhere you look. Everybody on the take. Because of him.'

'Why don't you leave if you hate it that much?'

'*Leave!*' If he'd had a cigar, he'd have spat it out. 'Why should I? It's my city too. I pay taxes, I earn my living. Nathanael Mead moves for no man.'

'Nathanael Mead,' I repeated. 'I'll remember that.'

'Do,' he sniffed, then let me off at Shankar's a couple of minutes later. I thought he might refuse the tip, me being one of the anti-Christ's footmen, but he took it, albeit grudgingly.

The maître d' was all smiles when I introduced myself. He treated me like a favourite regular and escorted me to table nineteen, waving aside the aides who normally seated the guests.

Shankar's was owned by Leonora Shankar, the woman behind The Cardinal in his formative years. The hippest restaurant in the city, where everybody who was anybody wanted to eat. But all the money in the world couldn't snare you a seat unless you were part of The Cardinal's crew. It was reserved for his people, from the shoeboys to the Troops to the executives. The food was great, the atmosphere delightful, and The Cardinal always covered the tab. One of the perks of the job. Occasionally the doors would open to a non-member but outsiders were rare and carefully monitored.

It was a huge, one-room complex, divided into two levels. The upper floor was made of glass and completely transparent – women with skirts and dignity usually dined below. It was a place of glass, marble and steel. Leonora Shankar was renowned for her cold tastes. There were no carpets or rugs. Lots of people complained about the decor, but when you were getting your meals gratis it was hard to be too critical.

There was no privacy in Shankar's. Everybody was there on The Cardinal's business and had nothing to fear. It was the safest spot in the city, short of Party Central. Impossible to bug or infiltrate. There was an unwritten law that nothing heard in Shankar's could ever be discussed outside. It was a law everyone paid strict attention to – the cost of breaking it was instant execution.

There was a man with Sonja when I arrived, as strange a figure as you were likely to find, swathed in sweeping robes and scarves, sandals, hair long and plaited with colourful ribbons, face covered in tattoos which looked real from a distance but were just paint. He sprang to his feet when I reached the table and before I could speak he jabbed a bony finger at me. 'Are you Capac Raimi?' When I nodded, he shrieked theatrically and threw his hands in the air. 'Too soon!' he yelled, then spun around and dashed off.

'Who the hell was that?' I asked, bemused.

Sonja smiled. 'He'll introduce himself when the time's right. I'd hate to steal his thunder.'

'That guy works for The Cardinal?'

'He used to,' she said. 'He was a high-flier once, but then he quit and now he's a nobody. He's left alone on The Cardinal's orders, comes and goes as he pleases. A lot of people would like to see him dead. Ford Tasso's one. There's nothing Ford hates more than a quitter. Personally I like him. I think you will too. Did you sleep well?'

'Not really. I nodded off in a chair, waiting for dawn to break.' I rubbed the back of my neck, trying to massage out the stiffness. 'How about you?'

'Same as usual. Popped a pill and slept like a baby. Do you want anything special for breakfast or do you trust me to order?'

'I place myself at your mercy.'

She ordered toast and cornflakes, low-fat butter and skimmed milk on the side. 'This is it?' I asked, disappointed. I was expecting something more exotic.

'I believe in simple starts,' she said.

I buttered my toast, milked my cornflakes and ate. 'Tell me,' I mumbled, 'and please interrupt if I'm being rude, but what you said last night — was it true?'

'About being a prostitute?'

'Yeah.'

'True.'

'Oh.'

'You don't approve?' she smiled.

'I thought it was something people fell into when all else failed,' I said. 'You made it sound like a career move.'

'It was,' she said. 'I'd never go back, and I wouldn't have started if I thought I couldn't move on to something better, but I'm not ashamed of my life. I did what I had to.'

'But surely it affected your love life. What did your boyfriend think?'

'I didn't have one,' she said. 'My current girlfriend wouldn't have approved, but I didn't meet her until later, so that wasn't an issue.'

'You're a . . . ?' I coughed uncomfortably.

'Yes,' she laughed as I blushed. 'And in case you were going to ask, I didn't turn to women because of my traumatic experiences with men while on the game.'

'The question never entered my mind.'

'I bet.' She poured some milk into a crystal glass, took a sip, wiped around her mouth with her satin napkin. 'This is Adrian,' she said.

I turned and looked back. A young man was standing directly behind me, a baseball cap held between his joined hands in a stance of mock respect.

'Hi, sis,' he said, drawing up a chair. 'What's hanging?'

'This is Capac Raimi. You're going to be assisting him.'

'Nice to meetja,' he said, nodding.

'Likewise. You're Sonja's brother?'

'Yeah. Can't you see the similarity?'

'No.' The two were as different as mud and gold. While Sonja was cool and sophisticated, this guy was dressed in jeans and a creased shirt. She was dark, he was pale. Different hair and faces. Plus she was a couple of decades his senior — he couldn't be much more than twenty.

He chuckled. 'You're thinking of the age gap, right? She looks old enough to be my mother.' Sonja punched his arm. 'I was a late arrival,' he said. 'A gift from the gods. Surprised the shit out of Mom and Dad, eh, sis?'

'To put it mildly.'

'So, what's the brief?' he asked.

'Capac's our latest recruit. He'll be under my direct supervision. I want you to take care of him, show him around, introduce him to the fun people and places. See to his needs. Educate him. Be his friend.'

'See?' he whined. 'She even tells me who my friends should be!' He pretended to cry, then shrugged indifferently. 'I don't care. It'll be nice to have someone my own age around.'

She wiped her mouth, placed her utensils neatly on one of the side plates and got up. 'You can start by driving us back to the office, so I can set him up with a cubicle and get him started.'

'Can you wait a couple of minutes? I haven't had breakfast.'

'Tough,' she snapped.

He shook his head sadly and clicked his teeth. 'All part and parcel of working for your sister,' he sighed. 'Family and work should never mix. Coming?'

'Might as well,' I said, finishing my toast. 'I wouldn't want to miss my ride.' I looked at the table and put a hand in my pocket. 'Do we leave tips?'

'Not in Shankar's. Nor the Skylight. The big guy pays the waitresses top rates. They sign a contract when they join, promising not to accept gratuities.'

'It's strange not tipping,' I said. 'I feel like a cheapskate, like Steve Buscemi in *Reservoir Dogs*.'

'Great movie,' Adrian said. 'They don't make them like that any more. Don't worry,' he said, clapping me on the back, 'you'll get used it. There's lots of differences when you sign on with The Cardinal.'

The next few months were tedious and long. I'd never sold anything in my life, or had to deal with the public face-to-face. Never had to go into a meeting with somebody I knew nothing about, whose trust I had to earn and then slyly exploit.

I was expected to be a great salesman. I was under orders

to pick up in weeks what others spent years learning. Sonja chose my clothes, enrolled me for elocution lessons, worked on my posture. She taught me to read people at a glance, how to scrutinise faces, note nervous tics and shrugs of fake confidence. A couple of nights a week were devoted to security footage. She'd bring home a box full of discs scavenged from some of The Cardinal's many shops and stores. We'd watch face after face, body after body, analysing, discussing, theorizing, until I wished I'd been washed up on a desert island at birth and never seen another human.

I blew a lot of my early meetings. I'd lose my way in the middle, the paperwork would become overwhelming, my tongue would run away from me. I'd forget what I was selling. Sonja didn't mind. She said I had one thing most other sales people would have killed for — the freedom to screw up. I didn't have to worry about a mortgage, my job, a family, bills. This was mere education.

In time I improved, learnt how to read faces, to fish around until I found the right bait to make the sale. Every customer was different, each wanted something unique, and the trick was tapping into that. There was no set patter, no definitive approach. Some needed coaxing, some bullying, some bribing. Sometimes you had to throw every policy in the book at them, in the hope one would stick. Other times you needed to focus on one lone premium.

The most important thing I gleaned – the reason The Cardinal put me there – was that it's *re*action which makes a man powerful, not action. I thought plans could take you to the top, that success came from knowing more than everybody else, preparing better, moving faster.

Wrong. Power came from watching others, standing back, studying, waiting, reacting. Let your mark make his case. Never be first to speak. Plan nothing until you knew what your foe had up his sleeve.

The computer records were the worst. Sonja drilled me in the ways of every legal procedure she could access, hammering home law after law, regulation after regulation. She said there were two types of people in any company – those who knew a bit about how everything worked, and those who shovelled shit. She said I'd either learn all there was to know or she'd pimp out my skinny, no-good ass.

An average day would start at seven. Down to Shankar's for breakfast. Back to the office, power up the computer, read until my eyes burnt. Douse them with water and read some more. A few trips round the city with Adrian, meeting potential customers, putting the preparation into practice. Shankar's for lunch. More customers and lessons. Late supper at Shankar's. Home to the Skylight to work from my bed until eleven or twelve. Lights out.

I travelled all over the city, though most of my time was spent near the centre. It was a different world to the quiet south-west. The streets were full by seven-thirty every morning, clogged with every make of car under the smog-obscured sun. Driving was a nightmare. The city wasn't designed for modern traffic. The roads were built around the buildings, twisting and intersecting at random. They were narrow, badly lit, many in poor condition. Gangs of kids amused themselves every day by rearranging street signs, shuffling them around like paper cards. If you didn't know an area, the rule of thumb was to take a cab.

People were constantly trying to improve the city's image. New buildings, fresh coats of paint, massive renovations, new roads, roundabouts and flyovers. On the outskirts it was working. But here, in the middle, it was a waste. No matter how fast they worked, others worked faster — squatters, gangs, dealers, pimps. They took over new buildings, defaced freshly painted walls, tore down street lamps, chipped the roads away with pickaxes. This was their city. They liked it as it was.

Brief respites from the insurance world came courtesy of
Ford Tasso, who turned up every so often and dragged me
out into the field, taking me along on one assignment or
another, testing my skills, teaching me a few tricks of the
trade. I loved those trips, the men in dark coats and shaded
glasses, the slit eyes, the cold guns, the casual stories of death,
robbery and old criminals. I felt at home in Ford's company.

I got to know Adrian like a brother. We spent most of the
days together and – once I'd settled in and found my stride
– often much of the nights, hitting the club circuit. He never
seemed to tire, though he worked the same hours I did. He
must have napped in the car while I was with customers,
though I never caught him.

One night, while we were relaxing in one of the Skylight's
massage parlours, I asked what his secret was. He twisted
around, wiped his long hair out of his eyes and said,
'Cartoons.'

I propped myself up on an elbow. 'What?'

'I watch a lot of cartoons.'

'What's that got to do with anything?'

'We've all got to laugh. Laughing is vastly underrated.
Clears the lungs for a start. Did you know there's a supply
of bad air in the lungs, a load of crappy gas which accumu-
lates in the lower sacs? That's what causes cancer and loads
of other illnesses. Check the statistics — most cancer casual-
ties are people who rarely laughed. Laughter's good for your
health. Plus it keeps your blood flowing freely. Clowns don't
have heart attacks.'

'Bullshit.'

'It's in the journals.'

'What journals?'

'That's the secret of my vitality,' he said, ignoring my question. 'I watch cartoons and laugh. I fit in at least two or three
hours worth a day. Any sort, old or new, good or bad. You

don't have to watch them the whole way through. A couple of minutes here, a couple more there. They all add up.' He lay back and smiled at the ceiling. 'You should try it sometime. Man wasn't meant to be serious.'

I thought he was kidding me. Adrian liked to spin yarns and you had to take his word with a generous pinch of salt. But a few weeks later we were on the town and got lucky. Picked up two beautiful exchange students, tall, lithe, golden and eager to experience the wonders of the new world. We normally retired to the Skylight on such occasions, but we were closer to Adrian's apartment that night.

They were both called Carmen (so they said). Mine was clumsy in bed — she'd had too much to drink and couldn't concentrate. We messed around for a while, but when she went to the bathroom to brush her teeth, I felt let down. I heard giggling and the low sound of a TV coming from Adrian's room. Grinning, I sneaked over to the door and quietly opened it a crack.

Inside Adrian was laughing and rubbing his Carmen's head fondly as she pleasured him with her mouth. On the TV screen, Wile E Coyote was lugging his latest destructive device from ACME up a hillside.

Shutting the door, I returned to the spare bed, smiling, and made a note to ring down for a Bugs Bunny feature the next time I was courting.

There were four classes of people in Shankar's. You didn't notice the divisions until you'd been there a few months. At first it looked like everybody was on an equal footing, no social discrimination. But that was just on the surface.

The first class was small and distinguished. Leonora Shankar, Ford Tasso, a few others. These were people you never approached, the cream of the crop, with inestimable power or influence. They were a law unto themselves, the gods of the company. We'd have sold our souls to get in with them but the Devil had no pull where The Cardinal was concerned.

The second class incorporated the majority. These people came to Shankar's occasionally. They liked the restaurant, some dropping by three or four times a week, but when all was said and done it was just another place to socialize and do business.

The third and fourth classes were regulars, men and women who came every day. To them Shankar's was home. Some stayed from opening until the early hours of the next morning. Others, with work to do, were absent for long stretches, but made at least a couple of daily appearances.

The third class was made up of veterans. The soldiers and generals from the early days, those who'd pushed The Cardinal to the top and had been put out to grass. This was where they spent their retirement, the one place where they still meant something. They were popular among the younger regulars, sought out for tales from the past, secrets which could be divulged now that they were no longer integral to The Cardinal's operation.

They were a mine of information. They knew everybody, where the real power lay, which avenues were shut and which were worth exploring. They knew all the big deals going down and would make introductions if you asked nicely. You found them all around Shankar's, alone or in small groups, silent, watching, waiting to be approached and activated.

They could have been mistaken for magical statues which mysteriously came to life when the right words were uttered, were it not for their shaking hands and trembling lips, products of old age and a life in servitude to The Cardinal. They could be spooky at times. I'd look at them and think, *Is that me? Thirty, forty years down the road, will I be sitting here, hands*

shaking on the head of a cane, eyes wet with tears, living off the
dreams of somebody else's youth?

I was part of the fourth and final class. There were about
forty of us, in our twenties or thirties, hungry – no, *starving*
– for success. We were the dreamers, the Roman conspir-
ators, each hoping to plot and scheme our way to the top.
We met every day in Shankar's, friendly, courteous, revel-
ling in the bonhomie, but ready to turn on each other in an
instant. We were best friends and bitter rivals. Some of us
would, one day, make it to the top we so yearned for, but
only at the expense of our companions.

We spent our time discussing the ins and outs of the
corporation, who was hot, who was fired, who was dead.
We followed every twist and caper avidly, treating our supe-
riors like idols, giants to be revered. When Gico Carl offed
his father and brothers and took over the western side of
the city, we debated his tactics for weeks, dissecting,
analysing, learning. Always learning. When Emeric Hines –
one of The Cardinal's best legal minds – went to court, we
taped his appearances and replayed them endlessly, marvel-
ling at his wicked tongue and shifting strategies, staging our
own mock versions of his cases, mimicking, practising, understanding.

The restaurant was our school. We studied, experimented
and made our mistakes where they didn't hurt us. Some of
the group actually brought paper and pens along, jotting
down notes. I laughed at first, but started doing it myself
before long.

Nothing was ever said by our elders – nobody told us we
should or shouldn't be congressing in Shankar's – but we
were aware of the watching eyes, the appraising gazes of the
men and women with power. In our line of study there were
only two grades — pass or fail. You got everything you wanted
or you didn't. Middle ground wasn't for us. We wanted it all.

Every day we gathered, gossiped, swapped notes and made plans, all the time looking around with envy at those who had made it, longing for one to pick us out, call us over and make us their own. We all wanted a Ford Tasso or Frank Weld to take us under his wing. No matter how much we learnt or how far we progressed, we couldn't soar until we were summoned. We could make all the moves we liked but until we were handpicked by someone higher up, we couldn't really exert any control over our futures.

When a call came, and one of our members waltzed off to a new life, the rest of us would group together enviously and measure the apprentice's prospects, the doors which would open, how high they could expect to fly. Usually it was easy to calculate. If Ford Tasso gave the nod, you were going straight to the moon. If Cathal Sampedro asked you to join his team, your ascent was limited to the lower stratosphere — you'd have a solid but unspectacular career.

Our futures were usually simple to predict, based on the standing of our patrons. But when my call came, nobody knew what to make of it, least of all me.

I arrived late that morning because of the green fog. The city was famed for its unique fog, the light green clouds which blew over the metropolis every so often. It usually lasted less than a day, but sometimes hung on for three or four. Nobody knew where the fog originated – industrial pollution was normally blamed – why it was green or why it hung only over the city.

The one thing everybody *did* know was that the fog made life hell while it lasted. You couldn't see more than ten or fifteen feet, so traffic ground to a virtual standstill. I was fortunate — the clouds had descended the night before and were beginning to clear, otherwise I wouldn't have made Shankar's at all.

I hurried to my regular table and hailed a waiter. Before I could order, he bent low and said, 'Table fifty-five, sir.'

Every head in my group turned. When we realized who was summoning me, a hush fell. All eyes settled on me, the same question in every pair — '*Huh?*'

I smiled an uncertain farewell and left for the new life ahead. It was as simple and final a parting of the ways as that. There was consternation at my passing. I'd only been there a few months, which was nothing compared to the years most spent milling around Shankar's before their big break. Even so, I don't think too many envied me. I'd been hailed by Leonora Shankar – the owner of the restaurant – and the mysterious man in the robes, who was the one person none of the older regulars would discuss. Nobody knew what my call meant or where it would lead. It was a bolt from the blue, as bizarre as it was unexpected. Where the hell did Leonora Shankar perch on the ladder of power? She was one of The Cardinal's closest allies, but what could she do for a young man's career? How far could you go with a restaurateur for a guardian angel?

My stomach tried to knot itself as I crossed the marble floor but I wouldn't let it. I'd stood up to The Cardinal without trembling, so I wasn't about to go weak at the knees now.

Leonora greeted me cordially and kissed my cheeks. The man in the robes said nothing, only smiled like a cobra and watched with glinting eyes as I sat.

Leonora Shankar was a tall Asian woman, dark and once beautiful. She was old, maybe eighty or more, but she moved with the grace of a woman in her forties. The rumours about her past were legendary. Some said she'd been slave to a Sultan and came to the city after killing him, or after saving his life and being freed. Some claimed she was The Cardinal's mother. A reformed whore. A deposed princess.

Throw a stick and pick one. What *was* known was she'd

been with The Cardinal from day one. She helped guide him from the gutters to the skies, but nobody knew how much active influence she now played in the growth of his empire, whether she was a pawn on the board or a sly queen watching from the sidelines.

Some said she'd only refined his manners and tutored him in the ways of form. According to others she was the brains behind his early rise. A few claimed The Cardinal was merely a front for the greater genius of Leonora Shankar, a puppet she manipulated to suit her own ends. But nobody knew for sure.

'I am pleased to meet you at last, Capac,' she said, her voice soft and alluring, her lashes fluttering flirtatiously. 'I see you here often. You like my restaurant?'

'Very much,' I replied.

'Splendid.' She looked around fondly. 'I feel like we are old friends, this room and I. Dorry offered to move me several times. He wanted me to find new pastures and explore new avenues.' She shook her head. 'I do not think he ever really understood my compulsion to remain here. To Dorry this was always a restaurant, nothing more.'

'*Dorry*?' I frowned.

'The Cardinal. That is how I always call him. From his surname, *Dorak*.'

I'd forgotten he had a real name, that he hadn't always been The Cardinal. Something-or-other Dorak. I couldn't remember his first name — wasn't sure I even knew it.

The robed stranger spoke. 'Aren't you going to introduce us, Leonora?'

'Of course. Capac Raimi, this is my dear friend, Y Tse Lapotaire.'

'A pleasure to meet me,' he grinned, leaning forward to shake my hand. 'The time is ripe, friend Capac,' he whispered seriously, clutching my hand tightly. 'I greet you with

a warm heart and the best of wills.' He pulled back, breaking
the grip, and smiled broadly again. 'A drink?'

'Beer, please.' I stared at him quizzically. He was in much
the same state as when first I saw him, covered in mock
tattoos, mascara, lipstick and paint. Red, black and green
were his favourite colours, teased into every line, smeared
around every curve. Purple by the eyes, pink lips, orange
streaks down either side of his nose. His ears were covered
with plastic rings. He was sporting a turban today, a couple
of knitting needles jabbed into it Oriental-style. His robes
shifted around him like a school of darting eels, layers
and scraps of cloth held together by colourful pins. His
toenails were in need of a serious manicure beneath the
sandals.

'I'm quite a specimen, aren't I, friend Capac?' he asked.

'You're not the sort I'd take home to mother,' I agreed.

'Y Tse likes playing the eccentric,' Leonora said. 'But do
not be fooled. He is little more than a dull duck dressed up
as a peacock.'

'Please,' he winced, 'don't give away *all* my secrets in one
fell swoop. Let the boy marvel at my weirdness a while.' He
took a sip from the huge yellow cocktail he was drinking.

'You've got an odd name,' I remarked. 'Is it French?'

He toyed with his glass, ignored the question and instead
said, 'How are you enjoying life with The Cardinal?'

'I like it. Although I wouldn't say life *with* The Cardinal.
I haven't seen him since our first meeting.'

'Really?' His eyes enlarged speculatively. 'That's a good
sign. The Cardinal only summons you when he thinks you're
doing something wrong. The less time he spends on you, the
better.'

'I doubt it's that,' I smiled. 'I'm only an insurance agent.
He probably hasn't thought of me since that first night.'

'Oh, I think The Cardinal has thought of you quite a lot,'

Y Tse said softly. 'I can tell you right here and now, as sure as my name's not Y Tse Lapotaire, he has more in mind for you than a life in the insurance business.'

'Like what?' I frowned.

'I don't know. I have my suspicions but what good are they?'

'How do you know he's got anything planned for me?' I pressed.

'Your name. I've heard things through the grapevine and the like. The Cardinal pulled an unknown off the streets for a personal meeting, then set him up under the guidance of the clever Sonja Arne. But the name would have been enough for me.'

'What's my name got to do with anything?' I asked, perplexed.

'My real name,' he replied, 'is Inti Maimi. I took on Y Tse Lapotaire when I fell out with The Cardinal and wanted to distance myself. Inti Maimi . . . Capac Raimi . . .'

'They sound alike, sure, but –'

'It's more than that,' he said. 'Do you know anything about the Incas?'

I paused. I'd heard somebody else namedrop them lately. 'The Cardinal,' I said aloud, remembering. 'He mentioned them at our meeting. He told me my name was Incan. Said he'd read about them.'

'I bet he did,' Y Tse huffed. 'He told me about them as well. Capac Raimi was the Incan phrase for the month of December. It means *magnificent festival*. Inti Maimi was June, the *festival of the sun*. Curious, don't you think? There's not many around with names like that. And both of us ending up working for The Cardinal . . .'

'It's odd, I guess, but I don't see what –'

'No,' he interrupted again. 'In another town, another time, we could pass it off as mere coincidence. Not here, when

The Cardinal's involved. He's told you about how he works, how he ties meaningless events in with bigger ones?'

'A bit.'

'He ever tell you the one about divination and the stock exchange?'

'No.'

'Ask him some time. It's a classic. Our names,' he said, 'mean something. They link us. You're more than just a wannabe gangster with dreams of grandeur. Inti Maimi was a real mover, up there with Ford Tasso. In the end I decided it wasn't what I wanted and walked.' He grimaced. 'How I survived is beyond me. I was a marked man. They'll stand for everything here – murder, rape, incest – but not ingratitude. That's a *Cardinal* sin. I had everything anybody ever wanted and I tossed it away with contempt. I should have been a dead man.'

'Dorry took pity on him,' Leonora interjected. 'He put out word that nobody was to hurt him or knowingly let any harm come to him. As much as many would have liked to kill him, nobody disobeys Dorry.'

'Pity?' Y Tse shrugged. 'I don't think he's capable of pity. I think there was a darker, selfish motive, but . . .' He stopped and was silent a long time. Eventually he lifted his head and gazed around. 'Have you seen Harry Gilmer recently?' he asked Leonora.

'Who?'

'Harry Gilmer. Short, fat guy, meets with me a few times a month. You know Harry. You've eaten with us plenty of times. He's always telling those awful mother-in-law jokes.'

'No,' she said. 'The name doesn't ring a bell.'

'You must!' he shouted, becoming livid. 'You know him, Leonora. You do!'

'I'm telling you,' she said firmly, 'I know nobody by that name.'

'Oh.' His face fell and his rage dissipated. 'That happens a lot here, friend Capac,' he sighed. 'Get used to it. People vanish. One day they'll be walking around, big and brash, the next . . .'

'Dead?' I asked.

'No. Dead would be fine — everybody dies, especially in this line. This is more than death. This goes beyond. This is *obliteration*.' He pointed at Leonora. 'She knows Harry Gilmer, but she won't admit it. Nobody will. If you go to his home, you'll find nobody there, no neighbours who'll ID him, no postman or milkman who remembers delivering. If you check the files in Party Central, you won't find anything on him. He's gone. Never was, never is, never will be. Understand?'

'I don't think so,' I said.

'They've wiped him out. They've taken Harry Gilmer and made it so he never existed. No records, nobody who'll say anything about him. Nothing. They've swept every file, forced or bribed everyone who knew him into denying his very existence. That's the cruellest thing there is, to take away everything a man ever was. It makes life seem so meaningless.'

'Who did it?' I asked. 'The Cardinal?'

'I suppose. Nobody ever talks about it, so I can't say for sure. But he's the only one with that kind of power. The only one who can coerce people like Leonora into denying a man the courtesy of a memory.'

'Y Tse,' she said calmly, 'I swear I never knew this Harry Gilmer. We have discussed this before. He has an illness,' she said to me. 'He invents people and makes accusations of this sort when nobody acknowledges them. Is that not so, Y Tse?'

He shook his head sadly. 'Maybe. There's plenty who'd say I'm wrong in the head. But I can remember him as clearly as anyone. Him and the others. I've seen the list, too, that damned Ayua –' He stopped abruptly and stared at his fingers.

'Take care, friend Capac,' he said bitterly. 'Watch out for this city. Don't let it do to you what it did to me. Don't become another Inti Maimi.'

I leant across the table, determined to push the point now that he'd brought it up again. 'Our names,' I said. 'What's the link? What were you going to say a few minutes ago?'

He smiled. 'The Cardinal hates guesswork. He'd shoot me here and now if he heard me guessing. But screw him. I stopped answering to him a long time ago. Here's what I think. I was The Cardinal's golden boy. He wanted me to take over when he passed on. There were a few of us – me, Ford, a couple of others – vying for pole position, but I was his favourite.

'I let him down. I proved him wrong. But he doesn't want to admit his mistake. I think he believes I was the right man, and if he could find someone like me – somebody with large dollops of the younger Inti Maimi – and train him, raise him up and make him the star *I* should have been . . . that'll justify his decision. It will prove he was right, that the failure was mine, not a reflection on his choice.'

He rose and stood beside his chair, adjusting his robes. Leonora was silent. 'I think, friend Capac, that The Cardinal has chosen you to fill my shoes, to prove to everyone – including himself – that his judgment is sound. I think you're being groomed to take over when he dies. This is the first step on a long, difficult road, but one which leads to gold, diamonds, all the riches you ever imagined. And more.

'I think he's planning to make you the next Cardinal.

'Goodbye, Leonora. Goodbye, friend Capac. See you soon.'

And he left, leaving me motionless in his wake, heart beating erratically, breath coming in jerks.

The next Cardinal.

He was mad, no doubt about it. His prediction was prob- ably the product of a wild, deranged mind. But still . . . *the next Cardinal!* Even if he was wrong, his words provided me with more scope for fantastic imagining than I'd ever known. And upstairs in Shankar's, surrounded by the echoing chatter and gabble of gangsters, veterans and young pretenders to the throne, I let myself dream.

paucar wami

Johnny Grace was an Irish Cuban who'd grown up in the harsh east of the city and headed a small but vicious gang, the Grace Brothers. They'd terrorized their home territory – no small feat – for three years and now Johnny had decided the time was right to expand west. He was looking for The Cardinal's green light. Ford Tasso wanted me to meet with him.

'Johnny'll be a little pissed when he sees you,' he said. 'He asked for me and he won't like having to deal with an underling. He might make a scene.'

'How big a scene?' I asked, worried. There wasn't much that frightened me, but a pissed Johnny Grace was near the top of the shortlist.

Ford smiled. 'Kid, would I send you in if there was any real danger?'

'Without even thinking,' I pouted.

He laughed and clapped my back. 'It'll be OK. He'll growl a bit but it'll be bluster. Stand firm. Let him rant. Don't show fear or apologize. In the end he'll calm down and you can talk.'

'About what?' I asked.

'Sound him out. Ask him how he plans to expand. What's

in it for us? Whose turf is he after? Will he create problems we don't want to deal with? Is he going to be a threat to our friends? Ask questions, make him talk, find out as much as you can. This is the first of many meetings. You don't have to pump him dry.'

'Any chance he'll attack me?' I asked.

Ford shrugged. 'He knows we'd come after him if he did. But he's a mad Cuban Mick. Who can tell?'

'Should I take a gun?'

He shook his head. 'You take a gun into a dark alley with Johnny Grace, and things go wrong, you're fucked. Without a gun he'll just kick the shit out of you if he loses his temper. But if he sees a piece . . .' He didn't have to finish.

Adrian and I dressed for the occasion in the Skylight. We'd been fitted for new suits earlier that week and eased ourselves into them.

'I feel like a pimp,' Adrian complained.

'You look like a pimp,' I comforted him.

'Do I *have* to come?' he asked. 'I'm just your chauffeur. I'm not paid enough to get involved with crap like this. Why can't I just drive, like I normally do, and sit it out in the car?'

'I want you there,' I told him. 'I might need you if things go wrong.'

'If things go wrong with the Grace Brothers, I won't make the slightest difference and you know it.'

I stopped trying to knot my tie. He was genuinely upset and I couldn't blame him. 'Adrian,' I said softly, 'you're the only friend I have, the one person I can rely on. This is a big day for me and I'm about a hair's breadth away from losing my nerve and bolting. I need somebody to hold me in place. You don't have to come. I won't force you. But I'm asking, as a friend, will you help?'

He considered it. 'No,' he said, then laughed and pulled up his socks. 'You'll owe me big for this.'

'I'll see that you never want for anything again,' I prom-ised. 'Neither in this world nor the next.' I paused. 'Which might not be as far away as we'd wish.'

We picked up Vincent in the lobby. He was coming along to observe me in action. He acted as if we were off to the movies. He lay in the back of the car and made us feel at ease with cute little stories. Like, 'I saw Johnny Grace chew a man's balls off once. No kidding. He stripped him, went down on him and gnawed the fuckers off!' And, 'Don't look at his feet. He's club-footed and hates it when people stare. You let your eyes drop below his knees, he'll come at you like a pitbull.'

The meet was on neutral territory in a northern section of the south-east. The streets were narrow, clogged with uncollected garbage, refuse from street traders, burnt-out cars. Every window was boarded over. The kids were dressed like Third World latchkeys, thin and mean.

We arrived first. Parked at the head of the alley, paid a few local teenagers to guard the car, and ambled down a dark, rat-infested stretch of street. It was day, the sun bright in the sky, but few rays penetrated the overhanging roofs and clothes-strewn washing lines.

Adrian and I stood against a wall while Vincent examined the layout. His hand kept going to the space at his side where his gun would normally be. I bet he would have brought one, regardless of orders, if they'd come from anyone other than Ford Tasso.

'You've never been on a gig like this?' I asked Adrian.

'Hell no,' he said. 'I've only been in this business a couple of years. And it's only temporary. A year or two more and I'm out of it. Out of this job, out of this city. I've only stuck it so far because of Sonja. She wants to see me doing well. You know how big sisters are.'

'Can't say I do.'

'Don't have any?'

'No.'

'Brothers?'

'No.'

'You're an only child?'

'Obviously.' I glanced at him. 'Why the interest?'

'You never talk about your parents, old friends, school or anything.'

'I don't?'

'No.'

I scratched my head. 'Didn't know you were so interested in my history. Let's see, I was born in . . .' As I thought about what to tell him, I noticed movement and stopped. 'We're in business,' I whispered, tapping his arm and pointing. Four men had stepped into view and were heading towards us. Vincent coughed and signalled for us to join him.

They reached us and stood looking, three or four feet distant. Johnny Grace was small, light skinned, but muscular. I didn't look at his feet to check if Vincent's story was true or not.

'Who the fuck are you?' Johnny snapped.

'Capac Raimi. This is Adrian Arne and Vincent Carell.'

'Where's Tasso?'

'I'm Mr Tasso's representative.'

He spat into the dust. 'Fuck. You hear that?' His three men nodded seriously. 'I come here, ready to do business with a man I respect, and get a fucking flunkey. You think I'm a nobody? You think Johnny Grace wastes time on fucking boot-boys?'

'Let's go,' I said to Adrian and Vincent. I turned my back on Johnny Grace, praying he wouldn't stick a knife in it.

'Hey! Where are you going?' His voice was startled, uncertain.

I half-turned. 'If you're not prepared to deal with me and my colleagues, we have no business here. I'll relay your dissatisfaction to Mr Tasso and maybe next time he'll come personally.' I smiled thinly. 'To sort things out himself.'

Johnny twitched and looked at his gang. They were all uncomfortable now. I waited. 'Shit, no need to get your feathers ruffled,' he said in the end. 'I was just disappointed, you know? I thought he'd come himself. But he's busy, he's got commitments, I know what it's like. Guess he couldn't make it, huh?' I said nothing. 'OK, fuck it, I'm sorry,' he shouted. 'I apologize, alright?'

'You want to talk?'

'Yeah.'

'Good.' I started back. 'I think we should begin with –'

Someone dropped from a nearby fire escape. A shadow fell by Johnny's feet, an arm slashed at him, then the shadow was among the other three Grace Brothers. More slashing hands, shouts, confusion. Then all three men were lying in the dirt, silent, still. Their assailant rose lithely to his feet.

Johnny was staring at me, eyes wide, mouth open. I stared back, stunned. His hands were over his throat but I saw blood pouring through the cracks between his fingers.

The man who'd dropped from the fire escape turned Johnny around. His hands fell by his sides. He tried to say something, to express shock, hatred or fear. But he couldn't. Johnny Grace was beyond words.

The man drove a knife into Johnny's stomach, held it there a second, withdrew, let the body drop, walked past and stopped in front of Vincent.

Vincent gulped deeply, his face ashen. '*Wami*,' he croaked.

'You know me?' the stranger asked. He had a smooth, mocking voice.

'I recognize the snakes,' Vincent said. 'I've heard stories.'

'You work for . . . ?'

'The Cardinal. Ford Tasso. I'm with Tasso.'

'Then you may live.' The man sheathed his knife and

smiled. 'Carry a message to Ford. Tell him I'm back. I'm here for my own reasons, but if he wants me, he knows how to get in touch.'

'I'll do that. I'll –'

The assassin brushed by Vincent and looked at Adrian and me. He was black, one of the darkest men I'd ever seen, about six feet tall, moderately built, completely bald. He had no facial hair but sported a tattoo on either cheek, colourful snakes which streaked down the sides of his face, came up under his chin and met in the centre beneath his lips. His eyes were a striking green. He was ageless, maybe thirty, maybe fifty. He was the most terrifying person I'd ever seen, and that included The Cardinal and Ford Tasso.

'You,' he said. 'What's your name?'

'Capac Raimi,' I stuttered.

He smiled. 'An Ayuamarcan. I thought so. And you?' he asked Adrian.

'Adrian Arne. Sir.'

He slid closer and gazed into Adrian's eyes. 'Yes,' he muttered. 'You're one too. A lesser specimen, I suspect. Interesting.'

With that he made his way back to the fire escape. He leapt, caught the lowest rung and hauled himself up. Within seconds he'd returned to the roofs of the city and disappeared from sight.

I looked around at the corpses. I was reminded of the scene with Uncle Theo at the warehouse. Could I expect this every time I attended a meet of gangsters?

'Fuck!' Vincent spat on Johnny Grace and stormed back to the car. Adrian and I followed.

'Who was that?' Adrian asked but Vincent ignored him.

'Who was he?' I repeated but Vincent didn't seem to hear. He was too busy cursing. 'Vincent!' I snapped. 'Who the fuck *was* that?'

He looked up. 'That was Paucar fucking Wami, man.' He
paused and shook his head. 'That was death on fucking legs.'
And he wouldn't say any more during the whole ride back.

When I wasn't working or hanging out with Adrian, I spent
most of my time with Y Tse and Leonora. They'd set themselves up as my sponsors and were doing their best to guide
and instruct me. While they weren't the powerful players
I'd hoped to be headhunted by, both had been close to The
Cardinal and knew him as a man, not a master. They were
able to describe at least part of his state of mind, something
nobody else in the city could have.

'Always stick by your guns,' Y Tse told me. 'Stand up for
yourself and say what you think. Everybody here –' he waved
around the restaurant '– wants things done the correct way.
They want you to obey their rules, follow orders, think and
speak as they dictate. They don't want dissent.

'You've got to ignore that. Be prepared to spit in their faces
and laugh at their rules. Discreetly if possible but openly if
not. You can't let them order you about. If you do, you
become their servant. You might go further faster by being
a yes-man, but The Cardinal has thousands of them, so what's
one more?'

'I've got to confront and antagonize him. Take no shit.'

'Yes.' He sounded uncertain. 'But you mustn't push him
for the sake of it. I'm not telling you to fire him up whenever you get the chance. Just speak your mind. If he asks
for your opinion, give it. You don't want to make an enemy
of him, but you mustn't be afraid to risk his wrath by contra-
dicting him.'

'You cannot play safe, Capac,' Leonora added. 'Dorry will
kill you or king you. If you are determined to strike for the
top, you must accept that it has to be one or the other.'

Another day she told me how to deal with The Cardinal's

fits of rage. 'He can fly off the handle any moment. There is no logic to his tantrums. He does not care who is present, what he says or does. Dorry cannot control his temper. There is a fury in his soul which can neither be explained nor quenched. It drives him on. In an earlier age he would have carried a sword and ravaged heedlessly. In these more civilized times he has to channel those urges. He does. Barely.

'It is not easy. When I first met him, he was a teenager, yet already he had killed more than twenty men. He was roaring through the streets, out of control, on his way to an early death. I was able to calm him. I taught him to suppress his anger, keep his fists in his pockets and fight his inner enemies. The effort almost broke him but he kept struggling and eventually he reached a point where he could sit at a table with a foe and debate their differences, rather than rip the other man's jugular out with his teeth, which is his natural reaction.'

Her eyes were soft. Even describing him at his worst, enraged, bloodthirsty and murderous, she spoke of him fondly. She loved him.

'But he cannot control his anger all the time,' she went on. 'Every so often it bubbles up and he rips into whatever is closest. If there is furniture and blank walls, he will vent his rage on those. If people are present, they suffer the consequences.'

'He doesn't look that tough,' I said. 'I think I could take him in a fair fight if it was one-on-one.'

She laughed. 'Nobody can take The Cardinal. His rage lends him strength. It is frightening to watch. He changes before your eyes. His body does not get bigger but it seems like yours gets smaller. I have seen him punch holes in brick walls, lift men twice his weight above his head. That strength comes from somewhere beyond the realms of fleshly bounds.'

She leant forward and spoke softly, her face ashen, the

only time I ever saw her truly afraid. 'He is a *god*, Capac,' she hissed. 'He does things the rest of us could never mimic, manipulates the world and the people in it like a magician. When all is said and done, it is as simple as that. Dorry is a god.'

About a week after the failed meet with Johnny Grace, Adrian dragged me out of the office, bundled me into the car and drove east. He took me further into the city's heart of darkness than I'd ever been, down streets a vampire wouldn't stroll alone. I felt uneasy and kept as low in the seat as I could. This wasn't our ground. These people respected The Cardinal but would think nothing of taking out a couple of his men.

'Are you sure about this?' I asked Adrian.

'Trust me,' he said, turning down a lane barely wide enough to accommodate the car. 'This guy knows everything about the city. He's ancient, over a hundred according to the rumours. He was big, decades ago, before The Cardinal. These days he takes it easy. He's got a couple of girls working the streets for him – more for information than money – but apart from that he just sits back and talks.'

His name was Fabio and I could well believe he was the other side of a hundred. When we pulled up he was sitting on the porch in a rocking chair, listening to old jazz music on one of those vinyl record players I dimly remembered from the far past. Adrian hailed the old man, who waved back pleasantly. He warned us with a finger not to say anything until the record was finished. A few minutes later, when the last trumpet had sounded, he examined my face, stuck a pair of false teeth out of his mouth and leered at me. When he sucked them back in he said, 'So you ran into Paucar Wami.'

The hairs on the back of my neck bristled. Nobody would

tell me who Wami was, not Vincent, Leonora, even Y Tse, who'd normally be quite happy to tell me what colour under-pants he was wearing.

'You know him?' I asked.

'Sure. Know him from way back, before you were born most prob'ly. He a bad mother, the worst I've seen, and I seen plenty of 'em pass in my time. That guy'd kill his own folks, then chop 'em up and make a stew of the bones. Prob'ly did.'

'Who is he?' I asked.

'He Paucar Wami.' Fabio smiled. 'He got more names than that. Each time he comes back he has a new name. Police have plenty of names for him too. The Black Angel. The Weasel. The Carver.'

'The Carver?' Adrian frowned. 'I heard about him. Some serial killer back in the 70s or 80s. I heard Sonja talk about him once.'

'That him. He didn't kill too many as the Carver, no more'n nine or ten.'

'You're saying this Paucar Wami has been killing people since the 1970s?' I asked. 'And he's never been caught?'

'He smart,' Fabio said. 'Never sticks to one identity too long. Keeps moving. Only comes back here every three or four year, if that. It's been nearly seven since his last visit.'

'That's all he is? Just a serial killer?'

'Just!' Fabio laughed. 'Murder ain't enough for you, boy?'

'I mean does he work for anybody? The way he took out Johnny Grace and his boys, it looked like he was on a job.'

'He for hire,' Fabio said. 'Sure. Most of the time he does it for fun but he don't mind killing for pay too. But he don't exactly advertise. Anybody want him, they spread the word and he gets in contact if he likes. Mostly he don't.'

'Has he ever worked for The Cardinal?'

Fabio shrugged. 'I heard tales, long ago, that he was The

Cardinal's man first and foremost, and everything else was a sideline. But who knows?' A car drove by and Fabio peered in the windows, noting the passengers. 'Why you so interested?' he asked when the car was gone.

'I like to know who I'm dealing with,' I said.

'Dealing with?' Fabio laughed. 'Boy, you don't deal with Paucar Wami. He the one does the deals.' He rocked forward in the chair and pointed a cracked old finger at me. 'And you better hope to shit he never does a deal with you, 'cos his deals always end the same way, him on top, the other dead. You be safer doing a deal with daddy death himself!'

Adrian dropped me back at the Skylight. He was going on to a party. He'd invited me along but I didn't feel up to it. My head was throbbing and all I wanted was a good night's sleep.

'You sure you don't want to come?' he asked for the tenth time. 'Liz'll be there. Remember Liz?'

'Not tonight,' I told him. 'Another time.'

'Your loss.'

He drove off, blowing the horn, loosening his tie, firing himself up for the night ahead. I entered the hotel.

I was in the lift when I saw *the woman* again. It was a face I'd been glimpsing at odd moments. A woman's face which would flash across the back of my eyes, leaving a vague impression. When I tried to focus, the image slipped away like a gypsy in the night. There were no memories to go with it. I didn't know where I'd seen her or why she was cropping up in my thoughts. Probably just my brain playing tricks. I'd more than likely passed her on the street one day and filed her image away for one obscure reason or another.

The lift stopped, the doors slid open, I stepped out and the shadow of *the woman* was gone. I tried to focus on it again, couldn't, shrugged it off and walked to my room.

I checked the TV stations — nothing on. I accessed the Skylight's movie database and scrolled through the titles. In the end I went for *Singin' in the Rain*. I'd seen it a hundred times but great is great. I set it to begin in five minutes, enough time to let me go to the toilet and wash my hands.

I heard it starting while I was soaping up. I rinsed, splashed my face with cold water and hurried back.

There was a girl sitting on my bed, watching the opening credits with wide eyes and a smile. 'This is one of my favourite pictures of all time,' she said, her voice curiously tinny and cracked. I thought maybe she'd had her tonsils out recently.

'Uh, yeah,' I replied uncertainly. 'Mine too.' I shifted closer to get a better look. She had a bright face, very little make-up. Shiny blonde hair, long and sweeping. Heavy clothes covering every inch of her below the head — a polo-neck jumper, long trousers, white gloves. She couldn't have been more than thirteen or fourteen. A sweet-looking girl.

'I'm not that fond of musicals,' she said. 'They're dumb. People bursting into song every moment . . .' She snorted. 'But not this one. Gene Kelly's so perfect. I wanted to run out and marry him the first time I saw it.'

'But then you found out he was dead,' I laughed.

'He wasn't when I first saw it. He was still going strong. I wrote him a fan letter and he sent a lovely reply. I still have it.'

I smiled, dismissing it as a flight of fancy. We watched the players dance and sing for a while, Gene and Debbie and Donald.

'So,' I asked eventually – I was still standing, afraid to sit beside her in case my actions were misconstrued – 'have you lost your way? Are you in the wrong room?' I looked at the door, which she'd left ajar when she came in. I was glad of that. I didn't want to be caught alone in my hotel room with a fourteen-year-old girl and a locked door. For all I knew she could be a trap. You had to stay on your toes when you worked for The Cardinal. There were a lot of people waiting to bring you down, not least The Cardinal himself, who'd sometimes sacrifice one of his pawns simply for the pleasure of watching them squirm.

'I'm not lost,' she replied blithely. 'I like running round the hotel, visiting the guests, seeing what they're up to. It helps pass the time. I can leave if you want.' She looked at me with sad eyes. 'Do you want me to go?'

I did. Like I'd told Adrian, I had a sore head. But she looked so lonely, I couldn't turn her away. 'You can stay until the end of the film,' I told her.

'Thanks.' She rewarded me with a smile that would have broken a choir of teenage hearts. I pulled at the neck of my shirt uncomfortably.

'Won't your parents be looking for you?' I asked after another couple of songs.

'I don't have any. They died ages ago.'

'I'm sorry.' She didn't seem to mind and waved away my condolences. 'Who are you staying with?' I asked. 'Guardians? Foster parents?'

'Friends,' she replied, then pulled a face. 'Not *real* friends. Ferdy just pays them to act that way. Do you have a girl-friend?' she suddenly asked, throwing the full weight of her young but alert eyes on me. I was on guard immediately.

'No.'

'Could *I* be your girlfriend?' she asked swiftly.

'Christ, no!'

She looked hurt. 'Why not? Am I too old?'

'Too . . . ?' I laughed. 'Girl, I don't know what movies you've been watching, but you're definitely not too old. You're too young. Way too young.'

She pouted. 'That's what's wrong with men today. They want rich old ladies they can sponge off. I bet you play up to grannies, right? Won't touch one below seventy for fear she might spend her money before she dies and leaves it to you in her will. Am I right?'

I shook my head and laughed. 'My name's Capac Raimi, by the way. What's yours?'

'Conchita Kubekik,' she replied airily. '*Miss* Conchita Kubekik. Pleased to make your acquaintance.'

'Likewise, I'm sure.'

We watched the rest of the film, laughing and singing along. It was a tonic, just what I needed, and my headache bubbled away long before the rain dried up and the singing stopped.

I flicked off the set and coughed. 'Isn't it time you should –' I began, only to have her hush me with a flick of a wrist.

She rushed to my phone and dialled room service. Lowering her voice, she mumbled, 'An egg and salamander sandwich for Room 863, please.'

She handed me the mouthpiece and raised her eyebrows competitively. Without thinking I said, 'And a goose and snuff salad on the side.' I hung up and we laughed at the silly prank.

'Who's in Room 863?' I asked.

'A dirty old man,' she said. 'I wandered in there a few weeks ago and he was lying on his bed, naked, with a pile of smutty magazines. He smiled when he saw me and waved me over with his dick. Dirty old pervert. I was half-tempted to go and punch him in the balls, but he might have caught me and had his wicked way.'

She was young and had all the appearance of innocence, but she was no frail snip of a girl. She was well acquainted with the seedier side of life. Wise beyond her years.

'How long have you been here?' I asked.

'A couple of hours,' she replied with a smirk.

'Ha, ha. You know what I mean. How long have you lived at the Skylight?'

'A couple of months shy of forever. Guess how old I am.'

'I don't know.'

'That's why I said *guess*!'

'Thirteen?'

'Nope.'

'Fourteen?'

'Not even close.'

'Fifteen?' My final attempt.

'I'm fifty-eight!' she roared, her voice almost shattering.

'You look well,' I complimented her, playing along with the game.

'I bathe in magic water every day,' she told me in tones of strictest confidence. 'Imported from Egypt. The water keeps me forever young, beautiful and virgin.' She cocked an eyebrow in my direction. 'Though that last needn't be a permanent condition. The right man, the right place, the right time . . .'

'Careful,' I warned her. 'You don't know where games like that might lead. What if I was one of those perverts like the man in 863?'

'You're not,' she said. 'Bad guys don't watch musicals.'

I didn't push the point. She'd find out for herself one day how deceptive appearances can be.

'Do you know any good games?' she asked.

'Chess?' I couldn't remember playing chess before, but as I said it I saw a chequered board and lots of pieces. In my mind I was sitting beside an open fire, *the woman* opposite, laughing, taking my queen with her bishop, unaware I'd tricked her and was two moves away from mate. How the hell did I –

'Pooh! Chess! No thank you,' Conchita said, holding her nose with one hand, waving the other underneath, fanning

away the stench of the idea and breaking my train of thought.
'Chess stinks. I like Snakes & Ladders, Twister, fun stuff like
that. Have you got any of those games?'

'No, but I have a pack of cards. We could play Snap.'

'Yes!' She clapped her gloved hands with delight. 'I'm great
at Snap. I'm the world champion!'

She could have been too. I let her win the first few hands,
the way adults do when they play with kids, but when I
tried to win a few back, I couldn't. She was lightning fast,
with a steady eye and hair-trigger reflexes.

'I'm bored,' she yawned after winning the umpteenth
game. 'You're useless. Are there any other games we can
play?'

'Poker?'

'I don't know how to play. I used to, but it was such a
serious game, and Ferdy got sore when I beat him and took
his money. I gave it up and made myself forget. I know how
to play *strip* poker . . . but it wouldn't be fair on you. I'm so
good, I couldn't lose, and it would be so embarrassing for
you, stripped bare in your own apartment, humiliated on
your own turf.'

'Besides,' I said, 'you'd have an unfair advantage.'

'How so?'

'All the clothes you've got on. Why do you wear so many?
Cold-blooded? Afraid of catching germs? Or could it be . . .'

I stopped. Her smile had vanished and her confidence evaporated. She'd become a frightened bird, ready to flee at a
second's notice. I'd somehow touched a nerve. She said
nothing for a while, deciding whether to leave or stay.
Eventually, tentatively, in a voice so small it was painful, she
asked, 'Can I trust you, Capac?'

'Sure.'

'I mean *really* trust you, with the most important secret
there is? I've never shown anyone. Apart from the doctors.

They said I should show my friends but I didn't have any, not like you. I've only known you a couple of hours but I feel like I could trust you with my life. I don't know why but I sense it. Will you promise not to tell anybody, ever, if I show you?'

I knelt down before her. 'I give you my word, Conchita. Whatever it is, I'll say nothing to anybody. Honest injun.'

She took a deep breath, glanced around the room, then peeled off one of her long white gloves. The hand beneath was wrinkled, covered in brown splotches. The fingers bent inwards arthritically. It was an old woman's hand. I knew now why she kept herself covered and why she seemed so mature. She had a disease. I'd read about it in magazines. I didn't know the name but it was where the body grew old prematurely. I'd seen a picture once, of a young boy all shrivelled up, a ten-year-old trapped in an old man's body, a kid who looked like a dried-out dwarf. The disease hadn't touched Conchita's face – she'd been spared that part – but the rest of her . . .

'Is it like that all over?' I asked gently.

She nodded slowly. 'All over. From my toes to my neck. Every bit except . . .' Her voice caught. 'Except for . . .' Tears were brimming in her eyes and she was starting to shake. 'Except for my face,' she wheezed, then fell to the floor and sobbed.

I stood by helplessly, not sure if I should step forward and embrace her, keep silent or what. In the end I bent, picked up her exposed hand, raised it to my lips and kissed it.

She stopped sobbing, looked up and stared at me, shocked at first, then delighted. A tiny smile broke through the tears. She threw her arms around my neck, hugged and kissed me, a little girl's innocent kisses.

'Thank you,' she whispered. 'Thank you. Thank you. I knew you were a good guy. Lovely and kind. I used to think Ferdy was like that but he wasn't.'

'Who's Ferdy?' I asked softly. She'd mentioned the name three or four times. I thought he must have been her father.

'Ferdy's my . . . he used to be my protector. He's gone now. Will you be my protector instead? I thought I was all alone and would be forever, nobody to look out for me when nights are dark and cold. Will *you* protect me, Capac?'

'Yes,' I said, patting the back of her head. 'I'll protect you. I promise.' I stroked the back of her poor diseased neck, not really knowing what I was saying, aware only that a small, fragile girl had asked for help. I was in a vicious business but that didn't mean I had to be a vicious man. Not all the time anyway.

Afterwards, when the tears dried, we cemented our friendship by going into the bathroom to play the *Singin' in the Rain* game. We stood in front of the mirror, one concealed behind the other, and performed. First up, I sang *Blueberry Hill* while she mimed it. Then I took to the stage and mouthed *Great Balls of Fire* while she sang behind me. I didn't know all the words but neither did she, so it evened out over the course.

'What do you want to be?' she asked as we sat down to *The Wizard of Oz* later. 'More than anything else in the world, what do you really want to be?'

'A gangster,' I smiled.

'You mean like Marlon Brando and Al Pacino in *The Godfather*?'

'Maybe more like Cagney, a villain with a heart of gold.' I stuck my hands out and did a rotten Jimmy Cagney impression. 'I liked Cagney the best. He always came good right at the end of the movie.'

'He didn't in *White Heat*,' she said.

'True.'

A lull in the conversation for a while. Then she said, 'That's a funny thing to want. It's not nice. Ferdy was a gangster. Then he said he wasn't, but he was really. Why do you want to be a gangster, Capac?'

I shrugged. 'You earn respect,' I tried to explain. 'You get power, privilege, a say in the running of the world. People look up to you.'

'Is that so important?'

'Yes,' I said fiercely. 'I've been a nobody. I've known what it's like to be one of the walking dead and I didn't enjoy it.' I was thinking of that night in the warehouse when death kissed my cheeks and let me go on a whim. 'I want power. I want the protection, comfort and safety that it brings. Without power you're nothing, a corpse waiting to be reaped.'

'Capac? *I* respect you.' She looked at me with sorrowful eyes, a lot like the young Judy Garland who was singing of life beyond the rainbow. 'Isn't that enough?'

I shifted uneasily and wished she'd drop this and get back to watching the movie. You were safe with movies. They can't hurt you. Not like reality can.

'You have to hurt people when you're a gangster,' she said. 'To get your power you have to take theirs. Isn't that right, Capac?'

'Yes,' I said.

'Would *you* hurt someone?' Her voice was low, steady.

'If I had to,' I answered truthfully.

'I don't think you could,' she said. 'You're too nice.'

'Maybe,' I said.

'What's your job at the moment?' she asked.

'I'm an insurance agent.'

'Ah,' she said, nodding. 'In that case, I suppose becoming a gangster is the next logical step.'

'Funny,' I said dryly.

'Were you always an insurance agent?' she asked.

'No.'

'What were you before?'

'I . . .' My mind flew back and I found myself facing a wall I'd been trying not to confront, though it grew in size every day. It was a wall I'd first noticed when Adrian asked me about my past.

What *had* I done before coming to the city? I couldn't remember. It sounded crazy but my past was a blank. I could recall every step since alighting from the train but not a single one before. I hadn't mentioned this to anybody, barely even to myself. I'd been hoping the memories would return if I didn't worry about them.

'Capac?' she tapped my shoulder. 'Are you OK?'

'Fine.' I coughed. 'Anyway, enough about me. What about Conchita Kubekik? What do *you* want to be when you grow up? A lawyer, actress, model?'

'I want to be a ballerina. They're so beautiful and graceful. There are no ugly ballerinas, not like . . .' She didn't finish. Didn't have to. I felt my heart lurch with sympathy. 'I used to go to the ballet a lot, maybe four nights a week, watching them spin and glide like angels. Yes, I'll be a ballerina. I'll dance all night, men will throw themselves at my feet and Ferdy will come and weep with joy. He'll see that there's more to life than . . .'

She stopped, blushed and looked to see what Judy was up to.

'You'd make a lovely ballerina,' I said softly.

'No,' she smiled flatly. 'I can't dance for shit.'

At one in the morning Conchita reluctantly said she had to return to her apartment. 'They come looking for me if I stay away too long,' she said petulantly. 'They like me to get out and about, but only if they're there to look over my shoulder. Not that I blame them. Ferdy would punish them if they disobeyed his commands.'

'Who are *they*, Conchita?' I asked.

'Doctors and nurses. My guardians.' She smiled. 'But I won't need them now that I have you. And you're so much better looking than those grumpy old men with their needles and stethoscopes.'

'Are you making this up?' I frowned.

'I'm a sick person, Capac.' She rolled up one of her sleeves and revealed the withered flesh again. 'They help . . . they stop me killing myself. I've tried a few times. Lots of times. I don't want to die but I get so scared sometimes, I just can't bear to live.' She smiled. 'But that'll change now that I have a friend like you.'

I didn't like it when she talked like that. We'd only known each other a few hours, yet she'd made up her mind I was some kind of Prince Charming. I recalled the promise I'd rashly made. I was genuine when I said I wanted to protect her, but could I keep my word?

'Can I come and visit you again?' she asked.

'Sure,' I said.

'Every night? Can I come and sit on your bed, watch movies and play games, laugh and be happy and not have to worry about my looks? You can tell me what's happening in the city. I've been in here so long, sometimes I believe the Earth was built with a pane of glass in front of it. I'll go whenever you're tired or want to be alone, because people get like that sometimes, I know.'

'You can come any time,' I told her softly. 'I'll get an extra card for you and you can let yourself in whenever you like. How's that?'

'Great!' She rushed out. Stopped and came back slowly. 'You're not a dream, are you, Capac? I've known dream people before. Here one day, gone the next. I knew dream people even before I got sick. You're not one of those, are you?'

'I'm not a dream person,' I assured her. 'I'm real.'

She grinned, then her face lit up with a new idea. 'Walk
me home!' she begged.

'What?'

'Escort me to my room and drop me off at the door with
a kiss, like they do in the movies. You can even come in and
meet my doctors. They can see how nice you are and not
nag me about coming to see you in future.'

'Is that a good idea? They might be suspicious of my
intentions. A grown man and a young girl, alone in a hotel
room . . .'

She laughed. 'I told you I'm fifty-eight. A woman that age
can do as she likes.'

She led the way to the lift and pressed the button for the
top. A sign lit up over the panel, asking for a code. She
pressed five buttons. I thought she was playing games but
the light blinked and we rose. I'd never been to the top floor
before. I expected Troops but it was the same as any other
hall, unguarded, ordinary.

Conchita walked ahead of me. I hesitated, not sure we
should be up here, then followed. There might be trouble
when we were found, but I was sure we could wriggle out
of it. I had contacts.

Conchita moved with confidence, not put off by the glass
ceiling and the black sky above. I paused a few times to look
down on the city. All I could see were tiny lights like stars
reflecting in a dark pond.

We went down two long corridors. I was starting to feel
itchy under the collar when she put her hand out, shoved
open a door and entered a seemingly random room. I rushed
forward to catch her, thinking the game had gone far
enough, only to miss, stumble in after her and find myself
in a huge room where all the furniture was covered with
white sheets and robes. Long curtains obscured the walls
and more had been draped across the glass roof to blot out

the sky. The entire room was smothered in wraps, just like Conchita.

There were four people present, a man and three women, clad in white. The man stepped forward angrily. 'Where have you been?' he snapped. 'We were about to ring security and you know how awkward we feel when we have to do that.' He eyed me suspiciously. 'Who's this?'

'My friend,' she said loftily, breezing past without a care in the world. His hands tightened and I guessed he would have loved to strangle her if he dared.

'*Friend*?' he barked. 'I wasn't aware you had any friends. Where did –'

She snapped her fingers and he shut up. 'That's enough, Mervyn. I'm allowed to have friends, am I not? I thought you'd be delighted.'

'Miss Kubekik, of course I'm happy that you –'

'In that case, please apologize to Mr Raimi.'

'Apologize for what?' he exploded.

'For being rude,' she growled. There was steel in her voice which I hadn't heard earlier. It sobered the doctor immediately.

'I apologize profusely, Mr Raimi,' he said, bowing to me, no sarcasm.

'In that case I'm off to bed,' she said. 'I'll see you again tomorrow, Capac?'

'Sure,' I smiled. 'Goodnight, Conchita.'

'Goodnight . . . protector.'

Then she was gone.

'One minute,' the doctor said stiffly as I tried to sneak out. 'You and I have a few things to discuss.' He gestured to one of the covered chairs. I sighed and sat. 'What happened downstairs?'

'Nothing,' I told him honestly.

He snorted. 'My charge spends hours away, comes back

with a man I've never seen, calmly announces he's her friend and waltzes off to bed as merrily as you please. This from a woman who's hardly spoken for five years. Cut the bullshit and tell me everything.'

When I did, he couldn't believe it. 'She showed you her arm,' he sighed.

'Is that such a big deal?' I frowned.

He laughed curtly. 'She hasn't let anybody look at her skin as long as I've been here. When we want to examine her, we have to sedate her. You must be a fakir, Mr Raimi. What's your secret?'

'I don't have one,' I said. 'We just clicked. She was lonely, I felt sorry for her and we became friends.'

'Just like that!' He shook his head and chuckled wryly.

'Where do we go from here?' I asked. 'She wants to visit me every night. I told her she could, but . . .'

'You don't want her disrupting your life?'

'It's not that. I don't mind her coming. I'm just worried it may not be the best thing. She might be better off with friends her own age.'

His eyes narrowed. 'Do you know what's wrong with Conchita?' he asked.

'I've read about it. The body grows old before its time and –'

'No, Mr Raimi,' he interrupted. 'You are thinking of progeria. This is not the same. There's nothing wrong with Conchita's body. The fault is in her face.'

'I don't understand. There's nothing wrong with her face.'

'She looks like any other teenager,' he agreed, then paused dramatically. 'But Miss Kubekik is fifty-eight years old.'

I did a double-take, then grimaced. 'She told me. I thought she was joking. But that means her body . . .'

'. . . is that of a normal woman her age,' he finished.

'How?'

'We don't know,' he said. 'We've been studying her for a quarter of a century and still don't know what's wrong. She was a beautiful young woman. In her late twenties she found she wasn't aging facially. For a while she was delighted, but as the years passed the implications seeped home. She wasn't growing older. In fact she was actually getting younger. She was a woman in her thirties but with the face of a teenager. She was cursed to never look her age.

'She lost her mind. She cut her face, thinking to scar herself beyond recognition. It didn't work. The skin healed in a matter of days. It has something to do with her unique DNA structure. I don't know all the ins and outs — I tend to her mind, not her form. She had a breakdown, the first of many. Later she painted her face to look her age. But she couldn't maintain the pretence. After several hard years, she left her face alone and went the other way. She looked like a teenager, so she *became* one. She bought youthful clothes, discarded her adult raiments, and began to act like a child. She convinced herself she was a girl, gave up her old life, her friends, her husband, her –'

'*Husband?*' I stared at him. 'She's married?'

'Yes.'

'But you call her *Miss* Kubekik.'

'Part of the pretence. There could be no place in her fantasy for a husband. To become a teenager she had to discard and forget him. She blanked him out, denied his existence, refused to look at him when he tried to see her. She took her maiden name and acted like she'd never lost it.'

'Christ.' I was glad I was sitting down. 'She mentioned him to me. Ferdy. That's him, isn't it?'

'Yes. She hasn't been able to wipe him from her thoughts as completely as she wanted. The memories return, remind her of the truth and plunge her into fits of despair. She's not exactly happy as a child but she's content. But when the fantasy breaks down and she remembers . . .' He shrugged helplessly.

We were quiet for a while, reflecting. Then a thought struck me. 'She wasn't desperate tonight,' I said. 'She talked about him, discussed him openly. She told me her age. She was sad but calm, in control of herself.'

'Yes.' He rubbed his chin slowly. 'That would seem to suggest a new phase. Perhaps she is coming to terms with her disease at last. She didn't actually tell you she was married, did she? Just mentioned his name. Still, it's a step forward. And admitting her real age. We weren't sure she still knew. We'll have to examine this carefully. I'll need to consult with my colleagues.'

'What do *I* do?' I asked. 'Do I let her come to my room?'

'Hell, yes!' he grunted. 'Turn her away now? You might destroy her. Let her come, Mr Raimi. Treat her like you did tonight. Be her friend. God knows, it's been long enough since she had one of those.'

aimuari

Conchita visited almost every night. She'd be there when I got home, curled up on the bed, glued to the TV. She only watched happy films. She'd had enough misery. She said movies should be for escaping the gloom and hardships of life. We played games but nothing too taxing. Conchita loved games of chance, where the toss of a dice decided all. She absolutely hated chess.

She talked freely about her illness and her past. She could remember everything but it hadn't always been so. At times she'd forgotten who she was, believed she was really fourteen, her whole life ahead. When reality intruded – as it always did – she hated herself all over again. That's when she tried to commit suicide.

She'd made attempts to accept her cursed condition a long time ago, but had failed and given herself willingly to illusions and lies. Now she was trying to be her real self again. She was scared and there were days when she felt she couldn't bear it, but she hadn't succumbed to fear as she had in the past. She said I gave her strength, that she wanted to stay sane for me. I never felt more honoured or more worried than when she said stuff like that.

I urged her to meet Adrian. She was reluctant but I sweet-talked her persistently and finally she agreed. They got on great, as I knew they would. I didn't tell Adrian about her disease. As far as he was concerned, she was just a strange little girl. Adrian didn't come every night but popped by a couple of times a week, played games and watched old movies with us.

'There's nothing underhand between you, is there?' he asked one day. 'You aren't doing her on the sly?'

'No!' I was shocked. 'What do you think I am?'

He shrugged. 'We move in dirty circles. You've kept your-self relatively clean so far, but we both know the day of reckoning isn't far off, that sometime soon you'll have to prove yourself to The Cardinal, show your ruthless streak. I hope never to hurt anybody as long as I live, but you're going to have to kill people one day. A man who'd do that . . . well . . .'

'I haven't touched her,' I said quietly. 'There are some things I'd never do, lines I'll always refuse to cross. I won't hurt innocents. Conchita's safe with me.'

'I hope you always feel that way,' he said softly.

We arranged a trip to the cinema one afternoon. It was the first time in years that Conchita had ventured outside the Skylight. She walked the streets slowly, awkwardly, like Neil Armstrong on the moon. I suggested calling in to Shankar's but she'd been there years before and feared people might recognize her.

Casablanca was playing. The best film ever. I looked around several times and almost everyone was mouthing along to the lines, like groupies at a concert. But for Conchita the best bit wasn't the classic movie – it was the simple walk in the open air.

The only part of her life Conchita wouldn't discuss was her marriage. I tried broaching the subject a few times but she made it clear she didn't want me prying. I asked her doctors and it turned out she'd been married to a mobster, Ferdinand Wain. I asked where he was but they didn't know. He used to visit but had given up on Conchita long ago. The doctors hadn't seen him in ages. But the cheques kept coming, so he must be around somewhere, and not doing too badly if he could afford a suite on the top floor of the Skylight. I kept meaning to ask Leonora or Y Tse about him, whether he was in the city or not, and if he was any relation to Neil Wain, the man who'd killed Uncle Theo. But I kept forgetting. It wasn't important. I was just curious.

Ford Tasso rang one day, told me to go home and get ready — we were going out that night. He didn't say any more. I rushed back to the Skylight, showered and changed clothes. I was nervous – I always got the jitters when Ford rang – and spent the time surfing the TV, wondering what lay in store. The trademark green fog of the city began to creep across the skyline as I waited. I studied it anxiously, afraid it would mean a cancellation, but then the phone buzzed and a receptionist told me a car was waiting. I expected Adrian but the driver was a stranger. 'What happened to Adrian?' I asked.

'Who, sir?'

'Adrian Arne. My regular driver.'

'I'm afraid I don't know him, sir. I only started a couple of months ago.'

'Who sent you?'

'The company, sir. Mr Tasso requested a driver. I was available. If you would rather another . . .'

'That's OK. Drive on . . . what's your name?'

'Thomas, sir.'

'Drive on then, Thomas.'

He negotiated the murky streets with great skill. The fog

was growing heavier all the time but he took no notice. He
drove to a building site where Ford and Vincent were waiting
by their own car, shrouded in green vapours. Vincent wasn't
glad to see me. 'You sure we should be taking him along?'
he pouted. 'He's still a beginner. What if he –'

'He's coming,' Ford snapped. 'If you don't like it, complain
to The Cardinal.'

Vincent pulled a sour face. 'I was only *saying*.'

'Don't.'

'So,' I said, trying to smile as if I wasn't nervous, 'what's
the deal?'

'Get in.' Ford opened the door. When we were out of the
damp fog he outlined the night's mission. 'We're after *him*,'
he said, laying a stack of papers in my lap. 'Aaron Seidelman.
Owns a stack of factories by the waterfront. We've been trying
to buy them for years. He won't sell. We've been waiting for
him to die – he's old as fuck and his kids would sell in a
second flat – but he's a tough fucker. We can't wait any
longer. The Cardinal wants those factories. We haven't come
down heavy on Seidelman so far but he signs tonight, one
way or the other.'

I scanned the papers while he talked. 'I'm going along to
see how it's done? Another lesson?'

'No. You're going to make him sell.' I looked up. Ford was
staring out the window.

'And if he won't?' I asked quietly.

'Your call.'

I was about to question him further when Vincent hissed
and drew a gun. 'Ford! We're being watched!'

Ford's head swung round. Through the rear window I
glimpsed a figure nine or ten feet behind the car. The muscles
in Ford's neck tensed, then relaxed. 'You're a dumb fuck,
Vincent,' he laughed.

'The fuck?' Vincent snapped.

'See his eyes?' Vincent squinted and so did I. As the fog swirled I saw a man in long white robes with blank, unseeing eyes.

'Shit,' Vincent growled, 'how was I to know?'

'I've seen him before,' I muttered, trying to remember where.

'Wouldn't surprise me,' Ford said. 'They're easy to spot.'

'*They?*'

'There's a group. All blind and dressed the same way. Religious nuts. They come out whenever the fog's up. I think they worship it. They're harmless. Still . . .' He tapped Vincent's shoulder. 'Let's go. Just because he's blind, doesn't mean he's deaf.'

I focused on the file as we drove. Aaron Seidelman was born in Germany in the 1930s. His parents died in the concentration camps. He was smuggled out by an uncle. Fled to France. Worked for a living from the age of twelve. Built up a small business, came here in the 60s, bought loads of old warehouses down by the docks, most of which he'd never done anything with. Old, past his prime, but wealthy and influential.

I burst into his house with Ford, Vincent and two others. He was in a robe and slippers, listening to some classical shit, sipping a glass of brandy. He tried to fight but one of our thugs knocked him down. 'Careful,' Ford said. 'Nobody hurts him unless Mr Raimi says so.'

I walked over to the old man and studied him as if he was one of my insurance customers. He was frightened, obviously, but there was strength in that face. A few broken bones wouldn't crack him. He'd been bullied and tortured before. He hadn't given in then and he wasn't about to start now. He held his tongue. He knew pleas wouldn't work on us, just as violence wouldn't against him.

'Well?' Ford asked. 'Do you want to talk to him here or do we take him out?'

'I've never had a Jewish takeaway,' Vincent giggled. 'Does it come with bagels?'

'Mr Seidelman,' I began, 'we want your factories. I know you want to keep them in your family but your children don't care. They'll piss away their inheritance or sell to the first bidder who waves a cheque under their noses. They only want the easy things in life. They're useless, selfish wastrels.'

'They are,' he admitted. His voice was firm, healthy, unharmed by the years. 'But I cannot control the world from my grave. I can, however, safeguard my business assets while I am alive, and I will never sell to one who plans to befoul what I have built. Your blasphemous Cardinal would turn my factories into whorehouses and opium dens.'

Opium. Was this guy behind the times!

'I will not let him soil what I have worked so hard for. There will be no revolution, no *new order*.' He smiled bitterly and one of his arms lifted slightly. I glanced down and noticed a faded smear, an old tattoo.

I stood back and studied him again, thinking about the way his lips had lifted, his peculiar choice of phrase. He was fit, healthy for his age, glowing skin, a fine head of hair. For some reason I fixed on the hair and an idea blossomed. I took Ford aside and whispered, 'You know how the Nazis destroyed the Jews?'

'Showers and ovens,' he replied, staring at me curiously.

'No. Before they targeted their bodies, they wrecked their spirits. Stripped them naked, humiliated them, starved them, beat them, covered them in filth. They deprived them of their humanity.'

'Interesting history lesson,' Ford snorted. 'How does it relate to . . . ?'

'I know how to crack him,' I said quietly.

'Then do it.'

'Whatever it takes?' I asked.

'Like I said earlier – your call.'

'I want him out of here,' I said to our thugs. 'Stick him in the car. We're going for a ride.'

I told Vincent to drive to one of our shops. I'd been there a few times for an old-style wet shave. Y Tse had introduced me to the place. It was late and the owner grumbled at being woken, but he shut up quick when he saw Ford Tasso. He got what I asked for, no questions; and stuffed it in a brown bag. I thanked him and left.

The others stared at the bag, wondering what fierce instrument of torture lay inside. I said nothing. Seidelman was trembling a little but was otherwise showing remarkable reserve.

We drove to the docks. I knew the sort of place I was looking for, a disused factory where the power had been supplied by coal-stoked fires. Large furnaces. We found one after a short search. Dragged Seidelman in and propped him by one of the cold, damp, metal walls. It had been a long time since one of these had been used in the name of evil, but memories last. I knew Seidelman wouldn't have forgotten the fate of his parents.

There were torches in the trunk of the car. We trained three of them on the shaking old warrior with more heart than sense.

'Strip,' I commanded. Seidelman hesitated. '*Strip*, you Jewish scum! Now!' The words came with frightening ease, I don't know from where.

Seidelman stiffened. Tears of fury glittered in his eyes. Sneering, he stripped naked and kicked his clothes away. 'So,' he snarled. 'You act the commander. Go ahead, young man. You would have fitted in well, *ja?* But I have dealt with your sort before. I did not crumble then, and will not crumble now. Your kind can never defeat mine. You tried once and failed. So try again. The fool never learns. Try and fail, bastard.'

Vincent and Ford were unsettled. They glanced at me sceptically. This wasn't their style. Tasso had tortured men, women and children. But not this way. He'd never tried to squeeze a man's soul.

I stepped forward. Seidelman was quivering like a leaf now, unsure of my intentions. He didn't know how far I was prepared to go. A faint breeze blew his grey hair into his eyes. He thumbed it away. I stepped closer, opened the bag and let him peer inside. He'd been expecting a gun or a knife, something brutal. He was ready for that. But not for this.

His body sagged. 'No,' he wept. 'You cannot do this. I am a human being. You are too. You must not resurrect the past. It is unholy.'

'Sign the document,' I said softly, running a hand through his hair, soothing him as if he were a child. 'Sign or I'll take this out and use it.' He stared at me with loathing and fear. '*Nein?*' I smirked when he hesitated and made a pass at his head. When he flinched, I said again, 'Sign.'

'You are a monster,' he sobbed.

'Yes. Me, Adolf, Hermann. We're all monsters. And you are our victim. Now sign and make the monsters go away. You have a choice this time. It's in your hands.'

'No,' he said, taking a pen from me. 'You destroyed my hands many years ago. And my will. I thought I was strong but I was wrong.' He signed his name, gave me the pen and paper, and said no more.

We left him alone, crying, naked, broken. The silence in the car was oppressive. Ford and Vincent thought they'd seen it all. I'd proved them wrong, shown them a new form of cruelty, an older kind.

When they stopped to let me out, Vincent grabbed the bag. 'I've got to see what's in it.' He opened it slowly, as if something alive and hideous was in there. His face dissolved into confusion as the object revealed itself. 'I don't get it,' he said. 'What's so fucking terrifying about hair clippers?'

Adrian didn't report for work the next morning either. It was Thomas again, silent, obedient, dour. The fog was clearing and we made good time on the way to my office. I rang Adrian's agency and asked about him. The woman on switch didn't know him. I looked for Sonja when I got to the office but she was out. I tried ringing him at home – no answer.

Worrying about Adrian, I lowered myself into my chair with my first café latte of the day. I'd barely sat down when the phone rang. Ford Tasso. 'The Cardinal wants to see you later.'

My heart jumped in my chest. 'Anything to do with last night?'

'Am I a fucking messenger boy?' Ford snapped. 'Just get your ass there for eleven and don't be late.'

'OK. See you –' But he'd hung up already.

I couldn't concentrate after that. I endured the office for forty-eight minutes, then had to get out. I rang for Thomas and told him to drive around for a while. I rolled the windows down and let fresh air sweep into the car. After a while that wasn't enough. I needed something to take my mind off my impending meeting with The Cardinal. 'Thomas, do you know any good sports centres?'

'Yes, sir.'

'Take me to one.'

'Any special preferences, sir? Bowls, badminton, gymnastics?'

'I don't care. I just want something that leaves me panting for –' Then I saw the face of *the woman* again and this time she was holding a tennis racket, laughing. 'Do you know a good tennis court?' I asked hesitantly, trying to hold the image but failing.

'Yes, sir.'

'Then get me there quick.'

The club was one of the best. Champagne on ice in the clubhouse, immaculately maintained courts, umpires and ballboys, ex-professionals to teach beginners. All the players oozed money, tanned and greased, sporting the chicest gear, pausing between sets to ring their stockbrokers.

The receptionist was snotty at first. They didn't favour blow-ins who turned up without appointments. But he warmed to me when I flashed my card from the Skylight. The Cardinal's reach extended everywhere. Only a fool turned away one of the Skylight's guests. You couldn't afford to make those sorts of enemies.

I had to shop for my equipment first — no rentals here. I'd picked up a few credit cards since my time with Theo (all arranged through illegal channels), so I put the skimpy T-shirt, shorts and trainers on one of them and tried not to look at the price.

My instructor had only played semi-pro but I didn't hold that against him. He asked if I'd played before. I had an impression of *the woman* serving to me, and could vaguely recall hitting a few balls back to her, but that was all. I told him to treat me like a beginner. He started me slowly, stressing that since this was my first lesson I couldn't expect too much.

I slipped him a tidy wad of notes and said I wanted to let off steam and while away a couple of sweaty hours without having to worry about work. I told him to hit balls at me hard. He was a practical man. He believed in putting the wishes of his clients first. Grinning, he pocketed the cash, moved to the far end of the court and let fly.

He slaughtered me to begin with. I chased hopeless balls, flew from one side of the court to the other, puffing and panting, feeling like an idiot. But towards the end of the first set I improved. In the space of a couple of games I shed my hunched pose, found my feet, adjusted my grip and shifted up several gears. A few games into the second set, I was returning everything he threw at me, beating him on my own serve, dictating play. He was chasing the game now. I was thrashing him soundly, ex-semi-pro or not.

I won the second set 6-4. The third 6-1. Match to me.

He stormed over angrily. 'You've played before,' he snarled.

'No,' I said. 'That was my first time.'

'Bullshit! You destroyed me!'

'Beginner's luck.'

'Like fuck!' He poked me in the chest. 'You're a pro. No amateur could have torn me apart like that. Who sent you? Did Sheryl pay you to humiliate me? Is this her idea of a joke?' He poked me in the chest again.

I grabbed his hand and twisted it back until it was a creaking bone away from snapping. 'Do that to me again,' I said as he yelped, 'and the only thing you'll be serving up is a plate of beans. Nobody sent me. I guess I'm a born natural or you're simply not as flash as you think. My advice — take that money I gave you, grin and bear it, and get the fuck out of my face.'

I let go and walked away, high on the buzz of the action. Not having wasted as much time as I wanted to, I hit the squash and handball courts. I wasn't as good there but surprised myself, displaying an athletic prowess I'd never suspected. If I was this good first time out, there was no telling where I might get with some practice. Maybe I'd missed my true vocation and a career on the tennis circuit beckoned.

I popped into Shankar's later. I was feeling fresh and alive. This was shaping up to be a great day. I could see The Cardinal throwing his arms around me, giving me the keys to his empire and the freedom of his kingdom.

I dined with Y Tse and Leonora. Told them about my ensuing meeting. They were thrilled, especially Y Tse.

'This could be the start of it, Capac,' he crowed. 'He probably won't say much tonight – it won't feel like anything big – but your entire future could depend on what happens at eleven.'

'How should I approach him?' I asked. 'Should I act casual, treat him like an old pal? Keep my eyes down and speak only when spoken to?'

'Act naturally,' Leonora advised. 'Dorry will have been monitoring you. He knows what you are like. Do not put on an act. Answer his questions truthfully. Be yourself.'

'Yes,' Y Tse agreed. 'There's no need to fawn or dazzle him. He just wants to see how his newest recruit is getting on. He might have a small errand for you. If he does, it'll seem no different to any other task, but it will be important to *him*. Treat it like any other assignment, like it's no big deal, but don't fuck it up.'

'Got you.' I bit into my burger. They cooked them magnificently here. Black as sin and packed with just the right amount of sauce and salad. 'Have either of you seen Adrian the last day or so?' I asked between bites.

'Who?' Leonora said.

'Adrian. My driver.'

'I do not think I know him. Have we met?'

'I'm not sure, but you've probably seen him with me. Young guy, always smiling, a bit of a clown.'

'It rings no bells,' she said.

'You?' I asked Y Tse.

'One young man looks pretty much the same as any other to me.'

'A lot of help you are,' I complained.

'It is our age, dear.' Leonora smiled. 'The mind starts to go when you are old. Memories fragment. Some days I struggle to remember my own name. Do you agree, Y Tse?'

'Who?' He laughed.

'If I ever live to be as old as you two,' I said, 'I hope someone has the good grace to put me out of my misery.' I stood. 'I'd love to stay but I've a career to build. See you later.'

'Good luck,' Y Tse said.

'Yes, luck, Capac,' Leonora added.

From there it was back to the Skylight. I had a shower, my third of the day — the city knew how to make a man sweat. Conchita was waiting when I stepped out, towel wrapped round my waist. 'Hello sailor,' she said in a passable Katharine Hepburn impression. 'I'm up for *The African Queen* tonight. You game?'

'Sorry,' I said. 'That's one river trip I'll have to skip. I'm meeting my boss. Could be in for a promotion.' I opened the wardrobe and searched for clothes. Nothing fancy. Neat trousers, a shirt, a loose tie. No jacket — too hot.

'What time will you be back?' Conchita asked.

'Don't know.'

'Should I wait up?'

'Not too late. Stick around a few hours. I'll ring from Par – the office if I get away before midnight.' I didn't want her hearing about The Cardinal. She still thought I was an insurance agent. I wanted to keep it that way. What she didn't know about me couldn't hurt her.

Thomas drove silently to Party Central. He didn't speak much, responding to my conversational questions with short, curt answers. The sooner I got Adrian back, the better.

Party Central thrummed with the sounds of the night shift. It wasn't as hectic as it got in the middle of the day, but it was by far the liveliest building in the city at that time of night. The Cardinal's interests stretched across the face of the globe. His company was a twenty-four hours a day machine, an economic monster that required constant feeding.

The Troops were on guard, cold and alien as ever. There'd been a bit of bother in the press lately. It happened every few years as young politicians tried to make names for themselves by pushing for the disbanding of The Cardinal's personal army. It normally went on for a couple of weeks, giving the citizens time to vent their anger and get it out of their systems. Then the aggravating hotshots were either bought up or ploughed under and that was the end of it.

I checked in at reception and passed over my shoes. There were bottles of foot deodorant for those who were feeling the effects of the heat but mine were fresh from the shower. I was in loads of time – thirty minutes too early – and waiting for the lift to arrive when I noticed the door to the stairs. I'd been in the building a lot since my first night, dealing with the administrative heart of The Cardinal's empire. In the beginning I'd had to come for new papers, official forms and ID cards to legitimize me (I must have left my own papers behind when I came to the city). I'd also done a lot of business here, making use of the building's enormous records rooms – spread over eight floors – which were the most comprehensive in the city, with files on everyone who was anyone, as well as lots of people who were nobody. Access was limited and I was only allowed on three of the floors, but the amount of paper I'd encountered was incredible, enough to account for a rainforest or two. The Cardinal didn't believe in transferring his files to computer — hacking was too easy and the risk involved far outweighed the benefits.

In all my visits I'd never used the stairs. There was no need, when the building was equipped with a fine array of efficient elevators. But I was feeling brisk after my exercise

earlier in the day. The thought of jogging up fifteen flights
appealed to me. It would waste some of the time and I could
slip into a toilet up there and dab under my armpits to get
rid of the sweat it would draw.

The staircase was dimly lit, the darkest place in the otherwise luminescent building. I didn't encounter a soul until
the eleventh floor. People simply didn't use the stairs, even
if they were only going up or down a flight. It wasn't so
much general laziness, more the decree of The Cardinal,
which said that in his building, on his time, you better damn
well get to where you were going in a hurry.

Somewhere around the seventh floor I began to think
about *the woman* again. I slowed, narrowed my eyes, and got
my best picture of her yet. I saw her in a variety of situations and poses, each segueing into another after a few
seconds. She was in a kitchen, over a barbecue, serving a
tennis ball, kissing me, lying by an open fire with a chess
board before her and no clothes on, driving a car, making
love (I guessed to me), tossing a pancake, nervously twisting
her wedding ring, watering flowers, laughing — laughing a
lot of the time.

Whoever she was, real or a phantom of my imagination,
she liked to laugh. A genuinely happy person, lines around
her eyes and mouth from smiling so much. Every time her
lips lifted, my chest constricted a notch, as if I was in love
with her. I couldn't understand it. Why should I feel so
strongly about a dream woman?

I tried recalling past girlfriends. Maybe she was one of
them, one I'd forgotten, or a conglomerate, my ideal woman
pieced together from all of those I'd loved and left behind.
I moved even more slowly, almost coming to a bemused stop.

I couldn't remember them.

My girlfriends and previous lovers. I could recall many
since coming to the city but before that, *nada*. I was drawing

a blank again, the blank I'd been noticing more and more these last few months. There were gaps in my memory. I must have had girlfriends before I came to the city but I couldn't remember any of them. Hell, it was hard enough for me to remember what my parents looked li–

With a sickening lurch I stopped short on the eleventh floor. I *couldn't* remember! My mother, my father . . . Did I have brothers or sisters? *I didn't know!* Everything was a blank. Every day, every face, everybody I may or may not have known before I stepped off the . . .

Out of the corner of my eye I noticed a woman above me. I wouldn't have bothered with her if she'd been moving normally, coming down loud and clear like a person with nothing to hide. But she was skulking, sneaking down the stairs. When she saw me, she stopped and tried to slip back into the shadows. Ironically, it was this attempt to conceal herself which alerted me to her presence.

She froze when I looked up. She was clad in black. As I stared, moving up a step for a better look, she resigned herself and came out of the shadows, affording me a proper look. She was tall, maybe my own height, long legs angling up to wide hips, narrowing to a trim waist, building up to what looked like a nice pair of breasts. She had a long face, not beautiful by any standards. Quite dark skin, though that might have been a trick of the dim light. A triangular chin, ears hidden by a long mane of black hair. I felt myself hardening as I looked her over and it took an effort to focus on the business at hand.

'What are you doing?' I asked sharply. She obviously wasn't here on legitimate business. But how had she entered the building? I thought Party Central was impenetrable. 'Who are you?' I let my right hand travel to the small of my back, giving the impression – I hoped – that I was carrying a weapon. 'What's your name? Why are you –'

I stopped. She'd moved forward and was eyeing me intently, head bent to one side. Her face creased, as though she knew but couldn't place me. Then, with a sexy grin that disarmed me completely, she brought her hands to her hips, undid her buttons and wriggled out of her trousers.

My hand fell away from my imaginary gun. She was wearing large, white pants. Nothing sexy about her choice of underwear but I didn't have long to look at them, because seconds later they'd joined the trousers in a heap at her feet.

She moved down the stairs, her dark pubic hair the only thing my eyes could fix on. She probably had a knife but I didn't care. I was like a man hypnotized.

She stopped four steps above me. 'Hey,' she said softly. I tore my eyes away and looked up. She licked her lips and fell on me.

We went down instantly, kissing and tearing. My hands grabbed her breasts, then pushed down her body. She bit my neck hard. Found my zip with her hands, ripped it open. Her fingers were cold as she pulled me towards her, urging me on (like I needed any urging!).

We rutted like cats. Rolled across the stairs to the wall, where we found our feet. I pushed her up against it, then she reversed our positions. Down again a few thrusts later. I'd never fucked so wildly. I freed one of her breasts and moaned as I sucked. I climaxed but kept pounding, still hard. She clutched me closer and bit my ear, muttering obscenities. Neither of us wanted to stop. Neither of us *could*. Until –

Suddenly I rolled off, breathing hard. I was dizzy and had to give my head time to clear. When I looked at her again she was sitting up, shaking her head, one hand on her knee, the other touching her groin softly. She grinned shakily, stood and pulled on her pants and trousers. Blew a kiss to me and left without a word.

I lay there like a fool and watched her go. She might have

left a bomb in the building but that didn't matter. I could no more have stopped her than I could have stepped off the roof of Party Central and flown.

After a while I rose in a daze and buttoned up. I checked my watch — I still had time. The romp had only lasted a few minutes. I hurried to a washroom and cleaned up. And then, red-faced and breathing raggedly, I went to see The Cardinal.

There were several people waiting outside his office. They were from every social strata, dressed in suits, rags, even clerical garb. The receptionist waved me past the lot. They stared jealously as I walked by, eyes smouldering.

The Cardinal was playing with his puppets when I entered, squatting behind a small table. There was a white sheet of cloth stretched across the front, lit from behind by a bright bulb. The Cardinal had two stick-puppets mounted on the ends of long rods, which he pressed against the sheet and jigged about, so from the front it looked as though they were free-standing shadows.

'Chinese,' he told me, not looking up. 'Three hundred years old.' He swapped one of the figures – a man with a large hat – for a small dragon.

'Not the most sophisticated form of entertainment,' I said.

'Who needs sophistication when you have . . .' He pulled the models away and set them down, then crossed his arms and smiled. On the screen the shadows still danced, the dragon and a man with a spear, circling each other, lunging in fits and spurts. '. . . magic,' he finished.

'How . . . ?'

He let me look behind the screen. There were no mechanical devices and no sign of the shadows on the back of the sheet. I leant round and there they were on the front. I looked over my shoulder but couldn't spot any cameras.

'Is it a screen?' I asked.

'Touch it,' he said.

It was just a simple cloth. Then, dimming slowly, the shadows vanished and all that remained was the glare of the light which The Cardinal soon extinguished.

'How did you do it?' I asked.

'Belief. Willpower. Using my mind.'

'You're not going to tell me?'

'Are you hungry?' he brushed my question aside. 'Thirsty?'

'I could do with a beer.'

He crossed to his desk, flicked a switch and told the secretary to bring some sandwiches, a beer and a mineral water. The sandwiches looked tasty so I had a couple. We sat munching and drinking, discussing the weather and football results, a couple of ordinary Joes.

'Just what the doctor ordered,' he said, finishing off the last of the bread. 'I've been on the go since five this morning and forgot about eating. I do that a lot. My doctors are always criticising me but where would we be if we lived life only for our doctors?'

'You work a long day,' I said, impressed. 'You must be ready to wind down soon.'

'No, Mr Raimi. Not for another thirty hours or so.' He wiped crumbs from his lips, licked his hand and burped. 'I don't sleep much. A couple of hours every other day. Sleep is a vastly abused talent. People sleep seven, eight, nine hours a night.' He shook his head morosely. 'Dreaming their lives away. It's fine for animals to sleep for hours on end — not humans. I think apes evolved when they stopped giving in to the powers of sleep. Where would the world be if people slept sixteen hours a day? Nothing would get done. Nobody would be awake long enough to invent anything. We'd still be swinging from the trees.'

He was serious, so I kept a straight face. But it was a struggle.

'We don't need to sleep so much,' he continued. 'We can push on when we force ourselves, and we should. Imagine an extra eight hours to play with every day, fifty or so a week, two and a half thousand a year. Then imagine everybody working that way. Multiply the hours by the talents of the workforce. Think how much more we could achieve. The key to success, Mr Raimi, lies in the controlled manipulation of sleep.'

'Maybe we should ban it,' I quipped.

'No,' he said seriously. 'Sleep's necessary. There has to be a place for the mind to retreat to and refresh itself. But we only need small quantities. Anything more than three hours a night is gluttony. It weakens and undermines us. There should be health warnings fixed to every headboard, like on cigarette cartons.'

'That's going a bit far,' I smiled.

'I've built an empire going too far,' he snapped.

There was no response to that, so I said nothing for a while. He let me consider his words and I got the feeling he wanted me to contradict him. If that *wasn't* what he wanted I was in deep shit, because I felt compelled to argue.

'That line of reasoning falls down in certain cases,' I said tentatively.

'Name one.'

'Einstein. Greatest brain since who knows when. He slept a solid eight hours every night and swore blind by it.'

'Einstein was a wastrel,' The Cardinal said dismissively. 'How much money did he make? How much power did he wield? What did he ever do in practical terms? Where was the profit?'

'They built the nuclear bomb based on his theories,' I said.

'Yes,' he agreed. '*They*. Men like me, Mr Raimi. Men with power, aims and both feet planted on the ground. Einstein made nothing from the bomb. He even warned against the dangers of it. He could have designed the A-bomb, held the world to ransom and made a fortune. But he slept too much. If ever there was a man who needed an extra eight hours a day, it was Einstein. If he'd figured out a way to use his theory of relativity to control the stock market, *that* would have been clever!'

His mention of the stock market reminded me of something. 'I was speaking to Y Tse Lapotaire a while back. He said I should ask about a deal you had going with shares and divination. He . . .'

The Cardinal's darkening features silenced me. He raised a hand, the one with the crooked little finger, and pointed ominously. 'Don't ever mention that fucking name here again. I don't acknowledge it. I knew a man named Inti Maimi once. As far as I'm concerned, he left my employ and is of no further relevance.'

'Sorry.'

'Don't be sorry!' he snapped. 'Be silent!' The Cardinal moved to the window, face black, and brooded silently.

'Inti Maimi,' he sighed eventually. 'A great man surrounds himself with greatness. I rule this city because I own its strongest men. Inti Maimi was the best. I had so many plans for him. I saw us ruling the world together, side by side. But he threw it away, wrecked my plans, set me back years. I'd planned to be out of here by now. I meant to exert the same control internationally that I do here, a king of countries, not just one lousy city.'

He shook his head sadly. The words would have been ridiculous coming from anyone else, but from him they were chillingly plausible. I caught my first glimpse of the empire The Cardinal hoped to build, a world of slaves under his control. He wasn't going to bother with the Master Race. No, The Cardinal wanted it all for himself.

'Why didn't you kill him?' I asked.

His jaw started to tic alarmingly and he clenched his fingers into fists. He was struggling to check his temper. That gladdened me immeasurably — The Cardinal usually didn't bother holding back.

'Don't test my patience any further,' he growled. 'I told you not to mention *his* name. Let that be the end of it.'

'OK,' I said softly. 'But what about the stock market and divination?'

He smiled and I knew I was safe. For a while. 'Very well. I'll let you in on my secret. But this is for your ears only. I've been king of the market for a decade and a half. There are men who'd pay any amount you asked for my secret, bankers who'd go down on their knees for it. Inti Maimi should not have shared such a gem so carelessly. I'll have to take steps. I'd advise you not to get too close to that particular fallen angel in the near future. But now that the cat is out of the bag, why not reveal all? Wait here a few minutes. Finish your drink. I have a call to make.'

When he returned (more like a quarter of an hour later), he led the way out of the office, past his secretary and the waiting crowd, to the elevator shaft. He pressed a button and the doors slid open. 'Six,' he growled at the shivering attendant and we descended.

'Have you been to the Fridge yet?' he asked.

'No.'

'But you know about it?'

'Sure.' The Fridge was a huge, private morgue, owned and operated by The Cardinal. Many of his friends and foes had wound up there over the years, and according to the rumours thousands of bodies were stored there still, though nobody knew why.

'I've ordered a takeaway,' The Cardinal said with a wink.

Downstairs, after a short walk, we arrived at a large set of sliding doors. The Cardinal tapped a code into the console to one side. The doors opened and we entered a long room with simple benches set along opposite walls and what looked like an operating table in the middle of the floor. The Cardinal took a seat on one of the benches and told me to sit on the other.

For about half an hour we waited, hands on laps, The Cardinal humming tunelessly. Then the doors slid open again and three Troops entered, pushing a gurney with a bagged body on top. They transferred it to the table in the centre of the room, then withdrew without a word.

The Cardinal rose and strolled towards the table, nodding for me to join him there. He unzipped the body bag and peeled it back to reveal the naked corpse of a man in his late thirties or early forties. Impossible to tell how long he'd been dead, since he'd been frozen like a turkey.

'Simon Spanton,' The Cardinal said. 'A high-flying executive with a major software company until his sudden, unexpected demise. I suppose it was a stress-related heart attack or a drugs overdose. Those are the killers of most execs who die young.'

The Cardinal slid open a drawer in the table which I hadn't noticed. He produced a set of scalpels. From a hook around the side he fetched a saw and other heavier instruments to slice through the dead man's breastbone and crank the two halves of his chest apart.

'I'd never have made a good forensic scientist,' he said as he set to work on the man's pale blue flesh. 'I enjoy myself too much. You have to be serious for this job. I'd have forever been playing around with guts and bones, making puppets or funny shapes out of them.'

I said nothing while he sawed, gritting my teeth against the crunching sounds. I kept waiting for him to ask me to give him a hand but he was having too much fun. He wanted to do it all by himself. For which small mercy I was grateful.

When he'd opened up the dead executive's chest, The Cardinal set his tools aside and wiped his hands on his trousers. He hadn't bothered with gloves and took no notice of the stains he'd left. His attention was focused on Simon Spanton's guts.

'I was always interested in divination,' he said softly. 'The ancients swore by it. They thought they could see the secrets of the universe in a person's innards if they looked hard enough. They thought we were all connected on some level, that what was within mirrored what lay without.'

He glanced up at me. 'I'm sure you recall what I said about connections when we first met. I think the ancients were right. If you know what to look for, everything is linked. It's simply a matter of knowing how to connect these –' He grabbed the corpse's guts, hauled them out of their stomach lining and dumped them unceremoniously on the floor. '– with this.' He waved a hand at the walls, indicating the world in general.

The Cardinal knelt over the mound of guts and began poking through them, ripping them apart, studying the patterns they formed. I felt queasy but I bowed over him politely, as if he was a collector of bottle-tops showing me his latest finds.

'I made a study of divination,' The Cardinal huffed as he worked, 'but I wasn't impressed. Most of those who'd dabbled were fools. They wanted to tie our innards to the elements, the spirits of the dead, wacky shit like that. I mean, who gives a flying fuck if you can tell what the weather's going to be like tomorrow? Carry an umbrella and sunglasses at all times if you're that worried — you'll be covered for every emergency.'

'I think they were more worried about famine or flooding, not what it was going to be like on their walk to the office,' I said drolly, but The Cardinal only grunted.

'Since most of the evidence – as such – was pretty flaky, I decided to make up my own rules and applications.' He stopped to pick up a purplish morsel that looked no different from any other part of the unfortunate Simon Spanton's innards. He studied it curiously, then licked it and smacked his lips together, eyes distant. I came very close to throwing up, but I just about managed to keep my supper down.

'I decided to connect divination to the stock market,' The Cardinal said casually, as if it was no big thing. 'I had the corpses of several executives from major companies delivered to me. I sliced them open, studied what I found, looked at how the patterns played when set against the fortunes of their companies before and after their deaths, and took it from there.'

'I don't get it,' I frowned, staring at the guts on the floor. 'I don't see any patterns.'

'It's all in the eye of the beholder,' The Cardinal chuckled. 'Like with a Rorschach test. I look at Simon Spanton's remains and find a picture of a troubled man. He wasn't at ease when he passed. Problems at the office. He was stressed, even though he had no obvious reason to be. His company's been performing well of late, but appearances can be deceptive. I own a substantial share of their stock already and was planning to buy more. But if Spanton's guts are anything to go by, it's time to sell.'

I blinked but I still couldn't see anything. 'So you're telling me this is how you determine what to buy and sell, how you trade? You study the guts of a dead exec and base your plans on what you see in his entrails?'

'Crazy, isn't it?' The Cardinal grinned. 'But it works. Maybe it's coincidence. Maybe I'm just on the luckiest roll ever. But for fifteen years I've yet to make a serious wrong call. I rule markets around the world. This is how.'

'What if nobody dies?' I asked. 'Executives can't be dropping like flies. How do you make a call if there aren't any company corpses?'

The Cardinal smiled like an angel. 'They say only God gives and only God takes away. But Cardinals can give and take too. If the grim reaper needs a helping hand from time to time . . .'

As I stared at him wordlessly, he slapped my back and thrust his tools aside. 'Come on,' he said. 'Let's get back to the office. I don't know why, having eaten just before we came down, but I feel devilishly peckish all of a sudden . . .'

Back on the fifteenth floor, he ordered and wolfed down a plate of ribs. A few memo sheets were stuck to his desk. He examined them briefly as he ate. 'Miss Arne tells me you're a natural salesman,' he said, licking sauce from his fingers. 'Already one of our best agents. Says you'll be running her office this time next year.'

I smiled. 'That's nice, but bull. I make my share of sales. But I've no stomach for it. As a learning exercise it's fine, but beyond that . . .'

'Yes, Mr Raimi? What lies *beyond that*?'

'I was hoping you'd tell me,' I said.

'In time,' he said teasingly. 'You've got a few more tricks to pick up before I think about moving you anywhere. You're learning quickly. Mr Tasso told me how you handled our Jewish friend. Impressive. Brutal, merciless, sly. I like that. Most would have beaten the signature out of him — effective but so unstylish.'

'I did OK,' I said smugly. 'Better than I fared with Johnny Grace.'

He waved the matter away. 'No blame there.'

'You heard about it?'

'I hear about everything, Mr Raimi.'

'You're not angry?'

'Better men than you have run up against Paucar Wami. Nobody's ever come away any the stronger. I would have preferred Johnny Grace alive, but I'm not about to get into a fight with Paucar Wami over him.'

'Wami seems to be a taboo subject round here,' I noted. 'Nobody wants to talk about him.'

The Cardinal nodded slowly. 'There are people who never worry about walking under ladders, spilling salt or stepping on a crack. Then they meet Paucar Wami and cross themselves whenever anyone mentions his name.'

'Is he as bad as that?' I asked seriously.

'Yes.' He paused. 'How much do you know about him?'

'He's a killer. Been around for thirty or forty years — though he looks much younger. He used to work for you, I think. Maybe still does.'

The Cardinal smiled. 'That's more than most people ever find out.' He gazed at his hands and watched his twisted little finger wiggle about. 'Paucar Wami was my greatest . . . *creation*.' He chose the word carefully. 'I discovered him, encouraged him, set him on his way. He's a lethal killing machine. Death is his coin of choice.

'I used him in the 70s and 80s to rid myself of troublesome opponents, those who stood in my way, who were stronger than me, too well guarded to be attacked in the usual manner. Wami's unstoppable once he starts. Nothing can deter him. He took out sixteen of the most powerful men in the city in a couple of years. Killed them in their beds, their mansions, at parties for their children.' He shook his head admiringly.

'We haven't worked so closely since,' he went on. 'Wami is too hot for one master to handle. He travels the world, killing for money, for fun. Whatever. He still works for me when I need him, which isn't often these days.

'Now,' he changed the subject abruptly, 'what about a home? You've been in the Skylight long enough. Time we did right by you. What are you interested in? I'll pay for it. No mansion – not yet – but I'll stretch to a nice top-floor apartment in the business district. Or perhaps you're a river-front man?'

'Actually, I was hoping you'd let me stay on at the Skylight.'

He smiled quizzically. 'What's the attraction? Do you like the food, the room service, the fact you don't have to lift a finger? I'm sure you can get a maid when you –'

'It's not that,' I blurted. 'It's a . . . a woman.'

He laughed snidely. 'I see. A femme fatale has her claws in you at last. It had to happen, an eligible bachelor like you. Enjoy her. I hope it works out. But surely she can move with you? Unless you're reluctant to commit?'

After a brief hesitation I decided I might as well tell him about Conchita. 'It's not a romance. She's sick. I'm her friend. That's all.'

'I didn't think sick people were allowed in the Skylight. I'll have to look into this — don't want people thinking I'm running a health spa.'

'Conchita's an exception. She –'

'*Conchita?*' he barked, then frowned as if racking his memory. 'Conchita . . .' He stirred in his chair and brought one hand up to rub his forehead. '. . . Kubelik?'

'Kubekik,' I corrected him. 'You know her?' I was mildly surprised, but then again her husband had been a gangster and The Cardinal was an expert in his field. This might be my chance to learn more about Ferdinand Wain.

'I knew her once, yes.' He sounded distracted.

'Her husband was a gangster, right? Ferdinand Wain.'

'Yes.' He half-turned away from me. He looked confused for a moment, but a second later he faced me and his con-fusion – if it had existed at all – was a thing of the past. 'Yes, I knew Ferdinand and his tragic young wife. Conchita Wain was exceptional. She used to light up a room like women do in trashy novels. Every man bent over backwards to please her.' He was smiling at the memory.

'Then her disease struck.' He grew sombre. 'A terrible thing. I tried to help. For once I acted selflessly, put Ferdinand in touch with some of the finest doctors in the country, loaned him the money to pay for their services. But they couldn't cure her. When all hope faded, I gave her a room on the top floor of the Skylight, so she could at least suffer where no one could bother her. Not many people have found a soft spot in my heart.'

He stopped talking and directed his thoughts inwards.

This was an unexpected turn-up. The Cardinal acting like a human? Maybe he wasn't so terrible after all.

'Was Ferdinand any relation to Neil Wain?' I asked.

'Cousins, I think.'

'What happened to him?'

'Dead. Long dead. Killed.'

'How?'

'The money I loaned him to cover Conchita's medical bills? He fell behind on the repayments.'

He said nothing further and I was too shocked to break the silence. *Human? The Cardinal?* Not a chance.

'Anyway,' he started up again, 'back to business. There's an old acquaintance I want you to visit. Cafran Reed. He owns a restaurant not too far north of here. He's an old adversary of mine. Not a foe, you understand — I like Cafran and want no harm to come to him. We're sparring partners. Every so often I send one of my agents out to him with a new insurance offer, and every time he sends it back unsigned. It's a game, an interesting little battle we've been staging for years. He's one of the few men I haven't been able to get on my side, one of the rare birds I haven't tagged.'

'Is he wealthy?' I hadn't heard of him before, and by that time I knew most of the major movers and shakers.

'No. I don't want to snare Cafran Reed to make money. I

want him because of the challenge. He doesn't want insurance or protection. He believes in taking life as it comes,
dealing with crises only as they arise. If you can convince
him – by fair means, let me stress again, not foul – that it
would be in his benefit to take out one of our policies, I
would be most impressed.'

'And if I fail?'

He sniffed. 'As I said, I've sent my best people to him
before. I don't expect you to win him over. I'm more interested in the manner of your failure than the slim possibility
of your success. I want to see how you handle a man like
Reed, how you try to crack an impenetrable nut. There will
be no penalties. Look on it as a trial test, where the experience is more important than the result.

'Now I'm a busy man, Mr Raimi.' He motioned to the door
but I stayed in my seat.

'I've a couple of questions, if you don't mind.'

'Oh?' He glanced at his watch, considered tossing me out,
decided to humour me. 'Very well. Ask quickly.'

'What sort of deal do you want me to strike with Cafran
Reed? Any particular policy?'

'No. The cheapest or dearest, or any in-between. Hook
him any way you can, as long as it's legal. Next question?'

I nodded over my shoulder. 'The people outside. I wondered
who they were, what they were doing here.'

'Informants,' he said. 'My eyes and ears in the city. They
come from all over, every walk of life, with all manner of
tales. They tell me what their neighbours are eating, what
their bosses are wearing. If they see a murder, they come
here. If they hear a rumour, they let me know. If their spouses
change their hairstyle, I get the lowdown first. I'll listen to
anybody who cares to talk. They keep me in touch with the
spirit of the city, its mind and emotions. Through them I get
to know the people I'm master of, their whims, wishes, fears.

I listen, store the information away, let it swirl around inside my head, and occasionally use a tab or two.'

'What do they get in return?' I asked.

'Favours. Sometimes money. Mostly just the promise of a good turn. I'm a worthy ally, a generous friend. These people tell me about their lives and in return I help them if they ask. I get their children jobs, make houses available, swing deals their way. The usual carrots one hangs before a human horse.'

'How do they know to come? Who tells them?'

'Word spreads, as it always does. I hold court a couple of nights a week. They come. They speak. I listen. You can send the first one in on your way out. Good night, Mr Raimi.'

And that was the end of that.

inti maimi

I had breakfast with Y Tse and Leonora in Shankar's the next morning and gave them a full report of the meeting. Y Tse was delighted that I'd been set a test by The Cardinal — more confirmation, if any were needed, that he was genuinely interested in me.

There was still no sign of Adrian. After leaving Shankar's I rang my office, told them I'd be late and went to check his flat. Thomas drove swiftly and silently, disinterested as ever. I rang the bell a few times when I got there, pounded on the door when that failed, and ended up shouting through the letterbox. No answer. I tried peering in the windows but there were heavy curtains draped across them. I was giving serious thought to putting a foot through a pane of glass when a voice out of nowhere surprised me. 'Hey! You got business round here?'

I looked around but couldn't see anybody. I studied the rooms above Adrian's – he lived on the ground floor of a five-storey building – but the windows were shut. Then I noticed a staircase to my left, leading down to a basement. I moved a few feet over and peered into the shadowy recess.

A fat man was glaring up at me. Stubble, unwashed hair,

baggy trousers, stringy shirt and braces. He spat on the floor – there was a lake of spit down there – and nodded a curt hello. 'You got business here?' he repeated.

'Are you the landlord?'

'I'm the supervisor. You want a room?'

'I'm looking for Adrian Arne. He rents this apartment.'

'Uh–uh,' the guy said. 'That's been empty for months.'

I glanced at the number on the door and it was the right one. I began to frown, then it clicked — kids had rearranged the plates.

'Somebody's been screwing with the doors,' I said. 'Switching the numbers.'

'The fuck they have,' the supervisor growled. 'I'd crack shin-bones if they tried that and they know it. Who were you looking for?'

'Adrian Arne.'

He spat again. 'No Adrian Arne here. We got an Aidan Aherne up top. Could be him you're after?'

I stared at the supervisor, then examined the door again. I'd been here several times and there was a scratch beneath the letterbox that I remembered Adrian making one night when he'd lost his bottle opener. This *was* the right place.

I shuffled down a few steps towards the basement. The supervisor raised a hand to shield his eyes and edged back-wards, squinting at me suspiciously. 'I've nothing any good to you,' he said quickly. 'No money, drugs or any of that shit.'

'I've not come to rob you,' I assured him. 'Could you let me in the apartment to check around?'

'What for? Nobody's there.'

I reached for my wallet and pulled out a fifty. Snapped it flat a couple of times. 'That real?' he asked, taking the note with his fat, greasy fingers, lifting it to his nose, sniffing its creases.

'Real as Christmas,' I said.

The supervisor snorted, spat into the lake, then rumbled to the top of the stairs, muttering about missing a game on TV and crazy crackheads wasting his time. He jerked out a massive bunch of keys, spent a few seconds selecting the correct one, opened the door sullenly, flicked on the light and let me in.

The room was empty. No furniture, TV or video. No moustachioed Mona Lisa grinning from the wall. The bed was gone, the toothbrushes, Adrian's collection of empty beer bottles. It was as if nobody had lived here in ages.

I turned angrily on the supervisor. 'What is this shit? Where's Adrian?'

'I told you there'd been nobody here for months,' he said smugly. 'But you're not getting your money back, so –' I slapped him before he could say any more. 'Hey, stop! Fucking stop it, you –'

He shut up when I slammed him against the wall. I reached down and pinched one of his fat nipples. He squeaked like a mouse. I pinched the other, then lowered my hand and held it inches in front of his sweaty groin. 'What happened to him?' I hissed.

'I don't know,' he said, lips quivering, stunned by this sudden bout of violence. I was stunned myself, hardly aware of what I was doing. I watched as my hand slapped him again. 'I don't know!' he screeched. I undid his flies. 'Fuck you!' he screamed as I reached in and pulled his prick out. I held it between the teeth of the open zipper, then pulled the zip half up, catching him firmly and painfully.

'Adrian Arne,' I said calmly. 'Where is he?'

'You're a nut!' he sobbed. 'Fuck you! I'm not saying a –' I gave another quick tug and his face went purple.

'A few more notches and you'll never piss straight again,' I said cheerily. 'They'll have to put a tap in your stomach to let it out.'

'Please,' he cried, 'I don't know any Adrian Arne. I swear on my life, man. On my mother's life. On –'

'Don't try shitting me,' I snapped. 'I was here not a week ago, and plenty of times before. I'm going to ask one more time. If I don't hear the right answer, you better hope the ambulances are running on time.'

'No! I swear! Fuck it, man, I'll tell you whatever you want to know. Adrian Arne? Yeah, I know him, sure I do, only please don't . . .'

I released his prick and let him tuck it away, his hands trembling. There was fear in his voice, but also honest ignorance. 'Tell me truly,' I said, 'do you really know him? Don't lie to me. I won't hurt you if you tell me the truth.'

He hesitated, considered a lie, then shook his head, hands covering the front of his trousers protectively. 'No. But please don't do that again. Please!'

'Who's been renting this room?' I asked.

'No one, not since the Moores, I think, or the Sims . . . shit, it's been a while. There have been enquiries but the owner tells me not to rent it, so I don't. I just work here. I don't make the fucking decisions.' He was growing cockier now that the immediate danger was past. 'Come look at the register. That'll prove it.'

His living quarters stank of beer, piss and vomit. Empty beer cans and porno mags littered the floor. Posters of naked women on the walls. The kitchen was visible from where I stood, but I chose not to look. The TV was an ancient machine with a poor quality picture and those wavy lines you don't get on the newer models.

He yanked the register out from under a pile of dirty linen, sat on the couch and opened it. 'There. The Moores. I remember them now. The Sims were just before them. You want a beer? I've plenty in the fridge. A man can never have too much fucking beer, right? I'll get a couple bottles.'

I concentrated on the register while he rooted through the fridge for a beer. Handwritten entries, torn pages, stains and smudges from months back. No trace of any Adrian Arne. Nobody had been in that apartment – officially anyway – for months. I glanced at the supervisor as he came back, sweating, opening the beers. He probably knew nothing, but I called his bluff just in case.

'Do you think I'm a fool?' I snapped. 'This has been fixed.'

'No fucking way! Gimme it!' He snatched the register and stared. 'Nah, this hasn't been touched. That's my handwriting. And that jam stain . . . I remember making that. You trying to stir up shit, man?'

'Who owns this building?' I asked. 'Who pays your wages?'

'Some business corporation. They pay cash. Never volunteered their names and I never asked. I've been here six years and never had a spot of trouble. Don't put up with any shit. Now why don't you piss off and –'

'I don't care what this book says,' I told him. 'I've been here before. With Adrian. You can't tell me that room's been empty because I know it hasn't. Even if he was squatting, you'd have heard him. You're telling me you never heard any noises from above?'

'Damn fucking straight,' he replied, sipping his beer. 'Mister, I'm gonna tell you something and I'm gonna be blunt. You're fucked in the head. You've got the wrong house, wrong city or the wrong fucking world. I check the rooms a couple times a week. Believe me, there's no Adrian Arne here.'

He took a drink and waited. Could it be true? Had I got the wrong building? No! Damn it, they might all look the same from a distance, but they weren't. I knew one from the other. I knew Adrian's. There was no mistake and I wasn't crazy. The supervisor had to be lying. Somebody had put the frighteners on him. Someone so threatening, he wouldn't crack even when his prick was on the line. An expert got to him and fixed it so he'd never talk about his lodger. It took a lot to put a man in that state. Maybe he had a family somewhere, or a dark secret he could never risk emerging. Whatever it was, I wasn't going to get anywhere with him.

'Tell them Capac Raimi's after them,' I said softly. 'Tell them Adrian Arne has a friend who won't put up with this. Tell them I'm coming. I'll find them and make them sorry. Whoever they are.' I left.

The supervisor came to the door after me. 'Fucking nut,' I heard him chuckle. I almost turned back but he wasn't worth the hassle.

There was a beggar with a tin box standing on the street near my car. He was wearing dark glasses and carried a white cane. 'Some spare change?' he asked. I normally didn't bother with beggars – the city was full of them – but my mind was elsewhere and I tossed him a few coins. 'Thank you, Mr Raimi.'

I was four or five steps past before I realized what he'd said. I stopped. Turned slowly. 'How do you know –' I began.

'– your name?' He smiled and removed his glasses. His eyes were white blanks and I suddenly recalled the blind man I'd seen outside the station on my first day here, and the one at the building site during the fog. This wasn't the same guy if memory served me right – he was taller – but the eyes were the same.

'I know many names,' he said. 'Capac Raimi. Y Tse Lapotaire. Adrian Arne.'

'You know Adrian?'

'Who?'

'Adrian Arne.'

'I've never heard of him.'

'But you just –'

'There is no Adrian Arne,' the man said. 'Never has been, never will be. There is soil. Air. Blood. Strings. Nothing more.'

'Very poetic,' I sneered. 'Now cut the crap and tell me what you know about Adrian.' I took a step towards him. His cane came up immediately and he held it lengthways between his hands.

'Your search is only beginning,' he said. 'You have far to go and the way is hard, but the start is always hardest. Forget about your friend. You have more important matters to consider.'

'Listen,' I said, taking another step. He threw his cane at me. I raised my arms to knock it away, but all of a sudden it transformed and I was covered in plastic wrapping. It swirled around me, encasing me from head to foot. It stuck to my skin, smothered my lips, tripped me. I tore at it angrily, ripped holes in it, and was free in ten or fifteen seconds. But the blind man was gone. The street stretched away in both directions, no sign of any beggars.

I hurried back to the car and asked Thomas if he'd seen what happened. He frowned. 'A blind man, sir?'

'Yes.'

'Here, sir? A minute ago?'

'Yes,' I growled.

'No, sir. Do you want me to get out and look?'

I spat on the pavement in disgust, then got into the car. 'Just take me back to the office,' I muttered and covered my face from the sun with a hand. I spent the ride brooding and for once I was glad of the silence up front.

I pulled our files on Cafran Reed and tried to immerse myself. Reed had no middle name, was fifty-four, divorced fourteen years ago, never remarried, a few romantic entanglements but nothing incriminating. He owned his own restaurant which he'd been running for more than twenty years, a small joint, popular with a select crowd, average annual income of . . .

My mind wandered. Adrian in the trunk of a stolen car, blood oozing out the corners of his eyes, cold, alone, dead. Dumped in the river, strands of his bowels indistinguishable from feeding eels. In a field outside the city, pushing up nettles, ribs home to a family of foxes.

Or was he alive? Maybe he'd skipped town one step ahead of whoever his enemies might be. Maybe he was hiding, waiting for a safe moment to contact me. Shit, he probably wasn't even thinking about me if that was the case — we weren't *that* close. Still, he would have said something surely. And what had that blind beggar been mumbling about?

I pushed the papers away. I couldn't concentrate, not with this on my mind. My right hand flexed and I recalled its grip on the tennis racket. That's what I needed to clear my head. A few hours on a court. I grabbed the phone to ring for Thomas and only then remembered Sonja. She'd know about Adrian. If she was here, not home weeping and planning a funeral. If she wasn't caught up in the same trouble. If she wasn't feeding the fishes with her brother.

I rushed up two flights of stairs to her office, suddenly certain she was dead or MIA. I burst onto her floor, alarmed her receptionist and crashed through her door without knocking. She was there. Looked up nervously, a hand snaking to the intercom to press for help. Then she realized it was me and relaxed. 'Jesus, Capac,' she laughed, opening her drawer to take out a cigarette. 'You nearly gave me a stroke.' She saw my red face and the look in my eyes, and lit the cigarette slowly. 'What's wrong?'

'It's Adrian. He . . .' I was panting. She told me to sit. Held up a hand when I tried to speak again, said to wait until I had my breath back. I said nothing until I felt myself regaining control, then began again. 'It's Adrian. He's missing. I called round to his apartment and he was gone. The supervisor said Adrian had never even been there, but that's bullshit, I visited him there plenty of times, I know it was the right place, I –'

'OK,' she interrupted. 'Calm down. Let's go through this slowly and carefully. Who did you say was missing?'

I frowned and said it slowly. '*Adrian.*'

She tapped her teeth with a glossed fingernail. 'Adrian who?'

I said nothing for a moment. Then, bitterly, 'Is that your idea of a fucking joke?'

'Adrian *who*?' she repeated.

'Adrian!' I yelled. 'Your goddamn brother, Adrian Arne. He's gone.'

She stared at me, confused. 'I don't have a brother.'

'What?' I said hollowly.

'I'm an only child, an orphan since the age of six.' I could only stare at her wordlessly. Her eyes were filling with tears. 'If this is some sort of a prank, Capac, it's in very poor taste.'

'A prank!' I exploded. 'Your brother disappears and you –'

'Stop it!' she shouted, tears trickling down her cheeks. 'This isn't funny. Why are you being so cruel?'

'Sonja, what are you saying? You *know* you have a brother! You introduced us, for the love of Christ!'

Her face whitened. 'The joke's over,' she snapped. 'I don't know why you're doing this and I don't want to. I would have given anything for a brother or sister, as I must have told you, or else you couldn't target me like this. How dare you throw shit like this at me? Get the hell out of my office.'

I tried to say something.

'*Now!*' she screamed.

I stood, head spinning, and stumbled to the door. I tried one more time before leaving. 'Who got to you, Sonja? Who made you turn on your own brother?'

'If you don't leave,' she growled, 'I'll set security on you, Cardinal's pet or not.'

'Have it your way,' I said coldly. 'Deny Adrian. Be a Judas. But I won't bend. You hear me? I won't fucking bend or let this drop. I'll find out who's behind this and I'll make them pay. Nobody fucks with my friends. *Nobody!*'

I stormed out of the office, fingers clenched into fists. I pounded the wall as I went and cracked the plaster, but I didn't give a fine flying fuck.

I couldn't stay in the office, not with that bitch laughing at me upstairs. Her own brother! Somebody had wiped Adrian out – I was sure of that now – and she was playing along. To protect herself? She hadn't seemed scared, so I didn't think so. To move up another rung on the corporate ladder? She'd sacrificed her own body to get this far. Maybe sacrificing Adrian's would move her a step further along. It didn't sound like the Sonja I knew but maybe I was just a bad judge of character.

This was turning into a nightmare of a day. I'd come into it with high expectations. The Cardinal was rooting for me, I had a golden opportunity to impress, and I was still buzzing from my mindblowing bout of sex the night before. I'd wanted to concentrate on finding my mysterious lover – I was sure I could track her down – but here I was, stuck with a far less attractive mystery. The woman from the stairs would have to wait.

As furious as I was, I took the Reed file with me. Ignoring a direct order from The Cardinal wasn't on the agenda, regardless of all other distractions. He'd told me to visit Cafran Reed and that remained my number one priority. I could put it on the back burner for a few hours while I did some digging around for traces of Adrian, but I'd have to turn to it in the afternoon. I didn't want to be the first man in twenty years to tell The Cardinal he had to wait because I had more important things to deal with.

I popped into Party Central and checked the records on three different floors. I wanted to see what sort of background info they had on Adrian, who his friends were, if he was connected with any shady deals, if there were clues in his past. It took a while for me to believe what I uncovered, but in the end I had to face the facts — *he wasn't there*. The most complete records in the city, and not a word about him. No birth certificate, no record of his driver's license, insurance details, schooling or employment history. I checked twice on each floor but every search produced the same result. Officially Adrian Arne didn't exist, had never existed.

It wasn't possible. There had to be information somewhere, perhaps tucked away in files on one of the higher, restricted floors. But I couldn't get in there, so I had no option other than to resign myself to his bureaucratic non-being.

Then I recalled my encounter on the stairs. Was the woman in black involved in this? Strangers didn't wander into Party Central as and when they pleased. Getting an operative in here would require tremendous influence. The same sort it would need to eradicate a person's files. She could be a link to Adrian. It looked like I'd have to investigate my mystery girl sooner than planned, only not for the romantic purposes I'd initially envisaged. It would be difficult but I'd hunt her down. For Adrian's sake if not my own.

I rang Adrian's agency and spoke to the manager, John D'Affraino, who I'd met a couple of times. He remembered me and was all smiles down the phone. 'John, do you have an Adrian Arne on your books?' I asked after a while.

'Let's see.' I heard him tapping the name into his computer. 'Is that with or without an E? With? No, no Arne. We've got an Adrian Arnold.'

'Could you describe him?'

'Six-two, black, thirties, bushy beard.'

'No. Do you have a record of my drivers for the last month or two?'

'Sure. Just a minute . . . here we go. You've got Thomas at the moment. He's one of our best. Before him you had Pat Burke. Gregg Hapes before that.'

'Could you get Pat or Gregg on the phone?'

'Sure. Hold on a sec.'

Pat Burke was off duty but Gregg Hapes was there. I asked if he remembered driving me. 'Of course,' he said cheerfully. 'I'm due to take you out again next week for a couple of nights, I think.'

'Do you recall the last time you took me out?'

'I think so,' he said. 'Last Thursday, wasn't it? Or was it Friday?'

'One of those, yeah. Do you remember my date, a tall lady in a green dress?'

A slight pause, one I'd have missed if I hadn't been expecting it. 'Sure,' he said, cheerful as before. 'A nice lady.'

'She lost an earring, we think maybe in the car. You come up with anything like that lately?'

'No, Mr Raimi. And I cleaned it out just yesterday.'

'If you do, will you send it on?'

'Absolutely. I think I remember them. Green, right, like the dress?'

'Yeah. Like the dress.' I hung up and took a few seconds to collect myself. I thanked the receptionist for the use of her phone, went to the toilet, came down in a lift and set off to see Cafran Reed.

They'd even got to the chauffeurs. Why go to such lengths? Deleting his files, securing the silence of those who knew him, covering every track he ever made. What justification could there be for the cost, time and effort that must involve? And if they'd gone that far, bought out his building super-visor and workmates, his own sister . . . if they'd solicited everyone who knew him and warned them to deny Adrian's very existence . . . why hadn't they come after *me?*

Y Tse rang as I was on my way to Cafran Reed's restaurant. 'Hi, kid,' he boomed. 'How's tricks?'

'Fine,' I said. This was the first time he'd called. He hated phones. I guessed somebody had been talking.

'You sure of that? Someone told me you've been acting a bit strange today. What's up?'

'Who was it?' I asked. 'Sonja?'

'Well, tarnation's titties, Capac, how many other dames have you been freaking the living shit out of? She was sobbing, called you a heartless prick, threatened to cancel your contract. She'd been drinking and that's not like Sonja.'

'And she's blaming me? Fuck her!' I yelled. 'She won't acknowledge Adrian. Her own brother, and the bitch sat there and told me she was an orphan! Can you believe that shit? Then I go to Party Central and someone's wiped his files. I ring his agency and they say he never worked there — not only that, but they've drawn up an imaginary list of drivers for me. And there's some –'

'Whoa,' he laughed down the line. 'Get a grip, Capac. Are you high?'

'Y Tse,' I shouted, 'Sonja *has* a brother! Adrian has been my driver and best friend since I started working here. A couple of days ago he didn't turn up for work and now it's like I dreamt him up. Nobody admits they knew him, there's nothing to prove he was ever alive. How the fuck am I expected to react?'

'Listen, Capac – no, no anchovies –' he said to somebody on the other end of the line, '– let's talk this through calmly. I don't know Sonja very well but a few years ago I had an all-night session with her and Leonora. We got to talking about our lives and inner selves, all the shit you only discuss at five in the morning. She said she'd never had a family, would have loved a brother or sister. She got quite emotional about it.'

'But I saw him! Every fucking day, Y Tse! Are you saying I imagined him?'

'No. All I'm saying is a few years ago, before anyone had ever heard of Capac Raimi, Sonja Arne told me she didn't have a brother. That means whatever you've stumbled into predates you. There are three possibilities as I see it. One, Sonja was lying all those years ago and really does have a brother. I don't think that's the case. Why should she lie back then if it was? Two, you're going mad. Not a pretty thought, but the mind screws up on us sometimes. I don't think it's likely but we can't dismiss the possibility. Three, there never was an Adrian Arne, only a pretender.'

'But she introduced us. She told me he was her brother.'

'She was lying.'

His simple assertion threw me. It was so obvious. Immediately I knew it must be the truth and cursed myself for not having seen it already.

'She wanted you to believe she had a brother,' Y Tse went on, 'so she fed you a lie. He was in on it too. It's an easy deception to pull off — you had no reason to suspect something foul. Now they want the deception to end. So they stop lying. No trick to it. Who's going to notice the disappearance of a guy who was never real in the first place?'

'Why go to all that trouble?' I asked. 'What difference can it make whether I think Sonja has a brother or not? It serves no purpose. Why would they pretend?'

'That's something for you to unearth if you decide to follow it up. But I'll tell you, whoever's behind this, I doubt it's Sonja. I guess somebody else is involved, someone who likes to play meaningless games for reasons sometimes unknown even to himself.'

'The Cardinal?'

'It's got his crazy stamp all over it. You checked in Party Central's files and drew a blank? Well, ignoring the fact that if he's not her brother, his name wouldn't be Arne –' *Fuck!* '– who's got the power to tamper with those files? A handful of people, and every one of them's on the shortest of The Cardinal's many leashes. Nothing like that could be done without his knowledge.'

'There was . . .' I paused. Should I tell him of my encounter on the stairs? I trusted Y Tse but . . . no. I trusted him and that was that. I needed at least one person to believe in. 'There was a woman last night. I met her going up the stairs of Party Central. I don't know what she was up to, but it wasn't on the straight. She was dressed like a burglar and –'

'A burglar?' he snorted. 'Get off the cloud. Couldn't happen.'

'But it did. She got in somehow. She was coming down from a higher floor when I –'

'I'm telling you,' he interrupted, 'Party Central has the tightest security on the face of the planet. Apart from the Troops camped around it, there are sensor beams on every floor, remote-operated machine guns set behind the walls, canisters of gas in the ceilings, hidden cameras, secret traps, all manner of –'

'Hidden cameras?' My heart raced as I thought of The Cardinal sitting down before a TV set with his lunch, watching my bony ass going through the motions.

'Loads of them.'

'On the stairs too?'

'Of course.'

Fuck. Another problem I'd have to cope with. This was one week I wanted to take back and start over again. 'So you think The Cardinal's behind this? That he set Adrian up to fool me, or made him vanish like those others you told me about, Harry Gilmer and the rest?'

'Harry . . . ? Oh, him. Yeah, could be. Not beyond the –'

'Y Tse,' I cut in, suddenly thinking of something, 'do you know Paucar Wami?'

There was a long silence. Finally, 'How do you know Wami?' he asked quietly.

'I don't. Not really. I ran into him a while back and the name just jumped into my mind a second ago. He worked for The Cardinal, didn't he? He killed people for him, made them vanish?'

Y Tse hesitated. 'People rarely see Wami coming or going, and he can eliminate a man without leaving a trace, but I doubt it's him.'

'But he's worth checking out?' I pressed, not sure why my mind had linked him to this but certain somehow that I was onto something.

'I wouldn't,' Y Tse said. 'Wami plays his own games and they're not the sort you want to get mixed up with. If you want my advice, leave Paucar Wami well alone.' But he said it with more hope than expectation. Y Tse knew I wouldn't let this drop.

We talked some more, about trivial matters, then he hung up. Thomas got stuck in traffic – this was a bad time to be driving – but eventually I made it to my meeting with Cafran Reed and breathed a sigh of relief as I stepped out of the car. It would be good to get back to some ordinary business for a couple of hours. I'd taken all the craziness I could handle for one day.

The sign above the door simply read 'CAFRAN'S'. Inside there were rubber plants in a couple of corners, strong yellow lights, paintings of trees and rivers, pop tunes playing softly in the background. The pretty receptionist paged her boss and a waitress escorted me to a table by one of the walls.

Cafran appeared a couple of minutes later, smiling easily. He was short, plump and pleasant, bald as an elbow. His face was a mass of freckles. He wore large, red glasses. His suit was conservative but somewhat at odds with the orange braces and 'I LOVE CAFRAN'S' rosette pinned over his heart.

'So, Mr Raimi,' he said brightly as he sat, 'you're the latest designated knight. It's been a while since my last. I remarked on it only the other day to Ama – my daughter – and *voila!* here you are. Would you care to order? The steak is rather excellent this week.'

'Steak would be great,' I smiled.

'Two steaks, please,' he said to the waitress. 'I've had one already today,' he told me confidentially, 'but don't tell Ama if you see her — I'm supposed to be on a diet.'

He prattled on while we were waiting for the steak, telling me about his doctor, the business, his customers. I smiled pleasantly, arched my eyebrows, threw him a question when-ever he paused for breath. I hated this part of the sell. I couldn't wait to get down to the nitty-gritty. I kept glancing around, looking for the steak, taking in the staff and customers. There was a waitress serving dessert at a table by the window. A nice figure. Long legs. Cafran said something about a magician he'd seen on TV. Magic was a hobby of his — he knew lots of tricks and offered to show me a few later. I said that would be nice. My eyes flicked lazily at the leggy waitress again. She'd just finished dishing up the dessert.

The waitress turned and I immediately lost all interest in Cafran Reed, insurance deals and everything else. It was the woman from the stairs! She looked up from her trolley, smiling mechanically, and saw me. The smile cracked. One hand dropped the knife it had been holding and it knocked over a small trifle. She recovered, carried on serving, and made her way across to my table.

Cafran beamed when she arrived. 'Ama,' he said, 'I'd like you to meet Capac Raimi. Capac, this is my daughter, Ama Situwa.'

'A pleasure,' I said, reaching out a trembling hand to shake hers.

'Likewise.' The instant our fingers touched I got a hard-on. She felt it all the way through my palm and smiled. 'I think we've met before, Mr Raimi.' Her voice was exotic, an accent I couldn't place.

'Please, call me Capac. Yes, I think our paths have crossed. Once.'

'Really?' Cafran was excited. 'What a coincidence. Where?'

'I can't quite recall,' Ama said. 'Do you, Capac?'

'I think it was at a party,' I said, smiling leanly. 'Up in the city somewhere. The central region, maybe.'

'Of course. *We passed upon the stairs*, as the old song goes.'

'That's right.'

She had a smile I wanted to frame. Her tongue had a habit of flicking past her front teeth between sentences. 'We must get together again soon,' she purred.

'Just name a time and place,' I told her.

'I will.' She turned to speak to Cafran. I felt myself throbbing uncontrollably. I gripped the edge of the table and suppressed a shudder. I missed what she said to her father and the next thing I knew, she was facing me again. 'Nice to see you again, Capac. I might drop by later, perhaps for dessert.'

'That would be nice.' Hell yes! Her on a plate with a sprinkling of sugar and nothing else. The image set me drooling as she continued on her rounds, favouring me with short, wicked smiles every so often. It was going to be a nightmare trying to concentrate on work, but I had to make the effort.

'That's quite a pair of eyes you have on you,' Cafran said drily when I finally looked at him again. 'It doesn't pay to ogle a girl in front of her father.'

'Sorry, Mr Reed, I –'

He burst into laughter. 'I jest. Ama is quite an attraction. I don't blame young men for gawping. I even take it as a compliment.'

I smiled awkwardly. 'You said her name was Ama *Situwa*. Is she married?'

'No. Her mother and I went our separate ways some years ago. It was not an amicable split. She returned with Ama to her home country, took back her maiden name and kept the two of us apart.'

'Then how come . . . ?' I nodded at his mesmerising daughter.

He sighed. 'Ama's mother died four years ago. She told Ama I was a monster, so Ama found it difficult to approach me, even when she was left alone. Finally she came to judge for herself, found me innocent, and we've been together since, making up for those sad, lost years.'

The steaks arrived and we tucked into them. When we were finished we leant back in our chairs and nibbled some mints. 'So,' Cafran said, rubbing his stomach and smiling with content. 'You've come to try and sell me insurance.'

'That's right,' I smiled. 'I've got some great policies lined up, at prices you're going to sing over.'

'I very much doubt that. I've never paid for insurance, not since I got stung in my youth. It's a money-making racket. One of the main reasons I remain in this city is its lax insurance laws where businesses are concerned.'

'And that's largely down to The Cardinal,' I noted. 'He keeps the law off the small entrepreneur's back. Without him you wouldn't be able to operate so freely.'

'That's true.'

'So why not pay him back? Take out one of our options. Call it a gesture of friendship. One good turn . . .'

He laughed. 'The Cardinal doesn't set the city's insurance standards with me in mind. I owe him nothing, he doesn't owe me, and I like it that way.'

'But –'

Cafran held up a silencing hand. 'There's nothing better after a good meal than a magic trick.' He dug into a pocket and produced a stick of celery and a finger guillotine. He placed them on a white napkin in the centre of the table. 'This is one of my favourites. Simple, classic, timeless.

'Ladies and Gentlemen!' he boomed, startling me. I glanced around and noticed other customers smiling — they were used to these displays. 'Cafran the Great is proud to present, all the way from anarchist France, Madame Guillotine! Severer of heads, the blade with the thirsty edge, the killer of kings, most lethal of stings, the steel which kisses and never misses. The victim goes in.' He pushed the celery through the hole in the contraption. 'The blade goes up.' He pulled the small blade to the top. 'The blood-hungry hags get ready to sup. The lever's released, the blade comes down!' He slammed it down, chopping through the stalk of celery. 'The head of the victim spins around.'

The spectators applauded. Cafran picked up the two pieces of the celery, held them for all to see, then handed them to the waitress to dispose of. 'Now,' he said cheerfully, 'do we have a volunteer?' He looked at me and reluctantly I raised an answering arm. Cafran reached across for one of my fingers.

'You know,' I said as he eased the middle finger of my right hand into the hole, 'I *can* think of an excellent reason why you should take one of our policies.'

'Oh?' he asked, frowning, concentrating on the trick. 'What would that be?'

'Your daughter.'

Cafran's smile froze and he faced me slowly. 'Would you mind expanding on that remark?' His voice was cold.

'If you want to keep your daughter, sign for me.'

'Is this a threat?' His fingers were clutching mine and I suddenly realized this wasn't the best of times to play games. But it was too late to stop.

'No. I'm making you an offer. You buy insurance from me, I let you keep your daughter.'

He sneered. 'I thought you were a nice young man but a rat's whiskers always twitch sooner rather than later. But you forget, my young, vicious friend, that you cannot harm me or my daughter. The Cardinal forbids it.'

'I wasn't talking about harming Ama.'

'Then what, to put it bluntly, *were* you fucking talking about?'

I leant forward. 'I wouldn't harm a hair on Ama's head, but I can and will take her away from you if you refuse to come to an agreement with me.'

'You plan to kidnap her?' He was more bemused than angry now.

'No. I'm talking about marriage, Mr Reed.'

He stared at me uncomprehendingly. 'What sort of a salesman are you?'

'One who'll take advantage of any opportunity. I believe Ama and I are made for each other. There's chemistry between us. She'll love me, given time. In fact I think she'll come to love me so much, she'll do anything I ask. If I leave this city and head for some godforsaken corner of the earth, she'll follow. You'll never see her again if I do that, Cafran.' I smiled. 'Or can I call you Daddy?'

'You're mad,' he gaped.

'Maybe. But look in my eyes. Look in Ama's. Tell me I'm crazy then.'

He glanced across the room. Ama was watching us, an amused frown creasing her face, wondering why the act had paused in the middle. He licked his lips. 'She'd never leave me. We're too close. Even if you did marry her, she wouldn't just abandon me.'

'You're sure of that?'

'I am.'

I shrugged. 'Maybe you're right. You know her better than I do. Maybe she'll stick by you, regardless of what I ask of her. But wouldn't you like to be certain? Wouldn't you like to *insure* her long-term loyalty?' I gave him my sneakiest smile and sat back.

His nails were digging into my finger. His right hand hovered above the top of the guillotine. The diners were looking on curiously, whispering, catching whiffs of the tension. The magic might be on the point of turning nasty and they relished the prospect of some unexpected blood.

Cafran looked up, smiled abruptly and brought his hand crashing down. I convulsed reflexively, in my mind's eye seeing the finger cut in two, blood spurting, harpies and vampires converging to suck me dry. But the blade came to rest harmlessly at the bottom of the guillotine. The crowd gasped, then clapped as I withdrew my finger and flexed it. Cafran stood, bowed and sat again. 'Now,' he said, 'where are these papers you want me to sign?' A pause. A charming grin. He tapped me on the chin and winked. '*Son.*'

I thanked Cafran for the meal, shook hands on the deal and took my leave. He was still smiling ruefully. Ama was waiting outside, arms crossed, serious as a judge in a hanging case. I walked over. We stood, staring silently for a minute, uncertain of ourselves. For all I knew she was one of The Cardinal's assassins, on orders to seduce, tempt and murder one Capac Raimi. For all she knew, I was The Cardinal's man through and through, here to make up for last night's error. Neither of us knew if the other was a potential lover or killer. It would have been comical if our lives hadn't been on the line.

Ama broke the silence. 'Have fun the other night?'

'Fuck yes,' I said and then we were both laughing. 'I never did it on the stairs before.'

'Me neither. Kind of different, wasn't it?'

'Pretty exciting.'

'And intoxicating. Invigorating. And incredibly, ridiculously stupid.'

'I know. Screwing like rabbits on the stairs of Party Central. If anyone had chanced upon us . . .'

She chewed her upper lip. 'So you're Capac Raimi.'

'And you're Ama Situwa.'

'Ever hear of me before today?'

'No.'

'I'd heard of you.'

'Word of mouth?'

'No. I read about you in the files at Party Central.'

I hesitated, smile fading. 'Can you tell me what you were doing there?' I asked.

She looked around nervously. 'How close are you to The Cardinal? How loyal are you?' She watching closely for my response.

'I don't know,' I answered truthfully. 'Up to a couple of days ago I'd have said I was loyal to my last breath. He was the key to all I wanted, riches, glory, power. Now I'm not so sure. A friend's gone missing and I think The Cardinal might be implicated, that he's playing games with me. If pushed, I'd describe myself as loyal but wavering.'

'I broke into Party Central,' she confessed. 'There's an unguarded window on the second floor. I get up there with a rope. I've been sneaking in three or four nights a week,

searching the secret files on the top floors. I've enough
evidence set aside to tear The Cardinal to shreds. I could
destroy him in the blink of an eye tomorrow if I wanted.'

It was a tall story, a lone woman breaking into Party
Central unassisted, but I believed her. 'Are you going to attack
him?' I asked.

'Probably. Eventually.'

'Why? What were you looking for? Why did you go there?'

'I'll explain later. For now, know there's nobody behind
me. I've done this for and by myself. If you betray him, it's
for me, a woman you don't know, a woman you've screwed
once on a flight of stairs, who thinks she's in love with you,
though she doesn't know why.' She smiled sickly. 'If that
sounds reasonable, you're as crazy as I am for telling you
this.'

She was trembling. I was a total stranger yet she'd entrusted
me with everything she had, her body, her heart, her life.
Nobody had ever placed such faith in me before. I never
thought anybody would. I felt weightless. Torn. For some
reason I wanted to run with her madness and join her against
The Cardinal, but that would mean risking everything, putting
my future on the line.

'Do you know Adrian Arne?' It wasn't an important question, but if she lied the way others had lied, I'd shop her to
The Cardinal before the night was out.

'Not in person,' she answered. 'But I know the name. He's
one of the people on the Ayuamarca list.'

'What?' I'd heard that name before.

'*Ayuamarca*. It's what I went to Party Central to find. It's
the answer to the questions I've been tormented by since I
came to this city. I haven't been able to crack its secret but
I know it's the key. It's full of names. Mine, Adrian Arne's,
Leonora Shankar's, yours. Dozens of names and a puzzle to
go with each.' She checked her watch and tutted. 'I have to

go in. Father needs me. A couple of the regular waitresses are off sick.'

'We have to meet again,' I said quickly, afraid she was going to vanish like Adrian once we said goodbye. 'I want to hear more about this list and what you're looking for.'

'Of course.'

'Where? When?'

'Tomorrow. The docks. Pier 15. Come about six. That'll give you enough time to think things over. You might decide I'm too much of a risk and choose to remain true to your boss. I won't blame you if you do. I'm asking more than any stranger should. Maybe you'll come with Ford Tasso and a squadron of Troops.' She sighed. 'I can't stop that now. If I've made a mistake, I'm dead. I'm gambling on the chance that you love me — and that's so crazy that thinking about it makes me sick.'

She left. I stood staring after her, mouth hanging open. A couple of seconds later she was back for one last question. 'Do you remember your childhood?' I must have jumped because she smiled knowingly. 'Neither do I,' she said. And then she was gone again, this time for good.

I filed my papers back at the office. Sonja was there, sullen, glaring at me, but she brightened up when she saw the signed forms. She'd been trying to land Reed for almost as long as The Cardinal had. She asked how I did it, making an effort to bridge the chasm between us. I only grunted. She'd tricked me and lied to me. I wasn't prepared to forgive and forget. I gave her the forms to finish, made a curt excuse and left.

I wandered the streets of the city for a few hours before making my lonely way back to the Skylight. Could I really betray The Cardinal? It should have been an unthinkable question. He'd spared me. Brought me into the fold, set me up with a great job, told Ford Tasso and Sonja to teach me.

I was going to turn on him after all that, on account of a cat burglar who'd seduced me on the stairs? It was crazy.

I had to give her to him. For all I knew she was a plant, and he'd put her in my way to test my loyalty. If she wasn't – if she was genuine – revealing her was all the more imperative. I should go home, shower, pick up my phone and tell The Cardinal all about Ama Situwa and the threat she posed. Feelings – the stirrings of what might be love, but which was probably just horniness – be damned.

I'd about made up my mind when my mobile rang. It was one of The Cardinal's secretaries. He wanted to see me ASAP. He'd heard about my deal with Cafran and wanted to congratulate me in person. That was the deciding factor. I'd go there and tell him face-to-face. Ama Situwa was finished. The hell with Adrian too. I had my own neck to worry about and that mattered to me more than any other's.

Just when my future had been settled, my phone rang again. This time it was one of Conchita's doctors. She'd had a visit from her husband, suffered a relapse and tried to kill herself. He said she'd nearly succeeded. He asked me to come as swiftly as I could. They'd drugged her but she was still conscious. If I couldn't help her, she'd have to be taken some place where professionals could care for her. He didn't come right out and say I was the only thing between her and the nut-house but it was what he meant. Forgetting all my other troubles, I barked at Thomas and we made it to the Skylight in record time. The Cardinal would have to wait.

When I reached Conchita's apartment, I was told she'd calmed down since they rang, due to exhaustion, drugs and the blood she'd lost. She was in her bedroom, resting, crying, staring at the ceiling, half-dozing. The doctors wanted me to come back in the morning, but then a nurse came out and said Conchita had been asking for me, so they decided I'd better go in after all. They warned me to be gentle with her, comforting, understanding. As if I needed telling.

I entered, closed the door and crossed the room to the frail figure stretched across the bed. 'Hey, little one,' I said softly.

Her eyes opened and she smiled weakly. 'Hi.' Her voice was faint and pained. 'I thought you weren't going to come, that I'd die alone tonight, that I'd lost you.'

'Don't be silly. You can't lose me. I have a homing device stitched into my skull. It always brings me back, whether I like it or not.'

'Silly.' She grimaced. 'It's been so long since I tried to kill myself. I forgot how much it hurts.' She began to weep. I cuddled her gently.

'Shh. Don't cry. There's no need. I'm here. I'll help. I promised to protect you, didn't I? Forever.' I backed off just enough so I could see her face. 'What did he say, Conchita? What did the bastard say to make you want to end it all?'

'He was awful, Capac,' she moaned. 'He didn't mean to be. He was trying to help, like you are now, only he doesn't know how. He wanted to prepare me.' Her eyes were brimming with tears. She shook her head sadly and some of the tears trickled out. 'Poor Ferdy. He always tried to do what was best for me. He was just never very good at it.'

'He's still alive?'

'Of course,' she sniffed. 'Ferdy will never die. He'll go on forever and ever, horrible and helpless as always.'

'I thought he was dead.'

'No. It was Ferdy. He'd lost some weight but otherwise he didn't look so different.'

'What did he say to make you do such a . . . a foolish thing?'

She stared at me coldly, the maturity of her age in evidence for once. 'He told me you were a gangster.'

My face fell. 'Conchita, I . . . I was going to tell you. I didn't want –'

'It's alright,' she said. 'I don't mind. I had my suspicions anyway. But he also said you were an Ayuamarcan.' That word again! It shocked me coming from her lips. 'He said getting close to you would be a bad idea, but I knew that anyway.'

'Why would it be a bad idea, Conchita?' I asked quietly.

'Because almost all the Ayuamarcans end up dead,' she replied. 'A few get to live – the chosen few – but the rest . . . By telling me, he hoped to soften the blow.' She snorted. 'Stupid monster of a man.'

'I don't understand,' I said, letting her go, moving away.

'Don't worry,' she said, following me. 'I'm not going to listen. He frightened me when he came. I tried to kill myself because I was scared. I couldn't face losing you. But you're different. You're not like the others. You can beat him, I know you can. You're not like them . . . or me.' She nodded when I looked sharply at her. 'I'm one too. I'm weak like the others. But you can turn the tables on him, Capac. You're stronger than the rest of us.'

'I still don't understand,' I said. 'What does Ferdinand Wain have to do with this? How can a nobody who's supposed to be dead wield so much influence? How does he tie in with this Ayuamarca list? What power does he –'

'Ferdinand who?' she interrupted.

'Ferdinand Wain,' I groaned. Was she forcing him out of her thoughts already? Shutting reality out again?

'Who's that?'

'He's . . .' I reached across and touched her hand. I didn't want to continue but I couldn't let her retreat, not until I had the information I needed. I had to push her, much as I might hate myself for it. 'He's your husband. Ferdinand Wain.'

She stared at me numbly and shook her head. 'No, Capac,' she whispered.

'Yes, Conchita.'

'No!' she screamed. Then grabbed my face and stared at me, horrified. 'I thought you knew. I thought that was why . . . God. I'm not married to Ferdinand Wain, Capac. My husband is Ferdinand *Dorak*.'

'Who . . . ?' My mind reeled. I knew the name but couldn't admit it.

'Dorak,' she repeated. And then, sitting back, face ashen, eyes starting to well with tears, she said, 'I'm married to The Cardinal.'

ama situwa

I sat alone in Shankar's, as far removed from the morning
regulars as possible, and brooded over the events of the
previous night. I had no appetite. I'd ordered a glass of orange
juice but lost interest in it after a couple of bitter sips.

Ferdinand Wain didn't exist. The name was a cover, something to serve up to doctors, nurses, hotel staff and gullible
fools like me. Conchita was married to The Cardinal.

I still had trouble accepting it. How could that old monster
have won the hand of sweet, innocent Conchita? Then again,
maybe she wasn't always this way. The fragile, defenceless
woman holed up in the Skylight might be a result of the
illness which wrecked her body. What was she like before?

Conchita said nothing of importance after hitting me with
the bombshell. I asked a few more questions about the
Ayuamarcans but she waved them away with exhausted
mumbles, saying only that they were dead people. She fell
asleep in my arms. I held her for a long time, staring off into
space, feeling her weak heart beating softly. She didn't stir
when I left.

Three people had now mentioned this Ayuamarca file. The
killer, Paucar Wami — I'd recalled this morning that he'd

said Adrian and I were Ayuamarcans, and realized that was
why I'd instinctively linked him with Adrian's disappearance.
Ama Situwa, who claimed to have invaded Party Central.
And The Cardinal's diseased wife. An unlikely trio, uncon-
nected in any other way as far as I could see. But who were
the Ayuamarcans? What linked them? And why did so many
wind up dead?

A thin hand tapped my shoulder and disturbed me. I looked
up, startled, expecting the angel of death, but it was only
Leonora. 'May I sit with you?'

'Sure.' I stood and pulled out a chair. She thanked me and
sat, setting down a plate with a sliced pineapple on it.

'You look like a man with too much on his mind,' she
said. 'Is life with Dorry getting you down?'

'It has its darker moments,' I confessed. 'I never guessed
it would be this complicated. I thought I'd take a few months
to settle and after that it would be easy. I'd be told what to
do, I'd learn and rise through the ranks, same as any other
business. I wasn't prepared for the intrigue, the uncertainty,
the madness.'

She laughed. 'You face the same maze as all Dorry's
favourites. The higher one flies in this city, the stranger things
get. If it is any consolation, it is a sign you are going places.
He is testing you.'

'I wouldn't mind a test but some days I feel like I'm being
set up for a fall. Like he's planning to exploit me and toss
me aside when he's finished.'

'It is possible,' she admitted. 'I do not think those are his
plans, but I have been wrong before.'

'That's a big comfort,' I said sarcastically.

She touched my arm sweetly. 'There are no safety nets
with Dorry. You knew that when you came aboard. It is too
late to complain now.'

'You're right. Sorry. It's been a hard week.'

'They will get harder,' she said gloomily. She ate a slice of her pineapple and glanced around the restaurant. A tiny flicker of doubt crossed her face. Then she dismissed whatever was troubling her and smiled. 'I love this place. It is my home. In many ways my life began the day I opened for business. I have watched the great men and women of this city sweep through, seen history in the making. Dorry was a nobody when I established this restaurant and only guttersnipes came. Then, as his power grew, this became *the* place to be. I remember the night he brought the president here. He looked so happy, the most powerful man in the country on one arm, Con–'

She stopped and grimaced.

'Conchita on the other,' I finished.

She blinked, surprised. 'You know about Conchita?'

'I met her in the Skylight. We're good friends.'

'Does Dorry know?'

'He does now.' My face blackened as I thought of her almost killing herself. 'What's the story with them?' I asked, moving my glass to one side so I could lean closer. 'Did he really love her?'

'As much as he could, yes.' She sighed unhappily. 'I thought Conchita would be the saving of him. He was so violent in the early days. When I first met him, he was a common thug, a brutal bully. He'd never learnt to suppress his rage. He lashed out like a hyperactive child. He was an animal. I spent years coaching him. I saw the potential, the man he could become. I devoted myself to him. I am not sure why. There was simply something about him which drew us together.

'He was suspicious. He had never trusted anybody before. I do not think he knew his parents. He grew up on the streets, sleeping in garages and deserted houses. He could not read, could barely talk coherently. I changed that. I taught him how to speak, read, reason, act. The one thing I could not teach him was how to love. He had no interest in companionship. Then Conchita came along.'

Leonora was lost in the world of the past. I hardly dared breathe lest I disturb her. 'She was so lovely. Petite but full of life. She persevered with Dorry as I had, put up with his tantrums, overlooked his rages, loved him wholly. They were like Beauty and the Beast. He roared at the world and she laughed. In public she would tickle his stomach and rub her nose across his neck. Nobody dared smile.'

'She calmed him?' I asked.

'No. She helped, as I had. But he went on killing people as if they were flies. His private life never distracted him. When the disease ruined her mind and drove her away from him, many people expected him to fly into a rage and take it out on the city. He did not. It was business as usual, no matter how much he was hurting inside.'

'*Did* she hurt him?' I asked.

'I think so. It is hard to tell with Dorry. He was certainly sullen when she left, and distant on occasion. But he did not grieve for her. I think he is incapable of grief. I cannot say how close he came to loving Conchita, but he was as far from loving her in the way you or I can love as this planet is from the sun. He has no true human emotions except for hate and rage.'

Leonora fell silent after that and by the way she concentrated on her pineapple I knew she didn't want to talk about this any more. I didn't mind. I'd already learnt more about The Cardinal than I expected to. I gazed around the restaurant as I mulled over our talk. 'Have you seen any sign of the Lap man today?' I asked.

She laughed. 'Who on earth is the *Lap man*?'

'Y Tse,' I chuckled.

'Who?'

I stared at her, heart sinking.

'Leonora,' I said, voice shaking, 'don't you dare sit there and –'

She raised a hand. 'Quiet.' She thought for a few moments. 'I want you to tell me about this "Lap man".'

'But you know –' I began angrily.

'Please,' she snapped. 'Humour me.'

Sighing, I described him, then went on, 'He used to be The Cardinal's right-hand man. He spends most of his time here, a lot of it with you. He acts crazy but he's not. The two of you are close friends. I have a feeling you might have been more than that once, though neither of you has ever said anything. His real name is Inti Maimi. Shall I go on?'

She was staring at the table, quiet as a corpse. When she looked up, her face was haggard. 'I cannot remember anything about him.' When my lips twisted into a sneer, her hands shot across the table and gripped mine. 'Capac, I swear that name means nothing to me. I am not saying he does not exist. I do not doubt your description. But I do not remember him.' She released me.

'It has happened before,' she said softly. 'But never so strong a sense of it. When I woke this morning, I felt something wrong, that something was missing. Like when you go into a room and forget what you wanted when you get there. There was a gap in my mind that I could not account for. I now know what it was.'

'What are you saying, that you've forgotten him? That's impossible. You don't just forget a person. You can't.'

She smiled bitterly. 'You have much to learn, Capac. I *have* forgotten him. And it is not the first time. Conchita often mentioned names that meant nothing to me, people she insisted I knew. This was a long time ago. I thought it was her illness, that she had concocted imaginary friends. But as the years passed, I began to think she was the only one who did *not* have a problem.

'Conchita berated others in our circle, insisting we knew people when we did not.' She shook her head. 'I am old and have seen many strange things in my life. The brain is complex, twisted. It can be manipulated. I have seen men walk on live coals, hold their breath underwater for an hour, recall events that occurred before they were born.' She finished the last of her pineapple and waited for me to speak.

'Y Tse remembered people too,' I said. 'He sometimes argued with you about it. He thought you were playing along with The Cardinal. I thought that of Sonja when Adrian – one of my friends – went missing.' I looked at her pleadingly. 'What does it mean, Leonora?'

She shrugged softly and rose. 'I do not know what is happening, but only two people apart from you ever spoke of the people the rest of us had apparently forgotten — Conchita, who went mad, and your Y Tse, who has disappeared.' She bent and kissed my forehead. 'Dorry's world is darker and deeper than even I can imagine. Be careful, Capac.'

I stared at her as she walked away, my head spinning. This was getting crazier all the time. I wanted to sit and pick at the puzzle all day but I had an appointment to keep. The Cardinal had summoned me the night before. I'd already kept him waiting and I knew he wouldn't be too happy about that. I'd hoped to clear my head before I faced him, but that evidently wasn't going to happen and there was no point delaying our meeting any longer. Pushing my chair back, I went to find Thomas and told him to drive me to Party Central.

The green fog was smothering the city again, so it took us longer than usual to get there. Ford Tasso was coming out of the building as I headed in. He grabbed my arm and jerked me to a halt. 'Where the hell have you been?' he roared.

'He's seething like the fucking Anti-Christ! Nobody stands up The Cardinal. What the fuck were you thinking?'

'I had other things on my mind,' I said.

'You . . . ?' He gawped at me but I didn't care.

'Do you want to drag me up to make it look like you tracked me down?'

He shook his head. 'Just get the fuck up there quick as you can.'

I took my time checking in my shoes – little rebel that I was – then took the lift and paused outside his door. The secretary was eyeing me wickedly, ruffling her papers. I didn't care. After what he'd done to Conchita, I thought the bastard deserved a bit of comeback. I waited until I heard the secretary grinding her teeth, then knocked once and entered.

The Cardinal was prowling in front of the window like a bull. He even snorted when he saw me. 'Well, Mr Raimi,' he growled, 'you finally decided to grace me with your presence. I hope I haven't torn you away from anything important?'

I opened my mouth and let the words flow without thinking. 'I'm late. Live with it.' Then I sat.

The Cardinal stared at me flatly, then closed his eyes and rubbed the lids with his fingers. 'Are you testing me, Mr Raimi? Do you want to know how far you can push me before I snap?'

'No. I just don't have any sorry excuses to offer. I couldn't come until now. That's the end of the matter as far as I'm concerned.'

He opened his eyes and scowled. 'I've killed men for looking at me crooked. Why should I let you get away with insolence like this?'

It was probably a rhetorical question but I began to answer it. 'Because you want me to be your . . .' Then I stopped, thinking I'd gone too far.

The Cardinal cocked his head. 'To be my successor?' he said mockingly.

'Maybe,' I said softly, deciding to push it now that the issue had been raised.

'You really think I'd choose you ahead of men I've known for decades, who've proven their loyalty a hundred times over?'

'Maybe,' I said again, a whisper this time.

'Are *you* loyal?' he asked.

I thought of Ama Situwa. 'When it suits me.'

'A strange answer. But I like it.' He smiled suddenly, startling me. 'Yes, Mr Raimi, I've singled you out as a possible heir.' My heartrate shot up but he raised a cautionary finger before I got too excited. 'But I hope to live a long time yet and others will undoubtedly come along. Plus there are several who already have a strong claim. Don't get carried away. I'm not about to hand the reins over any time soon, certainly not to one so immature. We'll see how you progress over the next decade. If you're still going strong, if you still want it, we'll talk about it then.'

'Of course I'll want it,' I said.

'Don't be too sure. The man who replaces me must be cruel, heartless, self-centred. He must live for and love nothing more than this empire. Is there anybody you would die for, a mother, sister . . . *friend*?'

'Yes,' I answered shortly, thinking of Conchita, maybe Ama too. 'There is.'

'In the end,' he said softly, 'you'll have to betray that person. If you hope to replace me, you'll have to learn to let go of those you love. Can you do that, Mr Raimi, sacrifice those you are closest to, renounce your humanity and become a monster like me?'

I thought about it for a full minute before I answered. 'I don't know.'

'One day,' he said, 'you'll find out. On that day you'll learn if you are fit to succeed me.' His eyes flickered as he added bitterly, 'Pray for your soul's sake that you are not.'

We discussed business after that. I told him about my deal with Reed, how I'd used his daughter to seal it. The Cardinal was worried I might have threatened her, but I assured him it had been above board.

'He believed you could persuade her to marry you?' he asked incredulously.

'Who knows — it might prove to be the truth.'

The Cardinal grinned wickedly. 'Pursuing romance so soon after my warning about getting involved with people?'

I shrugged. 'Like you said, it'll be a decade before I get anywhere. Why not have a little fun in the interim?'

We talked more about the future. He outlined the route he expected me to travel. A few more months in the insurance line, then a year or so with his legal team, learning everything there was to know about the law, 'or at least enough to fake it'. After that I'd be free to flit between one area of the company and another, feel my way around, find my niche, specialize or generalize as I saw best. He said no man worth his salt could be led about by the nose. I'd be guided while I was learning the basics, but after that I was on my own.

It was a magical meeting. He addressed me like an equal. Clapped me on the back and beamed as he poured drinks. Expounded on his long-term plans and investment ideas. Talked briefly of his national strategy, pinpointing the fields he dominated and those he needed to expand into. His international dreams were a long way from fruition. He didn't think he'd live to see the day when his men ruled the global economy and appointed or dismissed political leaders as they saw fit. But he was sure that day would come.

He said his heir would have the freedom of the world. He'd confined himself to the city because you had to be a big fish in a small pond before you could be a shark in a sea. He'd been tempted to leave, to branch out and gamble, but that would have meant spreading himself too thin, leaving himself open to attack from too many quarters.

'A true dreamer must be prepared to make any sacrifice for his dream,' he said. 'Even if it means sacrificing himself. The dream must be everything.'

Near the end of his speech he left to use the toilet. I took the opportunity to examine the room a little more closely. If – *when* I took over I'd have to make a lot of changes. It was too bare. A few plants and paintings would do wonders. More computers and telephones. And those puppets would go straightaway.

I walked to one of the walls and studied the miniature people, smiling condescendingly. Every man has his own particular folly. The Cardinal, a builder of empires, destroyer of men, would-be ruler of the world . . . and here he was with a load of childish toys. Why do even the greatest of men have . . .

I stopped dead, my train of thought dissolving.

Adrian's face was staring back at me.

I took a step away, blinking. When I focused again, it was still there. I moved closer, took down the model and studied it carefully. It was a tiny Adrian, perfect in every detail. I turned it around, amazed. The maker had even known that Adrian's left ear was slightly smaller than his right.

I edged along, clutching the puppet, looking for other familiar faces on the walls. And there they were. Leonora. Y Tse.

Me.

The toy Capac Raimi was as carefully constructed as the Adrian. I examined the hands and found slender fingerprints.

I tried comparing them to my own but I'd have needed a magnifying glass.

I wandered further along and found the killer, Paucar Wami, as well as Ama Situwa. My heart lurched when I found her puppet — it seemed I cared more for her safety than my own.

I was looking for more when I realized the puppet in my right hand – the mini me – was ticking. I held it to my ear and detected a thin, metallic heartbeat, as regular as the real thing. I raised Adrian's model but it was silent.

I returned the puppets to their rightful resting places before The Cardinal returned. I decided it was wiser not to ask about them. There was something ominous about them which disturbed me greatly. The Cardinal had been incredibly open with me, but I had a feeling his mood would turn in an instant if I quizzed him about the puppets.

He dismissed me shortly after he came back. I emerged from the room in a daze, head spinning from our conversation and the discovery of the puppets. On the one hand I was delighted – The Cardinal had singled me out for potential succession – but on the other I was fearful. He'd spoken of prices to be paid, sacrifices that must be made. What had he meant? And why did he have my effigy pinned to the wall? And why had my breast ticked and not Adrian's?

Ford was waiting downstairs. 'Still alive?' he grunted.

'Seems so. And I think I'll be around a while longer. He's preparing me to take over from him.' I had to tell someone.

Ford's eyes were black. 'What about me?'

My face dropped. I'd just shown my hand to my main rival for the post. Ford was a lot more powerful than me. He could make me disappear in a minute.

'You think you can crowd me out?' Ford growled as I flustered. 'You think you can brush me aside without a fight?'

'I didn't mean . . . maybe he was talking about something else and I . . .'

He laughed aloud and the darkness in his eyes faded. 'Don't worry, kid. I've known for a long time I wasn't going to be stepping into his shoes. He told me back in the early days. Made it clear I wasn't the kind of man to run his empire. Which is fine. I'm happy where I am. This way I don't have to worry about young punks like you coming along to knock me off. There's much to be said for playing second-fiddle.'

'I'll look after you if I get in,' I promised.

He chuckled bloodlessly. 'I admire your optimism but you need to trade those rose-tinted glasses for another pair. In the first place, I'll be an old man with a cane and a bladder problem by the time you'll be in a position to follow on from The Cardinal. He's older than me but still hungry. He'll go on another twenty years, easy. I won't be there when he drops. You might not be either. You're not the first successor he's lined up and you won't be the last. He's been looking for one ever since I can remember. Picks a fresh face every couple of years, gives them the rigmarole, raises their expectations, then dumps them when they don't measure up to scratch. No one has ever satisfied him. I don't think anyone ever will. The man who fills his shoes will just happen to be around when he topples. It's all a matter of timing. You're well on your way but it can end in a second.'

'Like it did for Y Tse?'

'Who?'

'Y Tse Lapotaire. Inti Maimi?'

He shook his head. 'Don't know who you're talking about. Any case, it doesn't matter. They're all the same. Front runners one day, fish food the next. Don't get carried away. You only need to make one mistake, then it's over.'

'Thanks for the pep talk,' I said sourly. 'Can I go now?'

'Yeah. Get out of here . . . *boss*.'

So Ford wasn't going to mention Y Tse either. Not surprising, given he'd always hated him and had probably fired the bullet personally. What was I going to do about Y Tse and Adrian? I wanted to find out why they'd vanished and make the bastards who'd killed them pay. But if those bastards were The Cardinal and Ford Tasso . . .

There was Ama too. I'd planned to squeal on her. I would have, I think, if I hadn't discovered those damn puppets. They'd thrown me all over again. I wanted to be The Cardinal's chosen one, but I wanted to know what was going on too, why Adrian and Y Tse had disappeared, who Ama was, what the Ayuamarca list was, why I couldn't recall my past. I could live with failure but not with uncertainty.

I decided I'd go to pier 15. Hear what she had to say. Find out who these Ayuamarcans were. Maybe even track down Paucar Wami and see what he had to say on the matter. After that, when I knew where I stood and why I was there? I'd cross that abyss when I came to it.

I left the car in the middle of the city — I didn't want Thomas seeing where I was going. I walked around a while, trying to determine whether or not I was being tailed. I didn't know how closely The Cardinal was monitoring me. I didn't think he was having me shadowed, but I wasn't about to chance it.

I entered a phone booth for privacy and began dialling on my mobile. I could remember the name of the man I wanted but not the firm he worked for. It took a while but finally I found the right company. He was off duty and the operator didn't want to divulge private information, but I persuaded her to connect me with the manager and sweet-talked him into patching me through. I told him I worked for The Cardinal and had left some papers in the taxi, papers he wouldn't want his firm to be associated with. Railroading people is easy if you speak sharply and threaten vaguely.

'Who is this?' the cabbie snarled when he came on the line. 'And don't give me no secret papers shit. Did Margaret put you up to this?'

'Mr Mead,' I said, pleased to hear that snapping voice again, 'my name's Capac Raimi. You don't know me but you've given me lifts a couple of times. I lied about the papers but I do work for The Cardinal. I need your help.'

He said nothing for a moment, pondering my words. 'What do you want?' he finally asked warily.

'You mouthed off about The Cardinal a while back –'

'So what?' he yelled. 'You gonna kill me for that? Fuck you. Come and try. I don't care shit for –'

'Mr Mead,' I said, 'I need a ride.'

'What?'

'I have to meet somebody and if The Cardinal finds out, I'm in trouble. Can you help me? It's dangerous. You'd be risking a lot. If you don't want to hear any more, I'll fully understand.'

He said nothing for a few seconds. 'You want a ride?' he asked in the end.

'Yes.'

'Why the fuck didn't you say so in the first place? Where do you wanna be picked up?'

I leant my head against the wall of the booth, thanked the gods, and told him where to get me. He drew up to the kerb smoothly half an hour later, appearing out of the fog like a ghost. He glanced around suspiciously. I sidled up to the back door and slipped in. 'You Raimi?' he asked.

'Yes. Nice to meet you again, Nathanael. I'm grateful to you for coming. It means a lot.' He had a wool cap pulled over his ears and dark glasses. 'Nice disguise,' I joked.

'No sarcasm in my cab,' he snapped. 'Where are we going?'

'The docks. Pier 15. You know it?'

He snorted derisively. 'You wanna go there quick or slow?'

'Normal. I don't want to draw attention.' He nodded and set off briskly, barely allowing for the fog, cutting across traffic without a second look.

I kept peering out the back window, searching for the cars I was sure must be following, in the throes of a paranoia attack. 'Do you think we're being tailed?' I asked.

'In this fog? I doubt it. Besides, unless they put up a neon sign, I wouldn't notice. I'm just a cabbie. I don't know shit about cloak and dagger.'

The fog began to thin as we got closer to the docks and it became easier to spot mysterious followers. There weren't any. All the same, I had Nathanael drop me at pier 16 as an extra precaution. 'You'll wait here for me?' I asked.

He tapped the running meter. 'Take all the time you need. I can wait. Got the radio and my papers — what more is there in life?'

'I shouldn't be more than a couple of hours,' I told him. I felt the handle of the knife through the fabric of my jacket. I was going to bring a gun but decided on the knife in the end – quieter, cleaner. 'If you see any cars circling, or anything that looks suspect, take off. I don't want you getting killed.'

'You're all heart,' he said. 'A true humanitarian.'

'No,' I replied, 'but I might need to use you again one day.' I slapped the roof of the car. 'See you soon. I hope.'

I left Nathanael Mead with his radio and papers and made the trek across to pier 15. There was a breeze blowing in off the river, dispersing the covering fog. There was nobody in sight but I skulked along in the shadows of enormous, empty warehouses anyway. They smelt of salt and dead fish. I'd need to bathe for hours to rid myself of the stench.

I was early but she'd got there before me nonetheless. She was leaning against a rotting wooden door, eight times her height, held together with the huge steel bolts they were so fond of back in the old days. She was dressed in blue jeans, a white Aran sweater and a long black trench coat. The wind caught the tails of the coat when she turned at my call, whipping it into the air.

I tried not to think about how she looked. This woman might be able to clear up the mystery of Adrian and Y Tse. And whether she did or not, I had to keep in mind that she was an enemy. Once I'd heard what she had to say – unless it was something truly extraordinary – I'd slit her throat and dump her in the river. She'd be my first kill. I wasn't certain I could do it but I'd give it a damn good try.

'You came,' she said. 'I didn't think you'd show. How'd you get here?'

'I know a guy who's no fan of The Cardinal. He brought me. You?'

'Scooter.' She pointed it out. A small model, nestled behind an abandoned skip.

'So what do you have to tell me?' I asked. 'What's the Ayuamarca file?'

'You don't beat about the bush,' she commented. 'Don't worry, I'll get round to that. First I want to know more about you. I don't really know anything except you work for The Cardinal, you sell insurance, and you're a pretty good lay. Tell me about yourself. Don't hold back.'

I thought for a few seconds. 'My name's Capac Raimi. I came to this city about a year ago to be a gangster with my Uncle Theo . . .'

I told her about the early days, Theo's untimely demise, meeting The Cardinal, Adrian, Y Tse, Leonora (I left out Conchita). I even told her my favourite foods and movies. I talked for twenty minutes solid.

'All done?' she asked when I ran out of breath. I nodded. 'Good. I'll know better than to ask you such a vague question again. Jesus on an accordion! But for all you said, you left much out. You didn't tell me about the *real* Capac Raimi.

All I got was recent history. How about your youth? Was your father a gangster? What were your brothers and sisters like? When did you decide to embark on a life of crime? Come on, Capac, fill me in. I'm fascinated.' She was taunting me, trying to make me feel uncomfortable. She was succeeding.

'That stuff's not important,' I waved it away. 'Who cares where I was born and how I grew up? It's old hat.'

'I like old hats. They keep my ears warm.'

'It doesn't matter.'

'Everything matters.' She tickled my nose, then quickly licked it. 'Come on,' she breathed, 'tell Auntie Ama all about it.' I tried to grab her but she danced away. 'Uh-uh, not until you've told me about your past.'

'Fuck the past!' I shouted angrily. 'I don't care about it. The past didn't matter when we were screwing like rabbits on the stairs.'

'True,' she said. 'But rabbits always end up with a bullet in their brains and their bones on a plate.' She left the shadow of the building and crossed to the edge of the pier. Picked up a handful of small pebbles and skimmed them across the face of the calm river. I followed her into what little sun was managing to creep through the eddying clouds of fog. We could have been the last man and woman in an post-apocalyptic ghost town. She spoke without looking at me.

'I went to Party Central again last night. I wanted to check on you. I pulled your files, the special ones that The Cardinal keeps hidden where only the elite can find them. Have you seen those files?'

'No.'

'They're incredibly detailed. Obsessively so. Lists of your clients, your friends and associates. A full itinerary of your time in the city, going back to when you were working for your uncle. Clubs you went to, women you've fucked, deals you were in on. Your favourite drinks and hobbies, notes on the way you walk and talk. Pictures of you, from pissing in urinals to making love to sleeping. Where you shop, what you buy, what you eat. Samples of your handwriting, with specialist assessments. They note the shaving foam you use, how often you wash, how often you change clothes. Details of your finances. The most complete files I've ever seen. But there's one thing missing. One minor discrepancy.'

'Go on,' I told her grimly. 'What's the punchline?'

'There's nothing about your past.' She got a stone to skim eight times. I counted each jump automatically. 'Nothing about when you were born, where you grew up, who your parents were, where you went to school.'

'That's not so odd,' I said. 'Like I told you, my past isn't important. My life before I came here doesn't mean shit. I was just an ordinary hick.'

'That's bullshit and you know it,' she snapped. 'Everybody in those files has a past, from the cleaners up to Ford Tasso. You think The Cardinal wouldn't have copies of your birth certificate, your school grades, letters from previous employers? You don't take someone on without knowing *anything* about him. Where are your medical records, your national insurance number, your driver's licence, your passport details? There's nothing. It's like you never existed. Every name in that building has a past. Except yours.' She paused. 'And mine.'

A filthy trawler passed. One of the crew was standing at the rail nearest us and waved. Ama waved back but I couldn't muster the enthusiasm. I kept examining her, saying nothing, waiting for her to go on. She watched the boat sail out of sight around a bend in the river before proceeding.

'I was happy when I came to this city,' she said. 'I was with my father, delighted to be reunited after so many years apart. I made new friends, played around with a few men, worked in the restaurant and took to it with ease. Life was simple and enjoyable. I felt I was where I belonged. Thought I was going to live happily ever after, like in the fairy tales, take over the restaurant when Cafran passed on, have kids, raise a family of my own.

'Then, one day, my friends were discussing their youth, schools, teachers and boys. I usually kept quiet in those kinds of conversations, always feeling awkward. One of the girls tried to draw me into the debate. She asked what my home town was like, my family, my friends. I brushed her enquiries away as I normally did, with a few half-hearted mutters, but she persisted. The others saw my reluctance and joined in, thinking I had something deep and mysterious in my past.

'I scoured my memories for some small titbit to toss them. I didn't ask much of myself. All I wanted was a simple anecdote they could laugh at, my first kiss or a row I'd had with my mother. Something like that.

'I couldn't think of anything.' She turned and I saw she was forcing back tears. 'There was nothing. No images of my mother, home or friends. I knew the story of how Cafran and his wife had split, how she'd whisked me away and reared me, but it was a tale I'd heard rather than experienced. I couldn't remember growing up. Everything before coming here was a blank.

'I went to Cafran. I thought he'd be able to jog my memory with reminiscences of his own.' She shook her head. 'He knew nothing either. He spun me the same old story but couldn't embellish it. He didn't know where I'd lived, when I'd been born, or which relatives I'd lived with after my mother's death.

'I thought he was lying — maybe there was something terrible in my past, like I'd killed somebody and could never be told. Something crazy like that. But the more I pushed and the more he had to defend himself, the more confused he became, and I saw he really didn't know anything about my years abroad.

'After that I went looking through city files. I figured there had to be something somewhere. I bounced between libraries, newspapers and bureaucratic departments. Not an iota. No Ama Situwa or Ama Reed. Cafran was there, and his wife, Elizabeth Trevor. *Trevor*, not Situwa. I found copies of their divorce papers but no mention of a child. I tried tracing Elizabeth Trevor's life after she left the city but I got nowhere.

'Do you realize how unsettling it is to find out you don't exist? That as far as official records are concerned, you're a nonentity?' Her lips twisted into a snarled smile. 'Actually, I think you might. And if you don't yet, you soon will.'

As I listened, I tested my own memories, forcing my mind down the cavern it normally shied away from. I started with the day I'd arrived here and worked back. Only there was no place to work back to. Like she'd said, there simply wasn't anything there.

'I hired a detective to search further,' she continued, 'but he couldn't do any more than I'd already done. He said either the records had been tampered with or else I was an illegal, adopted orphan. He'd come across it before — a couple who could neither have children naturally, nor adopt, sometimes bought a child on the black market. That would explain why I didn't exist in the files.'

'Sounds reasonable,' I agreed.

'Very. It made perfect sense, and might even be the truth, except it still doesn't explain the gaps in my memory.'

'Maybe you come from a forgetful family.' I smiled but she didn't smile back. 'Sorry. Go on. What did you do next?'

Next she went to her doctor, who couldn't find anything amiss. At her insistence he'd recommended a specialist who dealt with amnesiacs, but that led nowhere either. Several pricey sessions later, no further informed than she'd been at the beginning, Ama decided to let the matter drop. After all, she had a life in the present to get on with. If the past clicked into place one day, great. If it didn't, she'd just have to live with that.

'And then I met The Cardinal.' Her words caught in her throat. She knelt to skim a few more pebbles. I moved up behind her and ran my fingers through her hair. Cupped her face in my hands, bent and kissed her.

'Go on,' I said softly. 'You've taken it this far. Don't stop now.'

'He dropped by the restaurant one evening,' she said. 'His visits are rare. This was his first since I'd come to the city. He was courteous and charming, the exact opposite of what I thought he'd be. I found myself drawn to him. He flirted a little with me. I began to think he'd look great with a woman like me by his side. I was starting to pick colours for our wedding. You know the way foolish dreams go.

'Then, as he was leaving, he pulled me aside. My heart skipped. I thought he was going to invite me round to his place for a private drink. But he only said one thing to me. "How's life with your . . . *father?*" In exactly that tone, with the pause and stress on the *father*. He grinned as he said it. I knew immediately that Cafran and the city officials might know nothing about my past, but The Cardinal did.

'So I went after him.'

She'd gone to Party Central to look it over. She wasn't sure what she planned to do or what she was hoping to find. She just knew she had to do *something*, take control of the situation and not sit at home feeling sorry for herself. The front of Party Central was a dead end. Nobody could get near the place without attracting attention. So she went round the back. Found a large fence, regularly patrolled but not as carefully guarded as the front. The Troops back here were spread thinly. And although the fence was electrified, there was a small gate towards the end of the building which wasn't, which the Troops used to get in and out.

She waited until things were quiet, crept up and tried the lock. It was firm, but she discovered a gap between the top of the gate and the fence, one she could just about squeeze through if she sucked in tight. She didn't go in that first night, but came back a few times to observe the Troops. When she'd determined their routines, she walked up to the gate one dark night, brazen as anything, and slipped in.

The area between the fence and the building was used for parking and it was easy to pass undetected. She came to the rear wall of Party Central and walked along, examining the fortifications for weak spots. She found none. Though she searched for hours and checked every possible point of access, there was no way in. On her way out, as dawn approached, she was discovered. She was squeezing through the gap at the top of the gate when a voice from the darkness called to her. 'Miss Situwa. We have been observing you.'

Her stomach turned to slush. She wanted to run but she couldn't move. A figure appeared out of the darkness and a hand was extended towards her. Not having any other option, she took hold and slipped back into the compound.

The man was dressed in the uniform of the Troops, but was smiling pleasantly and his gun remained hidden. 'Would you follow me, please, Miss Situwa?' he asked and led her back to the building, to a spot near the middle, where he stopped and stepped back. He pointed upwards. Ama saw another person above them, opening a window. The Troop – if that's what he was – said, 'This window will be left open every night from now on. Use it as you wish. We are no friends of The Cardinal but we have his trust. We cannot protect you if you are caught, but we have taken steps which should make evasion easier. Come and go as you please. Goodnight, Miss Situwa.'

And he'd returned to his business. When she looked up again, the window had been closed and no one was visible. Dazed and feeling sick, she went home.

'Have you seen him since?' I asked.

'No.'

'Can you describe him?'

'Not really. All I noticed was the uniform. Every Troop looks the same in one of those.'

'What about the one above?' I asked.

'I don't know,' Ama said. 'I didn't get a close look. But . . .' She frowned. 'It might have been the glare of the sun on the glass, but it looked to me like he was blind.' She laughed shortly. 'Crazy, huh?'

I didn't think it was crazy at all. I considered telling her about the other blank-eyed men I'd seen, but decided against it. I wanted to think about this a bit more before I shared my thoughts with her.

Ama continued with her story. She hadn't taken the stranger at his word, but had come back and studied the site over the next few nights, trying to spot what she was sure must be a trap. Eventually, left with no other option, she scaled the wall – a simple rope with a hook on the end did the trick – and was in.

She'd expected sirens to blare, lights to blaze, Troops to crash down and haul her off. It didn't happen. Five minutes passed. Ten. Nobody came, no alarms sounded, there was no sign that she had been detected. Eventually she plucked up the nerve to try the stairs. She went slowly, sure she'd spring a trap every time she took a step. But one flight passed without incident. Another. And soon she was past the fifteenth floor, with all the secret files of Party Central at her disposal.

The upper floors of the building were deserted. The occasional secretary would wander through to take out a file or put one back. And Troops patrolled the floors several times a night on their regular rounds. But they always used the elevators and, if you were careful, you could hear them coming and hide before they were close enough to pose any danger. There was ample hiding space. The files were arranged in huge stacks of paper, towers reaching up to the ceiling in some places. All she had to do was squeeze between two of the piles to become invisible.

She spent hours every night rummaging through the monstrous towers. They seemed to be arranged in no apparent order. Ancient newspapers were bunched together with birth certificates, census copies, industrial figures going back to the 1700s, gang lists, property records and more. She took photos of anything that looked important, figuring it would be useful to have proof of The Cardinal's secret dealings. If he ever discovered her and tried to take action, she could blackmail him, trade the photos for her life.

Although she'd unearthed enough after a week to send the king of the city down or make a fortune by selling him out, she hadn't found anything pertaining to her own situation. She found plenty about Cafran and his restaurant, but not a word about his daughter or an orphan he might have bought.

Finally, among a pile of yellowing magazines, she found a file with her name on it.

'It was just a few scraps of paper,' she told me, 'bound by a cheap cardboard folder. The name was handwritten in capitals on the cover — *AYUAMARCA*. Inside was a list of names. I almost passed over it without looking. The only reason I didn't was the strange header. I opened it and skimmed through. There was nothing apart from the names. Leonora Shankar came first. Mine was one of the last. A hundred or so in all, each neatly typed. The first couple of sheets were old, brown, crinkled round the edges.

'Most names were crossed out, a neat line through the middle. Only nine were untouched. I didn't recognize any of the lined names, so I looked up a few — there was nothing on any of them. No files, no records, no mention anywhere. I think they're people who've been killed.'

'What makes you say that?' I asked.

'The first time I looked, Adrian Arne was one of the unlined names. When I checked last night – after you mentioned him – it was crossed out.'

'Was Y Tse Lapotaire on the list?' I asked.

'I don't recognize that one,' she said.

'Inti Maimi?'

'Oh sure. His name crops up twice — early on, crossed out, and on a later, second sheet. That one's untouched.'

'Not any more, I bet.' I looked down into the murky water · of the river. I could see an old shopping trolley in the mud at the bottom, tiny fish swimming in and out between the bars. I wondered if Adrian and Y Tse were down there somewhere. 'What about the unlined names?' I asked. 'You checked them?' She nodded. 'Any connection?'

'None that I could find. Except, like us, they've got short histories and don't seem to have a past. Plenty of information about their recent lives but nothing about their childhoods or families. The older ones – like Shankar and some guy called Paucar Wami – have long histories, going back decades, but not a word on where they came from or how they –'

'Paucar Wami's on the list?' I asked sharply.

'You know him?'

'I'm beginning to feel like I do. Find out anything about him?'

'Not much. Most of his files are coded. The bits that weren't made me hesitant to learn more. He was The Cardinal's main assassin in the early days, the man for the big jobs. But he's not around anymore. He's off somewhere else, touring the world.'

'No,' I said. 'He's back.'

'You're sure?'

'Yes. Wami's back, and Adrian and Y Tse have vanished.' I moved away from her and considered her story. 'You know, I'm not sure I believe you.'

She bristled but managed to check her temper. 'What makes you think I'm lying?' she asked coldly.

'People don't break into Party Central. It's a fortress. Cameras on every floor and flight of stairs. Sensors everywhere. They know when a fly flaps its wings. A crack squad of army vets would have a tough time getting past first base. An amateur like you couldn't simply waltz in like you claim.'

'I thought that too,' she said. 'But maybe The Cardinal's too sure of himself. Maybe he's too busy anticipating a full frontal assault to bother with a tiny gap in the back.'

'I don't buy it.'

'Well, maybe those other two – the one in the uniform and his friend upstairs – have access to the systems. Maybe they've turned them off. It could be I've stumbled onto some huge conspiracy, a plot to wipe out The Cardinal.'

'A rogue Troop and a blind man?' I was sceptical. 'If they have that much power, what do they need you for? If they wanted to destroy The Cardinal by releasing hidden files, they could do it themselves. This doesn't make sense.'

'Nevertheless, I'm here. I did it.' Her eyes were defiant.

'Have you got a copy of the Ayuamarca file?' I asked.

'No.'

'Why not?'

'There weren't many unlined names. I memorized them. Remember, I only went there to find out about myself. I never thought I'd be sharing this with anybody.'

'I want to see it,' I told her. 'I have to come and check this out myself.'

'You're sure? If you get caught up there, The Cardinal won't like it.'

'I'll chance it.'

'Very well. But you can't come the way I do — you won't fit through the gap in the gate. Can you meet me inside? Tomorrow night, about ten?'

'Why not tonight?' I asked.

'I have to go to a party with Cafran. It's for one of his brothers. I'm hoping I'll find out a bit about my past — maybe one of his brothers knows something and will let it slip. I doubt it, but I have to check. Besides, I want to give you time to think this through and do some research of your own. Search the files. Check that I'm telling the truth. I don't want you going into this with divided loyalties. Did you bring a weapon today?'

I nodded slowly and flashed my knife. She laughed and produced a gun. 'Just as well for you this ended amicably,' she joked. 'You had to come armed — you didn't know me or the sky above me. But there's no room for suspicion from here on. If you come to Party Central with me, you're in for keeps. If you're serious about seeing this through, you'll have to cross The Cardinal. You can't play both sides off against each other. It's your future or your past, your career or the truth.'

'I know.' I kicked the loose pebbles around us. 'I didn't before. I thought I'd listen, kill you and it'd be over. But I can't do that. The need to know is too strong, even stronger than the need to succeed. I don't want to betray The Cardinal – I'm still hoping I won't have to – but if I've got to choose between loyalty and peace of mind . . .'

'I'm with you,' I said.

And that was that. On the word of a woman I barely knew,

I'd pitted myself against the most powerful creature in the city. It was crazy, illogical, suicidal. But I had no choice. The need to know who I was outweighed all my dreams, ambitions and plans. If I lost everything in my hunt for the truth, so be it.

We hung around the docks a while and tried discussing other stuff, but we kept coming back to The Cardinal and our missing pasts. I told Ama about *the woman* and the glimpses I sometimes caught of a world I couldn't remember. It was more than she could do. For her the past was a complete blank.

I thought I'd grow to love Ama Situwa. I didn't know why, or what attracted me to her so passionately, but I felt we were meant for each other.

'We might be old sweethearts,' I said as we wandered through one of the empty warehouses. 'We might have known each other in the past. Maybe that's why we . . . on the stairs . . .'

'Perhaps.' She kicked a hole in a rotten plank and smiled.

'I wonder if the other Ayuamarcans have memory gaps?'

'I think they probably have,' she said.

'Where could we have come from?' I frowned. 'Employees, brainwashed to do The Cardinal's bidding?'

'Brainwashing's not real,' she scoffed. 'You can maybe alter people's minds a bit, but not to this extent.'

'Science can do anything these days,' I disagreed. 'For all we know, we might have volunteered. Maybe the others – the ones with the lines through their names – aren't dead. Maybe they just regained their old memories and were withdrawn from the programme.'

'Sounds flaky, Raimi.'

'How else do you explain it?'

'Maybe The Cardinal scours hospitals for amnesiacs,' she said. 'Buys or steals them, feeds them false identities and . . .' I raised an eyebrow. 'It's as likely as your theory,' she sniffed.

'We're probably way off base,' I said. 'The rest probably have perfect memories and we're just two screw-ups who came together by chance.'

'You believe that?' she asked.

'I don't believe anything anymore,' I told her.

We parted eventually, reluctantly, having said nothing about our feelings for each other or any future we might have together. There was no time. Not until this Ayuamarca business was out of the way. How could we think about a relationship when we didn't even know if our names were real?

We agreed to meet on the nineteenth floor of Party Central at ten the next night if we were both still alive. We kissed once and parted, no heroic or amorous last words. Ama returned to Cafran Reed on her scooter and I went back to the less fatherly Nathanael Mead. He was reading a paper when I arrived. He glanced up when the door opened, folded the paper and started the engine.

'A productive meeting?' he asked when we were on the road back to civilization.

'It was . . . different,' I said.

'He's a dangerous man, The Cardinal,' Mead said. 'You wanna watch yourself. He'll chew you up if you don't.'

'How come you know so much?' I asked.

'I'm a cabbie. Been one all my working life. You hear things. See things. If you want to. Most don't — they turn a blind eye and mind their own business. I'm not like that. I like to keep in touch.'

'Speaking of blind eyes,' I said. 'You know anything about a gang of blind, religious nuts? They dress in robes and –'

'– come out whenever there's a fog,' he said, nodding. 'Sure. I don't know much about them, except they've been around as long as I can remember.'

'Have they got anything to do with The Cardinal?'

'No idea,' he said.

When we returned to the heart of the metropolis I told him to stop. I paid the fare and gave him a hearty tip for his trouble.

'Not bad,' he whistled appreciatively.

'If I ever need you again, can I call?'

'Sure.' He gave me a grubby card. 'My mobile.' He paused. 'You're OK, Raimi. You need me, call. I'll come get you wherever you are.'

'Thanks.'

I waited around a while, then hailed another cab, directed the driver to Party Central, and gave him a tip up front to break a few speeding regulations. I had investigations to make.

capac

I stayed through the night. Secretaries and temps came and went in shifts but I remained, hooked to one terminal or another, eyes glued to screens or pages, fingers flicking over keys or through books, searching, absorbing, analysing. The files were as detailed as Ama had claimed. Everything I'd done since coming to the city was listed. Bills, receipts, inventories. Transcripts of conversations with clients, friends and associates. Even the tennis scores from my day at the courts. The Cardinal must have spent a fortune compiling this.

But not a word about my past. I used the computers to cross-reference my name with everything they could muster, but it was like I'd asked them to find a ghost. As far as the records were concerned, before I came to this city I didn't exist. In the face of such a lack of evidence, I could almost believe that I'd blinked into existence that day. Except I had memories. They were vague and I couldn't get a proper fix on them, but they were there. The face of *the woman*. My familiarity with old movies, songs and books that I liked.

It had to be amnesia. The Cardinal must have found me in a hospital as Ama had suggested, mind frayed, a wreck. He brought me here to serve one of his obscure purposes, fed me a false identity and set me loose. It was like something out of a sci-fi flick but I could buy it. Just about.

But what about Theo, Cafran Reed and Sonja Arne? They weren't amnesiacs. Maybe it was a big pretence but Theo had acted as if he truly thought I was his nephew. Cafran had studied Ama with a father's loving eyes. Sonja had doted on Adrian before she denied all knowledge of him. Easy to think they'd been bought, that they were playing The Cardinal's game, but I didn't think it was that simple. If I was any judge of character, they really *believed* that we were their relations.

I looked up Theo's files. He had two sisters, neither living in the city. I rang both, my throat dry, not a hundred per cent certain one of them wasn't my mother. I told them I was an old friend of Theo's, that I'd been away a long time and had just learnt of his death. They were glad to talk about him. Neither recognized my voice. I probed gently, throwing innocent questions their way. One was divorced and childless, the other had six children, the eldest a mere seventeen years old. I thanked them for their time, promised to drop in if I was ever nearby, and severed my connections with my *uncle* once and for all. He wasn't my mother's brother. He'd probably never seen me before I arrived that dull and rainy day.

I searched for Y Tse Lapotaire and Adrian Arne. I figured they had to crop up somewhere. But not a whiff. I went back further. As Inti Maimi, Y Tse had been The Cardinal's righthand man. There *had* to be files on him. You couldn't go through a period of your life as the second most powerful man in the city without leaving some trace. Even if his files had been pulled, there had to be mention of him in the records, photos of him in the press, like Ford Tasso, Sonja Arne and every other major mover.

Nothing.

My last throw of the dice was a copy of the register from

Shankar's. It was a huge, gold-bound book. Every guest was invited to sign it when leaving the restaurant. Most didn't — it was there primarily for the occasional high-ranking visitor. Y Tse and I had signed it a few weeks back. We'd been drinking a bit more than usual. In our drunken state it had suddenly become vitally important to sign the big book, leaving our mark for future generations. Y Tse went first, taking up three lines with his scrawl. I followed less flamboyantly. We laughed, slapped each other's backs and stumbled out.

The copy in Party Central was updated a couple of times a week. They used a colour photocopier so nothing was lost in the transfer. I flicked to the end and sought our names. There I was, Capac Raimi. And right above, three lines high — *Samuel Griff*.

I cast my mind back. Samuel Griff was one of my customers. I sold him a policy after a meeting in Shankar's. We hadn't been there that particular day of course, since I remembered being there with Y Tse then. But I knew Griff would say we had been if I rang and asked.

It was hopeless. The Cardinal had covered every track. As far as history was concerned, Y Tse Lapotaire never existed. Adrian Arne never existed. Capac Raimi did, but not before coming to the city.

I spotted the first rays of morning through window blinds. I'd spent the entire night following trails that led nowhere. I rubbed my tired eyes and leant back, yawning, stretching my arms until my fingers seemed to touch the ceiling. At least I now knew where I stood. No avenue remained, apart from the one I was going to explore that night with Ama. I stood to lose everything but it no longer mattered. I'd been robbed of a past and that was something I couldn't live with. I had to find out who I was. Whatever the cost.

I logged out, switched off the light, rang Thomas and told him to meet me at the bottom of the building. I headed back to the Skylight to grab a good day's sleep before the night raid. I'd need all my wits about me at ten.

I was half dozing in the back of the car when Thomas suddenly broke the protocol and addressed me. 'Sir, I believe we're being followed.'

'I don't think this is the first time,' I said sourly, thinking about all those reports I'd read the night before. They couldn't have tracked me so easily if Thomas wasn't helping them out.

'True, sir,' he replied, 'but I was not informed of any tail today.'

'Where is it?' I asked, glancing into the mirror. The fog had cleared overnight and I had an uninterrupted view of the road.

'The motorbike, sir. You see?'

I did, and knew immediately who it was. Ama had obviously decided it would be safer to keep an eye on me. I smiled and made up my mind to play her at her own game. I looked around. 'That shopping mall,' I said to Thomas. 'Pull up and let me out. Head home after that. I can take care of this.'

'You're certain, sir?'

'I'll be fine,' I assured him. 'I know who it is.'

The early morning air was refreshing. The streets were quiet, most of the shops yet to open. I called into a twenty-four hour café and ordered a coffee, giving Ama time to park her bike. When I was ready, I strolled to the mall, which was just opening. I passed weary workers heading in for an early shift, a couple of guards watching the sports news on a store TV, and several cleaners going about their work cheerfully, enjoying the calm before the crowds.

I saw a stalled escalator and trotted up the steps. At the top, where I couldn't be seen, I broke into a sprint and scurried

down a hall, looking for a niche. I wanted to spring out on
Ama and give her a shock.

I noticed a small, inoperative fountain. The base was dry
and there was a narrow ledge that I could just about squeeze
under. The only problem would be identifying Ama, but
there was a decorative mirror hanging from wires nearby. I
climbed into the fountain and eased myself under the ledge,
then slid along until I had a good view of the hall in the
mirror.

She was a long time coming. I heard footsteps before I
saw anything. They came cautiously, pausing every few
seconds. She probably guessed I was onto her, but had come
too far to turn back. Her feet came into view and I edged
out a little. She moved further forward. Any second now,
I'd be able to see her face and . . .

My entire body went numb.

It wasn't Ama.

I squeezed back under the ledge, quietly as I could. The
steps came closer. I was sure I'd been spotted, that I was a
dead man, but then my pursuer sat down on the ledge and
whistled aimlessly. I glanced up at the mirror. He had his
back to me but whenever he turned sideways I could see
the snakes flashing. I remembered Johnny Grace and tried
not to breathe.

Finally, as the mall filled, he drummed his fingers on the
ledge a few times, tutted and moved on. I stayed hemmed
in and let several minutes pass before I slid out. I fumbled
my mobile from my pocket – my hands were shaking bad –
and rang Ama. There was no answer for ten, eleven, twelve
tones. My throat tightened and a heavy weight settled in my
stomach. As I was about to hang up, somebody answered
groggily. 'Yes?' It was Cafran.

'Could I speak to Ama, Mr Reed?' I gasped.

'Who?'

My heart nearly stopped.

'Who is this?' he snapped. 'Do you know what time it is?'

'Is Ama there?' I shouted. 'Ama Situwa. Is she —'

In the background I heard a voice asking who was on the phone. Cafran placed his hand over the speaker to answer. Then, seconds later, Ama was on the line. 'Capac, is that you?' She sounded sleepy.

'Get out of there,' I said levelly. 'Don't pack, don't wash, don't say anything to Cafran. Just get dressed and leave.'

'What the —'

'Paucar Wami's after me.' She said nothing. 'You know what that means?'

'I have an idea,' she muttered.

'I gave him the slip, but maybe I'm not the only one he wants. Get out. Lose yourself in the city. We'll meet later.'

'Where? The docks?'

'No. Ring me on my . . .' I stopped, thinking for the first time that my mobile might be tapped. 'Hold on, I'll call you back in a minute.' I looked for a public phone, rang Ama from it and read out the number. 'Ring me at two o'clock. That'll give me time to get to the Skylight, freshen up and make plans.'

'Is it safe to go back there?' she asked.

'He won't hit me in front of so many witnesses.'

'But —'

'No more talk. Move. And Ama? Take your gun.' I hung up and walked out, not looking around to see if he was waiting, doing nothing to appear conspicuous. I hailed a cab and returned to the Skylight.

The air-conditioned room was bliss after the sticky cab. My limbs were heavy and my head was foggy. I'd been awake far too long. I went to the bathroom and splashed cold water over my face and neck, which shocked a bit of life into me.

I wanted to hit the sack but decided to go and say hello to Conchita first. I hadn't phoned the night before and didn't want her worrying about me.

She was reclining on a couch, doctors and nurses nowhere in sight. She smiled when I entered, sat up and patted a space next to her own. The room had changed recently. She'd started removing the sheets and covers, exposing the walls and furniture. Her clothes had also changed and now her arms and legs were bare. She was no longer ashamed of her wrinkled old flesh.

'Hey, small fry,' I greeted her. 'How you doing?'

'Not so bad. Yourself?'

'Can't complain.'

'I missed you last night. Business?'

'Yeah. Sorry I didn't ring. You weren't worried?'

'No. I knew you were OK. I could sense it.'

'Telepathy?' I smiled.

'Maybe the bonds of love,' she winked.

'Or maybe because we're both Ayuamarcans?' I probed.

She pinched her lips together. 'No,' she said. 'I won't talk about that. It drove me mad before and I won't make the same mistake twice. My advice is to forget it. Forget Ferdy, your job and this city. Walk away from it all.'

'By myself? I'd be lonely.'

'You needn't be.' She brought her legs up and knelt on the sofa, eyes bright. 'I'm an old woman, Capac. You made me realize that. I've wasted my life hiding from the truth, fighting my body, slave to my face. I became a young Conchita Kubekik again, when I should have fought harder and been Conchita Dorak. It's almost too late, but not quite. I've still got time.

'I'm leaving,' she said. 'In a couple of weeks I'll pack my bags, dismiss the help and go. I've always wanted to see the world. I've been tied to this city by an ugly umbilical cord of my own making. Now I'm going to chew it up and spit it out. I'm through standing still. I'll go on long cruises, explore exotic countries, take a harem of young lovers. I don't know how much life there's left in these dry old bones, but I'll make good use of it. I'm going to *live* and have fun!

'Come with me.' The light in her eyes was intense, hypnotic. She was doing everything she could to save me. 'Leave Ferdy, the gangsters, the hurt, the death. Be my companion, my son, my husband, my friend.'

I held her hands softly, saying nothing, and slowly shook my head. 'I can't. I'm glad you're escaping. Maybe I can too one day. But I can't turn my back on it yet. Find somebody good to love, without my dark desires. I'd only be a link to the past. I'd destroy you all over again. I wouldn't want to but that's how I am.'

'I know.' Her head sagged. 'I asked anyway, hoping, but I knew.' She looked up. 'He'll kill you, Capac. Ferdy will ruin you. You can't beat The Cardinal.'

'You're probably right,' I sighed. 'But this is where I'm meant to be. I can't explain it, but there's something about this city, not just The Cardinal, and it's made me its own. I'd be lost anywhere else.'

She freed her hands. 'So alike, you and Ferdy. He was fiercer, less refined, less thoughtful. But he knew what he wanted and the price he must pay. You do too.'

'What price, Conchita?'

'You know,' she said.

'I don't. Tell me.'

'Your life,' she said, glancing away.

'I'll lose that anyway in the end. What else?'

'Your friends.'

'I've already lost most of them. What else?'

'Your dreams will sour and leave you embittered.'

'Most dreams do. What's the price, Conchita? What do I have to lose that's so terrible? Tell me.'

She finally looked back and said it. 'Your humanity.'

I couldn't reply to that. I just sat and stared and tried to convince myself that she was wrong.

I took every precaution I could when returning to the mall. I changed cabs five times. Walked a couple of miles along the most crowded streets I could find. Even called into a men's store and changed my clothes. When I'd done all in my power, I crossed my fingers and made my way back.

The phone rang on the dot. 'Any sign of a tail?' I asked, not bothering with preliminaries.

'No.'

'You sound sure.'

'I went out to the country,' she told me. 'It's open roads and uninterrupted views for miles around. Nobody could have followed unobserved. I came back by a different route. I'm safe.'

'I'm not so certain, but I think I made it unnoticed. No sign of Wami anyway.'

'What are we going to do?' she asked.

'I'm going after him,' I told her.

'Wami?'

'Yes.'

'Are you crazy?'

'I have to. If he killed Adrian and the other Ayuamarcans, he's the only one apart from The Cardinal who can tell us anything. If I can talk to him, strike some kind of a deal, maybe he'll talk. It's worth a shot.'

'You know where he is?'

'No. But I can find out.'

'I'm coming with you.'

'That would be stupid.'

'We're safer together,' she disagreed. 'We can watch each other's backs. I don't want to be alone, not with a killer like Wami in the game.'

I hesitated. 'I don't want to put you in any more danger than I have to.'

'Who broke into Party Central?' she snorted. 'I'm not a kid, Capac.'

She was right. This was her business too. She was in this as deep as me and had done as much – more – as I had to deal with it. 'Meet me in Belle Square, half an hour from now,' I said. 'There's a beer garden near the south side. I'll be behind it. Bring your bike.'

She was there on time and we took off with barely a word to each other. 'Where are we going?' she asked over her shoulder.

'Hmm?' I was feeling her waist, remembering her exciting flesh. She slapped my fingers and repeated the question. 'I don't know. Somewhere in the east. Keep going. Hopefully I'll remember the directions along the way.'

We twisted and turned through the convoluted east of the city for hours. I tried recalling the route Adrian had taken but my memory wasn't that good. In the end we stopped and asked for directions. The people were slow to respond, but finally we found one who knew the old man and was prepared to talk for a price.

He was out on the porch when we pulled up, rocking in his chair, watching the world. He glanced at us with interest as we dismounted and approached.

'Hello, Fabio,' I greeted him.

'Howdy right back,' he said. 'It's . . . don't tell me . . . Capac Raimi! Right?'

'The one and only.'

'Heh. Old Fabio don't forget much. Don't know your pretty girl though.'

'Ama Situwa,' she introduced herself, leaning forward to shake his hand.

He nodded, filing the name away. 'Nice to know ya. You attached to this guy or are you independent?'

'She's attached,' I told him, smiling. Then I dived straight in. 'You recall what I came about before?'

'Sure. Paucar Wami. I wouldn't forget anything to do with him in a hurry.'

'I need to know more about him, Fabio. Where to find him.'

The old man's eyes narrowed. 'Do you now?' he purred. 'Why?'

'I want to talk to him.'

'Talk to Paucar Wami?' Fabio laughed. 'He's not much for talking, not by any account.'

'Do you know where he is?' I persisted.

'If I did, I wouldn't tell. I'm not sending his enemies after him. I know only too damn well he'd kill you and come looking for the snitch. I ain't getting on the wrong side of that mother.'

'Please,' Ama said, squatting. 'We're not his enemies. We just want to talk.' She grasped his hands, rubbed them gently and smiled. 'Please?'

Fabio looked at the hands, at her, at me. And grinned. 'Ain't it funny how a pretty lady always thinks she can find out anything from an old fart if she smiles nice and throws him the eye? They must think we're fools.' He looked down at the hands again and his eyes crinkled with memories. 'And they're right.' He lifted his head. 'You really just want to talk?'

'That's all.'

'You'll keep my name out of it?'

'We won't say a word.'

'Hmm.' He considered the matter. 'Now, I don't know if

this is his place for sure,' he eventually drawled, 'but he was spotted there a few days back. Man who saw him only glimpsed him, but those snakes are distinctive. If he's not there, I don't know where he is.'

'Thank you,' Ama said softly, rubbing his wrists.

'Damn old fool is all I am,' he growled, then smiled and gave her the address.

We pulled up at the block of flats and killed the engine. If Wami was here, he was on the sixth floor. I took a deep breath, stepped down and confronted Ama. 'I'm going up by myself,' I said, quickly raising a hand as she tried to interrupt. 'Don't argue. There's no point more than one of us risking it. Besides, we don't know for sure that he's after you.'

'Chances are he is,' she snapped.

'Chances are,' I admitted. 'But if he's not, it would be crazy to draw attention to yourself. Leave this one to me, Ama. You know it makes sense.'

She didn't like it but she knew I was right. She pulled out her gun and offered it to me. I was tempted but shook my head. I'd be a fool if I thought I could barge in and overpower a trained killer like Wami. I remembered him dropping from the sky and dispatching Johnny Grace and his men like a tiger. I took out the knife I still had from the night before and gave it to her.

'Wait a couple of hours,' I said. 'If I don't return, or if you see a bald, black killer come out alone, get the hell out of here as quick as you can.'

'Do you think you can pull this off?' she asked.

'I doubt it.' I smiled and kissed her. A long kiss, slow and passionate. When we parted there were tears in her eyes. Probably in mine too. 'Is this where I say "I love you"?' I chirped.

'No. This is where I say, "See you soon",' she replied.

It was an old building from the early twentieth century. The walls were riddled with cracks, holes, damp patches, burns and faded bloodstains. The doors were barred. Several apartments had been burnt out. Squatters abounded. All the people I passed walked in a crouch, hunched over in anticipation of an attack. The only people here who didn't live in fear were the younger children who had yet to learn the cruel ways of the world.

The apartment I wanted was on the sixth floor. There were no bars, no bell, no letterbox. It had been green once but the paint was old, discoloured and peeling. I could sense Ama watching, though I didn't turn to check. Taking a deep breath, I rapped on the door with my knuckles.

There was silence. This was a largely deserted floor, most of the rooms along the landing blackened and bereft of occupants. I heard a noise to my left and, glancing over, spied a tiny old woman coming out of her home with a shopping bag. She looked suspiciously at me, turned and made for the far set of stairs. I smiled and faced the door again.

It was open and Paucar Wami was standing there, grinning, the snakes on his cheeks showing their constantly unveiled fangs.

'Capac Raimi,' he said softly. 'What a pleasant surprise.'

I gulped a couple of times, then gasped, 'I want to talk.'

'You didn't want to talk this morning,' he said. 'Do you make a habit of taking early baths in public fountains?'

'You saw me? But . . . why didn't you . . . ?'

'Come in,' he said, standing aside. 'We have much to discuss.'

I walked past automatically. Dimly I heard him close the door. He didn't bolt it. I noted that fact in case I had to make a break for freedom later.

It was a tiny, cramped pad. A huge freezer lay stretched along one wall, a tall fridge beside it, mattress and sleeping bag on the other side of the room, a cabinet covering the window at the rear. The bulb was barely bright enough to light the area directly beneath. It was a room of oppressive shadows. There was a door in one wall which doubtless led to a toilet and shower.

'It's not much,' Wami trilled, 'but it's home. You'll have to sit on the floor. I don't hold with chairs. In a tight situation a chair can be an obstacle.'

I sat on the bare floor and crossed my legs. Wami went to his mattress and sat on the edge, hands resting on his thighs. He was studying me with an unreadable expression. 'What do you wish to talk about?' he asked.

'You were following me today,' I said. 'Why didn't you kill me?'

'Why should I?'

'Isn't that what you do? Kill people?'

'I let *some* live.' He smiled and the heads of the snakes lifted menacingly a couple of centimetres. 'It would be a lonely world if I killed you all.'

'But you've been hired to get rid of me,' I said.

'No.'

'You haven't?'

'You would be dead if I had.'

'Then why were you following me?'

'You interest me,' he said. 'You're an Ayuamarcan. They're an old hobby of mine. I like to keep up with them when I'm in town. I've been following you since we met in the alley.'

'Adrian too?'

'Adrian?' His face was blank.

'Adrian Arne. The man who was with me.'

'Ah.' He smiled serenely. 'Some things do not change.'

'What's that supposed to mean?'

He looked at the cabinet and his eyes narrowed. He was pondering something. 'How much do you know of me?' he asked, fingers rising to stroke the tattooed snakes.

'Not much. You're an assassin. You used to work for The Cardinal. Everybody who knows you fears you. They say you're the meanest, coldest man alive.'

He smiled modestly, liking what he heard. 'It's not an easy task, being the most feared man in a city like this. I have had to work hard for my reputation. But I am only an occasional assassin. When I'm in the mood, or if an old acquaintance asks. Most of the time I kill for my own reasons. I am a pioneer. I was one of the first real serial killers, back in the days before it was fashionable. For more than forty years I've blazed trails others can only dream of. I've adopted more guises than the police can count. I've been the Black Angel, Moonshine, the Weasel, Eyeball Ernie and more. I've taken life in every corner of the world, rich and poor, young and old, male and female.

'I kill because I am a killer,' he said. 'It's that simple. It's who I am, what I do. When I kill, I'm being true to myself. There are no hidden motives, no perverse longings. Do you think it's wrong, Capac Raimi, to be true to oneself?'

'When you put it that way . . .'

'There's no other way to put it,' he said, then added conver-sationally, 'I keep notes of my killings. I write of every one. I have dozens of notepads, full of times and places, names, methods, results. That's how I relax in my spare time. I write about my work and dwell upon it at length. I enjoy reading about my old murders. The problem with being responsible for so many is one tends to forget a lot of the details. One death is much the same as any other. They blend.

'I'm thirsty,' he said. 'Will you fetch a beer from the fridge? You may have one yourself if you wish.'

I felt uneasy having my back to him, but I didn't think he was going to kill me, not yet. I opened the door of the fridge and looked for the beer. The fridge was full of jars with hand-applied labels and contents I didn't want to think about. I ignored those easily enough. What I couldn't ignore was the child's head near the top, staring out at me with ruined, innocent eyes. It had been neatly severed and allowed to drain. There was a bowl underneath to catch the last few drops and, as I stood rooted to the spot, I saw a pearl of blood swell and fall.

'The beer's on the second shelf from the top,' Wami said pleasantly. 'Behind the head.'

I repressed a shiver of revulsion. I had a feeling there was a lot riding on this. A wrong move now and that face would be the last I'd ever see. Reaching out, I gently took the head by the ears and moved it to one side. The flesh was cold, scaly, a texture I'd never forget. When there was space, I reached past and grabbed a couple of cans, then laid them on a lower shelf while I returned the head to its previous position. I looked into those young eyes – five? six? – one last time, retrieved the beers and closed the door.

Wami was emotionless as I handed him the can. But, as I was taking my hand away, he suddenly grasped it. I tried to jerk free but he was too strong. He smiled and shook his head slightly. I stopped struggling. Without saying a word he put his can down and closed my fingers into a fist. Then he took my index finger and pulled it out so it was pointing straight ahead. He leaned back so his chin was sticking up. Slowly he guided my hand forward, bringing the tip of my finger to the spot beneath his lip where the heads of the snakes twined around each other. I stared at their painted mouths, their venomous fangs. Then he touched my finger to the flesh.

There was a sudden burning sensation. I yelped and dragged my hand back. He let it go and picked up his beer, saying nothing. I rubbed the finger and examined it. There were no bite marks but there was a small red swelling. I sucked the finger and studied it some more. The flesh wasn't broken and the redness was already beginning to fade.

'How did –' I began, only to have him cut in.

'There's a file over there,' he said, nodding towards the cabinet. 'Bring it to me.'

The cabinet was loaded with files, notebooks and loose pages. I looked up and down a couple of times, wondering which he wanted. I was on the verge of asking when I saw it, a small file halfway up, *AYUAMARCA* scrawled roughly in the top right corner. I handed it over. He opened it and took out two sheets of paper. Turned to the second and studied it. Grunted, found a red pen and made a mark. He showed me the page, pointing to the bottom. The name he'd made the mark beside was Adrian's.

'Adrian Arne,' he said, passing me the sheets. 'Sit. Don't look at them yet.' I did as ordered. 'I don't know this Adrian Arne. As far as I am aware, we never met. I don't recall him being with us in the alley, or writing his name.

'I noticed something many years ago,' he went on. 'One day, perusing my older journal entries, I spotted a couple of names I had no memory of. I'd described killing them, so I must have, but I couldn't recall doing it. Confused, I went through my records – a lengthy task – and found six names, half a dozen murders which didn't fit in with my memories. I was disturbed, naturally, but also intrigued. Madness has always fascinated me. If I was losing my memory, it might be the first sign of a slide into something darker, an abyss I'd always longed to explore. I considered it an opportunity, a chance to experience life from a different perspective.

'Alas, the condition didn't worsen.' He looked genuinely glum. 'I was able to operate as efficiently as always. I didn't find myself making mistakes, drooling in my sleep or coming to my senses in strange places. I was the same Paucar Wami I'd always been, bar the memory lapses.

'Later, searching the files in Party Central, I discovered that.' He nodded at the sheets of paper. 'I had looked for the missing names elsewhere but found no trace. When I saw them there, I made a copy and brought it home to study. There were other names on the list I knew nothing about, people who had nothing to do with me. But I knew a few and found records on some of the others.

'I decided to play a game with myself. I made a red mark to the left of each name I knew or could find in the files. Then, every once in a while, I checked the sheets to see if the names still registered with me. Whenever I found one I'd forgotten, I made a red mark to the right of it.

'You may study the names now.'

I quickly scrolled through the names on the two sheets. There were fifty, maybe sixty in all. The majority had red ticks to the left, including mine and Adrian's, whose names had been added at the end by hand. There were five or six above us, also pencilled in.

'The list is old,' he said. 'Out of date. I have tried to find a more recent copy but it was moved after I found it and I've never come across it again. I add new names as and when I chance upon Ayuamarcans in my travels.'

Virtually all of the names with a mark to the left also had one to the right. I knew most of the ones which didn't — Leonora Shankar, Conchita Kubekik, Paucar Wami, my own. Ama's name wasn't there and I decided not to ask about it. If he didn't know of her, so much the better.

'What is this?' I asked. 'Who are these people?'

'Apart from the few unmarked on the right,' he said, 'I don't know. Their names mean nothing to me. There are the six my journals tell me I killed, and a further five since, but as for the rest . . .' He shrugged. 'I knew them once, according to those marks. Not any longer.'

'What's an Ayuamarcan? You said you recognized me when we met. How?'

'We share a certain look,' he said. 'An emptiness. I cannot explain it any better. I have studied so many of these people

– though I do not remember most – that I can spot one instantly. I don't know what it means, who these people are or what's different about them, why they keep disappearing both from memory and the physical world. But one day, if I continue searching, I will find out. That's why I was trailing you. I hoped you might lead me somewhere.'

I looked down at the sheets again. 'You didn't kill Adrian?'

'To the best of my knowledge, no.'

'And you've no idea what this might be about?'

He hesitated. 'I know one thing — where the name comes from. *Ayuamarca* is Incan.'

I remembered The Cardinal and Y Tse speaking of the city's Incan connections. I shifted uneasily and readjusted the position of my legs.

'It was the name the Incas had for the month of November,' Wami explained. 'Translated literally it means *procession of the dead*. Of course our names are Incan too — you are December, *the magnificent festival*. I am March, *a garment of flowers* according to the history books.'

'Are all the –' I began.

'– names on the list Incan?' he finished and shook his head. 'No. There are a few others – Inti Maimi, Hatun Pocoy – but most are not.'

I pored over the sheets as though persistent examination would force them to reveal their secrets. *Procession of the dead*. That sounded bad in any language.

'Have you ever asked The Cardinal about this?'

'No,' Wami said. 'He doesn't appreciate such questions.'

I cocked my head. I thought I'd heard something in his voice, possibly the slightest hint of fear. 'But he is involved, isn't he?' I pressed.

'Nobody else could order such a purge of the files in Party Central, except maybe Ford Tasso, but this isn't Tasso's style.'

'What about our minds?' I asked. 'Who purged them?'

'You have lapses too?'

'Sort of. I can remember people – like Adrian – but I can't recall my past before coming to this city. I thought it was just amnesia but after hearing you . . .'

'You believe it is more.' He nodded. 'That is my reasoning also. At first it is easier to suspect oneself, but when you notice the flaws in others . . . There are things beyond us. That is why this file interests me. I have always been captivated by the beyond.'

Beyond . . .

'Do you know anything about blind men in robes?' I asked.

'Who never speak?'

'What?'

'They never speak.' Wami nodded knowingly. 'Not in English. Even when tortured by an expert.'

One had spoken to me but I decided not to mention it. I didn't want him getting jealous.

'They've been around as long as I can remember,' Wami said. 'I don't know much about them – how many there are or what they do – but I've run into them from time to time. You think they're connected to this?'

'Maybe.'

'Interesting.'

I tapped the papers against my knees and handed them back, deciding I'd learnt all that I could. 'Well, if there's nothing more to add, I might as well be going,' I said lightly.

'Just like that?' He didn't move. 'I thought you might like to stay and chat a while longer.'

'What for? You don't know anything, nor do I. Why waste each other's time?'

'You know where I live,' he said softly.

I stiffened. 'Look,' I said, 'I'm not going to pretend I understand you. I've met a lot of warped fucks in my time, but none who've kept heads in their fridges and Christ alone knows what else in the freezer. I don't know what's inside your head and I don't want to. If you're going to kill me, kill me. But if you have it in your mind to let me live, then I have places to go and things to do.'

He pursed his lips and nodded thoughtfully. 'You interest me,' he said. 'You are different. Stranger. There's a light in you I have not seen in the others. I will let you live. I think I have more to gain that way.'

'Thanks,' I said drily and stumbled to the door. I paused and looked back. He hadn't moved a muscle. 'I could let you know if I find out anything.'

'You will not track me again this easily,' he said. 'I will be gone before this hour is out. I have been here – in the city – long enough. It is time to move on. But one day I may look you up if you're still around.' He mightn't have meant it as a threat but it scared the shit out of me all the same.

He finished his beer, then went for a refill. He opened the fridge and lowered his head to examine something inside. He was smiling and, in the light, the snakes on his cheeks seemed to writhe. I hurried out the door and managed to stop myself from running down the stairs. Just.

Ama and I roamed the city randomly the rest of the evening. I told her about Wami, his file and memory losses. I mentioned Leonora saying something similar a while back. Like me, she wasn't sure what to make of it. We discussed it over the gentle purr of the bike but made no real progress. We stopped at a quiet restaurant for dinner in the evening but ate little, our minds elsewhere.

'We shouldn't go,' Ama said. 'You've seen Wami's list. You won't learn anything new by seeing the one in Party Central.'

'Wami's was old. I want to see a recent copy.'

'Why?'

'Maybe I'll recognize some of the newer names.'

'Capac, have you ever . . . or would you . . . do you think you could kill a man?' She looked at me.

'I haven't yet, but yes, I will if I have to.' I didn't hesitate with the answer.

'Could you kill like Wami does? Women? Children?'

'Of course not. He's insane. I'd kill somebody who got in my way, but a kid? Never.' She seemed satisfied with that but I wasn't. Because I wasn't so sure. I'd been appalled by what I saw in Wami's fridge. A part of me cringed and was cringing still. But another part registered admiration. I didn't like to admit it, but inside, not as deeply buried as I wished, I envied his ferocious feats.

We booked into a cheap motel and freshened up. I needed a shower. The trip to Wami's had left me a sweating mess. I was pulling off my pants when I became aware of Ama watching me. 'What?' I asked, pausing.

'I never got a good look at you the other night,' she said.

'I don't want you ogling me,' I grumbled.

She laughed merrily. 'Modest?'

I smiled. 'I'll take off mine if you take off yours.'

She returned my smile, nodded slyly and unpeeled. We showered together, our hands exploring each other's bodies as they had that night in Party Central. Only this time we went slowly, fingers creeping along lightly as we kissed. I stroked Ama's breasts while her hands performed remarkable tricks beneath my navel, but we stopped short of sex, saving it for later.

As our bodies dried in the bedroom, we shoved the two beds together and explored some more. I was struck again by Ama's peculiar beauty. I didn't know how others would respond to her – she wasn't men's magazine material – but to my excited eyes she was perfection.

We made love slowly but just as passionately as the first

time. We were still new to each other but it was as if we'd
been partners for years. We knew exactly how to please one
another, moving without thinking, loving intuitively. We hit
climax at the same time and it was painfully blissful.

'If we could bottle what we have,' Ama said afterwards as
we lay on the beds, wrapped in each other's arms, 'we'd
make a fortune.'

'Who cares about money?' I said, nuzzling her neck. 'I
don't want to share. Let the rest of the world go hang.'

'That's not a nice thing to say,' she giggled.

'I'm not a very nice man,' I smiled.

'Is that the truth?' she asked seriously.

'Having regrets?'

'I just want to know. I love you but I don't understand
what it is about you that I love or why. There's so much
that's a mystery to me. I'd like to know what sort of man
I've pledged myself to.'

I sighed and propped myself up on an elbow. My fingers
made invisible circles on the flesh of her stomach while I spoke.
'I'm a gangster. I steal, bully, hurt. Kill if necessary. I don't
harm innocents. I believe in family and sticking by one's friends.
But I've done bad things, Ama, and I intend to do worse.'

She nodded sadly. 'I figured as much.'

'Is it too dreadful to bear?' I asked quietly.

She shrugged. 'At least you're honest.'

'Can you love a man just for being honest?'

'Yes,' she said after a moment's hesitation. 'But can *you*
love a woman who'd love a man like you?'

'I'm prepared to give her a go.' I smothered her with a
kiss and she kissed back. Soon we were making love again
and all worries and doubts were lost to passion.

We booked out of the motel and made our way across town,
then separated a few blocks from Party Central. Ama went

round the back. I strolled through the lobby and checked in.
Said I wanted to use the computers. That wasn't unusual. I
handed over my shoes and socks and started up the stairs.
I took my time, reflecting on the task ahead, ruminating on
Wami's words. While I was distracted, a good picture of *the
woman* formed in my mind. I tried using it to pry open the
locks of my past but they were as secure as ever.

I was walking along calmly when, on the sixth floor, a
shadow detached itself from one of the walls and grabbed
my left arm. I almost lost control and fell down the stairs to
an untimely, ridiculous death.

'Capac, it's me.'

'Jesus!' I snapped. 'Are you trying to save The Cardinal
the job of killing me? What are you doing here? I thought
we were going to meet up top.'

'I didn't want to go alone. I got nervous.'

I studied Ama in the dim light. She was trembling. She'd
seemed so brave before, I never stopped to think how
unsettling it must be. She was, after all, the daughter of a
restaurateur. It was only natural that she should feel intimi-
dated and unsure of herself in a situation like this.

'You want to call this off?' I asked. 'I can go by myself.'

'No.' She smiled shakily. 'It's just nerves. They'll pass.'

'You're sure?' When she nodded, I gave her hand a
squeeze and we headed up, Ama leading the way. The stairs
were deserted. 'Don't you ever run into anyone?' I whispered.

'Rarely. Occasionally I'll hear someone coming, slip behind
a door and wait for them to pass. You're the only one who
caught me. Lucky you, eh?'

I grunted and we continued past the ninth and tenth floors,
then the eleventh and twelfth. There wasn't even anybody
on the unlucky thirteenth. I was starting to see how Ama
had got away with this for so long, how easy it was to pass

unnoticed if you kept your nerve, when the door to the fourteenth floor swung open on us.

We were seven steps down with nowhere to hide. As my heart dropped to my toes, I recognized the stone features of Ford Tasso. Acting impulsively, I moved up beside Ama and thrust an arm around her waist. I buried my face in her hair and pretended not to notice The Cardinal's right-hand man.

Ford's hand went to his holster at the sight of intruders on the stairs so close to the fifteenth. His reflexes were way sharper than they should be — I hoped I'd be in such good shape if I lived that long, which didn't seem likely at the moment. When he saw me he relaxed and lowered his fingers, but his expression was harsh.

'Capac,' he snapped. I looked up as if surprised. 'What are you doing here? And why aren't you using the lift like any normal person?'

'I could ask the same about you,' I replied cheekily.

'Doctor's orders. I need to exercise. I don't have time for a gym, so I jog up and down these stairs as often as I can.' He glanced at Ama. 'Who's your friend?'

'This is Ama, my secretary. I'm moving up in the world.'

'What's she doing here?' he asked.

'I'm showing her the ropes. Introducing her to the staff, helping her get her bearings. You know.'

'There are people paid to do that.'

'Sure there are, but . . .' I patted Ama's butt in a way I'm sure she despised. 'There's nothing like the *personal* touch.' I winked slyly.

Ford chortled, the sound of a corpse having a seizure, and moved down past us. 'Use the lift next time,' he said. 'I might have shot you if it was darker.'

'Yes, boss,' I grinned and held the expression until he turned out of sight. Then we looked at each other and sagged.

'Christ,' Ama wheezed. 'I come here dozens of times by

myself, no hassles. The first night I bring you, Ford fucking Tasso turns up! Are you a jinx, Raimi?'

'Let's hope not,' I said. 'You've got to admit, though, I handled him pretty well.'

'You were OK.'

'Just OK? What would you have done if you'd been alone?'

'Dropped my drawers and fucked him placid,' she laughed.

We made it to the nineteenth without further surprises. It housed a huge room, the length of the building. It was dusty and I found myself coughing. Ama lent me a handkerchief. I thanked her between convulsions. It was dark up here, lights set at infrequent intervals, too few and weak to be much use. Ama drew a small torch from one of her many pockets and flicked it on. She moved away from the door, into the heart of the gloom. I followed quietly, gazing around with interest.

Boxes stood in huge piles like silent guardians wherever I looked. Each pillar was set apart from its companions by three or four feet. A maze of passageways ran through the towers.

'What's in these?' I asked, tapping one of the piles.

'Everything. There are no clear divisions. Maps, blueprints, newspaper clippings and personal files. Minutes from secret government meetings, stuff he must have paid a fortune for. Lists of kennels, retirement homes and schools. Medical records. Photographs of hobos. Anything you can put on paper.'

I moved between a few of the skyscrapers, brushed against one by accident and froze, expecting it to topple. But it didn't even shimmer. I gave it a harder push but it was solid. Samson would have had his work cut out for him here.

'This place is like a museum,' Ama said. She was gliding between the pillars too. 'Records going back centuries. Nearly all of it's original. I bet the curators in this city would keel over in shock if they knew a place like this existed.'

'What about the guards?' I was starting to feel edgy about the lack of security. The open window was hard enough to buy, but to move so easily up the stairs and through floors like this . . . How could The Cardinal's people be so careless?

'You have to listen for them,' she said. 'But they're easy to avoid — they carry lights and are noisy. Like I've said, the reputation of Party Central is its prime defence. People just don't believe anybody could ever get in.'

'Still . . .' I couldn't shake the feeling something wasn't right. I had a nasty suspicion that a regiment of Troops would burst in and spray us with lead. Well, it was too late to worry. I should have done that earlier. I was here now, far beyond the boundaries of caution.

'Where's the file?' I asked, not wanting to waste any more time. We'd tempted fate enough already.

'Over here.' She led the way to a smaller stack. 'I targeted it because of its size. The taller ones are a pain in the ass. You have to drag out a ladder to get to the top, then pick the upper boxes off and climb down, up again, down again and so on. It takes ages. I stick to the small towers as much as I can.'

She pulled the paper down, one stack after another. I assisted her and within a minute we were two thirds of the way to the ground. 'Stop,' she said. 'It's around here.' She began removing single sheets, then found the pot of gold and handed it across.

It was a slim cardboard file. Four A4 sheets nestled inside. Just as she'd said, no indication of importance. The name was on a white sticker, stuck in the middle of the front. *AYUAMARCA*.

I examined the first sheet. A long list of names, single spaced, a neat ruled line through the majority. Leonora Shankar was the first name, unlined. Paucar Wami was a bit further down. Then a mass of crossed out names. I recognized none of them, with one exception — Inti Maimi. There was one further unlined name near the bottom — Conchita's.

The second page. Two survivors. I knew one of them, a general in the Troops. Inti Maimi was here again, near the bottom, once more neatly crossed out.

Two more untouched names on the third sheet. One meant nothing to me. The other was the mayor. 'You see this? The goddamn mayor's part of —'

'Shh!' She put a hand over my mouth, flicked off the torch and crouched. I squatted beside her, though I didn't know what the emergency was. A few seconds later I heard footsteps. One of the Troops. He was carrying a torch and shone it around the stacks of paper, going through the motions. He didn't come near us and I soon heard a door flapping open and shut. We stood and stretched.

'Sharp ears,' I complimented her.

'You get used to it,' she said. 'I've been here so often, and it's so quiet, I really think I could hear a pin drop.'

I turned to the fourth and final page. This wasn't full. The names stretched a third of the way down. Three unlined names. One near the top that I didn't know. Ama's, a few lines above my own. And the third — some guy called Stephen Herf.

Ama gasped and clutched my wrist. She couldn't say anything. She didn't have to. The strength of her grip conveyed her shock quite adequately.

I looked at my name, just below Herf's, and traced the neat line through it with my left index finger. The ink was still fresh.

'Well,' I said softly, smiling grimly in the gloom, 'isn't that a bitch.'

coya raimi

I was striding down the stairs, one hand clutching the file, the other clenched into a fist. My face was a pale, furious mask. Ama was rushing to keep up, tugging at my shirt, trying to slow me down.

'What are you going to do?' she asked.

'Go home, Ama,' I replied brusquely.

'What are you going to do?' she repeated, quickening her pace.

'Go home!' I snapped.

'No!' She swung in front of me, blocking my path. 'Not until you tell me where you're going.'

I clutched her arms and gazed into her eyes. They were fiery, uncertain, full of fear, love and pity. I wished we'd met another time, when I could have loved her. But we hadn't. We were here, now, and dead men can't afford love.

'It's over,' I said. 'You were a test — I failed. You were a trap — I'm caught. Go home.'

'You're blaming *me* for this?' she said incredulously.

'I don't blame you for anything. You were just one of his pawns. He set things up so you'd draw me to the point where

I had to make a choice, and I made the wrong one. My mistake. All mine. Now go.'

She shook her head angrily. 'Ever think that maybe *you're* the bait?'

I frowned. 'What do you mean?'

'You think everything The Cardinal does revolves around you. Maybe you're not so important. Maybe I'm the one he's after, the one he wants to trap. Maybe *you're* the pawn.'

I thought about it. 'Perhaps. Your name appeared before mine on the file. But I've heard The Cardinal wax lyrical on the subject of women. I think it's safe to assume you're not that important to him. No woman is.'

'What are you going to do?' she asked again.

I ran my fingers along the spine of the file. Her eyes grew round as she realized I meant to confront him. 'Run!' she gasped. 'Run away with me. It's the only way. We can ring that driver friend of yours and –'

'No,' I said. 'Where would we go? Where couldn't he find us? And what sort of a life would it be, living in fear and doubt? Remember telling me you couldn't bear the present, not knowing about your past?'

'But we have each other now,' she said. 'We can build a future together.'

'But we'd still obsess about the past.'

'He'll kill you,' she switched tack. 'If you go down there, you're dead.'

'Probably. But if that line through my name means what we know it does, I'm dead anyway. This way I go down fighting. I don't have to wait for Paucar Wami to sneak up behind me in the dark.'

'But you can run,' she hissed. 'You don't have to fight. There's a chance.'

'There was never a chance,' I said sadly. 'Not when we came here and openly defied The Cardinal. We came to find the truth. We made our choice. Now we've got to die with it. At least *I* do. Your name's untarnished. He doesn't want your head yet. Go home. Forget about me, The Cardinal, all this. Try and live a normal life. You might still be able to.'

'I'm coming with you,' she said. 'I've come this far, I might as well –'

'No.' My voice was as firm as my resolve. 'This is my last stand. I'm going there tonight to face the end. I'll kill him or he'll kill me, and that'll be that. This is my battle, Ama. You might face your own later, but not tonight. Not here, now, with me.'

'What will you say to him?' she asked.

'I don't know. I might not get a chance to say anything. If I do, I'll probably ask what this is about, what the list is, who we are, who we were. Maybe he'll tell me before I die.'

'I'll ask one final time,' she said, pulling away and glaring at me. She was shaking and there were tears in her eyes. 'Come with me. Leave The Cardinal, your job, this city. Make a life with me somewhere else.'

'There is nowhere else,' I said slowly. I touched her one last time, her face, her nose, her lips. 'He's everywhere, Ama.' I tapped my head. 'He's in here. I can't run from him any more than I could run from myself.'

'Then fuck you, Capac,' she sobbed and fled, never looking back. I almost ran after her. My heart almost won the day and I opened my mouth to shout, 'Stop, wait, I'm coming!'

Almost.

But I couldn't abandon the mystery. I was destined to face him, provoked by nature and instinct. Having come this far, there could be no going back. I let my mouth close and watched her flee, listening to the fading sounds of her feet.

After a time I resumed my descent, concentrating, not thinking of Ama or the fragility of life. Thinking about *the woman* and the other faces I could dredge up from my obscure past. There were lots of kids in school uniforms or gym clothes, running around, climbing ropes, playing ball. I had a whistle in my mouth and then I was kissing *the woman* and then I was at a funeral and then I was laughing and then I was . . .

Then I was there.

His secretary tried to stop me. She said he was asleep and could never be disturbed when sleeping. I pushed past her. She tried to sidetrack me but I shoved her to the floor. She scrabbled to the intercom to warn The Cardinal or summon the Troops. I didn't care. It was too late in the day to worry about secrecy.

He was asleep on a bare mattress in the middle of the room. Curled up like a boy or a dog, snoring lightly, face twitching from one dark dream or another. Hatred and disgust swept through me. An overwhelming desire seized me and, crazy though it was, I stamped across the room, stood above him, drew back my right foot and kicked him in the gut.

'Wakey-wakey, mother-fucker!' I shouted, laughing in spite of myself. I'd gone over the edge and fallen into the abyss of madness which Paucar Wami was so interested in.

The Cardinal's eyes shot open and he rolled away from me, surged to his feet and staggered for a few seconds, blinking sleep from his eyes. As soon as he focused on me, his mouth foamed and he shook with rage.

'Got your attention?' I smiled. 'Good. Now I want to know exactly what –'

I got no further. He was on me, roaring, an enraged panther, striking to kill. I discarded the Ayuamarca file and met his charge. We clashed like colliding trains, screaming, kicking, punching and tearing at each other. His nails scratched my face and narrowly missed my eyes. He got his head close to mine and bit into my left ear, drawing blood, almost choking on it. I punched his stomach repeatedly, hoping to break a rib and puncture a lung.

When his head slipped, I bit for his jugular. It was slippery and my teeth slid off his neck, so I was forced to settle for his meaty shoulder. He ripped chunks of my hair out and beat my back. I spat into his eyes. Raised my arms and struck the upper part of his body, hitting his nose, his cheeks, cracking his lips. He kicked my shins and knees. My legs buckled and I nearly went down. He got two fingers up my nostrils, while I got one in his ear. We pushed at each other for a few seconds, trying to force our way through the orifices to the brains within.

As our initial fury faded, we broke and circled each other warily, panting, drooling, hunched offensively, eyes narrow and focused. He was surprised that I was still on my feet. Not many men had fought The Cardinal like this and lived so long. I knew he'd respect my strength. It wouldn't stop him killing me but it might stop him pissing on my corpse.

He ended the stand-off and charged, bellowing like a bull, head down, looking to smash me into the wall. I skipped out of his way but only just — he caught my side with his head and I felt something in my ribcage snap.

He was on me as quickly as he could turn. Which wasn't quickly enough. I threw myself at him and slammed my knee up between his legs. If I'd connected, I'd have driven his balls through his brains and the contest would have been over, but he brought his thighs together in time and trapped my knee just short of its mark. It made him scream in pain, but it wasn't the killer blow that I'd hoped for.

His fingers sought my eyes, thumbs pressing into the bones of my cheeks. I chopped at his throat and his breath caught. He withdrew slightly and I pushed after him, seizing the initiative, chopping again at his neck and arms. He lashed out with both fists, one aimed at my stomach, the other at my face. I moved quickly and blocked one of the incoming fists. The other smashed my nose to a pulp. Blood spurted everywhere, into my eyes and mouth, blinding and gagging me. I staggered away and shook my head, trying to draw air. The Cardinal gave a roar of triumph and came after me, fingers stretched to strangle, sure of the kill.

I had one last move. Gathering all the strength my battered body could muster, I swung my right leg up in a final blind kick. I couldn't see where I was aiming but knew the general region I wanted to strike. I caught him in the testicles with the full weight of my foot, clean and vicious. Beautiful. He screamed breathlessly and fell back, rocking, whimpering.

Before I could crawl after him, the door crashed open and several Troops raced in, guns levelled, fingers squeezing triggers. A few shots narrowly missed me, shrieking by my ears and striking the wall. I collapsed and waited for the end.

'Stop!' The Cardinal roared and the firing ceased instantly. 'Get the fuck out of here,' he snarled. 'Go!' he shouted when they hesitated, and they fled, closing the door behind them. I'd been spared death by firing squad again. It was getting to be a habit, one I wasn't in any rush to break.

'Before I rip your throat out,' The Cardinal panted, shuffling gingerly around the room, 'perhaps you'd like to tell me what this is about. Why the fuck did you come here tonight?'

'Recognize this?' I wiped blood away from my face, stumbled over to the mattress and picked up the abandoned sheaf of papers. '*Ayuamarca?* All those non-people with lines through their names? The line through mine? Ring a bell?'

He sneered. 'Some people are never satisfied. I gave you all you wanted — money, women, power. I spared your life and offered you this city. How do you repay me? You fuck some bitch on my stairs, plot behind my back, break into my castle and ransack my most private files. Ever hear of *gratitude?*'

'Why is my name crossed out?' I shouted. 'Why are you

going to kill me? What's happened to Adrian and Y Tse? Who are –'

'*Stop!*' he screamed, baying like a hound. 'Always fucking questions! I tell you not to question me, not to probe, and what do you do? On and on like a parrot.'

'Who am I?' I demanded. 'Why am I on this list? Where did I come from? Where did you find me? Why don't I have a past? Where does Ama fit in? How do you make people vanish? How did you make Leonora forget Y Tse?' I spat out the questions as fast as I could, striding forward, jabbing a finger at him, until I was close enough to jab his chest. 'Who am I? What have you done with my past? How are you –?'

He began to shake. His face trembled and his lips drew back over his teeth. His hands clenched and unclenched. His head swivelled, the bones of his neck creaking as he flexed them. He wanted to attack. He was building up for an onslaught so psychotic and fierce, I knew I couldn't withstand it. I'd reached my physical limits but The Cardinal, it seemed, was just warming up. I was years younger but I couldn't match him. Leonora called it right — he was superhuman.

But he didn't want to attack. He wanted me alive, at least a while longer. He tried to control his rage. He placed his hands on his head and squeezed so hard I thought his skull would shatter under the strain. His face was red and his nostrils dilated wide enough to deliver a calf. He turned away, looking for something to vent his fury on. His eyes were bulging. They settled on his large chair, the one he enjoyed lying back in when entertaining visitors. He picked it up and tossed it at the reinforced window that had been built to stop bullets. The glass splintered under the force of The Cardinal's missile and flew out into the night in a thousand pieces, down into the black unknown of the city.

He was calmer after that.

He brushed a hand through his hair, stroked his cheeks and began to breathe normally. Walked over to the window, examined the damage and tutted. 'If only I'd thrown that chair at you, Mr Raimi, I'd have saved myself the embarrassment of an ignominious stalemate and, of more immediate concern, would still have had something to sit on. Good chairs are hard to come by. Still, I have a certain amount of money and power. I suppose I'll find one eventually.' He grinned, the old Cardinal again, relaxed and in control. 'You're a halfway decent opponent.'

'Does that mean you're going to explain things now?' I asked. 'Have I earned that right?'

He laughed, pulled out a spare chair and sat. 'You're too much, Mr Raimi. Always pushing and prodding. Tenacious, like a bloodhound. That amused me for a time but I'm starting to lose interest.' He pressed a button. 'Miss Fowler? Send the Troops in please.'

'You're going to kill me?' I gasped.

'Of course,' he said, directing the incoming Troops to line up against a wall in the time-honoured way of firing squads everywhere. 'The Ayuamarca file never lies. I hadn't planned to kill you for a few more days, but now I think the time is ripe.'

'At least tell me who I am,' I pleaded. 'That's all I want to know, who I am and why this happened. You owe me that much.'

'I owe you nothing,' he barked. 'You were a man going nowhere, a shit-eating fly I took a liking to. I gave you a chance to make something of yourself. This could all have been yours. I wasn't joking about that. But you blew it, so you die and I search again for an heir. Are your weapons ready, gentlemen?'

'So you'll let me die in ignorance.' I spat at his feet. 'You're a prick.'

'We all die in ignorance,' he smiled. I sensed hope in that

smile. If I kept him going, I might stumble across the words that could save me. I knew they existed. He would have killed me already if they didn't. He was throwing me an invisible lifeline. He wanted me to save myself. But why? I couldn't be that important to him. My death wouldn't cause him any hurt or inconvenience. So why was he so reluctant to . . . ?

It came to me and I knew instantly this was my chance. 'OK,' I said, drawing myself erect, wincing at the pain, but smiling in spite of it, because I'd found the way. 'If you're not going to answer my questions, we'll stop it here. Let me go.'

The Cardinal burst out laughing. 'You're too precious! I should keep you as my court jester. Let you go, Mr Raimi? Why would I do that?'

'Because you can't kill me,' I said.

He stopped laughing. 'What makes you say that?' he asked suspiciously.

'Conchita.' That drove the wind out of his sails. He hadn't been prepared for that one. It wasn't the line he'd thrown but it did have a hook. 'She's the only person in the world you love, if you can call what you feel for her love. You went there the other day. Why? To warn her about me and spare her the pain? I don't think so. You wanted to see if she'd accept you again. You wanted to be part of her life now that I'd cured her. When you gazed into her eyes and saw only fear and loathing, you told her about the file to hurt her. You hadn't meant to, but you did. You're a monster — you couldn't have done anything else.'

His face was ashen. He pointed a hand at me, the one with the crooked little finger. 'You go too far,' he growled. 'Even the dead have limits.'

'No they don't,' I disagreed. 'You care for her. She's the only one who means anything to you. I bet it chewed you up inside when you realized what you'd said and done. I bet you sat up here and thought she was going to die, or would regress, that you'd destroyed the one thing you loved.

'Well, you didn't. I spoke with her today and she's leaving this city, going out into the world to live a full life for as long as she can. She's going to do her best to be happy. She was optimistic, actually looking forward to life for the first time in years.'

'This is true?' he asked hoarsely. He wanted to believe me but thought I might be tricking him.

'It's true,' I said quietly. 'Ask your spies. She can be happy now. There's no place for you in her happiness, but that's not so bad, is it? That shouldn't bother you. Having her would have been the icing on the cake, but her happiness is the main thing, right?'

'Yes,' he said softly.

'And I'm the man who made her happy.'

He looked at me, sly again, compassion vanishing. 'Now we get to the real truth of it. You saved her, so you think that entitles you to a reprieve.' He shook his head. 'Wrong. Doesn't work that way.'

'Not a full reprieve,' I said, stepping forward, ignoring the click of the guns. 'A couple of hours. Give me a chance. I probably can't escape but let me try. You won't be able to live with yourself if you don't. You're human, Ferdinand Dorak, despite your monstrous qualities. You feel like the rest of us. If you kill me here, in your office, it will destroy Conchita if she finds out. And she will — people always do in situations like this.

'You can send the Troops after me later, the whole city if you wish. Let them hunt me like a pack of rabid hounds. You know they'll get me. I can't escape. Hell, I've nowhere to escape to. But at least you won't have my blood on your hands. You can distance yourself from the murder. Let me go. Give me a chance. Maybe it will stop you having nightmares.'

He flinched when I mentioned nightmares. Suddenly I was

able to see the real man, born to be a monster, but a man all the same, trapped in his own shell, forced to be what he was, not liking it but incapable of change. If he wasn't so terrible he would have been pitiable.

'You're old, Ferdy,' I said and he flinched again. 'You've done so much evil, hurt so many people, including yourself. I'm not asking for mercy. I'm offering you the chance to evade the guilt. You gain nothing if you kill me here, just drive another nail into the coffin of your heart. Let me go.'

It was a passionate speech but passion had never worked with The Cardinal before. He must have heard pleas like this a thousand times. But Conchita and his nightmares made the difference. Each one of us has a secret code, a series of buttons which, if pressed in the right order, make us perform contrary to judgment, logic and instinct. I'd found and pressed The Cardinal's. If that didn't work, the game was up and I was dead.

'I'll give you half an hour,' he said, nodding at the Troops to lower their guns. 'Don't say anything more. Not a word. You've been very persuasive and it's earned you a reprieve, but if you speak now . . . Half an hour. Not a minute more.'

I made my stunned way to the door. 'Mr Raimi,' he said, stopping me as my hand was poised to open it. He had his back to me and was looking out of the window. I could see his battered face reflected in the broken shards of glass the chair had left behind. 'Nothing's carved in stone,' he said quietly. 'Use your time. Don't run blindly. Turn your escape into a quest.' I saw him smile. 'That's the best advice I've ever given. I must be going soft in my old age.' He looked at his watch. 'Twenty-nine minutes, Mr Raimi.'

I fled.

It was too little time. I knew that before I hit the ground floor, grabbed my shoes from a startled receptionist and sped out the front door as fast as my legs could manage. Less than thirty minutes. I checked my watch. Five of those had already passed. There was nothing I could do in so short a time. I might as well have let him kill me up there.

I stopped in the middle of a small park and sat on a metal bench. My cuts, bruises and broken bones were stinging but I ignored them. He'd told me not to flee blindly. Running would get me nowhere. I had to think. Was there a way out?

I couldn't stay in the city, that was obvious. I could expect to avoid the chasing mobs for an hour or two if I was lucky. But as soon as morning came and word spread, that would be that. Troops, hired hoods, taxi drivers, hookers, cops and kids on their bikes — the city was bulging with the eyes and ears of The Cardinal.

But where could I go? Grabbing the first plane out was no good. That would be the last recourse of a desperate man, and desperation would ruin me just as surely as Ford Tasso and his men.

I had to focus on the mystery of my past. That was the key. The Cardinal had spoken of a quest — he could only have been referring to that. I had to find my way home and search for the truth.

I thought back to my first day in the city, when I'd trundled in on the train. I'd begun somewhere else. If I could find that starting point, I'd be closer to solving the puzzle. The only way forward was back.

I concentrated. Thought of *the woman*, streets I could visualize vaguely, other faces, lots of kids again. I tried distinguishing street names, buildings, parks, anything which might help pin a name to the anonymous city or town.

It was hopeless. My memory was too muddled. With time I might be able to remember. But I only had – a quick check – fourteen minutes. Not enough.

I could remember my time here so well. Why couldn't I

go back a few days more, or a couple of hours to when I boarded the train? The first thing I could remember was seeing the city, passing through the outskirts, drawing into the station, leaving the train and seeing the peculiar rain shower. Then the cab ride and my meeting with Uncle Theo. Everything before that was . . .

Wait. I was missing something. I got off the train and left the station, but there was a pause in there, somewhere, which I was overlooking. I hadn't come straight out. I'd stopped to . . . hand over my ticket. But there was no guard at the gate, so I put it aside to show my children one day. *I'd kept the fucking ticket!* The stations of destination and departure would be on it. If I still had it, it would tell me where I came from.

But what had I done with it? I thought back. I'd pocketed the stub and forgotten about it. Found it later, when I went to do my first load of laundry. I rescued it in the nick of time and stuck it . . . where? My wallet? No. I used my wallet daily and knew I'd pull out the ticket and lose it sooner or later. I wanted to keep it safe, so I put it . . . in the money belt I bought a week after I arrived! And I kept the money belt at Uncle Theo's. I hadn't brought it with me the night of his murder and had never gone back to retrieve it. Hadn't even thought of it in the months since. It contained nothing of import, just some notes, a couple of photos, loose change. And the ticket.

I didn't know what had happened to the house in the wake of the shooting. If new tenants had moved in – and they probably had – I was done for. It was a long shot, but I wasn't spoilt for choices. It was Theo's or bust.

How was I going to get there? I checked my watch. Eleven minutes left. Theo's house was miles away. Walking was out of the question. A cab? Sure, but how was I to know the radio wouldn't blurt out a description of me halfway there? I needed Nathanael Mead again.

I hurried to the nearest pay phone (not daring to use my

mobile) and rang. He was at home. He listened carefully while I gave him the barest description of my predicament. He was reluctant this time. This was too hot for him. He'd be glad to help but a risk was one thing, suicide another. In the end, I resorted to bribery and the lure of cash swung him my way. 'Where will I pick you up?' he asked.

I was about to tell him when I stopped. The Cardinal might have seen me with Mead before. Maybe he'd guess that I'd go to him again. Hell, the cabbie's phone might even be tapped. Unlikely, but I didn't want to take the chance. 'Nathanael, will you go to a pay phone and call the following number?'

I fidgeted and rubbed my hands while I waited. I was sore from the night's fight and it hurt when I moved, but I didn't want to stay still — I might stiffen and never move again.

By the time Nathanael rang, I'd thought the situation through and had a clearer plan in mind. It was too risky for him to come. I asked if he knew anyone he could trust, someone he could send in his place. 'I do,' he said, 'but I wouldn't like them getting involved in this shit.'

'I'll pay them the same as I'm paying you.'

'Damn.' He considered it a moment longer. I wanted to rush him but kept quiet and let him reach a decision in his own time. 'OK, I'll do it. If the person agrees, where do you want to meet?' I gave him the address of a nearby street. 'You'll have the money with you?' I assured him I would, then hung up and went to get the cash.

There were no banks open at that time, but I was close to an all-night casino. The Cardinal ran most of the casinos in the city and it wasn't unusual for his higher level personnel to draw funds from them if a lot of cash was required in the middle of the night.

Three minutes of grace were left, according to my watch, when I hurried through the lobby to the cashiers' desk. I slid up to the counter, handed over my card and prayed The

Cardinal hadn't cancelled it yet or put out word that I was *persona non grata*. He hadn't. I withdrew enough to pay off Nathanael and his friend, buy some new clothes and get me to wherever it was I needed to go.

The car was a few minutes late. When it pulled up to the kerb, I opened the rear door and leapt in. The driver took off before I could close the door. 'Hi, I'm –' I began, then stopped. A woman was sitting behind the wheel. She saw my confusion and smiled.

'We *can* drive,' she said softly. 'Despite what many men think.'

'I'm sorry. Of course you can. I just wasn't expecting . . .'

'No problem. You got the money?' I counted off notes and passed them over. She pocketed the stash and grunted. 'Margaret Stravinki's the name.'

'Capac Raimi.'

'I kind of guessed that,' she laughed. 'Where to?'

I gave her directions, sat back and tried to lay low. My face was aching, as were my ribs, and after a few minutes of uncomfortable bending I had to straighten up. I leant forward and examined my face in the front mirror. I was a mess. My nose was destroyed, my eyes red, my cheeks purple with bruises. Long scratches raked the flesh in several places. One side of my neck was bloody from my savaged ear. My lips were torn and puffy. I hadn't lost any teeth, but that was about the only positive aspect. I rolled my jaw gently from side to side, flexed my arms and legs. I'd be tender for weeks but I'd live. Unless one of the ribs had punctured something and I was bleeding internally.

I checked my watch. The pursuit should be hitting full flight about now. The posses would gather, heed their instructions and the hunt would be on. I had to hope they'd overlook Theo's house in all the excitement.

We got there without complication. The lights were off

but virtually all the houses were dark this time of night. There could be a circus troupe in residence for all I could tell. 'You'll wait for me?' I asked Margaret. She'd parked several houses away and killed the engine.

'Well, I was gonna do a bit of fishing, but since you asked so nice . . .'

'Thanks. If there's any sign of trouble, split.'

'Don't worry,' she said. 'I will.'

The back yard was deserted and the door was locked. There was a loose stone nearby which Theo always left a key under. I couldn't see in the dark, so I had to get down on my knees and scrabble around. When I found the stone I nudged it aside and explored with my fingers. I hit metal after a couple of seconds and retrieved it quickly. The key was caked in mud. I wiped it on my shirt, picked off the worst dirt with my nails and tried the lock. It opened without a problem and I was soon standing in the familiar kitchen, remembering happier, simpler days.

I crept through the house. I knew my way around, even after all these months, and could navigate with my eyes shut. But if people were living here, they would have made changes — new tables, stands, statues. I had to be careful.

I went up the stairs slowly, wincing at every creak. The door to Theo's old room was half open. I tiptoed over and peeped in. There was somebody on the bed, under the covers! I tensed and tried melting back into the shadows. Then, as my eyes grew accustomed to the dark, I smiled. It was only the sheets, crumpled on the bed. Nobody was here.

I crossed the landing to my old room. I moved quickly, feeling safe for the first time. I'd kept the money belt under the mattress. Lifting it a few inches, I groped for the pouch. Nothing. My hand crept in further, reaching deeper, describing a widening circle. It wasn't there. Someone had found it and

. . . There! My fingers closed over the belt and withdrew. I had it. Everything would be fine now.

I worked on the zip. It was stiff and I had to struggle. I didn't want to jerk too hard and break it. As I was trying to tease it open, a noise outside attracted my attention. A car had pulled up.

I returned to Theo's room which had a better view of the front. The car was parked across the street. Two men emerged while the driver stayed seated. It was dark and I couldn't see very well but I was almost certain one of them was Vincent Carell, Tasso's pet goon.

They crossed the road, unbuttoning their jackets, reaching for guns. I searched the room for a weapon. I'd left my knife with Ama because I couldn't have snuck it through the doors of Party Central. I meant to get it back later but it slipped my mind.

Pieces of a broken vase littered the floor. I found the longest shard and gripped tightly, grimacing as it sliced a thin ridge in my palm. It wasn't much of a weapon but it would have to do.

I heard the front door opening. They had keys. I made to leave the room, then stopped. They'd see or hear me if I did. Besides, there was nowhere to hide out there. I dived under the bed covers and pulled them over me. Fluffed them up a bit and lay as still as I could. Some camouflage!

Voices drifted up from downstairs. They obviously didn't feel any need to tread softly. I recognized Vincent's voice immediately, complaining as usual. 'Like I've nothing fucking better to be doing. I mean, he's really gonna come back here, isn't he? He's halfway to Alaska or the fucking Alps by now.'

'Sure he is. But The Cardinal said come check, and when The Cardinal says come check, we come check.' I didn't know this guy.

'You're so right.' Vincent's voice dripped with sarcastic

venom. 'Go check the back door. Look for a beer in the kitchen while you're at it, make us a cup of tea or something if you can't find one.' The back door! I'd left it ajar in case I needed to make a quick getaway.

'Vincent.' The voice of the second guy came a few seconds later, softer, urgent. 'It's open. Someone's been here.'

'Fuck.' A long pause. 'OK. We'll search the house. You take the bottom, I'll take the top. Be careful. The fucker could still be here. You see anything, shoot. Don't fuck around with this guy.'

'You think we should call this in?'

'You don't think we can handle a fuck like this by ourselves?'

'We should let them know.'

'Know what? That the door's open? Hell, it could be a bum or a kid. We'll search the place first. If we find him, we'll kill him and call then.'

He came up the stairs slowly, flicking on the light as he did. The moron. I'd never known why Tasso kept Vincent around. He was dumb, plain and simple. If I got out of here alive, it would be thanks to his stupidity.

Vincent checked the bathroom first, then my bedroom, the spare room, then the closet. Finally he reached rainbow's end. Turned on the light and looked around. I held my breath and acted like a corpse. 'Shit,' he muttered, coming forward. He must be on to me! I tried to spring away but found myself paralysed. I couldn't move. He was going to walk up and kill me and there wasn't a thing I . . .

He sat on the edge of the bed.

'Fuck,' he said, lighting a cigarette. 'I could be out getting laid. Fucking Ford. One of these days . . .'

I didn't deserve this much luck. I'd screwed up by coming here and by rights should pay dearly for my mistake. But Fate can be kind occasionally.

I gripped the jagged shard, ignoring the pain, and sat up swiftly. I could see Vincent through the thin fabric of the sheets, so I didn't waste time throwing them off. He must have got a shock, seeing those harmless bedclothes spring to life.

I clamped one hand over Vincent's mouth, jerked his head back, jabbed the other forward and drove the point of the makeshift dagger into his throat. It snapped in half. I dug the second shard in and whipped my hand from left to right several times. Vincent's body writhed but it was too late. His warm blood gushed like swarming locusts from some biblical breach in the heavens, soaking his chest, the bed, the covers, me. Within seconds he was through struggling for all eternity.

I'd killed him.

My first kill. I'd thought about it for such a long time. I'd wondered, nights when I couldn't sleep, how I'd react when I finally crossed this bridge. Now I knew.

I pushed the covers off and raised a hand. Touched my mouth and felt a smile. I *liked* it. Killing suited me. This was what I was born for. In that moment I knew, whatever else I may be – whoever – I was a killer first and foremost. The Cardinal would have been proud.

I rolled off the bed, took Vincent's gun from his limp hand and made for the door, picking up another piece of vase along the way. I didn't want to use the gun unless I had to — too noisy.

I left the room, the sticky smell of death wafting after me. I meant to wait at the top of the stairs and knife Vincent's buddy as he came up. Then I could take my time deciding what to do with the one outside.

That plan went out the window because the man was coming up the stairs as I crossed the landing. Thanks to the light, he got a clear view of me. He began firing immediately, shouting something incoherent. But he panicked and his shots missed by a wide margin.

I stood my ground, let his bullets whistle by, took a bearing and fired. A duck in a bath would have stood a better chance than the unfortunate guy on the stairs. My first bullet ripped a fifth hole in his heart. The second tore his eyes out, smashed his skull and sent him flying backwards.

I rushed down the stairs, jumped the body at the base, knowing I had only seconds to act. I raced out the front door, into the street. The driver was out of the car when I burst into sight, crouched behind it. He fired as soon as he saw me. I dived for the thin bushes in front and came up shooting. My first bullet tore into the car inches from his head. The second must have grazed his left ear. The third would have been the killer.

But there wasn't a third. I pulled the trigger and hit an empty chamber. That asshole Carell had come without a fully loaded weapon! The driver smiled and walked out in front of the car, taking his time, knowing I was trapped. I glanced around, weighing my options. I could duck back inside the house, but it was open ground and he'd have ample time to put a couple of shots into my back. Or I could wait until he was closer and rush him. Neither option looked promising.

I was making up my mind when another gun disrupted the quiet of the night. It fired three times. The body of the driver jerked briefly, then dropped. I got to my feet, unable to believe my luck. It must be Margaret, come to my rescue. I looked at the cab. She was still inside, crouched down, only the tip of her head in sight, the windows rolled up. It couldn't have been her. Then who . . .

A motorbike kicked into life and pulled up in front of me. An unhelmeted Paucar Wami grinned and saluted. 'We must stop meeting like this.'

I stared at the bike, the driver, then the dead man. 'You saved me,' I said.

'I was asked to.'

'By who?'

'Your blind friends.'

'The ones in the robes?'

'Yes.'

'Why?'

He shrugged. 'They didn't say. Just gave me the address and said you might need me.'

'Why did you come?' I asked. 'Why go out of your way to help me?'

He smiled. 'Like I said, you interest me. Luck, Capac Raimi.'

With that he disappeared into the night.

I made my way back to the car, numb, head spinning. Margaret had already started the engine. I climbed in and stared at the useless gun in my hands.

'Who was that?' she asked.

'Drive,' I told her. 'Take me outside the city. Drop me at a train station. Any will do. You pick.'

'But who was –'

'You don't really want to know, do you?'

She looked at my face in the mirror. Glanced at the body in the road. Pulled away. 'Don't reckon I do,' she muttered and said no more as we sped through the dark.

I unzipped the money belt at last and examined the ticket. *Sonas* was the name. I held the stub between two reverent fingers. *Sonas*. It didn't mean anything. I'd expected bells to sound, memories to flash through my mind at the speed of light, everything to come back in the snap of a wasp's wing. But Sonas could have been the name of an Eskimo's ranch for all it meant to me.

As dawn broke above us, Margaret dropped me off about twenty miles outside the city. 'You ever need a lift again,' she said, 'get out your thumb and hitch!'

'Here,' I said and gave her an extra roll of hundreds. 'That's for sticking by me. You could have fled and nobody would have blamed you.'

'Thanks,' she said and looked me over. 'You've got blood down your front.' I realized I looked like something out of an abattoir. 'I've got a coat in the back. I use it when the weather's bad. You can take it if you like. It'll cover you until you find something better.'

'You're sure?'

'Mister, for what you paid tonight, you could have my dress and panties.'

The station was preparing itself for the morning rush when I entered. A tired man in his sixties swept the floor lifelessly. His uniform was crumpled and worn, like his face. He looked up as I passed, sniffed, returned to his work. A waitress was raising the grille of a café.

'We ain't open yet,' she snarled as I approached. 'Come back in ten.'

The newsagent was the only cheerful soul. He smiled, rambled on about the weather, studied my battered face with concern. I bought some chocolate, a couple of papers, a magazine and a map. I asked him about train times. When he was through talking, I thanked him, tipped and left. Cleaned my face in the washroom, bought a cup of coffee in the café, then purchased a ticket and caught a ride.

The train chugged west. I studied the map, trying to find Sonas. I had to search hard. It lay to the southwest of the city, about two hundred miles off. A small town like any of a million others.

I spent the day traversing the country. I'd hop on one train, go north, get off at random, head east, west again, then south. I avoided crowds, let busy trains pass, found the quietest compartments in those I boarded. I bought a new suit at one stopover, along with a pair of dark glasses and a hat to hide the worst of my bruises. I hid behind newspapers for hours on end.

I knew it was a waste of time. I wasn't being followed, so I had no one to throw off the scent. The Cardinal's men didn't need to track me — they'd be waiting for me at the other end. He knew where I came from and that I'd have to head back. The longer I took, the more men he could post. I'd be shot the minute I stepped off the train. I should just go and get the whole thing over with or forget about it all and flee for real.

But I couldn't forget, and moving around like this gave me a sense of working to thwart my destiny. I needed the distraction of the game. It gave me hope.

I thought about waiting. Leave things for a few weeks, wait for the flames to flicker out. There was no hurry. Staying away would give my body time to heal, my mind time to clear. I could formulate a plan, maybe get some more of my memory back. Nothing was compelling me to rush to a certain death.

But The Cardinal's patience was legendary. He might have none where personal dealings were involved, but on a broader scale there was no better man for sitting on a fence, waiting for things to swing his way. His talk of ruling the world proved that — he was prepared to wait beyond death to make his dreams come true. Hanging around in small towns and villages would be of no benefit. I could leave it for months, years, and the end result would be the same. I could walk into Sonas an old man, seventy or eighty, and there'd be a young punk waiting to put a dozen bullets through my head. Nobody could beat The Cardinal.

I caught some sleep, stretched across uncomfortable seats, waking every time the train lurched or jumped. People tried to enter my carriage several times. They all stopped, paused, then walked on when they saw me. I was grateful for the solitude.

I thought about the two lives I'd ended. One by hand, one with a gun. I'd enjoyed the stabbing more but there was a certain thrill in shooting a man, a voyeuristic pleasure in being able to stand back and murder from afar. You felt a bit like a god with a gun in your hand, dispensing death as you saw fit.

I boarded one of the night trains which passed through Sonas. It was twenty-four hours after my showdown with The Cardinal. I was still alive, courting death, moving another voluntary step closer to the grave. The grim reaper must have been shaking his head in disbelief, muttering, 'Some guys just don't know how to quit.'

The train was quiet, no more than a smattering of passengers. I found one of the many empty compartments and made myself comfortable. Leant over to close the curtains and stopped. The night was pitch black, so the window was almost as good as a mirror. I took my glasses and hat off, laid them on the chair to my right, and stared at my reflection, tiredly wondering when the madness was going to end.

The face before me, which The Cardinal had split, cut and ruined for good. The broken nose and raked cheeks. The chewed ear. The puffy lips and tender cheeks.

It had healed itself.

A bit of bruising round the eyes. The nose slightly crooked. A couple of small scabs. Otherwise good as new. I checked my hands. Knuckles which had been torn and busted — fine. Palms which had been lanced by the shards of the vase — pure. I stood and jumped on the spot. No pain or the creaking of broken ribs. All my bones were whole. My flesh was clean. It was like I'd never been in a fight at all, as if the savage battle in Party Central had occurred only in my mind.

uma raimi

I didn't alight in Sonas. I wasn't about to make things too easy for my pursuers. Let the bastards work for their money. I peered out of the window as the train rolled through the unexpectedly large station. No sign of a welcoming committee. They were probably waiting outside, covering the exits. I couldn't expect everyone to behave as foolishly as Vincent had.

I got off at the next station and hired a cab to Sonas. 'I don't know why you didn't get the train,' the driver grumbled. 'It's just one stop further.' Some people don't know a good thing even when it bites them on the ass.

He dropped me in the town centre and made his way back home. I absorbed the surroundings. A milk van passed. The driver tipped his cap to me and I nodded in reply. A cat skulked past, sparing me a dirty glance as it skirted around my feet. Otherwise the streets were undisturbed. It was quiet as a grave. I'd spent so much time in the city, I'd forgotten places like this existed, towns without hookers, shift workers, gangsters and clubbing teenagers all heading home in the early hours of the morning, where police sirens didn't blare at any given hour. Out here, with the sun blinking over the horizon, I felt out of place. The quiet was eerie. I didn't like it.

I walked around, hat and glasses shading my face from the dawn light. I tried not to gaze at my reflection in windows as I passed. I didn't want to see that unblemished face. Didn't want to think about what it might mean.

Memories flooded back as I slipped from one street to another. I recognized landmarks. There was the sports store where I bought my first tennis racket. I'd been a kid, six or seven. I could feel it even now, the wooden handle, the tight plastic strings.

The cinema. Scene of many a teenage sexual encounter. My first kiss, tucked away in the legendary back row. Here was where I cupped virgin breasts, where a girl first let my hand slide up from her knee without resistance.

That small corner shop. We used to steal candy when I was nine or ten, me and some bigger kids. I got caught. I had glimpses of my parents shouting, my father taking a belt to me.

There was where I bought my lawnmower, shears and hoses for watering the grass in the hot summers. My hairdresser. A visit once every six weeks, regular as clockwork, except for a couple of teenage years when I grew it long. The park — days of eternal sun, running around in shorts, firing water-balloons at irate mothers, knotting the swings, smearing jam on the slides, not giving a damn if we were caught. The pool hall, cobwebbed lamps, rickety cues, chipped balls, pimply boys and girls mating clumsily, too young to get into the clubs.

It was a town of memories. I'd spent years here, most of my youth, all of my adult life, but although my memories were opening to me at last, I still couldn't piece everything together. Many buildings meant nothing and I couldn't remember the people in any great detail. I could see some friends and family faintly, might recognize them in the flesh if we passed, but I couldn't have described them if I'd been asked. It was like a jigsaw puzzle which had just been started — I could see a bit of the picture here, another chunk there, but I had no way of telling what it was working up to.

I saw more of *the woman*, the one person I had to track down, who'd hopefully be the catalyst for the rest to fall into place. She was in a lot of the memories, eating ice-cream with me in a mall, making out in the cinema, digging hard in the garden. But no name or blinding flash of revelation.

I wandered further from the town centre, out to the suburbs. I walked without thinking, following routes my feet remembered even though my mind had forgotten them. The further I went, the more familiar I felt. This was where I'd spent most of my time, beyond the hub, climbing giant trees, playing football in the open fields, growing, loving, living.

On the far outskirts, where the trees outnumbered the houses and streams cut wet paths across the land, where birds and squirrels reared their young, I found my home. It was a small white house, tucked away behind a plethora of bushes, shrubs and draping vines. A bungalow built from rough stones, capped by a newly tiled roof which jarred with my memories. The windows were round. The path to the house was sentried by tall hedges, as green as those on the path to Oz. The short wooden gate was topped with a floral arch. One might think it was the mouth of a tunnel similar to the one Alice fell down. How fitting — at the end of my bizarre journey, I'd come to a cottage from the pages of a fairy tale.

I lifted the latch and moved closer to the truth.

The brass knocker on the front door was oiled and it swung smoothly. I tapped gently, too softly to be heard. Drew back and knocked again, louder this time. It only occurred to me then that the occupant might be asleep. I checked my watch. Not yet a quarter to eight. Maybe I should . . .

I heard rustling. Moments later the door opened. A woman stood there, dressed casually, arms crossed, smiling curiously, not afraid of this early morning stranger. There was little to fear in Sonas.

It was *the woman*. I recognized her immediately. The sight of her in the flesh sent a shock wave through me, a blow worth any ten of The Cardinal's.

'Can I help you?' she asked brightly.

I raised a quaking hand and removed my hat and glasses.

Her mouth dropped and her eyes widened. She backed away from me, gasping, mouthing the word, 'No!', shielding her face with a hand, like Macbeth trembling at the sight of Banquo's ghost.

I followed and reached out to touch and calm her. She jerked away from my fingers and sank into a rocking chair by a huge iron stove. Her eyes were burning question marks. Her lips shook from the force of a thousand unaskable questions. I closed the door. Walked over. Crouched and touched her knee. She gasped again, shied away, then brought one of her own hands forward and carefully, fearfully, touched mine, like someone stroking a rattlesnake.

'I'm not going to hurt you,' I said kindly. 'I didn't want to startle you. But you know me, don't you? You know who I am?'

'*Muh-Muh-Martin?*' Her voice was a wheeze. 'Is it yuh-you?'

I thought about it. 'Martin.' Tossed the word around, testing, liking the sound, feeling it fit. 'Yes, I'm . . .' And then there was a surname to go with it and I knew that much about myself at least, at last. 'Martin . . . Robbins? No. Martin Robinson. I'm Martin Robinson. And this is my house. I remember it now. And you . . .' I stared.

The woman stared back. She touched me again, firmer this time, moving up my arm, my elbow, biceps, shoulder, finally running the tips of her fingers over my face, brushing my lips, my nose, my eyelashes. She smiled hesitantly, starting to believe this might be real and not a dream.

'Martin? It's really you? But I thought . . . all this time . . . oh my god. *Martin!*' She threw herself on me, dragging me to the ground much as Ama Situwa had on the stairs of Party Central, but this woman wasn't interested in sex. She only wanted to feel me and make sure I was real, half-expecting me to vanish.

'Martin. Martin. Martin.' She repeated my name over and over. It became a mantra. She said it as she touched me, pinched me, felt my legs, my arms, my chest and back. As she caressed my face, gazing into my eyes through a veil of tears, trembling, crying, laughing. As she hugged and kissed my neck, pulling me to her, holding me in a grip as if she never planned to let go of me again. 'Martin. Martin. Martin.'

'And you,' I whispered, trembling as the memories flooded back. 'You're *my wife*,' I said wonderingly and for a long time I could say nothing more.

The stove was the only source of heat. We'd used it for everything, cooking, boiling water, keeping the place warm on cold winter nights. We'd argued about it occasionally, especially on frosty nights when the roof was leaking and gusts of wind were having their chilly way wherever they wished. Dee wanted to tear it out and get a modern oven and heaters, but I loved it. My grandparents and parents had relied on that old stove and it gave me a strong link to the past. I'd agreed, reluctantly, to upgrade when we had kids, but as long as it was just the two of us, the house would stay the way it had been for the last seventy years.

Some nights, curled up in front of the range, Dee and I would pretend we were animals and lie there for hours, saying nothing, touching, kissing, feeling, being.

Dee. Short for Deborah. She had to tell me. I couldn't recall it myself.

I raised the lid of the kettle, checked the bubbling water, moved it to a cooler corner of the stove. Dee loved a brew first thing in the morning. It had always been my job to make the tea, often bringing it in on a tray, breakfast in bed, a spot of quick loving if we had the time.

Dee was still in the rocking chair, hands in her lap, eyes fixed on my every movement. She'd always been a pale creature and now, so early in the morning, not yet recovered from the shock, she was white enough to put Caspar to shame.

I walked around the room, studying the ornaments, the hangings, imitation paintings, a Gary Larson calendar. Dee loved Larson. The house had never been named by my grandparents, their children or me. Dee soon put that matter right. *The Far Side*, she called it, loving the name, the house, me.

I poured the tea. She sipped, peering at me over the rim of the cup. Grimaced. 'You forgot the sugar,' she reprimanded me.

'You take sugar?' I frowned.

'Oh. That's right. I only began after you . . . left.' She hesitated on the word. 'Life was bitter enough. I needed something sweet. These days I can't touch a cup without a couple of spoonfuls.' She glanced down into the mug, swirled its dark contents, looked up and smiled. 'I thought you'd disappear. I thought you were a dream and I had to keep my eyes on you, like with a leprechaun. I used to dream of you so much. Sometimes they'd be nice dreams, memories of you as you were. Other times you'd be a monster — you'd creep out of the shadows and maul me.'

'Which do you think I am now?'

'I don't know.' Her eyes betrayed her fears and hopes. 'When I saw you, so real, so vivid, I thought you must be a nightmare. You were always more substantial in the dark dreams. Now, seeing you walking, whistling, brewing the tea . . . Martin, what happened? Where have you been? Why stay away for so long? Why come back now, without a –'

'Dee. Stop.' I knelt and tipped two spoons of sugar into her cup. 'No questions. Later, yes. Not now. I've got to hear *your* story first. I can't remember all this. A lot has come back but much is still dark. You told me your name is Dee but I have no memory of that. If you'd said Sandra, Lynda or Mary I wouldn't have known any different. I know we were married but I don't know when. I know we loved each other but I don't know why or how it ended. I want you to tell me who I am, who I was, what I did, what I was like, how I lived. How I disappeared.'

'OK. But not until you tell me where you've been. I don't have to know any more right now. But that much I need.'

I thought about it. 'A year ago, I got off a train in a city and went to live with a man who said he was my uncle. I joined his business.' I chose my words carefully. She might know more than she was letting on, but I didn't think so. And if she didn't know about The Cardinal and my education in the ways of crime and death, so much the better. 'I've been there ever since. I can remember everything from that day but nothing before. Little,' I amended. 'For a long while, I didn't know anything was wrong. When I realized I was missing a past, I found an old train ticket and followed it here. That's all I can tell you. For now.'

'Amnesia?' she asked.

'I think so. Delusion too. I'm not sure who I was here, but I'm pretty certain Martin Robinson bore little in common with Capac Raimi, the man I was in the city. Was I a bad man, Dee? Was I involved in shady deals?'

'No!' She was startled. 'God, no. Nothing like that.'

'You're sure?'

'Certain.' She began rocking gently, composing herself. It always helped her think better if she was rocking. 'You weren't born in this house but you grew up here. This was the family home, the Robinson castle. Your parents treated you like a young prince, but they reared you to be polite and compassionate. You were a cute kid.

'You're eight months older than me but we were in the same classes at school and our parents were good friends. You used to make fun of my hair and clothes – my mother had terrible taste, buying outfits you wouldn't put on a doll – while I'd mock your buck-teeth.'

'I had buck-teeth?' Not remembering my childhood, I assumed I'd always looked this way. It hadn't crossed my mind that I must have changed dramatically over the years, like anybody else.

'Not really,' she said. 'A bit protuberant, but you were very self-conscious. A few Bugs Bunny jokes usually had you in tears. We went through that pre-teen phase where we wanted nothing to do with each other. I hung out with the girls, you with the boys. We hardly saw each other for three or four years. At fourteen we discovered each other again and were soon going steady. We got engaged when we were seventeen.'

She shrugged and rocked a little faster. 'Crazy, I guess, but we were in love and wanted to prove it would last forever. At least we didn't rush off and marry. We agreed to wait until after college. We were going to different colleges and you told me years later that you expected us to split within a couple of months. That's why you proposed — you didn't think you'd actually have to go through with it.'

'No,' I laughed. 'I couldn't have been that shallow.'

'Oh, you were.' She laughed too. 'But we didn't split. We dated a couple of other people on the sly but neither of us felt comfortable doing that, and every time we met we fell in love again. So, figuring it really was true love and there was no cure for it, we tied the knot a couple of months after graduation and became Mr and Mrs Robinson.' She pulled a face. 'That was the only bad bit, being *Mrs Robinson*. They even noted it in the paper when they printed our wedding picture, saying you'd better be careful if you ever saw Dustin Hoffman hanging around.'

I tried to recall our wedding day, picturing Dee in her dress, imagining a sunny sky and the joy I must have felt. But nothing came back to me. 'I bet our parents were happy,' I said.

She sighed and I knew it was bad news. 'Your father died when you were six.' It should have been a huge blow, but since I could remember nothing of him, it meant little. 'That was when you began taking tennis seriously.'

'Tennis?' I said eagerly.

'You were great. Your father taught you while he was alive. When he died, you threw yourself into it. He used to say you'd be bigger than Borg and you were determined to prove him right. You considered going pro but in the end you chose to concentrate on your studies. You didn't want to bank on a career where the best peaked by their early twenties. You kept playing, but for fun. You won a lot of amateur contests over the years.'

That explained my performance back in the city. 'And my mother?' I asked.

'She died when you were at college. During your second year. Her heart. She'd had problems for years. That's one of the reasons we married so soon — you had a house for us to move into and you were all alone in the world. Can't you remember *any*thing about them?'

I shook my head. 'Just names. Mother. Father. Ideas. Not people. So we moved in here and lived happily together?'

'Yes. We'd argue sometimes, about the roof – it was

thatched – and the stove and getting new windows and doors. It needed lots of work but you were reluctant to make changes. You were sentimental and wanted to keep everything the way it was.' She sipped at her tea. 'I stayed here after you . . . went. At first because I didn't want to be disloyal. Later because I grew to love the place. It grows on you. You told me it would, that one day I'd be as loath to alter things as you were. I scoffed but you were right.

'We both worked in town,' she went on. 'Walked most days, cycled if we were lazy. We didn't have a car. Neither of us ever learnt to drive. I always hated cars, and you . . . well, your father died in a car crash. I loved our walks, early in the morning, back again in the evening at the end of a busy day.'

'What did we work at?' I asked.

'I worked in a travel agent's. You were a teacher.'

I blinked slowly. From Mr Chips to Al Capone? That was some trip. I could see now why I kept picturing loads of kids, but I had problems imagining myself as a teacher. Then again, I *had* been patient and understanding with Conchita. 'What did I teach?' I asked.

'Physical Education. You could have taught at a university if you'd wanted, but you preferred younger pupils. Less stress, no campus politics. We remained like that for years, happy, not moving, not changing. We hoped for children of our own, barrels of them, but we weren't in any rush. We'd married young and wanted some time by ourselves before we started a family. We were talking seriously about them when . . .' Her face clouded over and she coughed.

'We were going to build an extension – this place is too small for more than three people. We'd started checking out contractors and were on the verge of . . . then you . . .' She'd been avoiding this part as long as she could. She'd shied away every time she'd come close, refusing to deal with it until the last possible moment. That time had arrived. There could be no more skipping over my disappearance. It was painful, obviously, but I had to know how The Cardinal got his paws on me. 'Do you really want me to go on?' she croaked.

'Yes. I have to know, Dee. Everything.'

'You can't remember on your own?' She looked at me, pleading to be spared. 'Think, Martin. You must be able to remember. Something this important . . .' I shook my head hopelessly. 'Very well.' She sighed, resigned. 'Like I say, we used to walk to town nearly every day. In the winter we'd wrap ourselves up in furs and walk in like a couple of Eskimos. It wasn't winter that day but it was cold, so we wore light furs. Kissed goodbye when we parted, like we always did. I headed for my office and you went to school. You had a gymnastics class in the third period. You liked gym, especially the vaults . . .' Her voice cracked and tears leaked from the corners of her eyes. 'Please, Martin, don't make me go on.'

'You must.' I squeezed her hands, trying to be a comforting husband. 'You've come too far to stop. It'll only be waiting for us if you do. Let's get it out of the way, once and for all.'

She took a breath, blew her nose, wiped the tears away and went on without a pause to the finale. 'You liked to show off in the gym. At the end of most lessons you'd give the kids a display, go through your tumbling routines – you copied them from the silent comedies we loved to watch – and thrill them with your prowess on the bars and ropes. You'd always end on the vaulting horse. You'd take a long run, turn in the air, land on it with your hands and push yourself off. The kids always wanted to try but you wouldn't let them — it was too dangerous.

'That day, one of the children played a joke. Nothing nasty or vicious. The kids liked you. They were always playing jokes. You never came down heavy on them. A boy called

Steve Greer came up with the idea. He greased the top of
the vault. He thought you'd slide off and land on your butt.
He thought it would be a great laugh. You might have too,
if things turned out differently.

'You approached the horse in your usual manner, cocky
and strutting, giving the kids a laugh. You bounced off the
springboard, high in the air, twisting your body a hundred
and eighty degrees, so your legs were pointing straight up.
You put your hands on the wooden top, meaning to push
away. Only this time your hands slipped out from under you
and you crashed straight to the floor.

'Your head hit the vaulting horse on the way. Your neck
snapped. The kids said it sounded like a gunshot. They didn't
move your body – they'd seen enough episodes of *ER* – only
covered you with a blanket and sent for the nurse. But it
was too late.'

She stopped rocking, stopped talking, almost stopped
breathing. Her face was ashen. I held her cold, limp hands.
'Is that where I went missing?' I asked. 'In the hospital?'

She stared at me as if I'd said something obscene. *'What?'*
Her voice was ice.

'In the hospital. Was that where I disappeared?'

She blinked as if coming out of a dream and seeing me
for the first time. 'The hospital?' she repeated. 'You're not
listening, Martin.' She laughed, a sickening, chilling snicker.
'You broke your neck. You didn't disappear from anywhere.'
She began rocking again. Turned her face towards the wall.
'You died. You broke your neck and died.' She looked back,
her mouth torn between a sneer and a cry, her eyes wide
and crazy. 'You're dead, Martin,' she whispered.

I stood by the window and gazed out. I was looking for
snipers in the trees, spies behind the bushes, but the country-
side was clear as far as the eye could see. If I'd been traced

to Sonas, the search hadn't stretched this far. Unless of course the cottage was bugged.

I turned from the view and took my seat again. The room was icy cold, in spite of the heat from the stove. Dee's face was distant, numb. 'There must have been a mistake,' I said.

She smiled crookedly. 'How? You died. The doctors confirmed it. I saw your body myself. Hell, I wept over it long enough.'

'They were wrong. I didn't die. I was injured, that's all.'

'I saw you,' she insisted. 'Your eyes were open, your neck bent. No heartbeat, no breathing, no movement. You broke your neck and you died. No mistake.'

'There must have been!' I barked. 'Look at me — I'm alive. They buried somebody else, or I was taken before the burial, or I got out afterwards. Something bad happened. Something foul. But I didn't die.'

'Then what? *What?*' Her face was pale, her lips tight. She sat waiting for my answer. I didn't have any but I could tell she wouldn't twitch until I came up with one, so I thought hard.

'Can you bring me a mirror?'

She tilted her head at the unusual request but fetched one without asking any questions. I examined my face. The bruising was gone and my nose was straight. No cuts or scabs. Pristine. 'Does my face look alright to you?'

'How do you mean?'

'It's not cut or bruised?'

'Of course it isn't.'

'I was in a fight yesterday. I got the shit knocked out of me. I was a mess. Less than thirty-six hours later, I'm fine, like I'd never been touched.' I put the mirror down and stared at her. An idea was forming. 'Regenerative powers,' I said, grasping at straws.

'Come again?' she blinked.

'Maybe I have healing powers. I broke my neck and was medically dead, but I put myself back together and healed on my own.'

'That's crazy.'

'I know. But I'm here. How else could it happen?' Now I was the one asking an unanswerable question and she struggled with it.

'How did you get out of the grave?' she asked. 'If you healed, why didn't we discover it before we buried you? How did you escape? Did you claw through the coffin and tunnel upwards?'

'Someone got me out. They knew about me. Somebody discovered my powers, waited, jumped in when the time was right.' The Cardinal would know things like that. His files in Party Central, his interest in the extraordinary. That dream he'd told me about, when he saw a man who couldn't be injured, who walked through hails of bullets unscathed – maybe that wasn't a dream at all, but a clue to test my memory. Maybe this explained why The Cardinal had taken an interest in me. 'It's the only answer,' I said, halfway convinced. 'There are no alternatives.'

'There are,' she said softly.

'What?'

She crossed her hands and studied them. 'Do you want to get really crazy?'

'Tell me what you're thinking, Dee.'

'OK.' She began rocking. 'You could be a ghost.'

'You can't be serious.'

'I told you it was crazy.'

'Dee, I'm . . . Feel me! Do I feel like a ghost?'

'I don't know,' she said. 'Maybe ghosts are solid, indistinguishable from other people. You could be a zombie, a ghoul, some kind of vampire.'

I stared at her. 'You believe that?' I asked incredulously.

'No. I'm just giving you alternatives. You want more? I can go on.'

'Please do.'

'Aliens spirited you out of the grave and reanimated you. A mad doctor dug you up and performed his Frankenstein trick. A liquid seeped through and brought you back to life. You're a clone — scientists took grafts of Martin Robinson and built a new one.'

I began laughing but Dee didn't join in. 'That's ridiculous,' I said. 'Aliens? Clones? Zombies? We've got to be sensible. I'm here, I'm real, I'm alive. We have to find out why and how. We need to examine this seriously. I've spent a year living as somebody else. I need to know how I became Capac Raimi.'

'Maybe you didn't. Maybe you imagined the last year.'

'Dee . . .' I groaned.

'I'm serious. I threw the other stuff at you to show how crazy your own notion was. But now I mean it. You spend a year suffering with amnesia, don't even know you've forgotten your past, and nobody else notices, they don't ask questions or wonder why you haven't any identification? *This* is real, Martin. Your life, your death, our marriage, your past. You were a teacher, a tennis amateur, a good man, a loving husband. That's real. What were you in the city?'

I paused, thought about lying, then confessed. 'I was a gangster.'

She laughed out loud and I flushed, face reddening. 'You wouldn't harm a fly! But you loved watching gangster movies like *The Godfather, Once Upon a Time in America* and those old James Cagney and Humphrey Bogart films. How about this — you didn't die, the doctors called it wrong and you revived. But you didn't go to the city or become a gangster. That's all a delusion. Your face is clear? That's because you haven't been in a fight. That was part of the dream-world you built.

'Where have you been this last year? I don't know. Possibly

wandering in a daze, slowly returning to your senses, mentally fighting your way through hordes of gangsters, subconsciously working through your confusion, trying to lead yourself back here. No big mystery if this is the truth, no super powers, nothing supernatural, no conspiracies. You survived a lethal accident, lived in a fantasy fugue and came back when your brain repaired itself. Does your life as Capac Raimi seem real now? Were the people normal? Do things fit into place when you train the spotlight of reason on them?'

I thought of the strange fall of rain. Uncle Theo's death and how I was spared. Conchita's conflicting body and face. Ama on the stairs, diving into sex with a stranger. The Cardinal building an empire out of guts and coincidences. Paucar Wami, coldly merciless in a way only a fictional character could be. People disappearing, vanishing like they'd never existed. Real? Normal? Feasible?

Not even remotely.

'But the grave,' I said, desperately clinging to the only reality I could clearly remember. If I let the last year be stripped from me, I'd have no real sense of a past at all. 'How do you explain the grave? How did I get out?'

'That's a problem. I think . . .' She began to smile. 'No, it's not. You were on display in the coffin the night before the funeral. They closed the lid after the service but didn't tighten the screws. You must have got out during the night, stumbled out of the chapel unseen, staggered away, confused, lost. I don't know how you got out of town without being seen, how you walked with a broken neck, how you scraped by over the following months. But it explains things, Martin. It does.' Her eyes were shining. She was excited. She thought she'd cracked it, that she could truly welcome me back now and pick up where we left off. But I wasn't convinced.

'Wouldn't the bearers have noticed the difference in the weight?'

'It was a heavy coffin,' Dee said. 'The bearers were young, your friends. Only one of them had ever carried a coffin before. They wouldn't have known about weights.' Dee grew more confident with every word and I was beginning to think she was right. A dream world, a fantasy . . .

'The cemetery,' I said. 'Is it far from here?'

'A couple of miles.'

'I want to go.'

'To dig up the coffin?' She frowned. 'I don't think we should do that.'

'Why not?'

'That's desecration. We could end up in prison. Besides, it's *your* grave. I don't think I could dig up –'

'But it's not.' I clutched her hands. 'If you're right, Dee – and I think you must be – that coffin's empty. We won't be doing anything wrong, digging up an empty grave.'

'I'm not sure . . .' She was repulsed by the idea.

'It's the only way to be certain,' I said. 'When we prove that it's empty, we can deal with this. It'll have to be brought to the surface eventually — if we don't do it now, the police will when they find out I'm still alive. Let's beat them to the punch and use this time to prepare ourselves. Maybe I'll be able to trace my steps from there. It might jog my memory some more.'

She hesitated before finally, reluctantly, nodding her head. 'You're right. We have to.' She looked out the window. 'But we'd better wait till night. These things are easier when it's dark.' As if she'd been graverobbing all her life.

The more we discussed it, the more I warmed to Dee's theory. I'd lost control of my senses and dreamed my year in the city. Like that silly season of *Dallas* years ago, when they wrote off an entire series as a dream. But it had seemed so real. If I'd been prey to sporadic fits, slipping in and out of my constructed reality, like a schizophrenic coming apart at the seams . . .

But I could account for every day, every character, every meeting. It was a weird world, granted, and I'd acted strangely, but it had been as real as this one. No reality breakdowns. Not until today when the marks of my fight with The Cardinal faded.

I studied Dee, turning the theory on its head. Was *she* real? Maybe this place was the dream, a trick of the mind. Maybe The Cardinal had hit me harder than I thought. I could be lying on his carpet, playing out this scene in my mind as the Troops carted me away to finish the job. That's the trouble with picking at the threads of reality — the fabric tends to unravel and leave you floundering in a den of infinite threads, not one of which you can trust or cling to.

We spent the day exploring our past. Dee pulled out old photos of a young boy with my face, my parents, us as teenagers, my friends, shots of me in school both as student and teacher. I found touching helped me more than hearing and seeing. When I felt objects – sets of keys, trophies, diplomas, books – I remembered events and feelings associated with them. They reinforced the physical reality of this town, this house, this person — Martin Robinson.

'What if the coffin's not empty?' I asked.

'Don't think about it,' Dee replied.

'I have to. What if it's occupied?'

She stopped sorting through albums. 'It has to be empty,' she said. 'You can't be in two places at the same time. I don't buy any of that ghost or clone crap I was spouting earlier. You didn't die and weren't buried.'

Her logic was faultless. 'But if there –'

'Martin!' She slammed an album shut and glared. 'Don't talk about it. It won't happen. Things are tense enough as

they are. You'll drive us both mad if you keep this up. There'll
be no body.'

'I hope you're right,' I muttered.

'Martin,' she said firmly, 'I can't be wrong.'

We left for the graveyard at ten. The walk to the cemetery
was nerve-wracking. The night was black as my memory.
We walked apart at first, awkward around each other, not
wanting to touch. But after half a mile we closed the gap,
drawing warmth from the union. The shovels were heavy,
growing heavier with each step. Our breath rose above us
and mingled in the air, trailing in our wake. Owls hooted
and small creatures scurried to the sides of the road.

We encountered no other people. We didn't expect to, not
at this time of night, so close to the discotheque of the dead.
Kids were in bed, parents were dozing in front of televisions,
lovers were making the darkness their romantic own. Only
vampires, werewolves and graverobbers were at large on a
night like this.

'This reminds me of the walks we used to take,' Dee said.

'We strolled out *here*?'

'No, silly. But we'd often walk around this time, when the
weather was good. We liked the solitude, the feeling of being
the only humans alive.'

'Where we're going,' I said, 'we will be.'

'Yes.' It was a joke but she didn't laugh.

The gates were closed, cold metal barriers between the
worlds of the living and the dead. Ornamental gargoyles
adorned either post and I felt them glaring at us as we scaled
the low wall to the side. We jumped into soggy earth which
squelched under our shoes, and long wet grass which damp-
ened the hems of our trousers and tickled our ankles unpleas-
antly, like the caressing fingers of the dead. Slugs were sliding
slickly through the grass and every time I accidentally

squelched one I shivered. My foot snagged on a stone and I half fell. My hands hit the ground and I snatched them back quickly from the chill earth. I wiped my palms on my trousers, over and over, but they didn't seem to warm or dry.

Dee's hand fell softly onto my shoulder and I jumped nervously. I turned and chastised her with a frown. She smiled weakly. 'Sorry,' she whispered. 'Are you OK?'

I wiped my hands one last time. 'I'm fine. Come on. Show me where it is.'

We found one of the many crisscrossing gravel paths and slipped past monuments, headstones, statues. I had the sense that stone heads were swivelling slowly, following us. I heard rustling, though there were no bushes nearby. The clouds parted briefly and all manner of shadows leapt to life. I glanced at Dee. She was trembling but her face was grim and she barely paused before moving on.

'This is it.' Dee stopped at an ordinary headstone. I could have made out the name and dates if I'd bent, but I didn't. Instead I rolled up my sleeves, spat on my hands and took hold of the shovel. I looked to Dee for approval. She was staring at the headstone. One of her hands reached towards it, but then she yanked it back. She saw I was waiting, let out a shallow breath and nodded.

I drove the shovel into the earth, wincing at the sound it made, the way the earth seemed to suck on the blade. There was resistance all the way. The top layer of soil had been hardened by the long, cold nights. Further down it was stony, the soil full of pebbles and shale. Dee dug with me. It was a joint venture. We said nothing, digging like silent drones. We uprooted worms, slugs and insects of darkness on our way down. They squirmed blindly in the sods we tossed into the air, their world uprooted. Some dropped back into the pit, falling on our hands, in our hair, slithering down our necks. As I shook them off I vowed I'd get cremated when my time arrived.

Dee hit the lid first. The sound of her shovel striking the hard wood will stay with me to the end of my days. Nobody should have to hear that, especially when the coffin in question is (allegedly) their own. We shovelled frantically, wanting the torture to be over. We cleared the earth away, using our hands on the smaller clumps. Again I cursed myself, as I had in Theo's house, for not bringing a pair of gloves. But I was luckier than Dee — my fingernails were short, whereas hers were long and quickly collected semi-moons of the dark, damp soil.

The screws were hard to turn. I spent ages twisting and kicking at them. I cut my hands in several places, licked the blood away and studied the nicks in the thin night light. If my year in the city was a dream, I should carry these marks for the coming week. If, on the other hand, they'd cleared by morning . . .

In the end the screws yielded to my blows, kicks and curses. I sat back, panting. Dee looked at me. 'Scared?'

'Shitless,' I confirmed.

'Me too.' She was shivering. I pulled her close and gave her a hug. 'If there's something there . . .' she began.

'There won't be. You convinced me of that in the cottage, remember?'

'I know. And I believed it then. But out here, with the dead all around and the screws taken off . . . Martin, what if –'

'Don't say it. The time for talking and worrying is over.' I took a deep breath but it didn't help. 'Ready?' When she nodded wordlessly, I swung back the upper half of the coffin.

The skeleton inside grinned up at us.

Dee screamed and scrabbled backwards. She hit the wall of the freshly dug hole, turned and yanked herself out. I heard her being sick, sobbing, retching, tearing at the grass with her hands.

Having half expected it, I was calmer. I studied the rotting corpse, almost all bone now. The skull wasn't set as straight as it should have been — there was a crack in the neck. Its hands were crossed serenely across its chest. Scraps of hair clung to its scalp, refusing to accept the finality of the situation. Long, jagged nails. No eyes. Maggots feasting on the leftovers.

I abandoned the grave and stood over the gasping Dee. My face was blank, my hands were steady, my mind was set. Her theory had offered hope of a sane, happy conclusion, but I'd known all along it was pie in the sky.

She looked up, mouth slick with vomit and spit, eyes wild and dark. There was fear in those eyes, confusion and doubt. But mostly hatred for me, the thing with her husband's face but not her husband. 'What are you?' she hissed. 'What the fuck *are* you?'

'I don't know. Come back to the grave.'

'What?' she screeched.

'I want you to verify it.'

'You're crazy.'

'I need to know for sure. That could be anybody. You've got to identify him.'

'It's Martin's grave! Martin's coffin! Who the fuck do you *think* it is?'

'Please, Dee.' I offered her a friendly hand.

She slapped the hand away. 'Don't touch me,' she snarled. 'Don't come near me. You're not Martin. You're not even human. You can't be. You −'

I slapped her hard. I didn't like it but I couldn't have her cracking up. I'd been acting the part of Martin Robinson, but whoever I may once have been, I was now Capac Raimi, a gangster, henchman to The Cardinal. And I wanted answers.

She stared at me, horrified. 'You never hit me before,' she whispered.

'Things change. I asked nicely. Now I'm telling you. Check the body.'

Wordlessly, holding a hand to her cheek, she crawled across and stared into the grave again. She wept as she did and a couple of drops fell into the empty pits of the corpse's eyes. 'It's Martin,' she moaned.

'How do you know?'

'On his chest. His hands. He's wearing his wedding ring.'

'They could have put that on anybody. It doesn't prove anything.'

'That's Martin,' she said, hard this time. 'And if you ever say that it isn't –' She stood and glared at me, '– I'll kill you.'

I nodded wearily and sat by the grave, swinging my legs into the space below. I wasn't fearful or nervous anymore. I was once again the cold, detached, clinical operator who'd killed a pair of men two nights before. Something changed when I exposed the body. The possibility that I was Martin Robinson evaporated and, as if I was an actor quitting a role, I dropped the persona instantly.

'It could be a fake,' I murmured. 'If The Cardinal took my body, he'd fill the gap with an impostor. He likes to cover his tracks.'

'*The Cardinal?*'

'You know him?' I stared at her.

'I know *of* him.'

'You've never met?'

'Of course not.'

'Did I . . . did Martin ever meet him?'

She shook her head. 'Martin was a teacher. That's all.' She moved back from the grave and circled me. 'You really worked for The Cardinal?'

'Yes.'

'Then it was true what you said earlier? About being a gangster?' I nodded sharply. I wanted her to be quiet so I could think. 'Did you ever kill anybody?'

'Does it matter?' I asked.

'I want to know,' she snapped. 'You've stolen my dead husband's face. I want to know what you've been doing with it.'

'It's none of your business.' I rose and picked up the shovel. 'I'll leave in the morning. There's nothing for me here. I thought there'd be answers but all I've found are more riddles and questions.' I kicked a clod of earth into the grave and glanced at her. 'Are you going to help me fill this in?'

Her eyes were wide with disbelief. 'What sort of creature are you? You come to me looking like Martin. You drag me out here and make me desecrate his . . . my husband's grave!' Her voice was rising dangerously. 'And you think you can just walk away without . . . like nothing had . . .'

'What else can I do? I'm sorry I put you through this but I had no choice. I was in the dark and I needed to –'

'You think this is the end of it?' she interrupted. 'Think again, mister. I don't know who or what you are, but I'll be damned if I let you walk away like it's some game.'

'What do you want from me?' I sighed. 'What can I do to please you?'

'Stop talking like that for a start,' she growled. 'We've just dug up a grave, damn it! You could at least show some respect for the . . . the dead.' Her head fell and she sobbed into her chest. I did feel sorry for her. Truly. But inside I was burning. The fire had been building during my year in the city, slowly, gradually. When I killed Vincent and the other man, it flared. It dwindled when I wrestled with the mystery of my former identity but now it was burning fiercely again. Only the truth could quench this fire. Dee couldn't help me unlock the secrets of my past, so I had no time for her any more.

'Dee,' I said as patiently as I could, 'let's just fill in the grave and leave. We'll finish what we started, go home, put on the kettle, get a few hours sleep. In the morning I'll be gone and you can get back to your –'

'You're going nowhere,' she insisted.

'You want me to stay?' I asked uncertainly.

'Oh, you're staying,' she chuckled grimly. 'And in the morning – no, as soon as we leave here – we're going to the police.'

'That won't happen, Dee,' I told her flatly.

'You don't have a say in this. It's *my* husband you're masquerading as. I'm the one who decides. And I say we let the police handle this.'

'You don't mean that.'

'You can bet your eyes I do.' She was sure of herself now. She had a cause to keep her going. By focusing on that, she wouldn't have to deal with the wounds I'd reopened. In her head it was straightforward — go to the police, tell them all about me, and they'd sort things out, somehow, some way. Then she'd be happy.

'Dee,' I said, knowing what I must do but trying to find another way, not wanting to commit myself to a path of damnation from which I could never come back. 'If I leave right now and never return, will you let this drop?'

'Never,' she hissed. 'I'll follow you. I know where you'll be and who you'll be with. I'll send the police after you, drag you back and make you pay.' She was telling me too much. The Cardinal could have warned her of the need to play her cards close to her chest. But I had her husband's face. She hated me but she didn't think I posed a threat.

I nodded resignedly and looked down into the grave at the grinning skull. 'Dee,' I said dully in answer to an earlier question, 'I have.'

Her face crinkled. 'Have what?' she asked suspiciously.

'Killed,' I said.

Then I swung the blade of the shovel against the side of her head.

She reeled away from me, stunned, blood coursing from the cut to her scalp. I followed quickly and struck her again, full in the face, feeling bones crush. This time she collapsed. She tried to crawl away but I pinned her down and rolled her over onto her back.

She stared at me through disjointed eyes as I straddled her body and raised the shovel high. 'Martin . . .' she croaked, shaking her head, begging me not to strike. 'Martin . . . please . . .'

'No,' I said. 'Not Martin. *Capac.*'

And I drove the point of the shovel through her eyes and deep into her brain.

When she stopped spasming, I bundled her body into the grave, on top of her dead partner. They wouldn't both fit inside the coffin so I left it open. Working as fast as I could, I shovelled the earth back in, pausing only once to scoop up a sliver of brain and chuck it down for the maggots.

When all was done and I'd patted the earth flat, I stood back and studied the freshly dug grave. It would be obvious in daylight that it had been interfered with. But it wasn't conspicuous and it should be a few days before the police discovered evidence of the dark deed. By that stage I'd be long gone.

I hopped the wall easily this time and strode away briskly, tossing the shovels into a dark ditch. I felt no remorse, no sense of panic, anxiety or doubt. I'd done what I had to. That was all.

A few weeks earlier – even a few days – I would have been plagued by guilt. I'd have been thinking of my code of honour, my assertion that I'd never murder an innocent. I used to think I was a clean man in a dirty business. Now I knew better.

A man who might once have been Martin Robinson entered that dank home of the dead, but the one who left was definitely Capac Raimi. I no longer had any doubts about my identity. I was a killer, a monster, a man who could do anything and would. I was an Ayuamarcan, a cursed soul in league with The Cardinal. I'd thought that, beneath it all, in spite of what I did, I was good. But in truth I was as evil as they came, as cold-hearted as The Cardinal, Paucar Wami or any other you might care to name. All that was left was to find out how I came to be such a damned, twisted mockery of a man.

There was only one place that question could be answered. So, after I'd visited the cottage one last time and cleaned up, I returned to the train station, never once pausing to worry about the men who might be waiting for me. The way I saw it, it would be their bad luck if our paths crossed. I was going home to the city, to The Cardinal. It would be the death of me, I was sure, but before he killed me, he'd talk. I'd make him. And pity anyone who got in my way or tried to stop me. No ordinary mortal could stand against a soulless monster like Capac Raimi.

ayuamarca

I had to wait almost forty minutes for a train. I passed some of that by calling Ama. 'Capac!' she squealed. 'It's really you? God, when I didn't hear from you . . . Where are you? What happened with –'

'Ama,' I interrupted, 'listen carefully. Get out of the city and never return. Understand?'

'OK,' she agreed instantly. 'Where will we meet?'

'We won't,' I told her. 'We're through. We can never see each other again.'

She laughed uneasily. 'Quit fooling, Capac.'

'You remember what I told you? That I'd never harm an innocent?'

'I remember,' she said quietly.

'I lied. I lied to you and to myself. I'm a killer, Ama, as ruthless and bloody-minded as the worst of them.'

'That's not true,' she said. 'I know you, Capac. You have principles. You –'

'I killed a woman this morning.' I stopped her mid-flow. 'She was a widow, harmless, innocent. She got in my way and I murdered her, brutally and clinically. Caved her head in with a spade and dumped her in an open grave. Get out,

Ama. It's not just The Cardinal you have to worry about any more. Now there's *me*.'

'Capac,' she sobbed, 'you don't know what you're –'

I hung up. Leant my head against the wall of the booth and sighed. That had been hard. All the time we were talking, I wanted to tell her I loved her and arrange a final rendezvous, one last passionate coupling. But I couldn't allow myself that luxury. Because when the love-making was over, maybe Ama wouldn't want to let me go. Maybe she'd cling to me and beg me to stay. Perhaps she'd try forcing me. If she did . . .

Could I raise a hand in anger against Ama? I doubted it. But I wasn't sure. That's why I had to sever all connections with her. I didn't know myself any more, or what I was capable of.

The train was almost empty when I boarded but it filled as we chugged closer to the city, commuters from nearby towns dragging themselves in for another day's hard toil. It was a long ride. Plenty of time for silent deliberation.

What *was* I? A replica, a zombie, a ghost, the real Martin Robinson? Did I come from a pod, a lab or beyond the grave? Was I on my way back to reality or was this all a dream? Had killing Dee merely been my warped mind's way of separating me from reality forever?

I shut my eyes and let the crazy thoughts slip from my mind. It didn't matter. I'd be in the city soon, where all answers – or death – would come. Thinking was redundant. I let myself relax and nabbed a few hours' sleep.

Nobody was waiting for me at the station. I stood on the platform and breathed the fumes of this orifice of the city, much as I had a year ago. But when I'd come before, it had been to start a new life. Now I was here to finish one.

A hand fell on my shoulder. With a sense of destiny I turned to face my captor, only to find – surprising me once again – the ever-grinning Paucar Wami. 'I wasn't expecting you for some time yet,' he said.

'What are *you* doing here?' I frowned. 'You told me you were getting out.'

He shrugged. 'I changed my mind.'

'Why?'

'We will discuss it on the way,' he said, sliding in front of me and heading for the nearest exit. 'The Cardinal has revoked the call for your head, but that might only be a way of snaring you. I don't think anyone is watching but who can say for sure. There could be a dozen guns trained on us right now.'

It was a convincing argument. I followed him quickly, reserving my questions. His motorbike was parked outside. He didn't ask where I wanted to go, just hopped on and kicked it into life as I climbed on behind.

'I take it The Cardinal didn't send you to fetch me,' I said as we cut through the traffic around the station.

'Hardly,' Wami snorted. 'I killed one of his men. He doesn't take lightly to his pawns turning on one another without permission.'

'Then how did you know I was coming?'

'Our blind friends of course. They told me you'd return. They didn't know the exact day but they knew the place. They said it would be worth my while staying to ensure your safe passage through the city.' He turned down an alley. 'Damned if I know how they found me.'

'Why didn't you ask them?'

'I didn't speak with them directly. They sent a couple of messengers who knew nothing. I tortured both of them, to be positive, but neither could tell me anything.'

'Where are you taking me?' I asked as we turned down another narrow alley.

'Don't ask stupid questions,' he grunted.

Wami dropped me at the front door of Party Central. Reaching inside his jacket, he handed me a tiny transmitter. 'Wear this. I want to hear what he says. I haven't gone to all this trouble only to be excluded from the final revelations.'

'What makes you think there'll be any?'

'The blind men's messengers said that through you I would learn the truth.'

I pinned the transmitter to my shirt, just beneath the collar. I didn't look upon Paucar Wami as an ally – he'd rip my heart out if it served his purpose, and not think twice about it – but he'd saved my life a few times now. I owed him.

'Enjoy your meeting,' Wami grinned and peeled away.

Shocked faces greeted me in the lobby. I smiled at a startled receptionist and requested a meeting with The Cardinal. She buzzed up and stared with disbelief as I slipped off my shoes and handed them over. Moments later Ford Tasso appeared, face dark, eyes black, fists clenched. 'You came back,' he growled.

'I was homesick,' I shrugged.

He smiled viciously. 'You've got balls, kid. I like you, even though you killed Vincent and led me a wild goose chase. I think we could have been friends under different circumstances. I'll miss you.'

'I'm not dead yet,' I told him.

'Aren't you?' he said.

We boarded the lift and ascended to the fifteenth. Everybody we passed in the corridor shot us darting, curious glances. They were stunned to see me. Ford left me at the door to The Cardinal's office. 'See you later,' he said.

'You think so?'

'Of course. I always clear up the bodies around here.'

I entered.

The Cardinal's face was scarred and puffy, proof that our

fight hadn't been a figment of my imagination, that my healing was real, that my year in the city hadn't been a dream. His fingers were steepled, eyes hooded, mouth a neutral line in an impassive face.

'Looking good, Mr Raimi,' he said.

'Feeling good, Mr Dorak,' I smiled. 'No cuts, no bruises, no broken bones. I must be some kind of superman, the way I can heal, the way I can shrug off a broken neck as easily as a cracked fingernail. I'll have to splash out on some of those insurance premiums I've been hawking — I can suffer the injury, collect the money, heal up quick. I'll make a fortune.'

'You may just do that, Mr Raimi,' he said, then added eagerly, 'tell me what you've learned.'

'You can't keep a good man down. To get to the top, you have to dig to the bottom. *Now* means nothing without a *then*. Shit happens. I'm a killer.'

'The three men at the house,' he purred. 'Nicely handled. How did you feel when you killed them?'

'Happy. It was a relief to get off the mark.'

'And now?'

'I feel nothing,' I said.

'Very good. There may be hope for you yet.'

'Sure,' I said sarcastically.

'I detect scepticism in your tone,' he said, eyes twinkling.

'I detect ridicule in yours. You're goading me. We both know I've come here to die.'

'Do we?'

'I turned against you, betrayed you, beat you up. I'm a dead man. I've accepted that. All I want to hear from you now is the truth. When you're finished, you can wash me from your hair forever. Only spare me the crap. I'm sick of it.'

'Mr Raimi,' he sighed and tapped the arms of his new

chair, nowhere near as grand as his last. 'So sure of yourself. So stubborn. So wrong. Sit.' Warily I took a seat. I noticed
he had my puppet on the desk between us. 'I'm not going
to kill you,' he said. 'This has all been a test. I wanted to see
how you would react when you found your name crossed
out, what you would do, where you would go when you
had nowhere else to run, how long it would take you to
come back. Cruel, hard, horrible tests.

'But you passed.' He paused and waited for me to speak. I
said nothing. When he saw I wasn't going to respond, he
continued. 'I know what you're thinking. You want to know
what you've won. But isn't it obvious? *This.*' He waved an arm
at the office. 'Party Central, the city, my empire. I told you I
wanted a successor. I said you were in the running. That was
a little white lie — you were the *only* candidate, the only man
I'd hand this over to. If you passed the tests. Which you did.'

I massaged my eyelids with my fingertips. He was playing
with me still. 'I don't want this,' I muttered. 'I'm sick of the
games. Tell me how you got me here and tampered with my
brain. Tell me about the other Ayuamarcans, what happened
to Adrian and Y Tse, what links us, why you've gone to all
this trouble, how you fool people into forgetting us when
we're gone. That's all I care about. Save your promises for
the next guinea pig.'

'You don't believe me,' he said. 'How peculiar. But I will
provide you with answers anyway. Are you comfortable, Mr
Raimi? This is a long, strange tale and I've never told it
before. It might take a while. It's an outlandish story but you
will believe it because you are part of the proof. But before
I begin, tell me where you went when you left this city.'

'You know where I went,' I snarled. 'I told you — no more
fucking games.'

'But this isn't a game,' he said. 'You are my heir now,
believe it or not, and I will toy with you no longer. I don't

have all the answers. There are things which I too wish to learn. So tell me, where did you go?'

'I went to Sonas,' I snarled, 'the town I lived in when I was Martin Robinson.' I told him all about my trip. Dee, my supposed death, the graveyard, the body, the murder. I left nothing out. When I was finished, he sucked the ends of his fingers, one at a time, biting the nails gently, and considered my words.

'How do you account for it?' he asked.

'You snatched me from the morgue and replaced my body.'

'Any other theories?'

'I'm a clone. A ghost. His twin. A zombie. This – you, my time in the city – is all a dream. Come on, quit teasing. Are you going to talk or not?'

'What if I told you I've never heard of Sonas or Martin Robinson?'

'I'd know you were as full of shit as ever.'

'Nevertheless, I never knew Martin Robinson. You are *not* that man and never were. That *was* him in the coffin and everything his widow told you was true. Your theories are flawed. You're as far from the truth as you were before you left. You only came close to the truth when you suggested this might all be a dream.'

'I'm not Martin Robinson?'

'No.'

'Then who am I?'

'You're Capac Raimi.'

'Before that,' I hissed.

He shook his head. 'There was no before. You're not human, Mr Raimi. I created you.' Then he leant back and let me gawp at him for a while.

'It started when I was a boy of the streets.' He had his chair turned towards the window and was half-facing away from me. He was determined to tell this his own way. I couldn't rush him, so I sat back, bit down on my impatience, and listened.

'The city was different then. There was no central criminal force, only dozens of transient gangsters. Every neighbourhood could boast its own independent, self-determining gang. They fought and murdered without reason. It was uncivilized chaos.'

'I know some people who say otherwise,' I told him, thinking of Nathanael Mead.

He waved that away. 'Some people would look on the bright side if eagles ripped out their eyes and shat in the sockets. The city was a cesspit. Anyone saying different is a fool or a liar.

'You had to be vicious to survive,' he continued. 'People didn't respect youth or make allowances for it. Pimps peddled two-year-olds at street corners. Boys were indoctrinated in the ways of the underworld as soon as they could walk. The papers rarely reported it and the police never admitted it, but that's how bad it was.

'My mother was one of the lucky ones. She came from a good family, had a decent job, could have lived in happy denial like the upper classes always do. But she had an Achilles heel. Rather, an Achilles vein. One of those poor people who lose themselves entirely to the temptation of drugs. She lost her job, was disowned by her parents, moved into the east of the city, supported her habit by selling her body. I never knew my father. She didn't either. A client, a pimp or just somebody who fucked her while she was lying in a gutter.' I was glad his back was to me. I didn't want to see his face right then.

'I had to fend for myself from an early age. My mother rarely thought to feed me, change my clothes or wash me. She should have had an abortion. If she thought motherhood might prove the saving of her, she was wrong. She went on shooting up and selling her body while I crawled through mounds of garbage, scavenging, fighting cats and dogs for scraps of meat and potato peelings.

'When I was four I started stealing from her clients. I'd sneak into the room while they were busy fucking, scour their pants and coats, take what I could find. I was a sly child. I had to be. One night my mother caught me and beat me for going behind her back and not sharing. After that we worked together — she fucked them, I stole and we split the proceeds seventy-thirty. It was the closest I ever got to her.

'One night a customer realized what was going on. He kicked up a storm. He was a politician or a judge, someone with influence. He said he was going to put an end to our evil ways. So my mother pulled a syringe out from under the bed and stabbed him. He staggered away, gasping, shocked, over to where I was standing. He fell and looked at me pleadingly, fear in his eyes. I picked up his belt and strangled him.'

There was a long pause. 'When we were dumping the body, I cut a piece of skin from his leg and kept it, much as Indians kept scalps. I lost it after a few months but I've always remembered the feel of it as it dried, the taste when I put it in my mouth and nibbled.

'Anyway, this went on for some time. We killed a couple more — each time it seemed like an accident, but I think we let it happen because we enjoyed the buzz. My mother introduced me to drugs, tried to hook me, so she could take more of my money. But I was no fool. I saw drugs for what they were and avoided them.

'One night we killed a hooker's man. Bad mistake. She paid a call with some of her friends. They cut my mother to shreds before my eyes. It was slow and bloody. I watched it all. They let me go with a minor thrashing — I was a child and they thought my mother had killed alone. From that day on I lived by myself. Life was hard, I took many beatings, I was raped a few times — but I survived. I kept going and refused to give in. I was a few months short of my sixth birthday.'

I'd seen a lot in my time and heard even more, but never anything to match this. Nothing that came close. I listened with awe and horror.

'I was a violent, backward child,' he went on flatly. 'My mother never taught me how to speak. I spent most of my early years avoiding people, slithering round the alleys at night like a mute, lonesome rat. I could understand what others said but I couldn't respond, except to grunt and shake my head. I was an animal. I didn't wash, I wore rags, I had no friends, I fought anybody I could.

'Fighting was my only release, the only time I felt good. I was a fierce fighter, even though I was only seven or eight. I had strength enough to beat grown men. I developed quickly, toyed with clubs, ropes, knives, guns. A man came to me one day, a shopkeeper I'd often stolen from, and offered me money to leave him alone. I learnt about protection that day and never looked back.

'I discovered the glories of women when I was eleven. The streets where I lived were throbbing with prostitutes and junkies. I only had to reach out and grab. I liked sex — it was almost as pleasant as fighting. I fucked a lot after that, every time I got a hard-on. I didn't understand the concept of waiting.

'One day a couple of prostitutes asked me to be their pimp. I was tough, as I said, but backward. They thought they could manipulate me. They were wrong. I demanded nearly all their money, beat them if they misbehaved, fucked them more often than their clients. But there was nothing they could do about it. I was like a boulder on top of a slope — once pushed, I couldn't be stopped.

'My biggest problem was money. It clung to me and I couldn't get rid of it. By the time I was fourteen, I had more than I knew what to do with. I had no interest in cash but I knew that others would kill me for it if I just sat on what I had. I hid wads under stones around the city. Many would be stolen, or I'd forget where I left them. I didn't care. It was only money. I could get more whenever I wanted. I knew nothing of banks and business. I'd learnt to speak – just about – but I still couldn't read or write.

'Because it was expected, I invested in guns, drugs and whores. I opened brothels, established drug factories, traded weapons. Everything I touched turned to gold. Success hounded my every move. I took over gangs, killed their leaders, won men's allegiance even though I didn't care for it. I was growing into a force, attracting attention, lawless and otherwise, but I was still a wild beast. My temper was getting out of hand. I fought non-stop, attacking every possible target with a fury born of frustration and self-hatred. I was spinning into an abyss of my own making. An early grave beckoned. I'd fostered powerful enemies and taken no steps to appease them, to hold the gangsters at bay, to win over the money men. Everything was poised to crash down around me.

'And then I created Leonora.'

He was back to the mystery at last, and I was glad. I could have listened to his story all day and night any other time, but now I was growing impatient. I couldn't see how it tied in with the Ayuamarcans or my not being human.

'I needed a mentor,' he said. 'I recognized that, even though I knew little else. I believed I could *do* something if I had the right teacher. I had to learn to express myself clearly, read, plan, act meaningfully. I was amassing a fortune and I needed to know what to do with it. Men were stepping forward, offering their advice and services, but I couldn't tell the pearls from the parasites.

'One night in bed I thought of what I needed — a woman who could mother me, who'd love and care for me more than life itself, who'd never grow impatient, who would be wise and knowing. She'd know how to deal with money, where to invest it, which men to listen to, who to trust. With her help I'd formulate ideas, plans, dreams. She would nurture and direct me.

'As I lay on the verge of sleep, thinking of such a woman, I saw faces, then naked people. They floated through my mind like ghosts. Hundreds, maybe thousands. I searched for a friendly face, panning from one to the other. Finally I settled on a handsome woman, kind and wise in appearance. I thought this was the type of woman I'd choose if I could. She *seemed right*.

'As I studied her, I idly wondered what she might be called. Something exotic, surely. Leonora, I decided. Leonora . . . Shankar. I don't know where the name came from. It just popped into my head. A fitting name for what would have been a fitting mentor. If she'd existed.

'I fell asleep thinking of her, all the things she'd teach me, what I could do with the help of such a woman. The next day, walking at random, I found a shop.' He paused and his fingers drummed the window. 'Or I was led to it more probably. It was nothing to look at, tucked away in a dirty side-street. There was no name or sign hanging outside. The window was full of puppets. They were pretty. I moved closer and pressed my nose against the glass like a street urchin. Then, with a shock, I recognized the face I'd been dreaming of the night before. My brain churned. As I tried to make sense of it, a man emerged from the shop and bade me enter. I was wary, but then I saw another man inside, taking down the puppet I'd been staring at. My curiosity got the better of me and I went in.

'The man who'd welcomed me shut the door, put up the

CLOSED sign and led me to the rear of the shop. In a dark room with strange symbols scrawled on every wall, two more men waited. Both were blind, dressed in robes, and spoke in a foreign language. They performed a ceremony I couldn't understand and involved me in it. I went along with them because, once again, it *seemed right* — it was as if I was still dreaming.

'The blind men linked hands with me and chanted. They drew blood from their fingers and mine, mixed it and daubed the face of the puppet. Then they handed me the puppet and led me back to the street. I took it home, clutched to my chest, bewildered and dazed. I felt fear whenever I studied the puppet. I wanted to throw it away. But I couldn't. It fascinated and held me. So I kept it by my side and went to sleep with it that night.

'The next morning, when I awoke, Leonora was at the door. She smiled, told me to go to the bathroom and freshen up, not to come back until I was spotless. Strict from the start, Mr Raimi. Exactly what I needed.'

He stopped. I began to shout, to demand he quit the nonsense games and deliver the truth. But my protestations died in my throat as he faced me. His expression was . . . I can't explain. Maybe he was like an Egyptian who'd chased Moses and got caught between the walls of the Red Sea, torn between marvel and terror as the water fell upon him.

'Leonora was marvellous,' he said. 'All that my dream had predicted and more. She took me to a hotel, locked me in for six months and educated me. She taught me how to read, write, think and speak. We shot through books like wildfire. She'd pick out the main points, drum them into me, then discard them. She introduced me to the great thinkers and planners, the wondrous architects of the mind. We devoured books on economics, the military, politics, science, history. I didn't learn everything. There's only so much you can cram into six months, no matter how fast you work. But everything I now know stems from that time in the hotel. My life since has been a pursuit of ideas I was first introduced to then.

'With Leonora's patronage, I wasn't long slicing through the fabric of the city's underbelly. Soon I was lord of my patch. I expanded swiftly, surely, cruelly. I bought the best men in every field, bribed, bullied or blackmailed them. Leonora told me we didn't need to know everything about our business, but we needed people who did, who we could control, who'd do the hard graft and leave us free to dream and plan.

'Within two years I was a major force, buying up every policeman, killing competitors, bargaining with those more powerful than me. It was difficult at the time to see a day like this, when I could sit here and lord it over all. But I had my dreams and Leonora and, in time, my other Ayuamarcans. Within a decade I was king of the city. Five years later I was The Cardinal, feared by all, central to all, lord of all I surveyed.'

'But what about *me*?' I demanded impatiently. 'Conchita, Adrian, Y Tse and the Ayuamarca list? Where do we fit in? How?'

'Peace, Mr Raimi,' he said. 'We're getting there. I'm rushing the story as fast as I can but there is much we have to cover. Now, as to where Leonora came from, I didn't know. At the time I didn't even pose the question. I thought she was connected with the mysterious store owners, my vision of her a mere coincidence. I didn't think about it for the first year, not until I created my second human.

'I've gone through many competitors during my time. They rise and fall like waves, and I'm the beach on which they break. One of my foes back then was Elmer Chag. He operated a large sector of the city adjacent to my own. We fought regularly along a dividing strip of land. He was older than I, more powerful. He should have seen me off, and would have if he'd realized what a force I was growing into. Unfortunately for him, he found it hard to see past my dirty, manic exterior. Like so many others, he thought I'd burn out. So instead of throwing all he had at me, he held back and waited for me to crumple.

'My tactics were crude in the beginning. I resorted to bullying and torture wherever possible. It was the only way I knew — find an opponent's weak spot and hit him hard. No room for finesse. But Chag had hardly any weak points. No family, no friends, no pets. There was nothing to hit. One night – lying in bed again – I cursed the fact that he had no relatives I could kidnap and use against him. A brother would have been perfect, one who'd grown up with him and battled by his side through the years, so close that he'd do anything he could to protect him. As I thought about it, the ghost faces came to me again. I scanned them with half an interested eye, found an appropriate, big brother sort of face, and put a name to it — Victor Chag. On that image I fell asleep.

'The next day, obeying a deep-rooted urge, I returned to the shop of puppets. I'd been there a couple of times since but it had always been closed and nobody knew anything of the owners. This time it was open and, as before, I was led to the back where a puppet resembling the fictional Victor Chag was chanted over and daubed with blood. Again I returned home, fearful, confused. The next morning, Elmer Chag had a brother.'

'You're crazy,' I said softly.

He smiled. 'Maybe. But if so, what are *you*, Mr Raimi? A product of my madness?' I didn't reply. I didn't dare. 'As far as everyone was concerned, Victor Chag was real. I knew Elmer was an orphan but everybody else thought Victor had always been there, that the brothers were a unit. Their knowledge of him was hazy. Nobody could describe Victor clearly, they didn't know how he spoke, what he wore, if he was vicious or polite. But they knew that Elmer Chag had always had a brother. Victor was real. I was able to create people.'

He paused, hands clasped, eyes bright with magic or madness — I wasn't sure which. 'Leonora and Victor Chag had never been born. I made them. I conjured them out of nowhere, gave them limbs, tongues, personalities, roles. I didn't know how. The uncertainty ate away at me, drove me to distraction and the point of true madness. I went back to the store but it was shut and I found no clues when I broke in. I asked Leonora but she knew nothing of the shop, puppets or blind men in robes. So, putting my doubts to one side, I kidnapped Victor Chag and used him to bring his brother down.'

'Elmer believed Victor was his brother?' I asked incredulously.

'Implicitly. When he was paying the ransom, I tried convincing him he was an only child.' The Cardinal chuckled drily. 'He looked at me as if I was crazy. I experimented after that. I tried summoning the faces and found that I could, any time I liked as long as I was on the verge of sleep. I'd make my choice, give the ghost a name and the next day the shop would be open and the blind men waiting. I stayed away a couple of times, having summoned a face, to see if anything would happen. It didn't. I needed the puppets and the blind men to make the ghosts come alive.

'I explored further and found there were limitations. *This* drew my attention to the first.' He waved his bent little finger and smiled. 'Nobody ever asks me about this. I bet you thought it was a natural defect or the result of an injury. Not so. It bends whenever I create somebody and stays bent as long as I keep them alive. With every person I create, it bends a little more.

'That was the first sign of my constraints. When I had

eight people walking around, it was stretched virtually to breaking point. I made a couple more and was in agony. I can comfortably keep seven Ayuamarcans on the go. Eight hurts. Nine is the endurable limit. It's not just the pain — I could live with that. But they come apart if I make too many. They lose their minds, my control slips, people start to forget them. The reality unravels. I learnt that quickly and have kept to the limits ever since, never giving in to the temptation to push myself to the extreme, to try for fifteen or twenty.

'Paperwork is a nuisance. The Ayuamarcans exist in human minds but not in print. They don't come with birth certificates, credit cards or backgrounds. At first that didn't matter. The people I was working with were beneath such legitimacies — crooks, thieves, rapists and murderers. I could get away with such discrepancies. Later, when I branched into less shadowy fields, it was trickier. But by that time I had the resources to forge the necessary documents. It's a hard business. Creating an Ayuamarcan is the work of a lone night, but I have to spend months beforehand working on the papers. Public figures are the hardest. Mayors are a bitch. The lengths I have to go to in order to create solid backgrounds capable of standing up to the most rigid investigation . . .' He sighed with exasperation.

'Erasing Ayuamarcans requires a little pin and a lot of fog. You've seen the blind priests when our famous green fog is up?' I nodded numbly. 'Many think they worship the fog but they don't. They *summon* it. My puppets have heartbeats. When I want one to end, I prick the heart with a pin. That wipes the Ayuamarcan out of existence. The priests – who always seem to know my actions in advance – take to the streets and create the fog, which sweeps through the city and wipes every mind it touches, eliminating people's memories of the dream beings. That's why nobody remembers

Adrian or Y Tse. They were real for as long as I sustained them, but once erased, they returned to the land of nothingness. Sonja wasn't lying about Adrian. She simply forgot. To her and the others, he never existed.

'Ayuamarcans are *not* real. They're elaborate illusions, walking, talking, living, eating, breathing images of humans. But once I switch them off, they flicker out of existence. When the fog subsides, it takes the city's memories with it.'

'What about people outside the city?' I asked. 'If you're telling the truth and the fog can do what you say, what about people in the rest of the world?'

'They pay no notice. Most of my creations keep a low profile. Those in the public eye – my mayors for instance – stick to the city. National interest in them is at a minimum. There are occasional enquiries about eliminated Ayuamarcans, but those are simply dealt with. If you don't believe it's possible for a public official to disappear without creating a nationwide fuss, set yourself this riddle — think of five major cities and try naming their mayors.'

I thought about it and came up blank. 'OK, I can't name any. But I'm sure there are lots of people who can.'

'Of course,' he agreed. 'But keeping those small pockets of know-it-alls in check is an easy task. As long as I don't do anything stupid – creating a national president, for example – I can go on juggling Ayuamarcans from here to kingdom come.'

'What if you just kill them?' I asked. 'If you'd simply shot Adrian or Y Tse, that would have ended them, right?'

'No. The Ayuamarcans don't cease to exist until I and my blind friends usher them back to their own plane. They still count when dead.'

I considered what he'd told me. Crazy? Sure. Impossible? Of course. Yet part of me knew it was true. I wanted to deny it – if only to prove I wasn't as mad as he was – but part of me *knew*.

'Where do we come from?' I asked. 'You must have found out in the time since then. How do you do it? Why call us *Ayuamarcans?*'

'I don't have all the answers,' he said. 'I've discovered pieces down the years. Once I conjured a man with an intact memory, one who knew all about himself. It worked. He told me about his past life, what his name had been, where he'd lived, how he died — all of the faces I see in my dreams are dead people. He remembered dying, then waking – he could not say how much time had passed – in the airport here. I checked his story and it was true. But he couldn't tell me more than that — he couldn't explain the nature of the force behind my power. I tried it a couple more times, and each person told the same story — they'd lived, died, come back when summoned, with new personalities. No one mentioned a heaven or a hell, only blackness followed by light, blankness by consciousness.

'I got the name – Ayuamarca – from the puppet makers. We've spent much time together over the decades. They always speak in that strange language of their own. Although I can't understand them when they speak, I picked up a few words, like Uma Situwa, Atahualpa and Manco Capac. Incan words. I believe they are descendants of those who fled the Spanish conquistadors, but I have no proof of that. It is mere conjecture.'

'Did they give you my name? Ama's? Inti Maimi's?'

'No. I choose the names myself. At least, I *think* I do.'

'The shop,' I said. 'Do you still go there?'

He shook his head. 'I grew tired of the travelling. In the end I moved them in here. They dwell in the lower depths. They change every so often. The two I first met have been replaced several times over the years. They look similar and speak the same language, and each is as mysterious and blind as the first two. I have no idea where they come from or where the rest of them live.'

'They're *here*?' I snapped. *'Now?'*

'Yes. The pair in the basement never go out.'

I stood. 'I want to see them.'

'In time,' he said.

'No. Now.'

He studied me for a few seconds, then inclined his head. 'Very well.' He stood and strode out of the office. Ford Tasso was waiting outside. The Cardinal bent and whispered in his ear. Tasso nodded gravely. Then The Cardinal straightened and beckoned me on. He entered the lift and cocked a thumb at the operator. 'Out.' Once I was inside, he keyed in a code and we dropped smoothly.

'I have been selfish, Mr Raimi,' he said as we descended. 'I've abused this gift for all it was worth. I could have made eight scientific geniuses and sent the world hurtling into the future like a comet with a nuclear missile up its ass. I could have generated prophets to bring peace. It was in my power to create people who could have changed the nature and future of this planet for the good. But instead I used my power to make myself The Cardinal. I don't apologize – I'm glad I did what I have done – but some nights, when I lean over my balcony and listen to the city and hear the screams drifting up . . .'

The lift came to a halt and we stepped out. We were on the lowest level of the building. The Cardinal crossed to a locked door, keyed in another code and started down the stairs which were revealed when it opened. I hesitated, my stomach tight, but I'd come this far, so there was no backing out now.

At the bottom was another door. No lock on this one. The Cardinal let me catch up, then edged it ajar and eased through. I wasn't far behind.

I saw the two men immediately, sitting on rough stools, their eyes white blanks, faces expressionless. I gazed around the rest of the room. Lots of barrels, boxes and tins. I examined a couple. Paint, metal, paper, wood, string, cloth and so on. I studied the markings on the walls. They meant nothing to me. I approached the two men, stopped and looked to The Cardinal for guidance.

'Go ahead,' he told me. 'I've brought others here before. They won't do anything. They just sit, still and silent, staring ahead. You can poke them in the ribs if you like.'

I shuffled across until I was between the pair. I looked from one blank face to the other. They weren't the blind men I'd seen before but they looked similar. I opened my mouth to ask The Cardinal a question, but before I could their arms snaked out and clamped on my shoulders. I was instantly immersed in a vision I could only barely comprehend.

Their eyes flared and grew. They filled with colour, people, then with sounds. It was like gazing into four movie screens, which quickly merged and became one, at which point I slipped entirely into their world.

It was long ago, before the conquest by the Europeans. I don't know where I was, but it was high on a mountain, beneath a burning sun. By a strangely shaped stone, men argued over the future of their people.

Then I was on a platform, surrounded by mummies. A blind priest stood in the middle of a rain shower – the same as the one I'd seen on my first day in the city – and through him a decision was passed to the others. They were told to leave.

The scene shifted and the members of the mountain city were on the move. They travelled by caravan, far and long, their families, animals and goods in tow. At the centre were six covered tents. They were elephantine and required many men to lift them. I couldn't see who travelled in these tents but they were obviously people of great importance.

After a long, testing journey, the group came to a river and settled. They unpacked, laid out their wares and greeted their new neighbours, dark-skinned Indians who were suspicious at first but gradually came to accept the strangers. The tribes learned to live as one, hunting, building and breeding together. Only those in the six tents – still unseen – remained separate, never coming out to dance or laugh, play or work.

After what must have been many years – I could tell by the growth of the village – a young boy was brought to the largest tent. The flap lifted, he walked in and I moved with him. There were about twenty people inside. They were light-skinned and blind. They sat in curious order, their bodies aligned in shapes that resembled the scrawled symbols I'd seen on the walls in the basement of Party Central.

'We are *villacs*, priests, servants of the gods,' one of them said, and though he spoke in an ancient tongue, I understood perfectly. 'We are here to protect and guide. You will serve as our *Watana*, the hitching post of our community. Step forward.'

The scene shifted again. The next I knew, the boy was a man and leader of the village. He had his own entourage of helpers, men and women who were the same as me — created by magic, designed to perform specific tasks, Ayuamarcans. They were architects, builders, farmers, medics. They taught the villagers, devised new ways to till the land, developed medicines. They governed and helped the people grow, learn and develop. As they prospered, so did the village, and that made the *villacs* happy. I don't know how I knew these things — I just did.

As the *Watana* moved around the village issuing orders, I noticed that one of his small fingers was bent like The Cardinal's. Then the picture changed again and I was looking at a different man with the same bent finger. The village was larger now, a town, and many tribes came from miles around to trade. None ever attacked because it was known that these people were protected by powerful forces, and everyone was afraid of the unseen, blind priests, around whom legends had grown.

Then came a race who knew no fear, with weapons beyond the power of any in this country. They swept through the town, raping and pillaging, and there was nothing the *villacs* could do to stop them. There was no gold, no silver, no coal, nothing to interest the invading savages, but they destroyed regardless. Their kings and queens across the great ocean demanded it.

The new rulers had heard the legends of the blind men and were quick to dispel them. They wanted no opposition. They tore the *villacs* apart, capturing, torturing and killing many, proving once and for all – as they had so many times already – that they were the strongest force in existence.

But some *villacs* survived. A few found hiding places beneath the ground. Those who escaped the slaughter were slow to emerge. They waited for many years, letting the marauders settle. As the homesteaders gradually moved in after the warriors and built their own town over the skeleton of the old, they returned to the surface, though from that time on they clung to the shadows and kept their existence secret.

They found a new boy to be *Watana*, host to their magical powers. This one was white, the progeny of the usurpers. That didn't matter to the *villacs*. They didn't care for the murdered members of the old town. Their only loyalty was to the land and the spirits of the future. They built, not *for* people, but *upon* them. Colour, race and religion meant nothing to the once-Incan priests.

But they'd been changed by the new regime. They were

bitter, less certain of their place in the town, wary. They'd enjoyed being gods but now they stayed secreted away so that they might never again face extinction. Whereas before they'd chosen the wisest of people to invest with their power, the gentlest and purest, now they picked the strongest, the fiercest, the most determined.

As the decades passed and their control returned, the town changed. It had once been a peaceful place, a centre of learning and hope. Now it became a fortress, a stronghold, built to repel any attack. Time rolled on. The blind priests tried but failed to exert their old level of control. There were too many people, new ideas from abroad, new languages and gods, machines and factories. They could direct the growth of the town but not as cleanly as they wished. There were too many factors beyond their control. They adapted as best they could, but it seemed they'd never again be the commanding force they once were.

More years passed and the town became a city. I saw the modern version start to emerge. Electricity arrived, automobiles, movies, shorter skirts. A war came and went. Another trundled round. And as the world came to grips with a new form of horror, the *villacs* pondered their place in the greater scheme of things.

I watched them gather and discuss the situation. They could sense the change in the universe. Mankind had always been destructive, but a new breed had arrived and it was going to get worse. They looked ahead and contemplated a future of gas chambers and inhuman violence, a future they couldn't control if they continued as they were. They needed to alter their approach. If chaos was the face of the future, then they must use chaos to shape it.

So they cast their net again and hauled in a child of the streets, a brutal, vicious creature, so backward and bestial he couldn't even speak. They dragged him in, though he fought every step of the way, and initiated him, filling him with the power of the *Watana*. But when he was primed, instead of tutoring him as they had the others, instead of teaching him how to control the power, they set him loose, as ignorant as he had been before, and left him to his own devices.

The *villacs* then withdrew and waited. They knew he would eventually dream, unleash his ghostly power and come looking for them. When that day arrived, they would complete the birthing rites but that was all. They wouldn't interfere with his creations or guide his decisions. They'd never tell him who he was or where his power came from. In this manner they hoped to produce a servant fit to face the challenge of the corrupt new world, one who could take the city in hand and ensure its prosperity in the harsh, unpredictable environment of the late twentieth century and beyond.

At that point the vision ended. My final sight was of the boy, skulking through the menacing alleys of the city he would one day conquer. He was filthy, badly dressed, hair long and unkempt, lips bared in a perpetual snarl. The ceremony had terrified him, but he was resilient and hungry, and now that he was free again, his hunger took precedence. Already forgetting the blind men and their arcane rites, he made his way through the city, the only world he had ever known, and looked for a place to feast.

My arm was being tugged. Blinking dumbly, I realized The Cardinal was hauling me away from the blind men. He was saying something but I couldn't hear. I glanced one last time at the makers of the puppets, then shook my head and made myself focus on the real world.

'. . . hell happened to you?' The Cardinal barked.

'They . . . it . . . how long was I out?' I gasped.

'A few seconds. They clasped your shoulders and began

murmuring. You went stiff. I grabbed you but you didn't respond. What happened? They've never done anything like that before.' He was shaken. He hadn't expected to lose control like this, not on his own turf.

'I want to get out of here,' I muttered.

Silently he led the way to the short flight of stairs and soon we were back in the deserted basement of Party Central. 'Well?' he snapped impatiently.

I thought about how he'd react if he learnt he was a tool, a manipulated pawn of the blind priests – the *villacs* – a servant whose only function was to help them preserve their hold on the city. Figuring he wouldn't take the news kindly, I opted not to enlighten him — I didn't want him exploding into a rage.

'I saw nothing,' I said. 'Just lights. A small electric shock coursed through me. I think they were checking me over, examining me.'

He squinted and scratched his chin. I don't think he believed me but he didn't push for more information. I think he was frightened of what he might discover. 'Well,' he grunted, 'do you believe me now? Were they proof that I'm telling the truth?'

'Yes.'

'You believe?'

'Yes.' I hesitated. 'But I still want to know what my role in this is. You've talked a lot about yourself but there hasn't been much about me. Why am I different to the other Ayuamarcans? Why did my cuts heal? Why –'

'Soon, Mr Raimi,' he interrupted. 'This isn't the place for revelations. Let's return to the heights, shall we?'

We got back in the lift and said nothing as we ascended. We hit the fifteenth floor and didn't slow. I glanced at the buttons and frowned. The Cardinal caught my glance and smiled. 'I fancy some fresh air.'

We came to the top floor and stopped. The Cardinal stepped out and led the way to a small flight of stairs leading up. Within minutes we were on the roof of Party Central, gazing down on the city. The wind was sharp as it whistled past my ears. I moved to the edge and peered down. It was a long drop into nothingness. The Cardinal clapped my back and I nearly toppled over. He laughed and shied away before I could hit him.

'Over here,' he said, walking to a large, steel outcropping which housed the machinery for the lifts. There were a couple of chairs set in the snug shelter of the steel. 'I put everything I had into building this empire,' The Cardinal said as he sat down. 'I sacrificed all other desires in my quest for control. The only time I sought company was with Conchita.' He smiled sadly. 'I really fucked that up. I wanted somebody who'd love me, who could teach *me* to love. When I was making her, I gave her some extra special qualities. I can do that. For instance, when I made Paucar Wami, I decided he should be stronger and faster than any ordinary human. I said he should never lose his strength or agility. He's almost as old as I am, yet he doesn't even look forty. My creations become what I describe. I can give them superhuman powers if I wish.

'Wami's one of my most fascinating creations,' he said. 'Ayuamarcans can only survive a week outside the city. After that they come apart. Except Paucar Wami. When I created him, I invested him with the ability to survive in the outside world. He's also the only fertile Ayuamarcan. The rest of you are barren. Wami's the only one who can procreate. I wanted to test my powers, to probe my limits. Wami seemed like the best one to experiment with.'

I wondered what the eavesdropping serial killer was making of this. Would he be incredulous? Dismayed? Tickled pink?

'We can only survive outside the city for a week,' I muttered. 'So, if I'd stayed away a few days longer . . .'

'No more Capac Raimi,' he smiled.

'What about Conchita?' I asked.

His smile faded. 'She hasn't left yet,' he sighed. 'When she does, her days are numbered.'

'That doesn't bother you?'

'Of course it does,' he snapped. 'But I'd rather she die happy than suffer here for the rest of her life. I forgot about the temporal limit when you were last here. If I'd remembered, I wouldn't have been so taken aback by your threat. I'd probably have eliminated you. Be thankful that I'm prone to the occasional error, Mr Raimi, or your life would have ended then.

'As I was saying, I made Conchita warm, loving and sensitive, beautiful, kind, compassionate. The last thing I thought before falling asleep was that she should grow old gracefully. My exact phrase was, "I want her to look younger with every passing year."'

He shook his head, eyes downcast. 'That disastrous quest for love aside, I used all of my other creations to further my position. Whenever standard tactics failed – when bribery, blackmail and violence weren't enough – I sent one of my dream people in. They've served me well, as loyal, smart and self-sacrificing as I've needed them to be. They never get out of control and turn on me because I program them not to.'

'*I* turned on you,' I growled.

'But it all meant nothing without a successor,' he said, ignoring me. 'I knew I couldn't do all that I wanted in the time allotted. Even if I'd been able to create more Ayuamarcans, it wouldn't have been enough. I want my empire to last. I want my descendant to rule all, forever. I want what the Egyptians, Romans and Greeks had, only I never want my empire to crumble and fall. That's my dream, Mr Raimi.

'It was clear that no *real* person could succeed me. No matter how strong a person is, they'll always die, and weak men have a habit of following in the footsteps of the strong. It had to be one of my creations, a man with the power to control and sustain the fires of my dream. So I made the first Inti Maimi. He was powerful, strong and intelligent, no scruples or feelings. A robot who'd follow my plans to the last dot, who'd destroy and conquer all.'

The Cardinal sneered. 'The trouble was, a robot can only follow orders, not scheme by himself. My heir will need to change with the times, react to the new world he helps create. The first Inti Maimi couldn't do that. He would have sunk like a stone without my hand to guide him. When I realized that, I sent him back to his grave and plotted again.

'The second Inti Maimi – the one you knew as Y Tse Lapotaire – was also a failure, though his flaws were slower in coming to the surface. He was smarter than the first, less robotic. The first knew about my Ayuamarcan project and his role in my plans. The second didn't. I wanted him to have a degree of freedom, a sense of individuality. That's where I made my mistake. I made him *too* free-spirited. When he realized I had his future mapped out, and he wasn't as free as he thought, he rebelled and thwarted my plans by turning himself into a fool.

'I kept him on for a long time, in the hope that one day he'd come to his senses and return to the fold. I liked the second Inti Maimi — of all my creations, he was the closest I ever had to a son. But he never repented and, when I created you and saw how fine you were, I decided it was time to let him go.'

'Tell me about myself,' I said coldly. It was sickening to find out I was no more than a puppet, controlled by strings, manipulated at every turn. Even if I was meant to be The

Cardinal's successor, I wasn't sure I wanted it now. Why carry on in a role not of my own making?

'You're different from the Inti Maimis,' he said. 'I brought them in at the top, as natural heirs. That was a mistake. I introduced them to the intricacies of my world too soon. That's why the second one rebelled — he saw that he was no more than the sum of my desires, that he acted on my say-so, in line with my wishes. He felt like he had no say in his future, that he wasn't truly real. I realized there was no point handing the world to my heir, as nobody can appreciate a prize that comes too easily. I needed someone who had to work for it.

'This time I made a man who started with nothing. I made you younger than the Inti Maimis, brash, imaginative and unpredictable. I gave you the desire to be a gangster, but also the freedom to deny that desire. That's why I granted you the ability to gradually recall your past, so that you had a sense of history, so that you knew you were not tied to your destiny. When you understood that you started life as a different person, you could have returned to that life. You didn't have to come back here. You had a choice — Capac Raimi or Martin Robinson.'

'It wasn't much of a choice,' I scowled. 'I'd have died if I stayed in Sonas.'

'But you didn't know that then,' The Cardinal said. 'As far as you were aware, you were free to choose. And you chose to return. You chose Capac Raimi. You chose *me*.' He pointed a finger at me. 'Don't make the mistake of thinking you're my slave, my puppet. You're not. I gave you life, yes, but you came here today of your own accord. I didn't summon you. I have no more influence over you than a parent has over a child.'

'Bullshit,' I spat. 'You've been there every step of the way. You set me up in the company, gave Adrian to me

because you thought I needed a friend, removed him and
Y Tse to arouse my suspicions and lead me to question our
relationship. You arranged my meetings with Ama and
Conchita, planted the Ayuamarca file where Ama could find
it, knowing she'd show it to me. You let me escape from
the city and made sure I returned to Sonas, knowing I'd
have to come back here for answers. That was all your
doing, wasn't it?'

'No,' he said firmly. 'It wasn't. That's why you are special.
You did virtually all of it yourself. I brought you into the
company, yes, but *you* made your own way from that point
on. I meant for you to meet Ama – I made her for you, and
she will be a great help in the years ahead, as Leonora was
of help to me – but not here in Party Central, on the stairs.
You were never meant to meet Conchita — that was a twist
I hadn't imagined. Adrian had nothing to do with you — I
made him for Sonja, who was having personal troubles and
needed somebody to love.

'I never intended for Y Tse and Leonora to be your sponsors. Adrian and Y Tse's disappearances weren't related to
you. I planted the Ayuamarca file, yes, but it was *your* decision to come looking for it and face me. *You* found the words
to stay my hand when I fully intended to execute you — I
thought you'd spun out of control. I was set to wipe you
out and begin again, but you persuaded me not to.

'To be honest, Mr Raimi, you're something of a mystery
to me. I didn't mean for this day of reckoning to arrive so
soon. I thought I'd have years to prepare for this, that you'd
grow into your role slowly, feeling your way along, climbing
the rungs one at a time. I hadn't expected to have this conversation for at least another eight or nine years, when you
were experienced and established, ready to meet me on equal,
less hysterical terms.'

He scratched his scalp and shivered as a gust of wind

swept round a corner. 'That's what I like about you,' he continued. 'You're unpredictable. You've surprised me since the beginning. You cut corners and make leaps forward. You're instinctive, original, innovative. I saw your despondency when you learnt of your origins but believe me, you're no pawn of mine. You've forged your own path and thrown any carefully laid plans I had for you into disarray. You're here because you want what I want — the world. But you want it for your own reasons, not mine. You have free will like the second Inti Maimi, but whereas he turned away from my empire, you have embraced it.'

I thought about that. 'You really didn't set me up with Leonora, Y Tse and the others?' I asked. 'It was coincidence? You had nothing to do with any of them?'

'Only with Ama Situwa. I programmed you to love her. In that respect you're helpless. You love her now and always will, even when she's gone. Apart from that, and the desire to be a gangster with your *uncle*, every other relationship you have formed, every step you've taken, every goal you've set, every route you've followed has been of your own making. I created your body but your mind is wholly your own.'

My body . . .

'What about my regenerative powers? Are they common to all Ayuamarcans?'

He shook his head. 'That quality is yours alone. The others suffer, ache and die like normal humans. They need not – I have the power to spare them – but I like to keep my creations as mortal as possible.

'I told you I want my empire to last. That has always been an impossibility. Strong men die and their legacies unravel. In the end, everything falls apart and only memories are left. Death has been the constant leveller of kingdoms and empires. It has always limited the influence of great men. Until now.

I believe I've found a way to cheat death. I might be wrong but I think it will work.'

'What are you getting at?' I asked suspiciously.

'When I made you, Mr Raimi – when I described the type of man I wanted – I wished for a man who couldn't be destroyed by human hands, who could only be undone by me. I created a man who could recover from any wound, even a fatal one. A man who'd age for a decade, then remain that age forever, who couldn't be scarred, who'd never sicken, who'd be impervious to the effects of time. A man who'd never die. A man who could live forever.'

He sank back in his chair and smiled, the smile of a master magician revealing his final, deepest secret. 'You're immortal, Mr Raimi.'

Neither of us uttered a word for about an hour. We sat facing but not looking at each other. My head was spinning, the thought of eternity searing the cells of my brain. I'd never considered this. I'd planned to make as much of myself as possible in the time I was allowed. I'd hoped for long years, several decades if I was lucky. But *eternity* . . .

If it was true, if he could pull this off, I'd be stuck here forever, running his empire. At the moment I could live with that — the thought of being in control, ruling the world, having that much time to play with and that much power, thrilled me. But what if I tired of it in fifty years, a hundred, a thousand? I'd be stuck, unable to end things. Did I really want to be part of a neverending cycle, nothing to look forward to other than an inescapable future?

'It's a trap,' I muttered. 'If I accept this and it works, I'm trapped forever. No way out.'

'As with everything in life,' he said drily, 'there are drawbacks. That's one of them. Another is loneliness. Look at me, Mr Raimi. There is no room for happiness this high up. All

I have is my empire. If you replace me, you'll assume that lonely mantle. Only it will be worse, because you'll have to live with it forever. Can you do that?'

'I don't know,' I sighed. 'I think I can but how can I say for sure?'

'You can't,' he said. 'You have to gamble and trust in your instinct.'

'But will it work?' I asked. 'What happens to the Ayuamarcans when you die? Can any of us survive your passing?'

'I don't think the others can. Maybe they'll go on to live full, normal lives, dying of natural causes when their time is up. But I doubt it. I think they'll vanish the instant my heart stops.'

'Then what makes you think I'm any different? Surely I'll zip out of existence like the rest of them.'

'Maybe. But when I made you, I stressed that not even my death should halt you. I don't know if I can thwart death in this way but I think your chances are good. Not great but better than average. Look at Conchita. Paucar Wami. How your body healed after our fight. I *am* able to pervert the laws of nature. If I can go that far, breaking so many natural rules, why not further? We won't know for sure until the day arrives – and I'm not planning to shuffle off this mortal coil for quite a while yet – but the precedents allow us to be optimistic.'

I thought about it some more. I didn't have to – I'd reached my decision halfway through his last speech, as suddenly as I'd decided to kill Dee – but it would be unwise to jump the gun when the stakes were so high. When I was certain that nothing would alter my mind, I spoke.

'I'll run your empire for you, Mr Dorak,' I said slowly and deliberately. 'I'll be your successor, the new Cardinal, and do everything in my power to carry your dream on, to one day

rule all and become, as it were, *The Pope.*' His face lit up and
he began to rise. 'But there's a price,' I added and his smile
faded. 'I'm not prepared to wait. I've moved fast, pole-vaulted
all between myself and the top. I'm not about to ease up
now. If you want me to take over, you'll have to relinquish
control immediately. I won't be second to anybody, not any
longer.'

He frowned, then shrugged and tried to make little of it.
'If that is what you wish, I will grant it. But why ignore my
knowledge, experience and wisdom when you can benefit
from them and milk me for all I'm worth? You have so much
to learn. Wouldn't it be better to keep me around, if only as
a –'

'You don't understand,' I said. I rose and crossed to the
edge of the building, no longer feeling the wind. I stood
looking down at the city for a minute, *my* city, seeing it
through new eyes, feeling it beat with my heart, sensing the
links which existed between us. Sighing happily, I returned
to my chair and sank into it. 'I want everything. The power,
the city, the dream, the future. And freedom.'

'But you are –'

'Please don't interrupt when I'm speaking.' He stared at
me with eyes the size of runny eggs. 'I'll be your heir, but
on my terms. I'm not prepared to play your game any longer.
I won't wait for you to die and live every day worrying about
your health, making plans for a future which may never
come. I have to know for sure. If your experiment succeeds,
I'll take control today. If it fails, and I pass from this world
when you die, that will also be today.

'I came to this office thinking it was the end. And it is.
Perhaps for both of us, but definitely for one.' I steepled my
fingers, lowered my head behind them and shot him a sly
smile straight from his own repertoire. 'The edge of the roof
is that way, Mr Dorak.'

He began to laugh. Stopped. Looked at my fingers, then at his own, which were spread limply on his knees. The baton of power had passed and his reign was over. Decades of hard work and planning undone in a matter of seconds. 'You can't be serious,' he croaked.

'It's the price,' I said. 'I flourish or die. You can either accept that and jump or unmake me and start anew with another Inti Maimi or Capac Raimi. Choose.'

'What about Ama?' he whined. 'Conchita. Leonora. They'll die too. Come, Mr Raimi — Capac. You need me. You need all of us. If I jump, taking my creations with me, all you'll be left with is Ford Tasso and the other ordinary people. I can make soldiers for you, politicians, men who can work to advance your cause while I'm alive. I can be of use even if you don't want me around. I'm the goose that lays the golden eggs. Why sacrifice me so cheaply? You'd kill Ama and Conchita just for peace of mind? Please reconsider, I beg you.'

I closed my eyes and pictured Ama, Conchita and Leonora. The three women in my life — lover, sister, mother. I thought of all the times Leonora had helped me, her priceless words of advice, her tips on how to handle The Cardinal, her kindness and generosity. But ultimately she was The Cardinal's woman, not mine.

Dear Conchita. I'd brought her out of her madness. She was starting a new life and deserved time to live a bit, laugh a little. It wouldn't be fair to take that away, to whip the rug out from under her just as she was learning to walk. But Conchita was finished. As soon as she left the city, an invisible timer would start its grim countdown. One week and the world would do for her, regardless of the decision I made tonight.

And Ama, the love of my life. Without her I'd never have come so far, so quickly. I'd acted faster than The Cardinal planned, just as I was moving too swiftly for him now, and it was largely because of her. She was all I wanted in a woman, the one person who could truly mean anything to me. Demanding The Cardinal's death – and thus Ama's – was stupid, destructive and cruel. Only a monster would do it.

'Come here, Mr Tasso,' The Cardinal called loudly, out of the blue.

I glanced up, confused. From the other side of the steel structure, Ford Tasso emerged with a bound and gagged Ama Situwa in tow. I leapt to my feet but sat again at a gesture from The Cardinal. He was smiling now. 'Remove the gag, Mr Tasso.'

Ford freed the strip of cloth from her mouth and Ama immediately roared at me. 'Capac! What the fuck are you doing here? Why did you come back?'

'How did she get here?' I asked quietly.

'Of her own free will, I assure you,' The Cardinal said. 'Miss Situwa has always been a strong-minded lady. She came after your phone call this morning. I'm not sure why. What were you after, Miss Situwa?'

'Fuck you,' she snarled.

The Cardinal chuckled. 'I told Mr Tasso to fetch her when we went to see our friends downstairs. She was to be my gift to you, a sign of my goodwill. Untie her, Mr Tasso.' While Ford loosened the knots, The Cardinal said, 'She is yours if you wish, Mr Raimi. Let me live my life. Learn by my side. Walk before you run. And you can have her. You don't need to face this on your own.'

'How much does she know?' I asked softly.

'Nothing. They could not hear us talking from where they were.'

'Capac?' Ama started towards us, then paused when she saw my eyes. 'What's wrong? You look . . . What happened? What has he done to you?'

I stared at her frightened face and considered her loving

innocence. I studied The Cardinal and thought of the warped way he'd treated me. Finally I looked inside myself and found something even fouler than Ferdinand Dorak.

'Ama,' I whispered painfully. 'I'm sorry. If I . . . You could remake her!' I shouted suddenly, springing on the idea. 'Erase her, then bring her back, only this time make her like me — eternal.'

'Capac? What's going on?' Ama was bewildered.

The Cardinal shook his head. 'It would be too dangerous. One man might make it through eternity, alone, focused, outliving and thus defeating his enemies. But if I gave you an eternal partner and she turned against you? No. I will not risk my empire that way. Besides, it couldn't be done. I could create another, but not the same, not Ama.' He stood and clasped my shoulders as the blind priests had. 'You're torturing yourself needlessly. There's no reason for me to die now, for Ama or Conchita to suffer. Time is on your side, Mr Raimi. Don't waste it.'

I hung my head, looked within and saw what I had to do. My cheeks were wet. Raising my fingers, I discovered I was crying. Ama was still hovering, not sure what she'd wandered into, knowing I was different but not knowing how. She could be mine. We could have many wondrous days and nights together. We could explore and learn more of each other. So much to discover. So many possibilities.

But — no. If I had a future, it was cold. That was the one thing I knew for certain. The man The Cardinal had designed – the man I'd become – had no place for warmth or love, not any longer.

'Why did you come tonight?' I asked Ama.

'You sounded strange on the phone,' she said. 'I wanted to find out what was going on. I thought The Cardinal might know where you'd gone.'

'You wanted to track me down?'

'Yes.'

'Why?'

'Because I love you, stupid,' she said, smiling foolishly.

'Even after I told you what I did?'

Her face hardened stubbornly. 'I'm sure you had no choice. I have faith in you, Capac. Whatever you did, I'm certain it had to be done.'

I looked away from Ama and locked eyes with The Cardinal. 'She'll accept me no matter what I do, won't she?' I asked and he nodded in reply. 'Regardless of how low I sink, she'll stick by my side and love me. She'd kill for me if I asked her or if she felt it was necessary.'

'She's your woman,' The Cardinal said.

I shook my head slowly. 'No. I'm many things but not a slave-master. Not yet. I don't want her.' The words almost tore me apart but I forced them out. 'I love her. I need her. But I don't want her seeing what I've become. I don't want her by my side, watching me change. I don't want her aligning her soul with mine. If I'm to be damned, I'll be damned alone.

'I want you out of here,' I told him. '*Now.*'

The Cardinal nodded grimly. 'We're so alike, Mr Raimi. I would have made that decision also, were I in your shoes. You'll suffer for it, more than you know. I've had but a few decades and already I'm tired, worn, on the verge of madness. I'm not sure you'll be able to deal with an eternity of cruelty. I wish you well though.'

He walked to the edge and paused, staring down on his city for the final time. As he hovered on the brink, the door to the roof burst open and a dark figure raced towards us. It was Paucar Wami. 'Stop!' he roared, training his gun on The Cardinal. For the first time the killer looked scared, uncertain. In learning of his inhumanity, he had finally realized what it was to be human. He wasn't the master he'd believed, only a puppet, one about to have its strings severed. 'One more step and I shoot.'

Ford Tasso cursed and drew his own gun.

'Mr Tasso!' The Cardinal barked. 'Put it away.' Ford hesitated. 'Do as I ask, old friend,' The Cardinal said gently and Ford reluctantly obeyed. 'Wami knows?' The Cardinal asked me.

'He planted a bug on me before I came up,' I explained.

The Cardinal started to laugh and Wami's eyes narrowed hatefully. 'If you try to jump,' he growled, 'I'll –'

'What?' The Cardinal jeered. 'Kill me?' He raised a mocking eyebrow. Wami glared at The Cardinal, then lowered his gun. He was shaking with anger or fear, maybe both. 'You are powerless here,' The Cardinal said. 'I created you to take life, not to save it.'

'If you jump, and I survive, I will take a few lives yet,' Wami snarled, setting his sights on me now.

'Ominous words, Mr Raimi,' The Cardinal chuckled. 'I would not like to be in your shoes if my predictions about the other Ayuamarcans prove invalid.' His smile faded. 'If I *am* wrong about them,' he said quietly, 'will you care for my Conchita? Keep her in the city if you can, tell her I loved her, honestly, as much as I could. Despite everything, I loved her to the end.'

'You know I will.'

The Cardinal nodded glumly. Then his fingers twitched and his jaw jutted forward proudly. 'In that case, there's only one more thing to do. Goodbye, Mr Tasso.' Ford was staring at him, head cocked sideways, a peculiar expression on his face. 'Farewell, Mr Wami.' Wami spat at him in disgust. '*Au revoir*, Miss Situwa.' Ama ignored him and moved towards me, reaching out, mouth opening to say my name one more time. 'Here's to a long life, Mr Raimi,' he shouted, drowning out anything she might have said. 'Farewell!'

And with that final shout – Wami roared too, darting forward to drag him back, but too late, too late – The Cardinal stepped over the ledge and dropped through the night to his untimely death, hollering like a monstrous baby all the way down.

capac raimi

And that's where the story of Capac Raimi ends. A simple tale really — once upon a time a boy came to a city, met a monster, killed him and became a monster himself. I don't like the man I've become but I don't hate myself either. Truth be told, I'm moving beyond emotions — hatred, love, fear and desire are relics of an obsolete past, symptoms of a personality I'm in the continual process of shedding.

I survived Ferdinand Dorak's death. While they were scraping him off the kerb, I led a shaken Ford Tasso to my office and advised him of my abrupt promotion. He accepted the change with barely a murmur. Ford needed a master, he couldn't function without one. He'd been loyal to Dorak because he was the most powerful man in the city. Now there was a new Cardinal, he was pragmatic enough to accept it and blow with the wind of change.

Ama and Wami froze as The Cardinal hit the pavement. As swiftly and simply as that. One second they were closing in on me – for very different reasons – the next they were statues. Then their bodies drew in upon themselves as if they were shrinking. The lines of their faces grew tauter by the second. Their carcasses contracted, arms, legs and necks merging with their torsos, losing shape, becoming dense, ragged forms.

And then they exploded. Silently, their bodies came apart in showers of cold, green sparks, and formed seconds later into two clouds of familiar green fog which quickly spread and covered the whole of the roof, so thick and cloying it caused Ford Tasso to fall to his knees and almost choke.

Moments later – guided, I'm sure, by the unseen *villacs* – the fog flowed from the roof, down the sides of the building to the ground and through the streets, until the entire city was in its grasp. It hung over the city like a death shroud for ten days, eradicating all memories of the final batch of Ayuamarcans, bringing travel and commerce to a virtual standstill. A fitting period of mourning for the deposed Ferdinand Dorak.

I tried the large chair in the office. It wasn't as grand as his old one but it felt good all the same. I asked Ford if he recalled Ama Situwa. As tendrils of green fog swirled in his nasal passages, he said he didn't. I asked if he knew anybody called Leonora Shankar. 'She have anything to do with the restaurant?' he replied.

Over the coming weeks I wiped the files on Ama, Conchita, Leonora and the rest of the Ayuamarcans. It paid to be tidy.

Nobody from the outside world took much notice of the changes. As The Cardinal had said, no one was bothered. There have been a few puzzled visitors and enquiries in the years since, but they've been easily dealt with.

Ford's been a huge help. He directed me to Dorak's secret files, outlining his plans for world domination, the steps I'd have to take, the speed I should move at, the difficulties I would have to overcome. It'll be a long time before those plans are put to the test but I have faith in them. The Cardinal was a genius in his own crazy way, a dreamer like no other I've ever heard of.

I wonder occasionally if he was speaking the truth when he told me I'd forged my own way to the top. It seems unlikely, the more I consider it, that he'd leave so much to chance and circumstance. Logic suggests I was steered, that he knew I'd demand his death, that he always intended it to end this way. But then I think back to our earlier meetings, the way he looked when he spoke of his games with the stock market, and I'm not so sure logic can be applied in his case.

Ford's talking of retiring soon. I'll miss the grizzly bear when he goes. I've thought about making him vanish when he steps down – he'll know more than any outsider should – but I'll probably let him see out his days in dignified retirement. He's earned it.

The *villacs* . . .

We've had run-ins. They've kept a low profile but whenever we've met to talk business, I haven't liked what I've heard. They have plans of their own. They want me to stick to the city and forget the rest of the world. They're only interested in the city's well-being. They might cause problems one day. I'll have to keep a close eye on them. If they think they can manipulate me the way they used Dorak, I'll have to prove them wrong. They might live to regret the day they put such power in my hands.

For a long time I kept thinking the world would wake up to my existence, that reality would realize I shouldn't be here and remove me with a swift flick of its fingers. But it hasn't happened yet and, having survived this long, I now doubt it will. I think we got away with it.

Assassination attempts come frequently. In the months after The Cardinal's death, I was eliminated by ambitious competitors no less than six times. They shot me, knifed me, even blew me up. The attempts are growing less frequent – I've killed lots of the pretenders to the throne, and the others respect me now – but there's still one or two every few months.

I always bounce back, no matter what they do. Even if they kill me, burn my body and scatter the ashes over the seas, I turn up a day or two later at the familiar train station, ticket stub in hand. My mind's sometimes a touch cloudy when I return but it clears after a while.

The rain shower is always there to greet me, narrow, straight and strange. It's become a tourist attraction — people flock from all over to see it. I've asked the *villacs* about it but they're keeping tight-lipped.

People have started saying I'm a god, the second Christ, the Devil, an alien. I let the rumours grow. Fear does them good and enhances my reputation. It's part of the plan. Gangster, businessman, politician, God. A natural progression, yes?

I suppose it'll be a good life. I'll have countries at my feet, more money, power and influence than any man in history. If we ever head for the stars, my people will be there, ready to put the squeeze on whatever kind of lifeforms we find. No matter where mankind ends up, Capac Raimi will tag along in spirit, the infallible, foul Pope of the underworld, the gangster god who can't be shaken free. My voice will be heard everywhere and it will be obeyed.

It's not all fun and games. I have nightmares. Faces of the dead, berating me for my ruthlessness. Dee, Conchita, Ama — so often Ama. I still feel guilty for abandoning her so cheaply. I wish I could have saved her, that I could bring her back. In my dreams she haunts me, her eyes filled with pity, never hating me. Only wanting to be with me, to save me from myself.

I even have nightmares in which I'm accused and tormented by a younger Capac Raimi, the one who watched silly movies and knew how to laugh and love, whose dreams never ended like this. I wake screaming some nights, a cold sweat covering every inch of my body, feeling like a man who's woken up to discover he's been buried alive.

On nights like those I wish I'd done things differently, stayed in Sonas with Dee to face the music, stayed true to Ama and spared her, given The Cardinal the time he requested. I wish I'd run away with Conchita and shared her brief week of happiness. I wish I'd never been created or that I could change my nature. But the nights always pass and such thoughts never last long in the clear-headed world of the dawn.

I'm becoming the man I was born to be. Every day brings me closer to the cold, heartless, emotionless machine of The Cardinal's warped vision. One day I'll wake up, look in a mirror and see nothing human at all. On that day I'll know I've made it. Top of the world.

I'm finished with this tale. The past is an interesting place but I've had enough of it. The call of the present can't be ignored. There are things to do. People to kill. Countries to buy and sell. I mightn't be able to leave this city for more than a few days at a time – I *die* if I do and end up back at the station – but that won't restrict me. I can see forever from the top of Party Central.

Reflecting on the past has made me maudlin. I think I'll crack open a can of beer and call in some whores. I've a meeting with a rebellious pair of gang lords this afternoon. They've formed a coalition and are plotting to overthrow me. I think they'll kill me at the meeting. I'll probably let them — it'll be good for a laugh. Pay them a visit when I return and watch their faces drop.

What will the future be like? That's the towering question. I feel great right now, running this brute of a city. In theory it should be even better when I have the planet under my thumb, god of all I survey. But I'm not so sure.

What if I get bored? When I've done everything and conquered all, what will be left? How does a man who lives forever get any kicks out of a world that can't surprise him any longer? Maybe I'll wipe everything out and start over. Even now I have missiles of mass destruction at my disposal. Maybe I'll raze the lot when the world starts to bore me and build civilization up from scratch. New cities, new races, new religions, new histories. I could do it over and over, build and destroy, build and destroy, an endless cycle. Kill billions, raise a new crop, then slaughter them all again. God and devil, giver and taker, tormentor of all and eternal.

Can I really be so ruthless, so tyrannical, so cold? Take this world to the very end of suffering and beyond? Yes. Yes, I think I can, if I have to. If I get bored . . . if eternity weighs heavy upon me . . . if there's nothing else to amuse me . . . I'll do all that and more. Much more. Anything to pass the time.

E   N   D

18/10/1993 – 21/8/2007